ERIC SUMMERS

WORDS & IMAGES

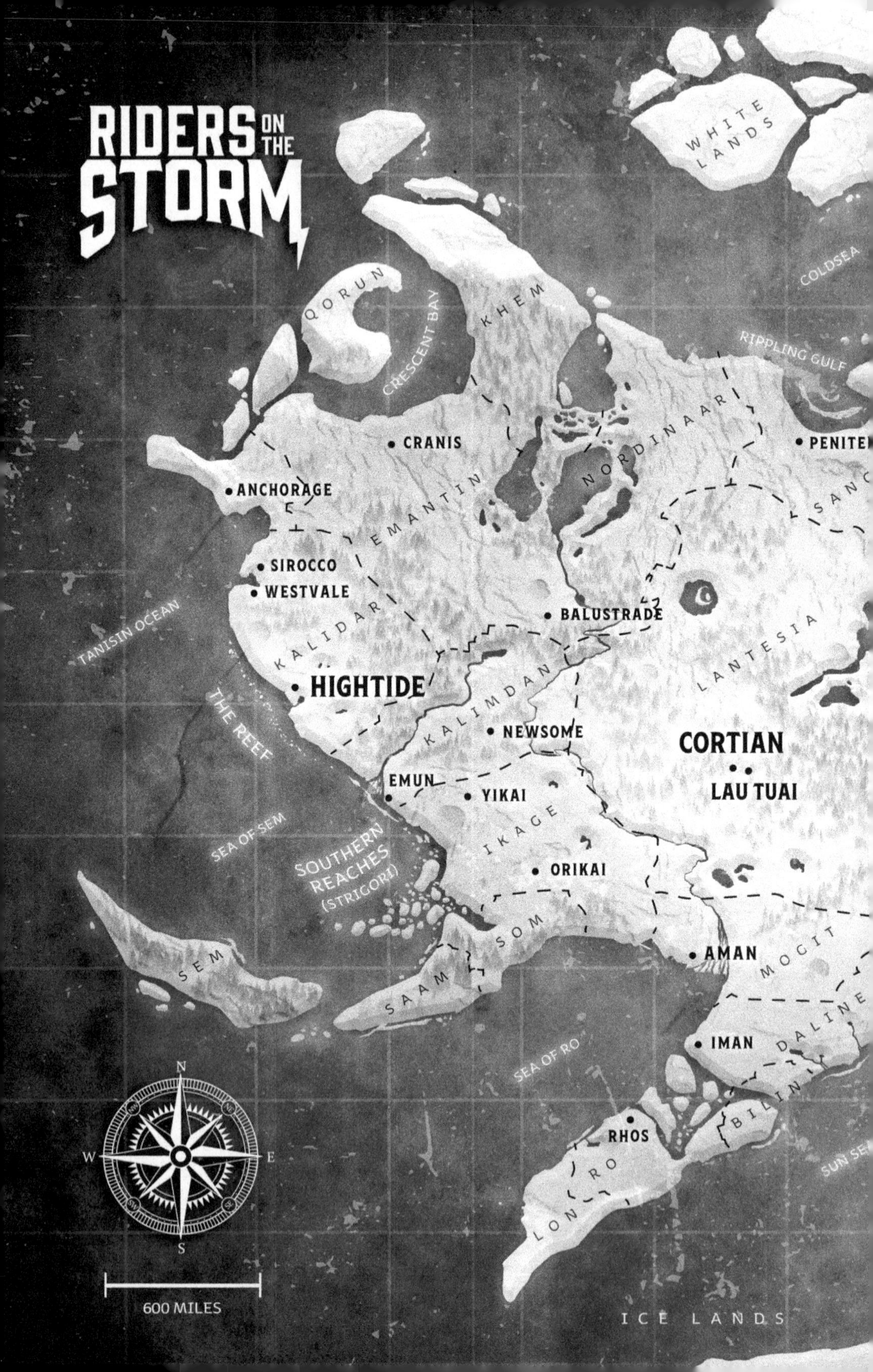
RIDERS ON THE STORM
WHITE LANDS
COLDSEA
RIPPLING GULF
QORUN
CRESCENT BAY
KHEM
NORDINAAR
CRANIS
PENITEN
ANCHORAGE
EMANTIN
SAN
SIROCCO
WESTVALE
TANISIN OCEAN
BALUSTRADE
KALIDAR
LANTESIA
HIGHTIDE
THE REEF
KALIMDAN
NEWSOME
CORTIAN
LAU TUAI
EMUN
YIKAI
IKAGE
SEA OF SEM
SOUTHERN REACHES (STRIGORI)
ORIKAI
SOM
SEM
SAAM
AMAN
MOGIT
DALINE
IMAN
SEA OF RO
BILIN
RHOS
RO
LON
SUN SEA
N
W
E
S
600 MILES
ICE LANDS

THE WORLD OF ELARIN

CHUNLAND
PERIL
BASIN
KINSHIP
LORDSDEN
AHRIMA
AHRIMACIA
DAGIN BAY
WHANIN
TARISIN OCEAN
DAGIN
JIPAR
KEANA
TEMPLE OF KOL
MOHAGAN DESERT
SUMI DESERT
CRONIS
STAGERI
SKYMOUNTS
KUBAL
LORN OCEAN

Riders on the Storm

This book is a work of fiction. Names, characters, places, and incidents are either the product of the author's imagination or are used fictitiously, except where I *totally* snuck in friends and family. I probably shouldn't say that, but nobody ever reads these things, right?

Cover, Interior Illustrations, and Book Design
by Eric Summers.
www.thatsummersguy.com

Edited by Rick Hynum.

ISBN: 979-8-9887224-0-3 (paperback)
ISBN: 979-8-9887224-1-0 (hardcover)
ISBN: 979-8-9887224-2-7 (ebook)
1st edition, 2023

This book is dedicated to Tracy and Brady,
my loves and my life.

To Heidi and Donny,
Mom and Dad,
for putting up with the neverending antics
of an idiot eldest son.

And to you, Reader.
Never stop chasing your dreams.

PROLOGUE

Cool water splashed around the children's ankles as they made their way back to the village, the slow, shallow river gurgling in time with their peals of joyful laughter after a hot summer's afternoon of swimming in the tide pools down by the sea.

Pyk looked back to where the trees widened out, enjoying the view of Longshore, sitting a few hundred yards off the coast, its garrison standing vigil over leagues of ramshackle docks stretching beyond sight to the northwest and southeast. Further past the thin island roiled the Sea of Sem, a seemingly endless expanse of blue. Masina Tamai—the Shattered Sister, ghostly yet brightening in the last of the day's light—wound its way above the horizon, the pieces of the broken moon's long arc glistening as they began their ascent. Masina Atoa, the Sturdy Sister, would soon follow.

Tall trees lining the banks swayed in the breeze, the rustle of leaves a soft counterpoint to the burbling of the river around them. Shinga, the mayor's thick-furred, spiky-tailed dobrin, barked as she frolicked in circles around the trio, further wetting them with her occasional shakes.

Pyk winced as water splashed, soaking him head to toe. He turned to glare at his companions as they roared with laughter, the large stones they'd just thrown rocking in the mild current as they settled to the riverbed.

"I'll remember that, Rabin, you drekface," he sputtered, wiping an ineffectual hand across his eyes. The mayor's son grinned even wider, jostling his shoulder.

"You said a bad word," Amiel giggled, wind rustling her curly locks—a golden brown nearly the same shade as her tanned skin—as she picked idly at a scab on one bony elbow.

Pyk sighed, feeling every minute of his ten years, scratching his shaggy blond hair as they resumed their hike uphill. As much as he enjoyed time with his friends and kin, he wasn't looking forward to the morrow. A week was a long time to spend on a fishing ship, but it was his duty to learn as much as he could. His father, Huk, was the best in the village, and Pyk was expected to live up to that reputation.

He knew something was wrong as they approached the tall wooden gates of Emun's western barricade.

They were closed.

The gates were *never* closed until after true nightfall. Sentries hailed them from the wall as the three drew near.

"Rabin, your pa's going mental! Get your backside in here on the quick, boy!" A muffled shout was directed at parties unseen within the fortifications, and the reinforced doors began to grind open enough to let them pass.

Pyk exchanged a glance with his companions as they entered the village. It was a beehive of activity, residents swarming at a dead run to all corners. Women hustled from their homes carrying bows, children following behind with armloads and full quivers of arrows as they headed for the eastern wall. Scarred old Mak Jinsin, Emun's sergeant-at-arms, spat orders as he handed out spears from the armory racks. Shinga barked and spun about wildly at all the commotion before running off with her pack mates.

As Pyk reached out to put his arm around Amiel—his nine-year-old cragcat of a sister—both his father and Rabin's sprinted toward them in tandem, as if the two were racing to see who could reach the kids first. Huk won, snatching up Amiel in a relieved hug and crushing Pyk to his hip.

"Order anyway, I'm glad you're all right," their father said, worry lining his sun-leathered face. "Did you run into any trouble on your way back?"

"What's going on?" asked Rabin, who received a much less affectionate welcome from his pa, Crixis.

"We don't rightly know, son," the mayor replied. "The scouts reported something massive appearing in that big clearing east of here. Some sort of enormous vehicle. There are Hostguard spilling out of it, on their way here now."

Rabin's eyes lit up at the prospect of glorious battle as only a child's would. Pyk's father, Huk, on the other hand, looked sick to his stomach.

Crixis eyed the children. "Pyk, Rabin," he said with authority, "go see Mak and pick up spears for yourselves. We'll need you on the lines with the men. Amiel, fetch as many arrows as you can and report to the wall."

Huk drew himself up and planted himself between his children and Crixis. "They'll do no such thing. They're kids, Crix."

"We'll be needing all hands, Huk," the mayor replied. "You don't have a choice in this."

"Chaos burn me if I don't. My wife is *gone*, Crixis. There's no one to stand for my young'uns except me, and I'll be damned if I let you drag them into *your* toss-up."

The mayor's eyes narrowed. "*My* toss-up?" he asked in a dark voice.

Huk stepped forward, almost nose-to-nose with Crixis. His voice dropped to a near-whisper. "I told you this crazy stunt of yours would bring down the wrath, Crix. I'm not letting my kids suffer because of your delusions of grandeur. You wanted my advice earlier? You do what the Hostguard ask, we go back to supplying the garrison like normal, and you forget this business of *demanding* concessions from the frokking Host!"

Crixis stared, face blank. "Are you refusing to fight for your friends and kin, Huk?" The tone was almost conversational, but a dangerous undercurrent ran beneath.

"I'm *protecting* my kin by—"

"Mayor!"

Huk was cut off as Jimen Lorca, the baker's teenage son, ran up in an explosion of heavy breath. "There's…the east gate…they're everywhere…"

Crixis gave Huk a dark look, then turned and bolted for the eastern wall. Rabin sneered at Pyk's father with a muttered "Coward," before scuttling after his pa.

Huk sighed. "I should be on the water," he murmured before turning to Pyk and Amiel. "Follow me. Do *not* leave my sight."

"Yes, father," Amiel replied, meeker than might have been expected. Pyk remained silent, not sure what to make of these developments. They trailed their father, reaching the eastern gate and climbing the thick log ramparts to peer over the battlement.

Pyk's insides curdled like spoiled milk at the sight before them. Outside the village walls, hundreds of armored soldiers formed orderly rows among the surrounding trees. Twice the population of Emun, at a conservative estimate.

Stunpikes thumped against the forest floor in pounding rhythm as the Hostguard chanted: a pumping "Aaa-OOO! Aaa-OOO!" in time with the drumming pikes.

"Gods above and below," muttered Huk. "Come on, you two."

They raced back across the village commons to an ancient redbark situated near the curving wall. It had been a few years since he'd last used it, but Pyk remembered well the treehouse, a small windowed hut built within its high boughs. The three rounded the backside of the tree and quickly made their way up handholds carved into the thick bark. Once inside the high hideaway itself, they were afforded a clear view of nearly the entire village and surrounding area. The columns of Hostguard stood poised outside the wall like an inbound wave bearing down to smooth out a sandy shore. Even including the women and children, the Emun resistance was a paltry thing compared to the Host's overwhelming force. Yet they had the advantage of tall walls and range.

The chanting and drumming increased in volume, a rising crescendo as a lone figure made its way through the ranks.

It was a woman, dark of hair and stunningly gorgeous. Enough so that Pyk—who as yet had little interest in girls—was taken aback by her beauty, even as he blushed at her attire. He was no stranger to scantily-clad bodies. No one who sailed the Sea of Sem was put out by the sight of bare legs or freckled arms, but the gossamer-thin gown worn by the lady left *nothing* to the imagination. It almost seemed a statement—contrasted against the heavily-armored Hostguard surrounding her—that she needed no extra protection.

Pyk jumped as Huk scrambled back from the window, breathing heavily, face contorted with the beginnings of panic.

"Dad, what's going on?" Pyk asked.

"Order anyway, it's the High Lady herself. Atia protect and preserve us…"

Amiel leaned her small face out of the window, fascinated. "*That's* Kaira? Atia's *bones*!"

Huk shivered, running his hands over his face. "We can't fight her," he mumbled, his eyes unfocused, struggling with some internal dilemma. "Gotta get them out…"

He turned the children to look at him. "The two of you stay here. Those people out there are our friends and neighbors, understand? I can't just leave them."

"What? Dad, no!" shouted Amiel.

"Stay. *Here*. Pyk, watch over your sister. I'll be back soon."

Pyk nodded, unable to tear his eyes from the mass of soldiers outside the wall. The door to the hut slammed as Huk left them.

Down at the wall, the eastern gate was open. A force of villagers had filed outside to form a battle line, spears and harpoons at the ready, led by

Crixis. The mayor stepped forward, and the thumping of pikes abruptly ceased. He jumped a little, clearing his throat.

"Mistress Kaira, High Lady of the Host," he shouted—voice trembling slightly—across the expanse of forest floor separating the two war parties. "We of Emun welcome you! We trust that you have come to negotiate our requests in good faith, but I can't help but feel trepidation that you'd need to bring so large a—"

He cut off as Kaira raised a manicured hand.

"Shut up."

Pyk clapped his hands over his ears. Her voice rang out loud enough to shake the trees. The walls of the hideaway rattled. His father staggered below, racing toward the gate and trying to round up anyone left within the walls. Huk was stabbing a finger toward the western exit, imploring those who weren't fighting to flee.

Nobody was moving.

The High Lady stepped forward, a single pace that positioned her ahead of the troops. Her amplified voice assaulted the ears of everyone present.

"There's a problem here, in this pile of drek you call a village. Your leaders, in their infinite idiocy, are under the erroneous belief that they are in a position to make demands of your regional Hostguard. If demands are made of the Hostguard, then by extension demands are made of the Host."

A cruel smile played across her lips.

"And no mortal in this world makes demands of *me*."

Her arms rose, and the east wall exploded.

Enormous logs shattered and flew, rending and impaling bodies mid-air. The Emun defenders were hurled like leaves in the wind, skewered by their own spears and raining down upon the village in a red monsoon. A great gaping hole was all that remained of the fortifications—walls, homes, and mangled bodies sprayed about in a rough semicircle by the blast. Pyk saw both Rabin and Crixis, broken and bloodied, land nearly on top of one another.

Kaira strode through the wreckage unimpeded. There were no fighters left to challenge her. Flames erupted as she moved further into the village, pointing at homes which blazed instantly. Bodies stumbled afire from within the infernos, shrieking and beating at themselves as they fell to the charring earth.

The Hostguard never moved from their ordered rows; the thumping began anew, chanting for their mistress, who alone wrought catastrophic destruction.

"Aaa-OOO! Aaa-OOO!"

Men, women, and children scattered in all directions, and wherever Kaira looked, they died. Jimen Lorca vanished in a spray of blood. Villagers fell by the dozens—flung, broken, or just flat-out ripped apart. Snarling dobrins were torn asunder, their yelps discordant against the Hostguard's chant. To Pyk's horrified eyes, the carnage both took an eternity and was over within just a few minutes.

"Aaa-OOO! Aaa-OOO!"

A lone figure stood before the High Lady. The last person left alive that Pyk could see.

His father.

"Aaa-OOO! Aaa-OOO!"

The chanting again quieted suddenly as Kaira paused in front of Huk. He didn't cower or beg; he just stood there—chest out, chin high, hands clasped behind his back.

Pyk reached out for his sister's hand, spinning in panic when he found only empty air.

"Oh, *Order above, Amiel!*" he screamed, and then he was bolting through the door and down to the ground at a reckless pace. He rounded the wide redbark just as his little sister reached their father, taking his rough sailor's hand with her tiny, unblemished one. Huk started, a pained expression crossing his face as he kneeled and placed his free hand to his daughter's cheek, filling his eyes with the sight of her.

Kaira snorted. Then she laughed, an evil crystalline chime made all the more terrible by her beauty.

Huk turned his head to see Pyk barreling toward them. He smiled at his son, a sad farewell holding all the unspoken lessons he would never be able to impart. Amiel met her brother's terrified gaze, eyes wide and mouth open, her hand outstretched as if to clasp his.

And then they were gone, father and sister alike, disintegrated in a shower of red mist that wet the thick grass with an unspeakable sound.

Pyk was on his knees, vision hazy and dark around the edges, a keening shriek splitting the air throughout the village commons. He was vaguely aware that it was coming from his own mouth. He felt pain and realized his fists were clenched tight enough to draw blood from his palms.

A delicate pair of sandaled feet stepped into view, and his sight cleared as he stood and stared into the face of the High Lady of the Host. Her eyes burned with an unnatural silver sheen as she smiled down at his small body, an almost tender expression of commiseration as false as anything Pyk had ever seen. He flinched as she reached out and tousled his shaggy, sun-bleached hair.

"Now you, pet..." Kaira began, "You, I believe I'll let be. I want you to render a service for me. Spread word of what happened here tonight in this..." She paused to gaze around at the wreckage of Emun—the shattered remnants of Pyk's life—and her lip curled in disdain. "This dreadful little place."

Pyk trembled in impotent rage and horror. He couldn't think, couldn't move. Her words were so much gibberish in his ears.

"Tell it far and wide that the Host will not suffer disruptions, distractions, or demands." Her hand clenched, bringing tears to his eyes as she pulled at his scalp. "The next time I'm forced to leave my Temple for an act of defiance as trivial as this, nations will tremble, and the land itself will be cast into the raging sea. Let everyone you meet know this, pet."

She flung him aside, turning to stroll her way through the ruination of everything and everyone Pyk had ever known.

He fell to his knees again, time passing unnoticed as he stared unblinking at the crimson-stained patch of earth that was all that remained of his family. Flames crawled sluggishly across the wrecked village, blackening the grass near him before petering out.

A low roar and stiff wind brought him to his senses. Pyk looked up to see a gigantic, boxy...*something*...rise above the treeline in opposition to gravity, bright lights flaring on its underbelly as it streaked through the darkened sky to eventually blend with the flickering stars. He didn't even have the mental capacity to wonder at what it was.

Guilt and shame and a crushing, unfathomable despair washed over Pyk as he threw back his head and howled, his anguish echoing skyward to the broken, uncaring moon.

ONE

The storm chased us toward port, a predator hounding flagging prey. Behind us, the darkening sky blazed—the deep, distant rumble of thunder shuddering louder than the short waves slapping against the prow of the *Quay*. Expansive sails strained taut against the masts, the boat spearing ahead of ruinous rain and gale.

Our ship reached the bay at Hightide less than two hours before the storm would hit, at my best guess. We'd been out for three relatively calm days, crewing for Old Craw Maggins on his homey fishing junk. There'd been the beginnings of a good haul, but the pickup of harsh winds and encroaching front—dark and pregnant with lightning—had forced us to turn back much earlier than the captain had anticipated.

Good thing, too, because the storm wall grew larger as we raced ahead of it. Gray-blue clouds stretched across the horizon, crashing thunder sounding ever closer as we approached the Reef, which stretched parallel to the shore for leagues in either direction.

The monolithic corpses of ancient vessels surrounded us as Craw guided his boat through the rusting maze, some extending hundreds of feet above the water line. As with every time we made the port approach, I was awed by the sheer size of the wrecked craft. Even the smaller ones, waves breaking around their bases with a shower of foam, jutted twenty, fifty feet into the air.

Supposedly—hundreds of years ago, back before the Ruin—the things had flown the skies and stars, wonders of technology and engineering virtually extinct in the modern world. Here and there you could spot the faded glyphs that marked the ships' names or designation numbers; writing that had long ago passed from memory, same as the archaic technologies that once powered the massive craft. Now they were just enormous hulks of chewed-up, hollowed-out metal forming the barrier which stretched along the western seaboard of Elarin, slowly disintegrating through time and tides.

But gods above and below, the things must have been impressive back in their heyday.

The *Quay* yawed its way through the Reef under Craw's steady hands as we avoided both the titanic husks and barely-visible wreckage of hulls lurking just under the waves. The craft themselves lay covered in a thick mass of lichen and other plants. White gulls screamed as they flew, and large, thick-shelled pua crabs scuttled about the ruins. I was constantly amazed at the variety of life that made a home of the wrecks, given that fishing wasn't advised within three leagues of the reef. The water itself held a virulent multicolored sheen from centuries of leaks and disintegrating polymers, a pollution that created some rather…interesting…mutations in the local fauna. Sure, they looked neat, but you damn well wouldn't want to eat them—as countless fresh-salt sailors of generations past had learned to their detriment.

I moved to the prow as we emerged from the gauntlet of sharp metal and oil-slick waters, taking up position next to Young Bil, our first mate and Old Craw's eldest son. He spared a glance before spitting tobacco juice over the rail as we took in the view.

"Something, ain't it, Pyk?" he asked. "Always gets me, that sight."

"Yup," I replied, grinning. "Like the dawn sun breaking a calm horizon."

Resting before us in the distance, sprawled across rocky shores and long white beaches, was our port of Hightide. Nothing like coming home. Soft waves—for now, at least—lapped against the extensive docks that abutted the merchant's district, filled with multi-story shops and warehouses. Stacked houses and avenues, built amongst the skeletons of ancient high-rise buildings, climbed the rocks nearest the water and wound their way up rolling hills beyond. Wondrously-carved stone bridges crossed the Canal, which meandered halfway through town before sprawling out to form Chanis Bay.

Dozens of small sailboats, canoes, and kayaks headed in to tie up before the blow. Sailors milled about the docks, unloading and stowing cargo and fishing hauls, while workers rapidly loaded mined gemstones and quarried marble from the nearby hills. Self-important clerks strode among the bins and crates, rushing their inspections, ticking checkmarks on their clipboards and chalking their slates.

Hightide was the very image of a thriving, prosperous coastal city. A small one, to be sure, but that only enhanced its charm. It was beautiful.

It was home.

And Order anyway, it was nice to be home.

There was hardly a stray splash as Craw navigated the crowded harbor and settled alongside our berth with a minute thump. Pretty impressive with such a wide, low ship against the strengthening winds and chop. The old saltwhelp knew his business. For my part, I was itching to get on with *my* business.

Even though I loved the call of the water, I never was partial to the grunt work of sailing. Some called me lazy. I didn't care. I didn't mind putting in early. There'd be opportunity to work the docks for a little while and make a few extra karani before the worst of the storm hit, then go relax with my buddy Mari while it passed. Mariyana was always great for a laugh or two. I might even cadge a bite to eat if she hadn't closed up shop for the day.

"Ho, Pyk!" Craw called to me from the wheel. I scrambled along the rigging so as not to disturb the other sailors trimming the last sheets and making ready to debark. Several of them tossed me disgruntled looks as I crawled past, but I paid no mind. Craw knew my worth. When you could dowse out and reel in a catch like I could—a natural aptitude for finding the thickest schools and best profit, honed under my father's tutelage—it allowed a certain leeway when it came to shipboard duties. Even the traditionally roughneck crew didn't give me much trouble beyond the occasional dirty glare. They knew that their bonus pay would be better with me along.

A loose topsail rope provided a good anchor as I pushed off the rigging to swing wide over the water and land at the wheelhouse. I skidded a bit on the polished wood, barefoot as I was.

"Ye did good out there per usual, boy," Old Craw said, his wrinkled face splitting into an inviting grin that poked through his long, bedraggled gray beard. That smile was missing far too many teeth, and the ones left behind had for sure seen better times. "Twice the catch of any others, including these salty old bones o'mine. I'll have the other lads finish up here, if ye'll promise to come back out again wi' me once this hair-trimmer's blown through." The old man's voice dropped to a conspiratorial whisper. "Pay and a half, if ye like. Can always use ye out there."

I liked Craw. In the nine years I'd lived in Hightide, and of all the captains I'd sailed with, he was by far my favorite of the lot. He wasn't nearly the mean-spirited drunkard that a lot of the other captains were, *and* he let me get away with mild dereliction of duty.

Besides that, he paid well and never skimped on letting me take a few fish for Mariyana to fry up whenever we made port. We had a mutually beneficial arrangement, so it was rare that I went out with other ships. I didn't tell *him* that, though. Better to let him think I was always being courted by the other captains and investor merchants.

"Sounds right by me," I replied. "Make sure they get everything iced down proper and I'll be back to help unload the catch once the rain dies down. Might even have a surprise for you."

The old sailor barked a short laugh, the sound like shallow stones grating along a hull. Though rough, it was endearing. He may have been my employer, but I thought of Craw as a friend. Not something I could say about any of the other merchant captains—very few people, being honest—in Hightide. My list of acquaintances was long, my friends short.

"I'll see they do, young'n. Get along, and tell the Chek I said hello. Bring me back some of her grub, would ye?"

I grinned. "Will do, Craw. Fair winds to you, old man."

"And fair winds to ye, young sir. Keep yer head dry in all this mess. We'll be seein' ye soon." With that, I hopped down a gangplank and began to make my way sunward.

I headed along dockside for a few blocks, calling out to various deckhand acquaintances and chatting briefly with grumbling shopkeepers closing up storefronts in anticipation of the blow. Many were sweating in the heat, straining to roll out their heavy-bottomed raincatcher barrels.

My stomach rumbled, so I swung over to The Bright Mercantile. The owner, Ardis, was a fruit and grain vendor I'd known…well, forever, since I was a kid still living on the streets. One of the few locals that had been kind enough to feed me first and then let me work off the debt carrying his goods from the ships to his storage cellar.

Oh, and he was a Thrane.

A fairly typical specimen at about eight feet tall, Ardis had the large crablike body of his forebears, and scuttled about on his six triple-jointed legs, battening down his store to protect against any damaging winds. His upper torso leaned back over a wide, multi-hued, and robed shell, centering his balance while his two smaller manipulating arms busied themselves with tie-downs and straps.

I could see the glint of his arm torcs, multitude of piercings, and the other assorted jewelry that he adored. Patterned silk robes flapped in the strengthening breeze, the snap of the fabric reminding me of taut sails and dangerous skies.

He was a bulky bugger, even for a Thrane, with a broad, toothy smile and a quick laugh—one of the few people I was genuinely fond of and willing to go the extra mile in helping out when I could.

"Ardis, how goes?" I called as he used his large pincer claws to pull down the retractable boards that would protect his windows. His flat head snapped up, black eyes widening as he flinched.

I'd be lying if I said it didn't startle me in turn. Ardis was the type of hail-fellow-well-met shopkeep who never met a stranger and loved to hear his own booming, gravelly voice. It wasn't like him to be jumpy or suspicious of anyone approaching his store. His mouth parted in a wide grin, the guarded look disappearing so quickly that I found myself wondering what I'd actually seen.

"Pyk Belloc! Didn't expect to see you back on land so soon, m'boy!"

"Yeah, I tried to get Craw to stay out, but no doing. Can't blame him, being honest. This one looks like it's going to be a bugger, and I've got no desire to try deep-sea fishing without the benefit of a boat under me."

"Yar, can't argue that, son. Hungry?"

"Starving. You wouldn't have an apple or something I could cadge, would you?"

Ardis chuckled. "I just might at that, lad. Get these last shutters for me and I'll dig up a good something for ye. One moment." He shuffled his flamboyant bulk through the Thrane-sized double doors, and I could hear him muttering to himself as he rummaged around in the bins behind the wooden slats. I busied myself securing the thick boards.

He appeared a moment later, a gigantic red sweetdew in his claw. I perked up. I'd thought they were out of season.

"Here you go, m'boy," he said, handing it over. As I cracked the rind and wolfed the fruit down with a muffled "Fanks, mate," I was surprised to see the bulky merchant pull a large keyring from his voluminous robes and lock up the shop doors. His apartments were upstairs, above the storefront, so why would he shut everything tight before getting settled in?

"Not staying here for the blow, Ardis?" I asked. Just trying to make conversation, but again his eyes widened and an uneasy twitch shook his head.

"No, I...uh..." His shoulders sagged. It was such a human gesture that I almost grinned. "Look, lad, I'm heading out of town for a spell. There's been more than a few travelers coming through the last few days with some right awful tales. Stories about the Host."

I frowned. The Host were a sore subject with me, and he knew it.

"What kind of stories?" I asked, although I pretty much already knew. There was really only one type of tale when it came to the Host: death and destruction on a horrific scale. It had been nine years since they'd last been seen anywhere near Hightide. Nine years of relative peace. If they were appearing again, it would mean bad things for simple folk trying to make a life for themselves.

Some of the idiots out there, like the Inori, actually worshipped the Host. Bloody fools. They weren't gods. Just small-minded, capricious tyrants with power. I spat on their so-called "divinity." I *hated* them. One in particular.

"The travelers spread rumors that Kaira is on the move again," Ardis said, shrugging his hard-shelled shoulders. "They say the High Lady is heading south, down the coast, searching for something. I couldn't confirm it, but I was told that Westvale and Sirocco have been destroyed down to the last man, woman, and child. Hightide is the next town in her path, so I'm honestly not of a mind to stick around and find out if the stories are true or a load of mulch."

My mechanical left hand clenched involuntarily, gears whirring as I popped the last of the sweetdew into my mouth. I chewed silently for a few moments. A faint metallic scrape was the only noise as metal fingers ground against the netanium palm.

Ardis's face was a mask of crustacean worry. He laid a claw on my shoulder in a kindly gesture I wasn't accustomed to receiving from many, much less from the Thrane—it was almost fatherly. "Look, lad, why don't ye come with me? I'm gonna head up to my cabin in the hills for a while, and wait 'til this is all blown over. I've already got a carriage waiting on me over at The Block and Cleat."

I softened a bit. "Thanks for the offer, Ardis," I replied. "That's generous of you, really, mate, but I couldn't just off and leave Mariyana. Not during a blow like this storm is shaping up to be. And *especially* not if one of the Host is making their way toward town."

"Order anyway, boy, bring the little lady along! Not like she'd take up much room in the wagon. Matter o'fact, it'd be good to have someone at the cabin who can actually cook. I haven't forgotten the last time ye tried to grill up a longbill ye brought off the boat."

I chuckled. That one *had* been a disaster.

Ardis sighed. "Ah, lad, I hope I'm wrong. I hope those rumormongers were full of drek. But better to be safe now than sorry later, y'get?"

I gave him a friendly tap on a pincer. His offer really did mean a lot to me, and it wasn't as if I actually *wanted* to be around if the Hostguard—or worse—showed up in Hightide.

But he was the first to mention the Host. In my brief chats with the other shopkeepers, I'd heard nothing else of the sort, and Hightide merchants were notoriously voracious gossips. I'd also learned my lesson years before that Ardis, while kind and giving, wasn't exactly a reliable source of worldly information. Lastly, there was no way I'd leave without Mari. My circle of friends wasn't exactly large, and she was by far the best of them.

"Thanks again," I replied. "Really, thank you. But I can't just take off. Craw's expecting me back on board after the blow, and Mari's not gonna want to up and leave her stall for a few days. You know she'd come back and all her stores would be cleaned out."

I grinned at the Thrane. "Besides, maybe there's nothing to worry about, right? Remember when you heard about those gem deposits that were supposed to be under the city hall? They ever get those foundations repaired?"

Ardis spat to the side. "Pah! That was Nathinn trying to put me out of business and ye know it. Don't change the subject. I want ye both to come with me out to the cabin. Don't stay here and get yourself exploded. Worst case, I'm wrong, and we come back after a nice restful vacation. I'll even front the cost to restock Mari's wares, if that's what it'll take."

I laughed and clapped him on the pincer again. "I appreciate it, old boy, but I think you might be wrong on this one. I *hope* you're wrong, at least. I haven't heard anything else of the sort, and there's just too much to be done around here."

"I hope you're right, boyo," he said with another sigh. "I do hope there's nothin' to worry about. Just...just be safe, okay?"

I spread my hands, flashing a broad grin. "Hey, it's me. Everything will be fine."

How wrong I was. How foolish.

TWO

With the wind strengthening, my hair whipped around my head as I made my way back toward the docks. Thick-trunked palms swayed from their cultivated gardens between—sometimes atop—the merchants' stores. It struck me that overall I was still in far too good a mood to spend my free time slinging grain off skiffs until the storm rolled in, so I turned east, heading into town and waving at various street performers trying to eke out a few more karani before the weather got too bad.

I passed a small congregation of Inori, my lip curling as the priest at their center pointed at passersby and bellowed out promises of the eternal fires of eternal torment in eternity, or whatever their nonsense creed dictated. His oddly-styled tall hair, a fashion statement to the Inori, seemed impervious to the thick breeze. The geometric mask he wore—bare gray metal aside from the two narrow eye slits—caused his voice to ring, as if he were casting hellfire and damnation through a message tube. One of his flock, maskless, eyed me with a hostile stare, ritualistic scars lining her face in those same strange geometries.

I eyed the weapons they carried on their hips.

There wasn't much love for their brand of faith in general. The Atia I'd always been taught to believe in was a stern but ultimately benevolent goddess; the embodiment of Order, purpose itself. Capricious, yet most likely to bestow her blessings and fortune upon those who made their own way in the world, doing more good than harm.

The Atia I knew didn't exactly *require* worship, but was said to keep her guiding hand over those who took care of her creation. Those who left the world a better place than they found it, whether by helping a neighbor, tending the herds, planting a garden, or so on. The service didn't really matter, as long as the outcome was a net positive to the general well-being of the community and advanced Order in all things.

On the other hand, the aspect of Atia worshipped by the Inori was a cruel and withered crone who brought no light or life to her creations, only vengeance and suffering. To all those who weren't her devoted flock, of course. All others were heathens, Chaotic pagans unworthy of salvation. Or mercy, or sympathy. And there were a great many *others*, to the Inori.

I couldn't fathom the type of mind who would gravitate toward that sort of belief. Poor, broken souls, they were. It always bothered me that they took such an opposing stance to the benevolent nature of deity. Who would *want* to follow such a bleak creed? To lean into exclusionary hate? Why would their vision of Atia differ so greatly from the accepted canon?

It went without saying that the Inori also believed the Host were lesser gods, and worshipped them accordingly. They believed that any atrocities committed by their demigods upon the people of Elarin were deserved as wages of sin. The particular sins changed like a child's swaddling—often and for much the same reason.

Hypocrisy wasn't a word in their limited vocabulary.

Bloody fools.

I shook my head, disgusted. I wasn't all that religious, given my history, but—with the majority of the Elarin people worshipping Atia and following the enveloping purpose of Order—I supposed I had picked up an appreciation for the concept of a compassionate being watching over and guarding us all. It sure beat the alternative.

The Inori priest shot a baleful glare and pointed a finger at me as I passed, named me a blasphemer and unbeliever who would face eternal judgement and pain, blah, blah, blah. I threw him a different sort of finger, then moseyed around the corner, thankfully dulling his ranting by a considerable degree.

"Hey, watch it!" I yelled as several small, tentacled baghdas raced past my feet, rubbery skin glistening wet and waterproofed message satchels strapped to their backs. Dorsals. Whatever they were called. I pulled my leg out of the way in a hurry. The damn things were friendly enough, but their secretions weren't too good for the integrity of one's clothing.

I climbed through the steep, wide thoroughfares of Hightide proper, looking out over the canal and bay, until I heard the familiar heavy ring of hammer on anvil. Good. Korbos was still working. We could ride out the chill of the storm next to the warmth of his fires. The old smith was gruff, close-mouthed and rather reclusive, but he'd become a friend over the years. Mari and I had always gotten on fairly well with him.

Kind of hard not to, with Mariyana's stall located just next door to his shop.

It didn't hurt that she plied him with food every chance she got. She'd gotten into a habit of prepping the day's leftovers and sharing them with the blacksmith. He in turn kept her shop in good repair and her oven blazing like the fires of his forge.

If I was lucky I'd be able to get in on the night's feast before the big man wolfed it all.

As I approached, the comforting orange glow of Korbos's forge leaked from the windows of his shop, contrasting with the smaller yellow cook fire coming from Mari's stand. Mariyana herself stood on a tall step next to the combination brick oven and grill that Korbos and I had helped her build a few years previous. Several customers milled about, savoring her food around the tiny bistro tables set out onto the cobblestones.

The sleeves on her white chef's coat—hemmed impractically short to show off her belly—were rolled up to the elbow as she worked the grill. It was a testament to her ability that she wasn't a mass of burns and scars, or so I thought. Various knives, tongs, and other instruments hung from the leather belt slung low across her hips. Her dark hair was pulled tight against her scalp, exploding behind the crown of her skull in two large, wild puffs. Rich brown skin and her overlarge pale purple eyes, combined with a tiny frame—almost childlike, if you overlooked the womanly curves—marked her as a Chek, those diminutive revelers of the lands of Elarin. Not that there were many of her kind left. Not after the Host's culls a generation back.

I could count the number of Cheks living in Hightide on one hand. If I were missing a few fingers. To a one, they were quick-witted, fiercely loyal, devastatingly cute. Party animals, too. The worst hangovers of my life had been spent in the company of one or all of Hightide's Chek population. I loved them, in my own way, although Mariyana had been my best friend since we were all kids running wild in the streets.

The other two Cheks in town, Rimple and Skot, were in a committed relationship—unusual for their highly promiscuous nature—and were expecting their first children, a set of triplets. Mari had sort of become a third wheel on the cart when it came to them, and I knew she felt left out the further along Rimple got through her pregnancy. I knew she felt lonely sometimes. Didn't help that they'd all grown up together in a Hightide orphanage after being abandoned as babies. I was probably the only person who knew her as well as those two, and it broke my heart a little to see her hurting. Thankfully, that wasn't too often, as Mari was almost rabidly cheery most days.

A raised voice drew my thoughts back to the moment. Mari was engaged in a conversation with a customer who seemed rather agitated. Her large eyes sparkled as I walked up, the ever-present mischievous twinkle within them flashing as she returned her attention to the patrons.

Some rich tosh and his wife, apparently; his brocade coat matched her parasol to an annoying degree. The cost of the coat alone could have fed us for several months. Minor nobility, no doubt, tapping their toes and looking put-upon as the man gesticulated wildly. I threw on my biggest smile as he glanced over, looked me up and down with narrowed eyes and an upturned nose, then turned back to haggle further with Mariyana.

I should've been offended at the quick dismissal, but—being honest—his type was hilarious to me. No better than anyone else, yet they thought their money and breeding gave them a right to look down upon the more common folk.

Idiots. They wouldn't last half a day out on the open water. But such is the world.

"Five karani?" the man asked in a haughty, incredulous tone. His brow contracted into a crease so deep that I wanted to do nothing more than stick a coin in the fold and see if it would stay put. I fought down a wholly inappropriate chuckle.

"I *never* pay that much for blackfin skewers. The very idea, really! You're just trying to rob me blind because of my good standing in this town, you beggaring minnow. I don't *care* if Lord Burkis recommended your food to us, I won't pay a whit over three. Magister Archa will *not* be taken advantage of!"

Now that *did* tick me off. I bristled on Mari's behalf at the insult and stepped forward to give him a sailor's lesson in manners. She held up her hands in a placating gesture, palms out, one angled slightly in my direction. I took the hint, stopping short and leaning against one of the stall supports. A tight smile made my cheeks hurt, and I stood ready to put the posh *bhaka* on the ground if needed.

Not that I was much of a fighter, but I figured I could take him. Maybe. He was pretty skinny.

Mari blinked her bright eyes in such a look of false innocence that I had to stifle an authentic grin.

"Good sir," she said, "Please give my thanks to Lord Burkis, I don't think he led you wrong. Please, try a bite—on the house—and if it's not better than any blackfin you've ever tasted you can leave with it free of charge."

"Well, I…humph. Very well, then. But *don't* think I won't be a fair judge of your quality!" He waggled a finger under her nose, entirely too close to her personal space for my liking.

"I would never presume, sir," she said, face studiously blank as she held out two steaming skewers. "Here you go."

My mouth watered, even though I wasn't particularly hungry after the sweetdew.

Magister Archa was still rambling to no one at all about his impeccable impartiality when he and his lady bit into the blackfin. I knew just how delicious it was, so it was no surprise when the magister went stock-still, eyes bulging. His lady savored the flavor, lids fluttering as her eyes rolled upward in ecstasy. I grinned wide, appreciating their delight on my friend's behalf as Mari tipped me a wink. I had tried a number of times to get the secret of Mariyana's cooking, but the chipper little Chek always found a way to dodge my prying.

"I *say*, small mistress!" Archa exclaimed around a mouthful of fish. He was shoveling it into his gob as quickly as decorum allowed. "Your reputation is well deserved, indeed! My apologies for my earlier brusqueness, you know how *these* places can sometimes be." He waved a hand vaguely about himself, as if to encompass the docks, the surrounding shops, homes—generally anywhere in Hightide that wasn't his manor. "Let it not be said that Magister Archa welched on a deal! Your coin, good madam."

With that, they paid and left, gnawing on their food as they walked. I shrugged. He might have been a *bhaka*, but at least he was honest about it. Mari's purse clinked as she dropped in the coins to mingle with the rest of the day's haul. Sounded like she'd been busy.

The ring and ting of hammer on metal beat its rhythm as I leaned on the stall counter and waited for the nobles to walk their way out of earshot. The rest of Mari's customers bled away as she hopped down from the lift platform rounding the inner edge of the stall and began to close up for the oncoming squall.

"Keep that up and you'll have all of Tallgarden coming down here," I said. "Who knows if those upturned noses could handle all the muck and dirt us lowly vermin are covered with?" I grinned. "I might have to start acting like them to blend in. Avoid undue notice when they're lined up twenty deep. Gods above and below help us, Pyk might even start talking about himself in the third person."

I stretched my neck out and turned my nose to the sky, adopting a haughty swagger. "Dunno if I could afford that vest, though."

Mariyana threw a playful swat at my arm. "You hush. He left a tip, and their coin spends better than most. And you know full well it allows me certain…leeway."

As if on cue, a small family crept from a nearby alley and hunched their way up to the stall; a father, mother, and two children, all clothed in patched rags that looked as if they might have been new thirty years ago. Mariyana's expression softened as they stepped forward, and from under the counter she brought out a tray heaped high with the last of the day's unsold food. Meat, vegetables, some paras fruit she'd bought from a vendor down the street.

Tears formed in the bedraggled mother's eyes, and the children each gnawed on a skewer quickly filched from the tray. "Order bless you, Missus Naribi. Bless you," the father said as Mari shoveled the fare into a burlap sack. His eyes were dry, but his voice was hoarse with barely-hidden emotion. They'd be able to eat for three days on the feast Mari had just provided. She solemnly stuck out a hand, and the father took it in a firm shake. Bowing, they took the sack then backed away and melded into the shadows of the nearby alley from which they'd emerged. I hoped with all my heart that they'd be able to hang on to the food and ride out the storm in safety.

Mari turned, a satisfied grin splitting her delicate dark features. "See?" she said, "The rich ones let me do *that*."

She fingered a small pendant resting in the hollow of her neck. An Atian medallion. She brought it to her lips and whispered a quick benediction for the well-being of the hungry family. Mari was always the more religious of the two of us. A small woman with a large faith, that one.

I chuckled and gave her head a good-natured rubbing. Her dark hair rustled under my knuckles.

"Atia's bones, you're a good woman, Mari," I said. "Even if you are shorter than a squirrel's nuts." I glanced about. "Speaking of squirrels, where's Bastin gotten himself off to tonight?"

She laughed brightly. I loved making her laugh.

"Oh, he's around," Mari replied with her usual smile. "He's been gallivanting all over town today, but I'm sure he'll be back soon. You know he doesn't enjoy leaving me alone for too long, and he likes to be by my side when storms roll through. Too much wind, even for him. And don't call him a squirrel where he can hear you, unless you want to lose some bits you might not care to."

She poked a stern finger into my gut, though her eyes sparkled. "And *don't* blaspheme."

I raised my hands in mock surrender. "Sure thing, Mari. Apologies."

The street pattered as a soft rain began to fall. All the other merchants had their wares packed away, storefronts shuttered against the oncoming winds. Korbos's shop had gone quiet; most likely he'd put away his hammer and was banking his fire. I busied myself with battening down the wood-and-canvas sides of Mari's stall as she stowed her day-to-day utensils and put out the oven.

As we were rolling down the final shutter, a howling breeze snapped our clothing taut against our bodies and a low hiss grew in volume. We turned to see a curtain of hard water rushing toward us. The storm wall had arrived.

We raced over to the main building of Korbos's mercantile and slammed the door behind us, dripping and laughing. I shook myself like a wet dobrin, taking in the shelves lined with spare boat parts. There was a gleaming multitude of fresh mooring cleats, oar stirrups, nails, lantern frames, nails, hooks, more boxes of nails; any metalworking a vessel might need, large or small. I even spied a few metal-banded wooden rudders leaning along the back wall, some taller than me.

Over his twenty years of business, the big man had definitely found his niche in one of the best seafaring markets in Elarin. The workshop was a good size—though not overlarge—and nicely appointed. Trim and clean, as smithies went. His rooms behind the shop were much the same. All in all, they spoke of a quiet, restrained prosperity for their owner.

Korbos looked up as I approached, his good eye marking me, and he inclined his head with his customary small grunt of greeting.

His appearance usually startled strangers and newer customers, but Mari and I had been hanging out at his shop for years, since we were small children. We had a deep fondness for the gruff bugger. Korbos had a massive blacksmith's frame, at least two hundred and seventy pounds and a full head taller than I was, wide in the shoulders with heavily-muscled arms. He was almost twice as tall as Mariyana, and easily three times her weight.

A wide patch of black cloth covered his missing left eye, the flesh surrounding it puckered and scarred in some long-ago fire or other horrific catastrophe. My desire to know the story behind it was maddening, but despite all the years of our friendship I'd never asked and he'd never told.

The blacksmith was a stoic fellow, for the most part, but his eye twinkled as he shouldered the gargantuan poker with which he'd been spreading his forge coals. Outside, the wind howled even louder and the rain began to pound against the stones in earnest.

"I suppose you two plan to hide out from the storm in my place of business?" Korbos asked in his rumbling voice, eyebrow cocked as he glanced sideways. Thunder crashed outside, a counterpoint to his rhetorical question.

"You know it, mate!" I said with exaggerated cheer. "Be a shame to let these beautiful golden locks drown. And you know Mari can't swim in anything bigger than a thimble." She swatted my arm again, harder this time.

Korbos snorted as he rummaged around a nearby cabinet. "Hmmph. Well, we can't have that, can we? Sounds like it's going to be a rough blow out there. Fortunate for you, it just so happens I've got a couple bottles of Ryaan Lee's whiskey that he gave me as payment for his barrel staves. You got any trade?" He turned, holding one of the thick bottles out to Mariyana. He took a long pull from the other, already opened. The man did love his drink.

Mari skipped forward, a sealed—though slightly damp—bag of blackfin held out in her tiny hand.

I laughed. The Chek always had food pocketed away on her somewhere. Chaos take me if I could figure out where she stowed it, since her belt pouches were always full of tools and non-perishables—not always in separate pockets. The scarred corner of Korbos's mouth quirked upward as he took the bag.

Mari bowed her head and closed her large eyes. "Atia, bless this nourishment which we take of your grace and blessing. Guide us to righteousness and generosity to our neighbor. As it ever was, so shall it be."

Korbos frowned. "You know I don't hold to that, Mariyana. I won't begrudge a woman her faith, but I'd appreciate you not doing that in my place."

Mari smiled wide, beautiful teeth flashing. "I *do* know you don't, Korbos, that's why I do it! If you won't seek exaltation, I might as well do it for you, right, because we all have to try and better ourselves sometimes and I figure we can all use a helping hand from time to time so I've got absoluuuuutely no problem doing it for you if you—"

"Right, right." He patted the air before him, interrupting. If you didn't cut Mari off before she got going, she'd never stop, and the two had engaged in their religious squabbles for years. They'd keep sniping at each other for hours if allowed. "Sorry, Mariyana, no prayer talk at dinner. I don't hold to any religion, and I *definitely* don't hold to the Path of Atia."

"Oh I know you've told me a million times before, but I—"

"*So*, Pyk..." Korbos turned to me with only a slight huff of exasperation. He clapped my shoulder, nearly knocking me from my feet. "I didn't think you'd be back for another couple of days. The squall drive Old Craw back in?"

"Yup. Gonna be a doozy." Thunder rattled the windows, to emphasize my point.

"Well and good, then. You can help me with the shop while you're in. I can always use a hand with the bellows. The sawdust could use some freshening, too."

I groaned around a mouthful of blackfin. "Boooooring."

Mari cackled. "I didn't realize we were that dull, Pyk."

"Well, better bored than drowned, that's what I always sa—"

That was when the door burst open.

Mari and I jumped in surprise, and I whirled around to see a slim figure, silhouetted against the pouring rain and lightning. Very dramatic, if I do say so. A fusillade of water blasted in around the figure, driven by the apocalyptic wind. The person stepped into the shop, dripping water on the concrete and sawdust, and by the light of the fire I could see it was a woman, well-built and muscular, cloaked and hooded in a dark, yellow-trimmed cape. Bright green eyes sparkled from the hood's shadows.

"Order anyway, what are you doing out in all that?" Korbos asked before recovering himself. "Can I help you, miss? The shop's closed, obviously, but if you'd like to place an or—"

"Yeah, you can help," she said, cutting his words short. A quick step forward brought her within a few feet of Mariyana, who took an equal step back. "I was told you'd pay me good money for this thing, but I gotta get out of here quick. So pay me and I'll go."

Korbos blinked, although his face remained impassive. "And...just what is it that you think I'll be purchasing, miss?"

The girl darted a quick glance back at the open door, then shifted her cloak aside and pulled a small linen-wrapped package from the pouch at her belt. She held it out to the smith and gently untied the string. The room grew brighter as the cloth fell away to reveal a crystalline cube, thick but small enough to fit in her hand, that radiated a soothing golden light throughout the shop. Ornate angular designs roiled in layer upon layer within the crystal. They appeared to be moving in multiple directions, the patterning almost hypnotic in its smooth motions.

Korbos went stock-still, his eyebrows climbing into his scalp. He raised his head with glacial slowness, his good eye locking the woman's gaze.

"Where did you get this?" he growled.

I'd known Korbos for years, ever since my miserable arrival in Hightide. He was generally a quiet one, but I'd have never said he was dangerous, even as big as he was. The chill in his voice, however, sent a rapid shiver up my spine. His eye narrowed, and his face went as dark as the thunderclouds railing outside. The girl opened her mouth to answer but was cut short by a muffled crash from beyond the door.

Raised voices sounded in the streets, barely audible over the pounding rain and gale. The hooded woman's head snapped around, darting like an animal smelling a predator on the wind. Korbos raised his eye from the cube with a noticeable effort. "Pyk, see what's going on out there, please," he said, a note of cold command in his statement that I was surprised to hear directed toward me. That voice brooked no argument; it demanded to be obeyed.

The woman's tanned face drained of color. "I need the money," she said. "*Now!* They're *coming.* Gimme the cash, hide the cube, and act like I was never here."

I was getting rattled at that point. What was the object to Korbos? Why would it turn the quiet-yet-genial blacksmith into a menacing brute with barely-checked violence in his voice? From the moment the girl revealed the cube, I could hear tension in his every word. And just what in the fires of Chaos was going on outside in the middle of this gutter-scrubber of a storm?

I tore myself away from the hypnotic light of the cube—which took more willpower than I'd care to admit—and went to the door, sticking my head out into the street as my clothes were immediately drenched by the sideways rain.

My blood went as cold as the water sheeting down from the eaves.

Through the haze of the downpour, I could make out a number of figures milling around a doorway four or five buildings down the avenue, dressed in insectile armor that gave their silhouettes a terrifying inhuman aspect. Water dripped from jutting protrusions and segmented plates, and a soft red glow emanated from multiple large round lenses set into nightmarish helms. A crack echoed as one kicked in the door.

The Hostguard. Looked like Ardis's anonymous travelers had been right.

I froze as a guard moved, revealing a woman standing off to one side. She stood with chin high and a haughty disregard for anything happening around her. The rain itself bent and rolled away—as if she was within a bubble that wouldn't allow the water to come close to her porcelain skin. Gauzy garments barely fluttered in the howling wind as she raised a glass of wine to her lips. I recognized her immediately. How could I not?

Kaira, High Lady of the Host. The beast who'd slaughtered my family, friends, and kin, then torched my entire village.

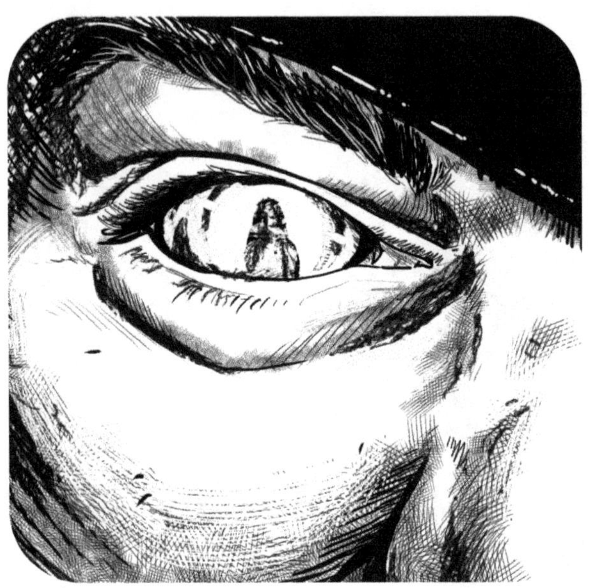

THREE

Pure fury blazed white-hot inside my chest, pushing away the chill of the storm. My ears rang with remembered screams. Skin burned with the remembered heat of blazing homes and people on fire, running to nowhere. My heart ached with the remembered agony of seeing my closest friends and family lying mutilated in the streets, some ruptured beyond recognition into steaming hunks of meat. The coppery smell of hot blood. My…my little sister, Amiel.

I wanted nothing more than to race out into the wind and rain, to hurl myself against the High Lady and tear her head from her shoulders with my bare hands.

Good thing I'm not a complete idiot.

I ducked back into the shop, dripping, shaking with wide-eyed rage and breathing hard as I closed the door behind me. Korbos, Mariyana and the hooded woman were all looking at me in expectation. The shimmering cube was engulfed in the smith's massive hand, golden beams dancing around and through his fingers.

"The Hostguard is here," I said, running to his side. "They're searching door to door. The High Lady is with them." My metal hand ground as it clenched hard enough to break stone.

Korbos's eye widened. He stepped forward, grabbing my shoulder and pulling me close. "Kaira? You're *sure* it's her?"

"Yeah, I'm not bloody likely to forget her. She looks exactly the same as the last time I saw her."

"She would," Korbos murmured, seemingly to himself. He glanced at his glowing hand. "Why has it appeared *now*, of all times? Gods above and below, we have to get out of here. She can't have the signara, it would be the end of all ho-"

"*Drek!*" the woman cursed. "I'm sure you're having quite the conversation with yourself, but for the love of Order, gimme my money and hide that thing! Nothing good will happen if they find it here."

"They're after *you*?" I asked. "Out! Get out!" I took her shoulder and started steering her toward the exit.

For the second time, the door to the shop burst open, and Hostguard piled through. We all froze. The lead soldier stopped, staring at the glow in Korbos's hand, then shouted over his shoulder.

"Here! It's here, my lady!" His voice was metallic, a synthetic tone distorted by his helm. The Hostguard fanned out, stunpikes pointed at us. There was a cacophony of orders for us to remain still and show our hands.

Korbos, his back to the guards, pressed the cube into my hands. I quickly stowed it in a hip pouch before they could see that it had been passed over.

"There's a door two rooms back," he said in a low voice. The fatal calmness in it scared me more than the threat of the soldiers. "It leads out to the alley on Tanner Street. Whatever happens, do *not* allow them to take it. *Run*."

I nodded. I knew the path.

He turned back to the door as the High Lady stepped through the row of guards. I stared at Kaira. She was as beautiful as the stories lauded, full-figured with an ageless heart-shaped face. She appeared to be anywhere from twenty to forty years of age, although I knew she was *old;* far older than all of us put together.

She wore a simple off-the-shoulder dress, slit up the sides nearly to her waist, over bare legs and calf-length boots. Golden jewelry adorned her neck and ears, with several studs piercing her eyebrows. Long shimmering black hair flowed straight and dry, contrasting oddly with the sopping guards to either side. Two plaits framed her face, colorful beads holding them tied. Her graceful poise was practiced and intimidating, especially considering her relatively small build. Sinuous tattoos resembling tentacles wound their way up her arms and legs.

The blacksmith stood protectively in front of Mariyana, the girl, and me, though I knew from experience that he had no chance against one of the Host. Kaira could tear him apart like a sheet of paper, if she chose. Given what I knew of her, she most likely would. It's what she'd done to my family. I tamped down my burning rage as best I could.

Kaira's large golden eyes widened at Korbos, and the beads in her long black hair clacked and clattered as she slowly shook her head in astonishment. Then her lips spread in a terrible grin and she laughed, a high delighted sound. Childlike, almost. She gave a little hop and clapped her hands, further enhancing the incongruity. It was both endearing and terrifying at once.

"Oh, what fortune is *this*?" she asked, wagging a finger at the big man, "All these years, and you've been *here*? Never would have taken you to become a tradesman, Korbos."

I goggled. They knew each other? Korbos *knew* how much I hated the Host. Hated Kaira in particular. And he'd never said anything?

The blacksmith's voice rumbled as he shrugged. "You overlooked me. That's what happens when you keep your nose turned up and away from the smelly parts of the world, Kaira."

"Indeed! Oh, I have missed you, pet. Now, as fun as this reunion is—and I'm sure we'll have *ages* to get reacquainted when you return to Kol with me—I'm only here for one thing. Give me the signara, Korbos my darling. I know it's here."

Korbos turned his head slightly so that he could see us from the corner of his eye. "Remember what I said, Pyk," he growled. "Don't wait for me. *Go, now*!"

Then his eye blazed silver as he hunched and an invisible force *pushed* away from him.

The three of us were shoved, hard, toward the back exit of the room, but the Hostguard were flung about like leaves in a hurricane. They bounced off the walls and ceiling as if thrown by the hand of an angry god, smashing the stones of the shop walls and crunching to the ground hard enough to crumple their armor. A bestial growl came from Korbos as his fists clenched.

I vaguely heard Mariyana calling my name, pulling at my arm. I stood, paralyzed and dumbfounded, my mind recoiling.

What in the name of Order had Korbos *done*? What was—? My thoughts scattered.

The High Lady stood her ground, unaffected by whatever had tossed the Hostguard. Another wicked grin shone out, enhancing rather than marring her terrible beauty.

"Really? We're going to do this here? Now?"

Some primal part of my brain was screaming at me to run, hide, get away at all costs, but my feet were rooted to the spot. The High Lady's eyes went blazing silver, as though the fires of Chaos itself were bursting from them, and her hair and garments began to rise around her. She looked like she was floating underwater. Korbos shifted his weight and bellowed in defiance.

I might have died, frozen like that, if not for the hooded stranger, who rushed back in and nearly yanked me off my feet.

"*Come on!*" she screamed in my ear, pulling on my mechanical arm and startling me out of my daze. We turned and stumbled into the next room, where Mari was already waiting by the far door, her large eyes wide and darting.

"Go! Go!" I yelled as we barreled through the common room, flinging aside chairs and other obstacles in our haste to escape. We made it to the alley door just as the wall behind us exploded and something came crashing past us in a broken tangle of limbs and debris.

"Atia's bones!" I screamed as I was pelted by debris. Chips of the wall *pinged* off my metal arm, raised to protect my face.

It was Korbos. He'd been flung through the wall, with far greater force than the guardsmen. His uncovered eye was open and staring, and blood from a hundred wounds mixed with the dust and debris covering him. I cried out in despair but kept moving, the stranger still pulling me by the arm.

We burst outside, the heavy rain and cold wind hitting me like a fist to the jaw and instantly soaking me to the skin as we ran for our lives down the alleyway. Mingled shouts came from behind us, where the battered Hostguard were regaining their feet and giving chase. A distorted voice cried out, "The Chek is mine!"

Mariyana kept pace with us for a few minutes, but her much shorter legs soon began to flag, and she fell behind. I glanced back, and she waved me on, yelling "Go, I'll find you soon!" Still running, she brought her fingers to her mouth and blew a shrill three-note whistle.

Moments later a large, furry form bounded down from a nearby rooftop before throwing its legs wide to reveal tent-like flaps of skin stretched between its limbs. With an almighty leap, Mari's scuridai companion rode the howling wind to the ground, skidding to a stop in front of her, his startlingly oversized eyes blinking in the rain. The size of a small, squat horse, Bastin looked like nothing more than an enormous squirrel, with the exception of the glide membranes and two short horns curving from behind his ears. Steel rings had been drilled into the horns, with a leather strop tied between the two as makeshift reins.

Mari took two hurtling strides and slammed onto the scuridai's back. "Up, Bastin!" she cried. Long climbing claws unsheathed from his toes and they scrambled back up to the rooftops, holes remaining in the bricks and plaster as he punched through them like butter. In a bound, Bastin was onto another roof and bearing Mari away from the danger.

"Where's she going?" yelled the cloaked woman.

"Don't worry about her, she'll be fine!" I replied, straining to make my voice heard above the crack of thunder and the roar of rain. "Keep going!"

We set a reckless pace as we careened down Tanner Street, dodging the detritus blown about by the storm. I was in excellent shape but honestly didn't know how long I could keep up such a speed. I could barely see through the torrential downpour.

Worse, I didn't know anywhere to go that the Hostguard couldn't eventually find. Hightide wasn't *that* big. All of the shops along the dock were barred and boarded against the storm. There wouldn't be time for me to pick a lock before we were caught. My belt pouch containing the crystalline cube beat against my hip as we fled.

I couldn't imagine how such a small thing was worth Korbos's life.

"Head for the south docks, pier twelve!" the woman screamed.

The docks? Sailing in a storm like this was suicidal at best, but still a damned sight better than being caught and slowly exsanguinated by the Hostguard.

"You're nuts! I hope to all the gods above and below you've got a fast boat!" I replied. I was beginning to tire, a small stitch burning in my ribs. I thought about the thicket of stunpikes that was almost certainly following us and pushed myself to run faster.

Minutes later we made it to the southern dock entrance, which followed the beach in a wide curve, stone and wooden boardwalks extending into the water. Ships bobbed in the churning ocean and tarps flapped in the strong winds from where they were lashed over cargo that couldn't be moved inside before the storm made landfall. Rain blew in sheets across the cobbled stones. Across the forms of three Hostguard, pikes leveled, waiting for us.

We hadn't been quite fast enough.

FOUR

"Oh, drek."

We skidded to a stop on the wet cobblestones. The soldiers were terrifying, their armor giving them the appearance of gigantic flesh-eating bugs—the type you'd see in your last moments just before they disemboweled you and burrowed into your carcass to birth their young; that sort of thing. Order anyway, I was creeping myself out.

Rain spattered from their helms, running across the multiple red-tinted eyes in rivulets. I knew they were just normal men underneath the carapaces, but the effect was intimidating in the extreme. Their stunpikes were pointed at us, and, before anyone could move, the leftmost guard sent a flare sparking into the clouds above us. The blinding crimson light bounced and scattered among the raindrops. The rest would know we were here.

Kaira would know we were here.

I was on the verge of turning and running when the hooded stranger let out a vicious roar and charged the Hostguard. For a half-second, I was stunned by the suicidal bravado. Then, because I'm an idiot, I charged after her. Crazy or not, I wasn't about to let a lady be taken by the guard.

Turned out, she really didn't need me all that much.

From beneath her cloak she whipped out a strange dagger, the hilt much longer than the wide blade. With a flick of her wrist, two more edged sections extended, locking into place to create a deadly-looking short sword. It looked almost like a cleaver—flat-nosed, without a stabbing point—and she gave a quick flourish on the run that indicated she knew how to use it.

She fell among the troops in a blur of hands and feet, vaulting over the middle pike and planting a foot into the guard's chest, sending him crashing to the ground in a grating clatter of armor and stone. Simultaneously, her sword clanged against the helmet of another, creating a bright spark but doing no serious damage.

One of the standing Hostguard stabbed at her, slicing her cloak as she spun out of the way and opened his throat with a vicious backhand swing. The guard dropped, blood mixing with the rain on the stones. The woman continued her spin, cloak flaring, and her left hand dipped beneath the swirling fabric again, emerging with—Chaos below burn us all—a pistol.

An actual, Order-blessed *handgun*.

She emptied three shots into the chest of the enemy, the rain magnifying the flare of the muzzle blast to an almost blinding yellow. He staggered back and fell without a cry, the bullets tearing through his armor like tissue. The air vibrated with the flat crack of the pistol.

I couldn't do anything but stare. The gun was a marvel, a miracle of long-forbidden technology. Gleaming machined steel shimmered as rain glinted off the barrel. A small optic was attached above the cylinder. The grip looked as if it was inlaid with redbark and fit her hand—I noted absently that her left hand was missing the last two knuckles of its ring finger—perfectly. I couldn't fathom where she'd gotten such a treasure, much less how she kept ammunition for it. Bullets were so rare as to be considered extinct.

"Atia's bits and bobs, lady, who *are* you?" I asked, my mouth hanging open.

Her cloak had fallen free during the fight, and when she turned I found myself staring at a beautiful raven-haired girl, skin tanned and freckled from the sun. Brilliant green eyes, exotically angled, glittered over a quirky grin set within mischievous full lips. She looked maybe a year or two older than me, thin, with ropy, well-defined muscles.

"Name's Cassidy," she said. "Guess I'm your ride outta this dump."

There was a glimpse of movement behind her, a flash of steel. The third guard, the one she'd knocked to the ground, had regained his footing. I didn't think, just barreled past her and slammed into the soldier before he could bring around the blade of his pike and bury it in her back. We hit the ground in a tangle of limbs and clanking armor. I wrestled the haft of his pike from his grip, then smashed the butt of the staff into the insect-like helm.

He tried to rise, so I hit him again. And again. And again. Yet he still tried to regain his feet, his helmet smashed and crumpled. In a frenzy, I reversed the pike and stabbed, opening his neck at the joint between breastplate and helm. He gurgled, clapping a gauntleted hand to his wound, and didn't rise as blood pooled beneath him and diluted into the puddles of rain.

I stood, panting, as he died. Water ran from my hair into my eyes, and I shook my head to clear them. Shock and adrenaline rushed through me in equal parts. I'd just killed a man. We'd just killed three of the *Hostguard*! I shuddered at the thought. The Host were merciless when it came to challenges to their power. Going by the stories—and personal experience—entire towns had been reduced to rubble over some small slight. I knew better than most the sort of destruction they were capable of; the stories did it no justice. We needed to leave, immediately.

Cassidy placed a hand on my shoulder.

"Come on, we gotta get to my ship. They know we're here."

Stinging rain blurred my vision as we ran past berth after berth along the crescent of the docks, each filled with ships lashed down against the storm. I passed a number of rocking boats that I knew by sight, and more than a few that I'd crewed at one point or another. We slid and stumbled, our footing treacherous on the rain-drenched cobblestones. The wind, howling hard enough to push us off-balance, didn't help matters.

Distorted voices and the stomping of hard boots came from behind us. I glanced back to see a full legion of Hostguard on our tail. Thirty soldiers, at least. There was no way we'd be able to hold them off long enough to get Cassidy's ship unmoored and cast off.

I was a moment away from kicking in the door of one of the merchants' stores on our left and praying there was a back exit when a tremendous explosion came from behind us. Metallic screams pierced the air, muted by the downpour as a huge fireball scattered Hostguard across the docks. A second explosion blew apart even more soldiers.

A blur streaked through the rain overhead and I let out a great whoop, punching the air as I recognized Bastin. Mariyana was perched on his back, a large sack slung over her shoulder. She waved to me with a fierce yell as Bastin wheeled, landed on a nearby roof, then launched himself back into the air with a quick bound.

Mari pulled a small ceramic jar from her bag, twisted a device set into the top, and then hurled it with all her tiny might toward the Hostguard. The resulting explosion threw five more guards into the water. Others crashed against the walls of a nearby banking guild office. Her homemade grenades were nothing to sneer at.

I cheered again, beginning to think we might actually have a chance. The Hostguard were powerful warriors and frightening hand-to-hand combatants, but they damned sure couldn't fly. Little they could do against an aerial attack. Cassidy and I raced ever faster toward berth twelve.

As I rounded the long, bulky hull of the *Pellegrin* in berth eleven, I was brought up short again, skidding on the wet docks until my feet slid out from under me and I hit the ground. I barely felt the sting on my bottom, I was so dumbfounded by the sight.

"Atia's bones," I muttered.

There was no ship at pier twelve. Not a sailing ship, at any rate.

It was a skipship.

It was beautiful, for lack of a better word. Yet another piece of long-forgotten technology that shouldn't even exist in the modern world.

Long lines arced down a neck-like cone into a wide body decorated with two vertical fins. Triangular wings swept forward from massive fan-like cylinders set into the fuselage. The engines, I assumed. A huge barrel, divided into sixths and reminiscent of Cassidy's pistol, hung from a swivel mount under the pilot's flight control deck. Blue-gray metal gleamed in the rain, a large symbol painted in orange on the side of the jutting cockpit—a lightning bolt within a circle.

Bright orange paint peeled in accented areas that contained writing like nothing I'd ever seen. No, wait, I *had* seen its sort before. It was the same incomprehensible language as the fading markings on the behemoths studding the Reef. Order anyway, this thing was *old*.

It was a miracle. A mirage of improbability. I'd never dreamed I'd ever see anything like it in my lifetime.

I looked up at Cassidy as she ran back and helped me to my feet. Who in Order's light was this woman, to have such riches at her disposal? The price a skipship would fetch would be enough to buy the entire town of Hightide, including all the ships and cargo on the docks. Those craft were the rarest thing in all of Elarin, far more rare even than the gun on Cassidy's hip. The only ones I'd ever even *heard* about were owned by the richest men on the continent, who liked to take them out for ostentatious showboat flights around far-flung cities like Ahrimacia or Lordsden. Who *was* this woman?

Cassidy followed my stare and her face brightened in an impish grin.

"A beaut, ain't she?" A large blast from behind us lit her face in the rain. It was a very pretty face, I admitted to myself.

I began a stammered reply as I scrambled back up, but at that moment a mid-sized skiff crashed to the docks just beyond us. We were pelted with splintered wood as the craft exploded against the cobbles, shrapnel stinging as it cut into my exposed living arm. A large piece missed my head by mere inches, the force of its passage puffing out my hair.

I spun. Mari had done a great job thinning out the Hostguard. There was less than half the previous number, and they were a good distance behind us, somewhere in the vicinity of pier five. But I could just make out the lithe woman strutting at their head, unconcerned by the explosions bursting around her.

Kaira.

She extended her arms to the side, her eyes blazing silver, and another small ship rose from the water as if lifted by an immense unseen hand, trailing rivers through the air as her incomprehensible powers hurled it at us.

We leapt out of the way as it crashed next to the skiff. Kaira was attempting to cut us off, block us from reaching the skipship. Worse, she wanted us alive, or she would have simply ripped us apart from the beginning. My body flooded with terror and adrenaline at the thought.

Each time we tried to scurry around the debris, another object crashed in front of us. She was herding us, penning us in as the Hostguard cautiously made their way forward. A blur flew overhead as Bastin passed and Mari threw a grenade at Kaira, who flung it back at them with a casual wave of her hand. I cried out, but Bastin was nimble in the air, twisting in a quick bank to avoid the explosion. The pair rode out the shockwave, disappearing past the roofline of a nearby building.

Kaira and the Hostguard drew closer. Cassidy's eyes were alight with fury and frustration, her sword and gun in her hands, ready to fight to her death. I realized I was still holding the pike I'd taken off the guard earlier. It might as well have been a toothpick, for all the good it would do me. Baring my teeth, I lowered my scavenged stunpike toward our approaching doom. She might be able to tear me open from the inside out, but I wasn't about to die without trying to take Kaira with me.

The High Lady prowled toward us with a nimble grace, in no hurry to finish off her cornered prey.

Blue light strobed from a window to my right, in a print shop halfway between us and Kaira. It flashed again, a stutter of brilliant blue, and then the front wall of the shop exploded outward. Hostguard that weren't knocked unconscious or felled by flying bricks scattered in every direction. Yet the High Lady remained unharmed, the bubble of an invisible shield springing up around her and deflecting the debris. Rage contorted her face as a massive figure leapt through the dust and rubble into the wind and rain. My jaw fell open as he took up position between us and the Host.

It was Korbos.

He *lived!*

The blacksmith—the quiet, gruff man who had been my friend and watched over me since my first days as an orphan in Hightide—was transformed. He wore a long black coat that flapped in the tempest. And—gods above and below take me—he had a gun against his shoulder; a long monstrosity of a thing that tossed giant bursts of blue energy at least two feet from the end of the barrel. Korbos had to hold it with both hands, the butt of the gun bucking against his bulk. His eye glowed silver, and Kaira—now fighting alone—fell back before his onslaught. I could see—actually *see*—glowing silver cracks spiderwebbing her shield.

Kaira's eyes flashed in blinding brilliance, lighting up the docks around her and reflecting off the wet cobblestones. She flung her hands forward and dozens of crates flew toward Korbos. And, I realized grimly, at me.

"Pyk, *go*!" Korbos roared, unleashing a volley of blue fire and disintegrating the projectiles posing the most immediate threat.

He didn't have to tell me twice. I spun and ran through the wreckage, thanking Order's light that I'd put my leather boots back on before leaving the *Quay*; the cobblestones were littered with shattered, stabbing boards and scattered nails. One day soon, if I survived this mess, I'd need to invest in a good pair of steeltoes.

A loading ramp was ratcheting down on Cassidy's skipship, and I could see illumination in the control room. Pilot area. Whatever it was called. Circular lights underneath the ship began to grow brighter, and the three support legs slowly rose from the ground as the ship hovered in the air. I bolted up the ramp, then turned and wrapped my free arm around a hydraulic strut, steadying myself and watching the chaos unfold before me. Cassidy swept past me toward the interior, shouldering me aside as she hurtled through the large bay at the top of the ramp.

Korbos was backing toward the skipship, his fire alternating between Kaira's shield and the debris being flung from every direction. It was...well, it was unbelievable. He never missed a target, the azure bolts incinerating an insane amount of projectiles at a rate my eyes couldn't begin to track. He dropped his enormous gun to his hip, firing with one hand as he stretched out his left and—with a sweeping gesture—brushed the skiff wreckage behind him off the dock and into the water.

I gaped. He *was* using Host powers. What I'd seen him do in his shop was real. My brain refused to quite process what it was seeing.

He was almost to the ship, but Kaira was beginning to overwhelm him. Bits of debris clanged off the skipship's hull as Korbos missed some of the projectiles. He reached the rising ramp, hopping up and never ceasing his steady stream of fire. I had no idea how he wasn't running out of ammunition. Even as rare as they were, I knew guns needed bullets.

The skipship quickly rose into the air. High Lady Kaira, her rage palpable, stopped her barrage. Korbos likewise stopped firing.

"You can't run, Korbos!" she screamed. "Wherever you go, however long it takes, I will *hunt you down*!"

He scoffed and raised his voice to be heard over the torrent of rain and the thin whine of the skipship's engines. "You've been hunting me for decades, Kaira. What makes you think that'll change?"

They stared at each other for what seemed an eternity, and then she turned and stretched out her arms. I heard a loud groaning as an enormous sailing ship—four masts and at least a hundred tons—slowly rose from the water. Kaira wasn't taking any more chances. Rarity be damned, she'd obliterate the skipship before letting us escape with the cube. A faint cry of fury came from her as the giant vessel rose over her head, water sluicing off to part around her shield. Beams split and rivets popped along the keel of the behemoth.

"That's the *M'aiq!*" I barked with a wild, uncontrollable laugh as Kaira turned back to us. "Jen's going to be *ticked!*" I couldn't stop laughing. I was scared that if I did I'd break down into sobs. The skipship hadn't yet crested the roofs of the dockhouses. We'd be knocked out of the sky, assuming the *M'aiq* didn't just mush us into a thin paste.

Korbos, still standing at the edge of the ramp, put his fingers to his mouth and blew a shrill, piercing whistle. Three notes. A lot like the trill used by—

"Mariyana!" he bellowed.

Bastin's silhouette leaped from a nearby roof, Mari riding high on his back. She held one of her homemade grenades at the ready. Korbos stretched an arm toward Kaira, and just as Mariyana launched her weapon a cavalcade of metal containers shot forward from a pile of cargo lying a few docks away. They converged on the High Lady, and I had a brief glimpse of a familiar triangular warning just before Mari's grenade hit.

Danger: Combustibles.

The blast was magnificent. Fire enveloped the docks, the shockwave demolishing cobblestones and counting houses alike as it washed over Cassidy's ship. The skipship listed as the wave pushed us to the right and briefly formed a calm bubble within the rain. Strangely, the fire didn't burn us, although I could see crates and fallen timbers igniting as they blew outward.

I stared, dumbfounded, until I noticed that the returning rainfall bent around the ship as if sliding down a curved piece of glass. Korbos stood unfazed on the ramp, rifle slung across his shoulder, not even holding on for support as the ship continued its ascent. Unreality washed over me along with the wave of diminished heat. Korbos had protected the ship, encasing it in a bubble like the High Lady's.

Kaira had kicked ten hells out of him in his shop, so just how powerful *was* he?

After the calamity died down, there was nothing but a gigantic pile of collapsed rubble where Kaira had been standing, the crumpled wreckage of the *M'aiq* topping it like a decoration on a cake. As the skipship continued to climb, I coughed out another bitter laugh. Jen really *was* gonna be ticked off about her boat.

FIVE

Korbos walked up the ramp and turned beside me to wait. A moment later, Bastin glided into the ship, his claws screeching against the deck plates as he skidded to a stop. Neither he nor Mariyana looked any worse for the blast. The blacksmith slapped a red button against the inner hull, and the ramp whirred to a close. How had he known what that would do?

The decking under my feet pitched, the skipship turning to starboard. The large drives kicked in, and I had to grab a wall strut to keep my balance against the sudden acceleration. Mari jumped from Bastin's back and threw her tiny arms around Korbos's waist. As far as they would go, anyway.

"I knew you weren't dead! There's no way you'd go out like that and how did you find us and oh did you see me bombing those Hostguard with my boompowder I really messed them up and I totally saved Pyk and that lady and is this her ship it's so cool and wasn't that *awesome*?"

She was literally hopping with excitement.

Korbos's good eye lit up as his teeth showed in a rare smile. After gathering Mari into a crushing hug, he scratched Bastin behind the ears. The scuridai, for his part, chirruped in satisfaction, as if he knew he'd done well and deserved the attention.

"If you say so, little one. You fought well out there." Mari's smile widened, and Bastin purred softly and nuzzled Korbos's hip.

With the danger behind us, the events of the last few minutes slammed home all at once. I fell back to lean against a stack of crates, pressing my netanium hand to my forehead in an attempt to cool my racing blood.

My heart lifted to see my friend alive, though I couldn't fathom how he'd survived. Every instinct I had told me he had been killed in his shop. Yet here he stood.

Another part of me, however, felt betrayed. Who *was* this guy, who could apparently return from the dead and wield the destructive powers of the Host themselves? Was he one of the monsters that had destroyed my life so many years ago? The old tales told of many Host, perhaps as many as ten, harbingers of doom and desolation. I was only familiar with Kaira and Kalos, but that didn't mean that others weren't out there somewhere.

Had I ever *really* known Korbos in all the years we'd been friends and neighbors? If he was a Host, why would he save us? The Host only looked out for themselves. Power, pleasure and control were the only things they desired. They were abominations plaguing the world. I could barely think, my mind warring between revulsion and relief.

He turned to me, mouth open to speak. I took a step back and held up a hand to stop him.

"Don't," I said. "I don't want to know, not right now. Maybe not ever."

The tone was harsh enough, but the betrayal must have shown as well in my expression. His face fell in a weary sadness I'd have never expected from the stoic smith. The big man sighed, giving a curt nod and turning to walk the gangway to the skipship's cockpit. Lightning cracked and thunder shook the ship as I followed, wary of *all* of this drek.

We were already underway, heading west out to the Sea of Sem and away from the ruins of the Hightide docks. The ship was low to the water, having already skimmed over the Reef, and I marveled at the speed of the waves whipping past. Volumes of rain sluiced off the thick glass of the pilot's viewport. Innumerable lights blinked and gauges shifted as Cassidy gently adjusted our course from the pilot's seat.

She turned her chair, a wry smile quirking a corner of her mouth. It really *was* a pretty one. Her green eyes, large and tilted, glittered with humor.

"So do I get my money for that cube now?"

Korbos looked over to me. I nodded and took the cube from my hip pouch, handing it to him in much the same way as I'd hand over a poisonous snake.

He grunted, then remained silent for a long while as the skipship passed through the storm and into almost blinding sunlight.

The sun lit his face as he finally spoke.

"Do you have any idea what this device is, child? How important it is? For everyone?"

"Nope! Don't care. I just want my money. That cube's still mine until I get paid and you all get the hell off my boat. And don't call me child, old man."

The blacksmith stared out the wide windscreen, his features carefully blank. "You'll get your money soon enough. But I'd like to hire you and your ship. We need to get to Cortian as soon as possible."

Cassidy's eyes widened. "Cortian! That's a two-month-long journey inland, to a frokking Devoid city! There's no way."

"Yes, but that's two months by land. In a wagon. I'd wager that a ship such as this can make that distance in considerably less time. Say, maybe a few days? And the Devoid are a necessary risk."

I cocked my head. What were the Devoid? I glanced over to Mari, who gave a small *I dunno* shrug.

Cassidy's eyes narrowed, and she gave Korbos a more appraising look. "You're good for the coin, then? The price is twenty thousand karani. Plus twenty for the cube."

My jaw dropped. Forty thousand would have bought me a ship the size of the *Ma'iq*, with enough left over for three months' crew wages.

Korbos didn't answer, turning to me and Mariyana.

"We can drop you two anywhere you'd like along the way. I can't ask you to follow. I have no right to ask you to follow." He never broke his gaze from me. It felt uncomfortable. There was something there that I couldn't read. Was it guilt? Anger?

Fear?

I stared him in the eye. "We were seen with you. With her," I said, jerking my head toward Cassidy. "Atia's all-seeing eyeballs, Korbos… where could we go that the Hostguard wouldn't find us? You two got us into this mess, so I don't think we've got any choice but to see it to the end. I just hope it's not my end. Or Mari's." I tried to insert some authority into my voice, but it sounded more like petulance.

"Don't blaspheme," Mari whispered beside me.

Korbos sighed, holding the cube up to the light. Sunlight sparkled from enigmatic patterns and runes as they danced around the multilayered panels. "I searched for this data drive—this signara—for nearly five hundred years," he said, voice whisper-quiet. "It's the only one of its kind left in all of Elarin, as far as I know. I'd begun to think it had been lost forever."

Mariyana and I started. Cassidy's head whipped around, eyebrows climbing into her scalp.

"I've given up my left eye and more good people than you'd ever care to know about in pursuit of this...thing. If you knew half the things I've done while trying to find it, you'd rightly call me a monster. But I'd given up. I quit. I was content to live out the rest of my long days, quietly creating useful tools and providing help where I could. And, for the first time in more years than I can count, I made friends. You."

He looked around slowly, taking us in one at a time.

"I'm tired of losing people I care about, so listen up. This drive is the key to ending the Host, forever. If you decide to follow me I cannot begin to overstate the danger we'll be facing. But I'd be glad to have you along. All of you." He glanced at Cassidy before turning back to me.

"I didn't want this burden any longer, but since all the powers of Order have seen fit to drop it into my hands, it appears I don't have a choice. But I can't *tell* you to come. If you do, there's a high likelihood you may never see home again. I can only protect you so far. Would you be willing to leave everything to follow me, Pyk? To see this through to the end, either the Host's or ours? *Could* you do that, my friend?"

Confusion and doubt raged through my brain as I stared at the floor. My hands—both mechanical and flesh—clenched and released.

Five hundred years, if he was telling the truth. I couldn't even conceive that amount of time. That much *life*. The number twisted through my mind like a bluegill circling a baited hook. I couldn't grasp it in any meaningful way. I knew the Host were long-lived, practically immortal, but still…

I remembered the second-worst day of my life, not long after I'd arrived in Hightide.

Ten years old, orphaned and alone, I was honestly naive to the ways of the world at large. Even the Host's attack on my village had only exposed me to nightmares that seemed surreal; terrors out of a monstrous fairy tale. Not the horrors, lesser and greater, that men can willingly inflict upon one another.

I'd been attacked, robbed of my few meager possessions, severely wounded and left for dead in an alley. My last sight was of a giant standing over me as I blacked out. When I came to, I was strapped to a table, in a great deal of pain. My left arm had been removed, and in its place was a synthetic limb—a lean approximation of an arm; netanium plating, pistons, and servos where flesh should have been. When I cried out in terror, the shape of the giant loomed over me, whispering calming words and offering cool water laced with painkillers.

As the days and years passed, Korbos taught me how to use my new Seeker arm, spending his own money and replacing it whenever I outgrew the previous iteration. He was always kind, although gruff, and never expressed any desire for repayment. Most merchants would have considered my debt high enough to consign me to a life of indentured servitude, but the blacksmith waved off my efforts with a meaty hand.

It never really occurred to me to consider him a father figure, but I realized he was the closest I'd come to one since my family was butchered.

This was Korbos. My *friend.* I owed him my life, and he'd saved our backsides at least twice tonight. He wasn't an evil man. Not like the Host. I was sure of it.

Something in my chest loosened, and I raised my head to meet his eye. "It's true, then. You're one of *them.*" It wasn't a question.

He hesitated, then nodded. Cassidy whistled low through her teeth.

"Well, then," I sighed after a thoughtful moment. A grin broke as I clapped him on the arm. "Good thing you're on our side!"

Korbos seemed to deflate as he released a held breath and relief slackened his face. He smiled his tight, thin smile and clasped me by my metal shoulder in a warm gesture.

"I can't speak for Mariyana," I said, "but I'll go with you as far as the road ta—"

"Of course I'm coming!" Mari leapt forward and tried to wrap her arms around both of us, failing spectacularly and causing us both to chuckle. She clapped her small hands together with far too much enthusiasm for my taste. "Just think, Pyk, it'll be awesome! Hostguard chasing us, stuff to blow up, grand tales of adventure to tell our kids well assuming we have kids one day kids with other people I mean not each other oh if we're going on a quest I need to get some treats for Bastin and I'm out of boompowder I kinda used the last of mine on that big bang back ther—"

She quieted as Korbos laid a hand on her tiny back.

The three of us turned to look at Cassidy.

"Ah, *drek,*" she said, shrugging. "Why not, as long as I get paid? At least that *bhuta* Kaira is dead."

"Dead?" Korbos asked, tilting his head. "Oh, no. No, it would take one hell of a lot more than some bombs and bricks to kill someone like her. We most likely only made her angry. She gets pretty mad when she so much as gets a hair out of place, so it's probably for the best we didn't stick around."

Everyone stared blankly for several seconds, then Cassidy and Mariyana burst out laughing together. I quickly followed, holding a panel to keep from doubling over. It was terrified, relieved laughter—almost hysterical—but it felt good all the same. A release of tension from the close call we'd all just gone through. Gone through *together*. Korbos stood stoic, a small, cockeyed grin his only acknowledgement of what we'd just survived.

Cassidy held out a hand to the blacksmith once the laughter tapered off.

"You give me your word that I'll get my forty thousand after we reach Cortian, and I'll get you there faster than you'd ever dream. No skipship on the planet faster than my girl here." She patted the console beside her.

"Well, there's only, like, four of them anymore, right? Not exactly an overwhelming sample size," I snarked. She stuck her tongue out at me.

Korbos, face studiously solemn, extended his massive hand and enveloped Cassidy's. They shook.

"Our bond is made, the bargain struck, captain."

Cassidy gave a single, slow nod, then broke into a wide, mischievous grin. "Okay then, pal, you gotcherself a skipship. I'm Cassidy Ryker. Welcome aboard the *Storm*."

SIX

"Rules of Order and Chaos *damn* it!" Cassidy screamed, an impressive stream of curses following as she hurtled through the *Storm*'s passageways. A steady beeping from the pilot's seat receded the further astern we jogged. I was about to ask if we were going to fall out of the sky when she rounded a tight corner to the sound of hissing. A thin white jet of gas expelled from an exposed pipe running down the bulkhead.

"Cover your face," she barked. "You don't want this drek on your skin if you can help it."

I couldn't do much about my bare arm, but I pulled my shirt up over my mouth and nose, trying my best not to breathe in the gas as Cassidy did the same. She snatched a black cylindrical device from a neighboring pipe, and slammed it over the break fast enough to avoid any prolonged contact with the mist. Two shining levers were pushed backward, tightening the clamp enough that she could twist a few knobs and seal off the breach. She hustled to the nearby lavatory to rinse off her hands and forearms.

"Should I be worried?" I asked. Hopefully my nervousness didn't show on my face.

"Nah," Cassidy replied. "The old girl springs a leak every now and then. The clamp will hold until I can either patch it for good or fabricate a replacement."

"How old *is* the *Storm*, anyway?"

She thought for a moment. "If I had to guess, I'd say about six, maybe seven hundred years. Order only knows for sure." She finished wiping down her hands and tossed the rags into a vacuum bin. "Probably been around since the Ruin."

My mind reeled at the number. I couldn't fathom how the skipship was still even skyworthy after that long. Between Korbos, Kaira, the *Storm*, and the gun resting in Cassidy's leg holster, it seemed like I was hip-deep in Elarin history lately.

"How is this thing not a total rust-bomb? Where'd you even get it?" I asked. Rare treasures aside, she didn't *look* like she was rich enough to buy a skipship outright.

Cassidy was quiet for a few moments as we walked back to the bridge. I ran my flesh-and-blood hand along the wall panels, admiring the craftsmanship of the vessel. The hall was wide enough for the two of us to walk side by side, covered in plates of some hard yet light—maybe hollow—material, broken here and there by inset piping and tubes. It wasn't quite metal, yet not something so fragile as ceramics. I'd never seen anything like it before.

Sliding cabin doors stood open, and I could hear music coming from one just ahead. As we passed, I saw Mari standing on her rumpled bunk, gyrating to a pounding rhythm and screeching caterwaul that emanated from a small box set into the wall. I shook my head at the wonder of it. Music in a box. Centuries-old music at that. Bastin lay curled on the decking at the foot of the bunk, the cabin barely large enough to accommodate his furry bulk.

"Well," Cassidy finally replied as we entered the cockpit, "thereby hangs a tale, if you've got time."

I glanced around, gesturing to the intricate panels surrounding the flight controls. "Where else am I gonna go? Not like I know how to do anything around here."

Cassidy chuckled, strapping into the pilot's couch and fiddling with a few knobs. "True enough. Grab a seat over there, and don't touch anything. The long-range comm station hasn't ever worked for me—just the intership comm—but I'd prefer you not accidentally set off a transponder or something and let the whole frokking world know where we are."

"Right. Got it." I had no idea what she was talking about. I dutifully crossed my arms, sitting down to what I assumed was the copilot's station, keeping them far away from the controls.

A peaceful quiet fell over the cockpit as we both stared out at the starry night sky. The two moons—Masina Atoa and Masina Tamai—shone bright; the former large and yellow-white, the latter small and broken, pieces scattered in a wide arc across the heavens.

"So?" I prodded. "Just who in the hells of Chaos are you, Cass?"

"Cassidy, please. I hate being called Cass."

"Duly noted, sorry."

"Eh, not like you'd know." She leaned back in the couch, throwing her feet up on the console. "Sorry, I really don't mean to come off as brusque. I've been on my own for a long time."

I grinned. "A long time? You're what, twenty? Twenty-one?"

"Twenty-two in a couple of days, actually."

"Mom always said beware the older woman," I said with a smirk. A bittersweet pang hit me as I tried to recall my mother's face. My memories of her and my father were becoming less and less clear as time passed.

"Ha-frokking-ha. You wanna hear about the ship or not?"

I waved a hand in a gesture of magnanimity. "By all means, proceed."

"So whaddya wanna know?"

"How'd you even *get* this thing? Are you some kind of secret princess who snuck out of daddy's castle with a few toys? Steal the keys to his prized skipship and too scared to go back?"

Cassidy sighed, pinching the bridge of her nose. "No. No, I'm not a frokkin' princess. Okay. So, in order for me to tell this, you gotta know a little bit about me. I *did* run off from home, but that's my business and none of yours, so just go with it when I tell you I've been on my own for a while."

I nodded in agreement, curious.

"I took up mechanicking—yes, that's a word—with Master Erbal Riekan in this little town called Newsome when I was thirteen. He fed me and clothed me and trained me to work on boilers and just about anything mech you can think of. It kept me off the streets, and I really enjoyed the work. I love figuring out how things operate."

I was surprised by that, but it made sense. Mechanic wasn't the most, uh, traditionally womanly of professions, but it at least explained how she could keep an ancient craft like the *Storm* from barreling into a cliff at a high rate of speed. Order knew *I'd* never figure out something like that without getting myself killed.

She scratched at her arm. "I spent a few years happy in Newsome, banging away at steam engines and assorted contraptions, but right after I turned seventeen, Master Riekan got sick with lung disease. When he died, the banks took his shop and kicked me out. I got more than a few bruises trying to fight off their thugs. Sorry…'collection agents.'

"I didn't have anywhere to go, but I had the contacts I'd made as an apprentice. Unfortunately, like a moron I picked the wrong ones and wound up fixing steamcarts for the Quicks Guild. That quickly turned into modifying and building shock lances and other weapons for 'em."

My eyes widened. The Quicks Guild was notorious in the western part of Elarin. They were a gang of reavers and robbers, responsible for a long spell of highway banditry. Most city watches were able to keep them out of the townships, since they operated openly, but they were a terror along the countryside trade routes. At least, up until—

"Wait," I interrupted. "I heard their base was found and burned out a few years ago. Didn't the Newsome mayor or somebody put together a watch coalition and go on the attack?"

Cassidy's green eyes looked down and away. "Yeah, that was my doing." She shrugged. "They forced me into building weapons for them, but I never really gave it much thought as to how they were using them. I was happy in the work. Until I heard about the Merin incident."

I whistled low, nodding. Tommas Merin had been one of the richest and most influential textile merchants on the western seaboard, until his family's caravan was ambushed on the road to Hightide a couple of years prior. The Quicks Guild had taken him for ransom, but they killed the rest of the entourage, including Merin's wife and seven children. After the ransom was paid by his company's bank, Tommas's head had been delivered to the Merchantmaster's office in a gilded box with a note that simply said, "Thanks." It had been the talk of Hightide for weeks.

Cassidy grew quiet. "After I heard about those kids, I knew I couldn't work for the Guild any more. But you don't just up and leave an organization like that. Not in one piece. So I waited a few months and managed to sneak away during a supply run. I went to the Newsome constabulary and told them everything I knew about the Guild and their location. The mayor put together his coalition and firebombed the place.

"Most of the Guild was wiped out in the attack, but I'm pretty sure Javi Quicks is still alive. In the years since, I've had a couple of his bounty hunters try to run me down. They're dead now, obviously, but they all bore the Guild mark."

She pushed down her glove to show me an old, puffy brand on the inner flesh of her right forearm—a stylized flaming comet.

"I knew if Quicks was still out there, he'd be looking for me, so I packed up what I could carry and headed out east. I wound up hooking up with a group of Seekers, and spent the next few years learning everything I could about their trade. Been doing that ever since."

"Wait, so now you're a tomb robber?"

"No! Well…yes, if you want to be crass about it. I prefer the term 'Preserver of Antiquities.'"

I nodded again, smiling to myself at her indignation. The Seekers were a band of treasure hunters—almost a cult—dedicated to reviving the technological wonders of the pre-Ruin era. It made sense that Cassidy, with her love of mechanics, would wind up joining them. Even if their successes were relatively few, Seekers were responsible for rediscovering the secrets that led to steamcarts and had made amazing strides in mechanical replacement limbs, such as my left arm. By and large, however, they'd had remarkably little progress in bringing back the true marvels of the past. They couldn't build stuff like skipships, for instance. Just found and fixed up what they could.

"So you picked up the *Storm* with them?" I asked. "Must have risen through the ranks fast if they trusted you with something as invaluable as a skipship."

Cassidy glanced away again. "They…don't technically know about the *Storm*." She sighed. "I left the main body of Seekers after a…let's say an incident…with one of the higher-ups not too long ago. He was interested, and I wasn't. Emphatically.

"Anyway, while I was with the Seekers I saw *so* many wonders. You wouldn't believe it, Pyk, seriously. Two years ago they discovered a man built of metal, buried in the desert sands a day's ride outside Qirim." She grinned, wagging her eyebrows before pulling a small flask from a pocket of the pilot's couch and taking a swig.

"A mechanical man? Like, a whole man made out of parts like my arm?"

"Yeah, except he was about five times the size of the *Storm*."

She was right, I didn't believe it. I scoffed, coughing as I took a burning pull from the proffered flask.

"So, I came across some seriously old military maps—I mean *crumbling* with age—while I was on an expedition. Order only knew if they were accurate or not—it wasn't like anyone could translate them, they were so old—so I held on to them for authentication rather than storing them in the Searching Library.

"After my falling out, I spent six months tracking down an old storehouse that was marked on the maps and nearly got myself killed in the doing. I literally fell into the base while I was digging around some hills looking. The ground caved in underneath me, and I woke up on the floor of an enormous room, like a big cavern. Pure lucky that my legs weren't broken, not to mention my neck.

"The place was absolutely huge and halfway to wrecked. I've no idea how long it had been hidden, so I can only guess that the original inhabitants tried to clean it out when they left, or died, or whatever. It was a Seeker's dream, though. Whether functional or not, the entire base was packed with old stuff. Vehicles, medical bays, crates upon crates upon crates of rations and Order only knows what. You wouldn't believe how well the old ones crafted some of this stuff. So much has been lost." She shook her head sadly.

"A lot of it was scattered to the winds and rusted beyond recognition, but while I was digging around I found a few things that were salvageable. One was Jasmin here." She patted the gun at her hip.

"Can…can I…?" I stammered, gesturing at the gun.

She cocked an eyebrow at me, but drew the pistol with care, flipping it around and handing it over grip-first.

"Here you go," she said. "Just try not to muss up that pretty face, sweetcheeks." Her lopsided grin appeared, crinkling her eyes and setting her freckles to dance.

I stared at the machine in awe, admiring its lines. The precise angles of its construction. I ran my fingers over the cylinder that held the bullets, the redbark of the grip. The delicate curve of the whatever that part was…

I was entranced. There was a vague impression of Cassidy reaching out toward me as I sighted along the optic, pointing the gun toward the ship's aft. From a distance, I heard her cry out "Don't!" as I gently squeezed the curvy bit.

KA-BLAM!!!

Fire shot from the end of the pistol as it bucked in my hand. I dropped it in surprise, shrieking as it bounced off the deck. I…I hadn't meant to set it off! I looked up to Cassidy's screaming face, but I couldn't understand her muffled words. The shot was so loud in the tight cabin that I'd gone temporarily deaf.

Cassidy scooped up the gun, returning it to its holster. Sound began to filter back in, primarily a stream of profanity spewing from her mouth as we walked over to survey the damage.

A large round hole had appeared in the bulkhead at the rear of the cabin, wide enough for me to put my first two fingers in. I put my eye close and stared through to another room. Cassidy's quarters.

"*Drek*, drekdrekdrekdrek*drek*!" she was shouting. We jumped up and rounded the corner to the hatch, where we skidded to a stop with an enormous rifle in our faces.

"Atia's *bones*, Korbos, wear a bell or something!" I yelled, trying to catch my breath and tamp down the adrenaline surge.

"I heard a shot," he rumbled, shouldering the rifle. "I thought maybe…"

Cassidy laughed. "Thought maybe I was going to go pirate on you? Not likely. You're too damned big and he's too pretty."

I tilted my head. That was twice she'd called me pretty.

We entered her cabin and turned to the wall abutting the cockpit, where a tall locker stood. The door was buckled outward with an alarmingly large hole in it, big enough to put my fist through. Order anyway, what kind of ammunition did that thing shoot?

Cassidy tsked and swung open the locker, examining the damage from both sides. There was an open crate underneath a disorganized pile of her clothing, stacked full of brass bullet casings. Hundreds of them.

That solved the mystery of where she got her ammo.

"Well, Pyk," she said, "you owe me a locker door."

"I'm so sorry..." I began.

"No, that was my fault," she sighed. "Probably should have given you a rundown *before* handing you a loaded weapon. Let's just chalk it up to an accident and be thankful nobody lost a spleen or worse."

"I can probably fix that locker when we have time," said Korbos.

"See that you do, my good man."

We returned to the cockpit, taking up our former positions, Korbos joining us in one of the two empty seats. My head was tucked and shoulders hunched in morbid embarrassment.

"So where was I?" Cassidy said. "Oh, yeah, all the fun stuff I found in that warehouse. Food, my Jasmin here, a few other assorted weapons—though this was the only gun—all kinds of historical stuff that set my little Seeker heart aflutter.

"The truly great find, of course, was the *Storm*. It took some doing, but she was still skyworthy. It took me way longer to figure out how to get her out of there. I spent three days combing through these dank stairwells trying to find my way back outside, and another two tracking down fuses to route power and open a gate. Atia and Order themselves must have been looking out for me, because I was lucky enough to find a bunch of sealed rations that hadn't spoiled. Otherwise I think I'd have starved down there."

She paused, taking a sip from a different canteen in her couch's cup holder. Looked like it wasn't water, judging by the slight grimace and small shudder she gave. Mari's singing, loud and off-key, kept the silence from being uncomfortable. Sounded like *she'd* been into a drink or two as well, given that she was singing along with words in a long-dead language.

I wondered how much alcohol Cassidy had stashed around the ship as I took another sip from the flask. Wouldn't be there for long if Korbos found it.

"So that was about...six weeks ago? Eight? In any case, Hightide was the first place I visited after figuring out how to fly my baby here. I'm starting to wonder if she's bad luck, honestly. Almost tore her straight into a mountain on our first flight, and then once I get the hang of it I nearly wind up in the arms of one of the frokking Host."

She took a longer pull from the flask, releasing a contented sigh that echoed through the cabin. "Not exactly an auspicious start to my solo career in adventuring."

I nodded, considering. Not that I was a scholar on skipships or their owners, but I think I'd have maybe heard of a nine-fingered rogue bouncing around Elarin with a gun on her hip and a ship nobody had ever seen before. It made sense that she hadn't been active and mobile for very long.

"Sounds like you fell into a Second Battalion storehouse," said Korbos in his deep boom.

"What's a Second Battalion?" Cassidy asked.

"The one right after First Battalion."

I stared. Had...had Korbos just made a *joke*? Cassidy gave him a wry look.

"Sorry," Korbos rumbled in what he must have considered a small voice. "Trying to develop a sense of humor, I suppose. Mind if I get a hit of that?"

He motioned for the flask. Sighing, I handed it over, and he took a long, long drink.

Eventually he lowered it back to me, exhaling in satisfaction, his eye a little bleary.

"Second Battalion was a military unit, prior to the Ruin, whose primary purpose was provisioning and logistics for the Imperial Dynasty. They had warehouses such as you describe dotted here and there throughout the countryside. I used them on occasion to rest and resupply while I was hunting the signara. Matter of fact, the storehouse you visited is likely the one where Kaira finally captured me about two hundred years ago. If it *was*, you're lucky there was anything left to find. We trashed the place pretty well during the fight, before she eventually subdued me."

His face darkened. "It took almost two centuries for me to escape her. After that, I gave up on my hunt. I've been hiding in Hightide ever since."

"Bloody hells, Korbos," I said. "Just how old *are* you?"

"I don't honestly know for certain, but around nine hundred years. It doesn't matter, my story isn't important."

"Nine hundred *years*? Not important? *Drek*, do you have any idea how much you can tell us abou—"

"My secrets are my own, Pyk!" The smith's face was thunderous. "And I'm telling you that they don't matter right now. What's important is that we get to Cortian with this signara and get at the data it contains. That's the *only* way we bring down the Host."

I nodded, that ever-simmering anger at the Host giving a slightly larger burble at the thought. I took one last chug from the dwindling flask. A small one. It was strong stuff.

Korbos turned to Cassidy. "Is that where you found the signara? In the storehouse?" He held up the cube, the golden patterns flitting about beneath the glassy surface in hypnotizing geometry.

Cassidy spun her pilot's couch slowly, silent a few moments before answering. "Yeah, found it in a triple-locked chest buried under a small mountain of supplies. In a sealed room three levels down from the hangar where I found the *Storm*. Took forever to break through the locks, but it looked shiny enough that I figured it'd be worth something to somebody."

Korbos grunted.

"So why Cortian?" I asked. "What's there that we have to get to so badl—"

"*Drek!*" The loud curse broke my train of thought.

We turned to Cassidy, who was fiddling with the ship's controls. A loud beeping was coming from the console. Her canteen disappeared back into the couch's pocket.

"Will this affect our trip time?" Korbos asked, placing his hand on the back of the pilot's couch and leaning over Cassidy's shoulder.

"At cruising speed, it'd be maybe two, three days, but we might have a slight problem. So yeah, I'd say so."

"What kind of problem?" I asked. " A 'fall out of the sky' problem?" I couldn't hide the tinge of panic that crept into my voice.

"No," she replied. "I dunno. Kind of?" She rocked her hand back and forth, then tapped a small red illuminated bar, which was blinking rapidly. "We're low on fuel."

SEVEN

I stood at the edge of an *extremely* high cliff overlooking the Southern Reaches, a chain of relatively small land masses that stretched out into the distant ocean horizon. Towering fingers of rock dotted the waters amongst them, reaching for the sky as if a multitude of enormous stone giants lurked just below the surface, ready to clench their fists and crush the unlucky sailors forced to navigate the narrows.

Korbos was irritated by our delay. He wanted to travel directly inland to Cortian, but Cassidy insisted that the *Storm* needed an annual refuel before we could begin the journey. The ship ran on salt water, she said. Something about electrostatic fusion, whatever that meant. Sounded like so much drek to me, but Korbos reluctantly nodded in agreement. I supposed he'd seen it all before, being ancient and all.

I'd asked why we couldn't just dip down on any random beach, but apparently normal seawater wouldn't work. Thus, our detour to the Reaches. The *Storm* rested in a small, grassy bowl valley, high on a plateau edged with spears of rock.

"These cliffs are the closest source of the tarbrine we need," Cassidy replied as she waved her arm to encompass the jutting stone around us. "The rain runoff leaches through the rock, which is pure saltstone. It becomes super-concentrated—almost a sludge—and collects in the volcanic springs dotting the lowlands. Once I meet up with my supplier and get it here, we'll fuel up and be on our merry little way."

That had been hours ago. I was briefly nervous that she'd taken the opportunity to ditch us, but my fears were allayed by the thought that no one in their right mind would just haul anchor and leave a skipship behind. Not that I was sure of Cassidy's sanity, after the way she'd charged those Hostguard back in Hightide.

So for hours I'd waited, pacing the ship. Pacing the tall grass around the struts. Pacing the field we were in. Mariyana kept busy by grooming Bastin and taking short flights around the rocks and natural landings of the plateau. Korbos passed the time by oiling his gun and the rather dizzying array of knives and other bladed weapons he produced seemingly from nowhere.

I was going stir-crazy, so I set out to climb an outcropping I'd spotted over at the western edge of the valley. Several minutes later I was enjoying a breathtaking view of the Reaches in all their splendor. The giant fingers, spotted with patches of shockingly green vegetation, stood proudly against the rising sun, the sky blazing with reds and pinks and oranges.

The soft susurrus of impossibly blue waves lapping against their bases filled the air. A rainbow of color, sound, and light assaulted my senses as I breathed in the pleasant scent of ocean air.

A man could get used to this sort of beauty.

It was during this deep and spiritually enriching moment of reflection that someone slammed into me from behind, carrying us both over the edge toward the ocean far, far below.

"Oh, *drreeeeeeeekkkkk*!" I screamed as we plunged toward the distant water.

I couldn't see anything of my attacker, but I felt a cold line slice across my forearm, followed by hot warmth as blood flowed. So, yeah, they had a blade. I thrashed, throwing elbows and bucking my back to try and break them loose. We separated just long enough for me to spin around, and I caught a glint of steel stabbing directly for my face.

I managed to get my metal hand in front of it, deflecting it away, but by then that water was coming up really, *really* fast. I shoved my knees up, putting them between me and the hard mass of white flesh in front of me, and pushed off as hard as I could. My enemy spun away in a tangle of flailing limbs, and I had barely a moment to straighten my legs, tuck my chin, and clench my bottom as I *slammed* into the water feet first.

The world went dark for a few seconds, then I was struggling for the surface. I took in a great gasp and coughed out seawater as I breached and spun to orient myself. Everything hurt. The shore wasn't too far away, so off I paddled. To my left I could see a pale body bobbing facedown in the waves.

Good. Hope they felt it.

I dragged my way onto a beautiful white sandy beach, panting and choking. Above the rush of the waves, I could faintly hear the booming fire of Korbos's gun echoing from above. Looking up at how far I'd fallen made my stomach roil. I should have been dead.

How in Order's light was I gonna get back up there?

I was still considering the unmitigated luck of my survival when I was interrupted by four figures striding out of a crevasse to my right. They were tall and lanky, with impossibly white skin—maybe powdered?—and long braided stark-white hair to match. Three were male—although one had the build of a youth—led by a female walking ahead of them. The woman appeared to be made of nothing but muscle and sinew. If it weren't for the dark tribal markings crisscrossing their skin, I'd have had a hard time distinguishing them from the sloping white sand rising to their backs.

Their shapes were vaguely human, but the faces were like nothing I'd ever seen. Brilliant yellow dots practically glowed inside large dark holes where their eyes should have been. No whites showed. Each had a small, stubby nose, and their mouths appeared to have no lips, teeth jutting every which way as they clacked together rhythmically.

So yeah, they were pretty freaky-looking, but my attention was captivated by the four extremely sharp obsidian spears they had pointed at me.

I raised my hands in a gesture of surrender as the woman shook her weapon in threat, grunting a string of vowel sounds and clacking her teeth in a peculiar rhythm.

"Look," I said, "I've got no quarrel with y—"

She let out an ululating howl, cutting off my words as she pointed her spear toward the body in the water, then followed it up with more of her grunts and clacks.

"Hey, sorry if that was your buddy, but maybe he shouldn't have knocked me off a bloody cliff!" I spat.

The female—chieftess, shaman, whatever—lowered her spear and charged.

I yelped, barely spinning aside. My metal hand came down in a chop, shattering the spear's haft, and I threw every ounce of strength into my best bar-fight punch, connecting just below her nose. Then I howled, shaking blood from my hand where her exposed fangs had torn into my knuckles. She just looked at me, head cocked like a dobrin. Then she laughed, the sound like a shaken bag of rocks, before stepping back and motioning for the others to take me.

I retreated two steps, a wave washing over my feet, wondering how in the world I was going to get out of this one. Nothing was coming to me. I could maybe hold my own with a spear or harpoon, but I never was the best brawler. I was a damned *fisherman*, for Order's sake! Maybe I could get lucky and grapple one, take their weapon...

A blur swept overhead, and then one of the attackers was down, Mariyana shrieking as she fell with the force of a boulder and buried a pair of knives into his back. She bore him to the ground, then smoothly rolled away and hamstrung the second attacker—the young one—who went down with a cry of pain.The final creature raised his spear, a hair's breadth from impaling the small Chek, when Bastin slammed into him in a frenzy of fur and claws. Blood flew as the thing wailed.

Within seconds, the only one left standing was the female who'd tried to stick me. I wheeled to make sure she wasn't about to rip out my spine, but she was beating a quick retreat along the shoreline. I sat down hard on the sand, suddenly exhausted and overwhelmed. There was an agonized crying coming from somewhere, and for a moment I couldn't be sure if it was the hamstrung youth or me.

Rapid footsteps padded on the sand, and I looked up to see Cassidy racing down the slope of the beach, white sand flurrying up behind her. She pulled up short as she reached Mariyana.

"Are you okay?" she asked the Chek, giving her a quick once-over for any cuts or bleeding. Bastin seemed no worse for the fight, gamely licking sand and blood from his claws. I tried not to look at the remains of the creature he'd set upon.

"Is *she* okay?" I belted, incredulous. "Atia's *bones*, she didn't just get *thrown off a frokking mountain*! What about *me*?"

"Well, from the sound of your bellowing, I think you're still pretty healthy," Cassidy replied.

I grunted, stood and brushed off my trousers. "Yeah, but my arm hurts," I replied, gesturing at the line of blood dripping down my forearm onto the sand. "So who are these guys?"

Cassidy bit her lip. "They're Strigori tribe. Local natives. They're my suppliers. I dunno why they'd attack us, though. They're relatively peaceful, for Reachers. At least toward outsiders. Usually you only have to worry about them killing each other. I didn't have any trouble out of my contact T'krill earlier, so I have no clue what brought all this on." Her thumb jabbed toward the top of the plateau. I didn't want to look.

She strode to the youth, who was still lying on the ground, clutching his leg and whimpering. He cringed as Cassidy kicked at his thigh and squatted down beside him. She rattled off a few sentences in the tribe's guttural, clacking language. It hurt my teeth just hearing her make those noises. The Strigori gave a much longer reply, and Cassidy's eyes grew steadily wider as he finished.

"*Drek*," she spat under her breath. "We've gotta get out of here."

"What's up?" Mari asked.

"The Host has already been here," Cassidy replied. "He says a god named Kalos came through a day ago and killed their chieftain and his entire family. The Strigori have standing orders to capture or kill us and recover the signara. My supplier's the one who set an ambush. Let's get back to the *Storm*, now."

My blood went cold. I had my own personal grudge against Kaira, but the stories about Kalos were absolutely terrifying. In the past, the tales said, he'd wiped out entire cities on a whim, slaughtering whole populations because a single person had displeased him. Nearly a thousand years ago, the Host had thrown Elarin into utter chaos, ushering in an apocalypse that the world was still suffering. According to the legends, Kalos was the prime architect of destruction during those times, responsible for the deaths of millions. Anchorage, a Thrane-held peninsula northwest of Hightide, was *still* a scorched wasteland from when he'd annihilated it three hundred years previous. He wasn't someone I wanted chasing us.

"Yeah, okay, let's go," I said. "What about this kid?"

"Right. Well... he *did* throw you off a mountain."

Cassidy's wrist flicked and her sword extended and locked. She started toward the youth, who cried out and raised his spear in warding. I stared, hand outstretched, but couldn't get out any words as I realized what she intended. Cassidy leapt forward, arm reared to strike as she swept the Strigori's spear away with her four-fingered hand.

"No!" Mari cried, stepping between Cassidy and the youth. Bastin, ever at her side, let out a low growl, backing the pilot away. "He's just a boy, leave him be! He can't hurt us." She pointed a finger at Cassidy. "Let's get

it straight, we don't kill defenseless enemies, much less kids. Or you can forget your payment!"

I wasn't too surprised.

Mari and Cassidy had hit it off really well during our short time aboard the *Storm*. Cassidy taught the Chek a bit about the ship's instruments, even going so far as to let Mari take the stick and actually fly for a short while. They'd become fast friends, but Mariyana was a pacifist at heart, like most Cheks.

As a race, they generally just breezed through life, partaking of any and every pleasure available to them—which I supposed was why Mari enjoyed cooking so much—but they'd grown harder after the Hostguard's culls. Mari could take a life if the need arose, but she'd never enjoy killing.

Personally, I could sympathize. I was still struggling with the fact that I'd killed a guard back in Hightide. Never mind the dozens that everyone else took out.

Cassidy shrugged and sheathed her blade. "Fine by me. He'll either hobble his way home, or someone will come find him."

Mari visibly relaxed. "Thank you," she said in a small voice as I snatched up a fallen black spear and we started our way back up a winding path carved into the plateau.

"I guess Kaira lived after all," Cassidy puffed as we jogged the switchbacks leading to the valley. "She must have told Kalos we were in a skipship. My guess is that he's hitting all the tarbrine repositories within the area. Order anyway, it's a good thing we didn't arrive while he was still here."

A memory clicked into place. "I heard Korbos firing up above. What happened up there? Is he okay?"

"Like he'd be hurt," Mari said, rolling her eyes. She rested comfortably on Bastin's back as he kept pace with us. A flash of envy raced through me. I was out of breath but determined to not slow us down. "We heard you scream—you have a really high-pitched scream, by the way—and then we were surrounded by all those pale folks. Korbos started blasting away when they charged us and I couldn't really do anything except get in the way, so he yelled at me to come check on you which was a great thing because I totally saved your life back there."

I turned to Cassidy. "And you?"

"I was just entering the valley with my supplier and the tarbrine when Korbos opened up on the war party," she huffed. "I hit the deck, then ran looking for you two as soon as I saw he had it under control. He's watching the ship and the fuel we brought. As well as T'krill, that…that scumbag."

We made our way up the last switchback and rounded the rift into the valley, our weapons raised. The booming of Korbos's gunfire had ceased long before, but best to be ready for any trouble.

Korbos sat quiet on a barrel-laden wagon, his enormous gun propped on his shoulder. Bodies were everywhere; at least twenty, maybe more. He gave me a curt nod and a grunt as we approached. "Glad to see you still walking, Pyk."

I shuddered. "It was a close thing. Everything okay with you?"

The big smith exhaled hard through his nose, a look of consternation crossing his face. "Just a little tired." He waved his gun toward a body—wisps of smoke rising from a giant hole in its chest—lying at the front of the wagon. "I was trying to keep the wagon driver alive, but he snuck up on me and shoved a knife in my back. Didn't have much choice after that."

"What?" Mari exclaimed. "You're hurt?" She sounded surprised.

"No," Korbos replied, turning to show a wide rip in his shirt. Blood stained the edges, but the skin beneath was whole and undamaged. I tilted my head in an unspoken question. "I heal fast," he said with a shrug. "Still hurt like hell, though."

A low growl and a thump drew my attention to Cassidy, who delivered a second kick to the wagon driver's body. Her posture radiated fury. She huffed, fists planted on her hips as she spat at the corpse.

"Aggravating that they'd throw me over just like that. I thought T'krill here was a friend."

I shrugged. "Well, they *did* have one of the Host threatening to wipe out their village. Not that it excuses things, but it's understandable."

"Oh, I understand. I just can't forgive. You don't screw over partners."

Korbos laid a hand on my shoulder, his visible eye dark and furrowed. "Did you say one of the Host threatened the village?"

"Oh yeah, one of the fellows that just tried to kill me down on the beach said they had a little visit from a god named Kalos."

Korbos's hand tightened for an instant as he frowned.

Cassidy stared into the distance before snapping her head around to the wagon. "Oh, *drek*." She ran for one of the barrels, unrolling a coiled hose and working the pumping mechanism to which it was attached. Cloudy water began to flow onto the ground as she stuck a finger into the stream and brought it to her mouth. She spat in dismay before taking out her short sword, extending it with a flick of her wrist, and twirling it around in agitation. The air swished as she swung back and forth a few times.

"Regular seawater," she said. "This just gets better and better."

"Wait," I said. "So we can't fuel the *Storm*?"

"Nope."

"Great. Just frokking *perfect.* Atia's *bones.*" I sat down on the grass and laid the salvaged black glass spear across my lap. "So what do we do now?"

"We're obviously not going anywhere without fuel," Korbos said.

"Yeah, but these Strigori guys are sitting on the supply, right?" I replied. "So how in the world do we get the tarbrine without having to fight our way through an entire village? Or worse, having an entire village kill their way through *us*?"

Cass frowned and tapped the flat of her blade against her leg. She looked at Korbos; more accurately, at the hole in his shirt. "So if you can't get hurt, you up for providing some distraction?"

Korbos growled, a deep rumbling in his chest. "I never said I couldn't be hurt. It just takes a hell of a lot to kill me."

"Mere details," she replied, flapping a hand absently.

My eyebrows shot into my scalp. Couldn't...be killed? Just how immortal *was* he?

Cassidy chewed her bottom lip for a moment, then turned to Mariyana and me. "Like the man there said, we're not going anywhere without fuel for the ship. The only place to get it is from the springs on the other side of the Strigori's village."

She cracked a wicked grin.

"So let's go steal some."

EIGHT

"I'd just like to go on record that this is a horrible, *horrible* idea," I said.

Cassidy, Mariyana, and I lay prone at the edge of a ridge overlooking the Strigori village. It wasn't very big by any civilized standards, but there were several dozen wood and grass huts, along with what looked to be at least a hundred pale figures milling about the dirt streets. There wasn't much to distinguish the males from the females; mostly the women wore more ornamental hairstyles and the barest of chest coverings. A majority of the adults carried those obsidian spears, and I could even see a few children play-fighting with sharpened sticks here and there.

The huts were arranged in rough concentric circles around a central green space, maybe two hundred feet across, the low-cut grass surrounding what appeared to be a wide communal fire pit. Within the green, a number of the adults were loosely arranged in what looked suspiciously like war parties. The rest stood around, I hoped, to see them off. If I was wrong, it could mean the four of us and Bastin facing off against hopeless odds. The war parties chanted and clacked in their gravelly tongue, beating their spears against the ground in flawless rhythm.

"What are they saying?" I asked Cassidy.

"'Warbringers, gird your loins, honor the gods, prepare for glory, death to the infidels, so on, so forth.' That sort of thing. It's funny, I never had any problems with them until you got on my ship."

"I'm sure you would have eventually done something to tick them off."

She swatted my arm.

A commotion sounded from the edge of the village, causing a number of the warriors to rush from the square. Squat, furry dobrins chirruped and squawked as they followed, tongues lolling from the excitement of running around and through their masters' legs.

"Here we go," muttered Cassidy. We crept back down to the brushy spot where we had stashed the barrel wagon. Rather than pulling it ourselves, we'd rigged up a makeshift harness for Bastin, who could move much faster than us if necessary. He sat patient, gnawing on some treats Mari had produced from Order knew where, the occasional low chitter sounding. As she reached him, Mari gave him a soothing scratch behind the ears to keep him quiet.

"You two be careful," I murmured, adjusting the strap of Korbos's gun, slung tightly over my shoulder.

"Hey," Cassidy replied with a smirk, "thieving is what I do best, One-arm."

"Funny, I thought it was 'antiquities preservation.'"

She threw me a wry grin that set my head spinning. I gave back a tentative smile.

They crept away, skirting low around the smaller hills and tiny farms encircling the village, and quickly vanished from sight. With luck, the rises and tall crops would keep them hidden from the Strigori. The distraction was up to Korbos. He hadn't been too happy about the plan, but he was taking much less of a risk than the rest of us, all things considered.

I made my way back up the ridge and waited. I could see Korbos enter the village, the Strigori boy from the beach slung across his shoulder. He was surrounded by hooting and clacking warriors, and, as I watched, one of them landed a vicious blow with the butt of his spear to the back of Korbos's leg. The big man stumbled but kept walking, grim face set in determination. More blows followed, but Korbos kept walking. The Strigori didn't seem too concerned about hitting their own as well. The limping boy cowered as several staves struck his arms and back. I could hear his cries of pain.

My heart sank. I'd been hoping the Strigori would be receptive to us bringing back one of their lost warriors, but I supposed they saw it as a failure on the boy's part. Korbos made his slow, agonizing way to the village square, where the boy was ripped away from his arms. A dozen spears immediately lowered toward them both. A tall woman stepped forward—I was a little surprised to recognize the one that had run from the beach—and exchanged words with the youth.

For several minutes, they just stood talking, and then—with a crack that I heard all the way up the ridge—the Strigori backhanded the youth across the jaw. The boy stumbled back, favoring his wounded leg, but didn't fall. Korbos stood silent, arms crossed in front of him. He'd left his rifle with me, claiming that he didn't want to use any more force than necessary. A dumb decision, I thought, but he wasn't to be dissuaded. At least I had it nearby, even if I had only the faintest clue how the thing worked.

The crowd encircling them all had grown even larger. It looked like the entire village was there to see the show. Hopefully it would make Cassidy and Mari's mission run smoother. Though I knew she could fight as well as anyone, I wasn't comfortable putting Mari in harm's way if it could be avoided. The tiny Chek had been the better option to go on the tarbrine run, though. I sneak about as well as a bulloc in a bell harness.

The Strigori leader beckoned, and the warrior standing behind Korbos prodded him forward. I couldn't make out what was being said—didn't even know if Korbos spoke the language—but there was a lot of waving back and forth between the big smith and the much smaller wounded boy. A spear was shoved into the boy's hands, another into Korbos's huge paw. The woman stepped back, bellowed a few words, then gestured at both prisoners. They were meant to fight each other. Just like Cassidy had anticipated. We'd hoped that wouldn't be the case, but here we were. The crowd murmured excitedly over the barking of the dobrins.

For a brief moment, I reflected on the nature of inevitable violence inherent in both man and beast, its usage in conflict resolution and relationship with societal development—or lack of—before a cry from below brought me back to the matter at hand.

Korbos had thrown down his spear, and the Strigori leader was yelling at him to pick it up and fight. Korbos responded with a slow shake of his head, and the woman turned to scream at the boy in obvious frustration. The kid looked back and forth between his leader and the big foreigner several times, then set his shoulder and shuffled forward as best his wounded leg would allow. His steps were unsteady, but the point of his spear never wavered.

Korbos just stood, stock-still, waiting. As the boy thrust, he calmly stepped to the side, avoiding the blow.

Another attack shot forward, almost faster than the eye could follow. Then another, and another. Each time, Korbos made a single, perfect movement to avoid the blows. Some he reached out and slapped away. For long minutes, the two eased their way around the ragged circle formed by the cheering and shouting onlookers. The boy's attacks came slower and slower, and he was obviously struggling for breath. Korbos didn't even look winded. His motions only expended as much energy as necessary, drawing out the fight and forcing the youth to wear himself down. The big man's objective in this fiasco was to delay, giving Mari and Cassidy as much time as possible to steal enough tarbrine to get the ship off the ground.

Blood streamed down the lad's leg where his wound had reopened. The big smith was saying something as he dodged, but at this distance I couldn't make out the words. Soon after, the boy planted the butt of his spear into the ground, leaning heavily against it and panting hard.

The leader, having had enough of the drawn-out struggle, stepped forward and ran her black spear through the youth's back, the obsidian spraying red as it exited his chest. Korbos let out a wordless exclamation, his hand outstretched as the crowd jeered. I stared in shock, frozen to my spot on the ridge. None of the villagers were supposed to be hurt in this, but we'd underestimated their aggression even toward one another. We'd known there was a risk of Korbos being injured, but he'd assured us that the Strigori wouldn't be able to kill him. This…this savagery…

wasn't in the plan. Why in all the hells of Chaos did Cassidy trade with these people?

With Korbos's attention drawn, a Strigori warrior took the opportunity to slam a spearpoint into the blacksmith's calf. His leg buckled, sending him to one knee as he bellowed in pain and rage. Pale bodies enclosed him, obsidian spears flashing. He had to have taken twenty thrusts in the time it took me to draw a horrified breath. I heard a low *click*, *click*, and realized I had risen to one knee, unknowingly raising his behemoth of a gun to my shoulder and pulling the trigger to no avail. The rifle wouldn't fire for me. I came to my senses and dropped back to my belly, hoping that none of the Strigori had spotted me. Damn fool. We'd known this was a possibility, maybe even likely. My one job was to witness, to wait. And to hold the damn gun.

A bestial roar echoed across the green as a bright flash of silver erupted from the center of the frenzied stabbing and the Strigori were flung away in a mass of flailing limbs and flying spears. Thick *whunks* sounded as some embedded into the wooden walls of the nearby huts; the rest rained down around the village like a flight of arrows. I curled into a protective ball as one impaled the scrubby ground less than a foot away from my head.

When I looked back, Korbos was gingerly rising, his clothes shredded. Blood dripped and halted as his wounds closed. The Strigori, for their part, stood frozen in awe and fear even as their companions slammed into the ground with meaty thumps. Korbos looked around slowly, and where his gaze met theirs, they dropped to their knees, prostrating themselves before him and babbling rapidly in their clacking tongue. The ones who had survived being flung away rolled to their knees as well, stretching out in reverence.

Korbos searched the crowd, limping only slightly, until he stood in front of the nominal leader—the woman who had speared the young warrior from behind. The big smith stretched out a clasping hand, and the Strigori rose smoothly from the ground, lifted by an unseen force until she floated before Korbos. Pale muscles rippled and strained as she tried to move against the binding force. The warrior spat several unfamiliar words at Korbos, rage and frustration evident in the strain of her neck. A shocked murmur issued from the crowd as Korbos's shoulders slumped. With a quick motion, his massive hand clenched shut, and the Strigori woman's neck twisted with a crackling snap that I could hear from my hiding spot.

I started again. That wasn't in the plan.

A low moan went up from the prostrate crowd, followed by a shrieking ululation from the returning war party which had picked that moment to stroll onto the green. They didn't seem too happy about their boss being killed. A particularly massive specimen—almost as big as Korbos himself—threw his arms wide, howling and shaking his enormous spear in challenge. Korbos didn't move, merely crossing his arms as the giant stepped forward. A swift thrust shot out, and Korbos leaned out of the way. Just enough so the spearhead slid past his tattered shoulder. His one eye went silver, and the warrior shot into the air, limbs outstretched as though he were roped and tied, head thrown back. Korbos reached forward with his hand.

"No!" I was on my feet and running for the green, the smith's heavy rifle bouncing painfully off my back as I stumbled to a halt before him, panting.

"This wasn't part of it, Korbos!" I yelled, shrugging the rifle from my shoulder. My back was sore from it banging against my bones. "We didn't come here to kill these people!"

"Hellfires and Chaos, Pyk, I told you to stay hidden, damn it," Korbos growled. The big Strigori thrashed against his invisible bonds, still hanging in midair. "You knew this was a possibility. What do you think *you'd* do if you got stabbed a hundred times?"

"Yeah, well, I'm not a walking calamity, either! You don't *have* to kill anyone. It's not like they can really do you any damage, right?"

"That's not the point, Pyk! Yes, the damage will heal, but that's not what leaves the scarrin—HURK!" His eyes went wide as a black spear tip emerged from his throat. I screamed as hot blood spattered across my face. A Strigori warrior, lean and muscular, stepped from behind Korbos, wrenching free the weapon as the smith fell to his knees, choking. More closed in, spears stabbing, and I fell back as more than a few turned their weapons in my direction.

Korbos rose from his stagger, the unseen hand again hurling the Strigori to the ground, although it seemed with slighter force than before. A wet growl escaped him as he stretched out his hand toward me, even as the new wounds began to close. I jerked sideways as his rifle ripped itself from my hands and flew into his ready grip. He rose, and blue fire erupted from the barrel, punching holes in at least five of the pale warriors. The closest of the crowd, watching the annihilation of their kinsmen, seemed to lose their worshipful manner. At least, I assumed that's why they let out a war cry and began brandishing spears. My shoulders dropped. This was *not* what I'd signed up for. I looked around wildly, searching for the main gate, when I spotted movement on the side of our not-so-distant plateau. The one hiding the *Storm*. Mari and Cassidy, leading Bastin and the fuel cart up the switchbacked paths. They'd done it.

"Korbos, come on—" I began. The sight of the smith stopped me cold. His eye, though not flaring, shimmered bright silver, and his face bore a pure cold fury, much unlike my friend of so many years. His terrifying gaze swept the Strigori, and he opened fire as they charged. Rows upon rows of warriors fell as he strafed across their ranks, yet still more came. His teeth were bared in a rictus that almost seemed a grin, then I realized he was *laughing*. Laughing as he slaughtered our attackers.

Something in my chest tightened as I realized again just how *old* he was. How little I really knew of him. I quickly retrieved a spear and stabbed at several Strigori, dropping them while I pulled away, making sure to stay at Korbos's back as we retreated toward the village entrance. I parried a thrust aimed straight at my face and skewered a warrior through the breadbasket. I should have felt sickened, but the surge of adrenaline and fear pushed such concerns from my mind.

I'd have to deal with the guilt later.

Still the pale warriors charged. Still they were cut down, massive blasts crashing around us. I watched men, women and children alike fall to the huge bursts of blue energy. Horror crept over me at the ecstasy sweeping across my friend's face. It probably wasn't the smartest move, but I reached up to grab Korbos by the arm, using a little more force than strictly necessary from my netanium hand to make sure I got his attention. For a moment I wished I hadn't as he turned his glowing eye to me and snarled. The gun stopped erupting.

"Time to go," I said, jerking my head in the direction of the plateau. His face cleared for a moment; he threw a quick glance to the distance and nodded before turning back to the Strigori. His shoulders slumped as they continued to press forward, albeit more tentatively than moments before. Spears shook in our direction in a threatening display. They seemed to be intent on herding us out of the village rather than mounting an all-out attack. Anger and fear played across the expressions of the vanguard, though I could see hands still raised in worship further back. But at least Korbos had stopped mowing them down.

I began to wonder if they were going to harry us all the way back to the ship, but the Strigori halted at the arching wooden wall that served as the village gate. Cries of anger, sorrow and awe mingled together as the tribesmen bunched up, the foremost warriors shooing us away with their spears. Others behind them wailed as they waded through the bodies of their kin. Korbos and I backed away until we reached a small foothill that blocked our view of the village, then turned and broke into a jog. I looked over to see an agonized scowl twisting his face. We ran the distance to the plateau in complete silence, but I was lost in my own thoughts anyway.

He'd been laughing as he mowed through the Strigori. Enjoying the carnage. Granted, I'd only known him for a small fraction of his exceedingly long lifetime, but that didn't fit my image of the big man. Didn't seem like the friend I'd spent so much time with over the past nine years. Definitely didn't fit the person who'd rescued a wounded young street urchin, replacing his shattered arm and saving his life in the process.

Every time I felt I was making peace with my idea of Korbos, some new revelation came and swept my legs from under me. It was a disorienting sensation, far worse than any storm-tossed deck heaving beneath my feet. Compounding that was the strange lack of guilt I was feeling, even after striking down several more living beings. I stayed in my own head as we ran through jungle brush and foliage, then laboriously climbed the switchbacks to the top of the plateau. As we crested the trail, we could see Cassidy pumping the last of the tarbrine into the *Storm*. Empty barrels lay discarded around the cart, which had been unhitched from Bastin and lay neck-down near the ship's stern.

"Hey, guys, did everything go okay?" Mari shouted from Bastin's back as we made our way across the grassy field. "We thought we heard shooting, but we figured you big bad men could handle the trouble and oh man that must have been rough Korbos, your clothes are all destroyed and Pyk where'd you get *that* spear is it new and how bad was the fight there's blood all over it and—OH!—we didn't have any trouble with the tarbrine, obviously, because Cassidy's over there filling up the hold but you should have seen her, she was great, knocked out the two guards at the springs—POW! BAM!—and then we just booked it around the back side of the village because you guys did great with your distraction and we didn't have a lick of trouble getting back to the *Storm* so everything went according to plan!" She heaved in a great gulp of air.

Korbos grunted. "We'll talk about it once we're in the air, Mariyana. Cassidy! How are we?"

Cassidy gave a thumbs-up from the rear of the ship. "Good to go!" she shouted. "Funneling the last now! This cragcat will purr for a year on this much fuel!"

Korbos nodded in approval, his head bowed and his feet dragging as he ascended the ramp. "Everyone on board. Let's get the hell out of here."

Mari shot me a questioning look as Korbos made his way up, and I shook my head slightly. *We'll discuss it later*, that shake said. She shrugged and guided Bastin up the incline and into the ship.

As I reached the stern, Cassidy heaved the last barrel to the side and clapped her hands together, brushing off dirt and wood chips. "So what really happened?" she asked.

"I'm…not sure," was my tentative reply. "Let's get into the skies, and I'll talk to Korbos. But for now, keep your eyes open. I'm not entirely sure we can trust him any more."

NINE

We spent over a day in the air, and I couldn't bring myself to confront Korbos. I kept a wide berth, staying out of the same cabins and avoiding him while I tried to get my thoughts together. Even on a ship as large as the *Storm*, it wasn't an easy thing to do. As I sat in the copilot's couch, Cassidy kept throwing glances my way. She didn't know what to make of the situation, and I didn't know how to explain to her that I was afraid of one of my oldest friends.

At least Mari was keeping the peace. The Chek's infectious optimism had helped keep me from snapping at everyone over the last hours, and she had provided the big blacksmith company and diversion from my mood. Korbos was wise enough to sense that I wasn't ready to talk and let me be. Order anyway, I didn't like being in such a funk. I much preferred my usual chipper and cheery self.

Sighing, I heaved myself upright and went looking for the smith. Our conversation didn't need to wait any longer. I found him, as expected, sitting cross-legged in the cargo hold, his gun disassembled and spread out before him for cleaning. Disturbingly, he still wore the clothes he'd been wearing in the village, shredded and holed from dozens of stab wounds.

A half-empty bottle of some dark liquor sat next to him, the loose cork rolling slightly on the floor from the motion of the ship. Mari sat on a nearby crate, jabbering and waving her arms in the throes of some long-winded story—Korbos didn't appear to be hearing a word she said—and Bastin lay curled in a corner. One large eye cracked open at the approach of my footsteps.

I caught the Chek's eye, jerking my head toward the door as I champed my jaw a couple of times. She took the hint and hopped off her crate, patting Korbos on the shoulder as she passed. He never looked up from his work, merely picked up his bottle and chugged. I sauntered over to her former seat, taking my time and considering how best to delicately broach my concerns to my friend.

"So what the *frok* was all that about back there?" I demanded.

Oh, well, I was never subtle.

Korbos looked up, the corners of his mouth turned down. I fought back a shiver. His scars shone palely in the harsh light of the hold, casting odd shadows and distorting his face even further. A flash of silver played across his eye, quick as a bolt of lightning, before it went wide in something akin to fear. I tensed in fear myself, taking an involuntary step back. He closed it, breathing a hard sigh and loosening the tension in his back. He looked bone-weary, deep shadows forming under his eye and a slight sag to his mouth. It wasn't a look I had ever actually seen on the big man in all the years we'd been friends. He was built like a mountain and always seemed to have a limitless reserve of energy.

"We might as well wait until Mariyana gets back with the food," he said.

I raised an eyebrow. He didn't miss much.

We sat in awkward silence for ten minutes or so while he reassembled his enormous rifle and nursed the bottle at his side. Mari reappeared shortly after, bearing fish for three and a bowl of kibble for Bastin. She'd swiftly made the *Storm's* galley her own domain, forbidding Cassidy from even entering after the previous night's culinary disaster.

Mari closed her eyes and folded her hands. "Atia, bless this nourishment we are about to partake, and Order, light the path for those with kindness in their hearts. Keep high the spirits of your followers, and receive us in love at our end of days. This we beg in humility and fervor."

Korbos took his plate with a frown. "I deeply wish you wouldn't do that, Mariyana."

She rolled her eyes. His frown deepened; he seemed to be weighing whether to push the point further, before finally looking down to his food in consternation. Silence thickened as he dug a fork into his fish.

We tucked in. Delicious as always. Order only knew how Cassidy stocked her larder with so many seasonings, but Mari had made excellent use of them.

"Is Cassidy occupied?" the blacksmith asked a while later, after finishing his repast.

"Oh, yes, I went ahead and took a plate to her first since she's all busy captaining and flying the ship and oh hey she wanted me to let you know we might hit some…what was the word—turbulence?—yeah, turbulence…soon, so don't worry if the ship starts shaking and she's going to keep it on manual so she can feel the winds, whatever that means." She was *such* a chatterbox when she got excited.

Korbos grunted. He got up and shut the thick door between the hold and the crew bunks, glancing down the hall to the cabin to make sure Cassidy was indeed strapped into the pilot's couch. He pulled up another crate and took a seat.

"Good. We need to talk, just the three of us." The bottle came up to his lips.

I crossed my arms, flesh overlaying mechanical. "You gonna tell me what happened back in that village? That didn't seem like you, mate."

He sighed. "Siddown. This might take a little while. Our little refueling jaunt put us behind schedule, so I guess we've got some time."

I ran my flesh-and-blood hand through my hair and resumed my seat on the crate, spreading out so Mari could rest on her knees between my legs. I absentmindedly rubbed her shoulders as Korbos slid over a larger crate and sat opposite us.

He was silent for a long moment before looking me straight in the eye. "So what do you want to know?"

My jaw worked soundlessly. "What…what do I want to *know*? Pfft!" I threw my arms wide. "How about *everything*?! I *saw* you back there, Korbos. You were laughing! You were slaughtering those people like chickens for a cookout, and you were *frokking laughing!*" My voice rose until I was near screaming. Anger and uncertainty warred in my mind, a rising incredulity of my friend's seeming disinterest taking over until I lashed out, picking up my empty plate and hurling it at his feet, where it bounced and rolled away. Bastin's head snapped up, a low growl rumbling in his chest as the plate spun to a halt against his forepaw. Apparently it was unbreakable, crafted for durable use on a maneuvering skipship. Definitely felt like an anticlimactic gesture.

Korbos didn't flinch; his eye never budged from mine. He just sat, elbows on his knees, as he stared me down. I panted, shoulders heaving, and forced my breaths to slow until I was calm.

"I want to know why you don't seem to *care* that you were annihilating those people, even though you didn't *have* to. Atia's *bones*, man! You handed me your gun and said to my face that you wanted to use as little force as possible. Did *that* seem like reasonable force to you?" Well, maybe not *quite* calm.

The blacksmith remained silent, accepting the chastisement and lowering his eye to the floor as a corner of his mouth twitched and his massive hand clenched and loosened involuntarily on the bottle. Mari—having jumped to her feet and backed away when I'd thrown the dish—looked back and forth between the two of us, worry on her face. Seeing that neither of us was going to throw a punch—or in Korbos's case, blast me clean through the hull—she gingerly stepped back and hopped up, taking a seat beside me.

"What in Order's balls and breath is that racket back here?" Cassidy stepped through the hatch, throwing it wide to clang off the bulkhead. She took in the tension between Korbos and me and raised her hands in placation. "Whatever your problem is with each other right now, I'd appreciate it if you didn't take out your frustrations on my frokking ship. Get me?" She eyeballed me in particular. I guess I *was* being the loudmouth. But dammit, I was *mad*.

Korbos grunted, frowning at her. "Just a little disagreement among friends. No need to concern yourself." He punctuated his statement with a glance toward the cockpit, obviously dismissing Cassidy.

"No, it's okay," I snapped. "Stay, Cassidy. Korbos was just going to explain to us why he went all murder hobo back at that village. I think you've got a right to be here, since you're our main method of transportation."

I held Korbos's eye. "Am I wrong?"

His eye dropped as he slowly closed it, shoulders rising and falling in a long sigh. He took another long pull from the bottle.

"I care," he replied in a low voice—almost a whisper. I had to lean in to hear him. He ran a hand through his salt-and-pepper hair, clutching at it for a moment.

"You've got to understand, Pyk, that I haven't had to use my Host powers in over twenty years. It's…difficult, but it's the best way."

"Best way to what?"

His voice quieted, barely audible.

"Stay myself."

I blinked, not following. "What do you mean 'stay yourself'?"

Korbos sighed again. "What I'm about to tell, you have to keep to yourselves. It's…not exactly a secret, but it puts me at a disadvantage. I'm only filling you in because you have a right and a need to know, if we're to be traveling together. And…I trust you." He gave a sidelong glance toward Cassidy. "Both of *you*."

She shrugged, not seeming to take offense at the implication.

Korbos wiped a meaty hand across his face, pausing for a moment to adjust the thick embroidered black eyepatch. Took another swig. He had to be well on his way to getting drunk. I was mildly surprised one of the Host could even *get* drunk, even though Mari and I had spent many a night huddled around Korbos's fireplace, laughing and enjoying his company. But his voice didn't slur, despite the slight glaze in his eye.

"Okay. Story time."

TEN

"I wasn't born, so much as created. We all were. The Host. A little over nine hundred years ago. Oh, I had a mother and father, I just can't remember them. I've forgotten their faces. I grew up a normal man, until I reached the age you see me as. At least I've always assumed so. There aren't any memories prior to my being made into…this. And much as I'd like to, I haven't been able to forget a single moment since then. Not quite a millennia, and I'd give anything to remember my family. Did I have a wife? Children? Order only knows.

"You two have to understand…all the legends and tales and myths of life before the Ruin? None of them do it justice. Order knows *I* can't describe it properly. Autocarts, aerowings—sort of like the one we're in now—along with buildings and cities larger and taller than you can imagine. It was the definition of a golden age. Of course, there was the occasional skirmish with the Thrane or the Na'don, but by and large everyone lived in peace. The ruling Imperium had kept things smooth and prosperous for hundreds of years, I was told.

"That all changed when we came along."

Another pull from the bottle. There wasn't much alcohol left.

"Our creator was a brilliant scientist, the brightest mind of her time. She was obsessed with the idea of pushing mankind through the evolutionary gateway, into some sort of godhood. She spent decades pioneering biotechnological marvels in her quest to 'uplift' us. She was the first genuine metahuman to ever live. The first of the Host. Well, no. She's not even a Host, technically, but *the* Host, the wellspring from which we all were created. Whatever it is that fuels our long lives, it stems from the experiments she eventually performed on herself.

"Somewhere along the line, though, she lost her mind; her goal switched from 'uplifting' to 'enslaving,' as she decided that mankind couldn't be trusted to responsibly use the wonders she was creating. And she *did* create wonders. Horrors as well. She and her entire lab team went rogue, performing biotech experiments on whole population centers before the authorities of the time even had the chance to realize what she was up to. Millions died."

Mari gasped. I leaned forward, hands between my knees. I couldn't realistically conceive of that many people. There were *maybe* five thousand residents in Hightide. The village where I was raised—the village where Kaira murdered my family—had held less than two hundred.

"Drek," I whispered.

"I assume," Korbos continued, "that those catastrophes were the final data she needed to complete her work on the Host. I just know that when I woke, strapped to a steel table in a hidden laboratory with no idea of who I was, the entire continent was in chaos. The Imperium had fallen, laid waste from within by a coup of Mother's followers. The *bhuta* had put together an alliance with key military leaders and formed an army of her own. I found all this out later, of course. When I woke, it was just me and her. She explained that I was a volunteer—which I eventually came to doubt—and that she and I were going to change the world. I was the first, you see."

He sighed. "The first to live, at least."

The bottle rose as he took a sip.

"I've never told you about my past for obvious reasons, but let's just say I was not a nice person in those early years. I was exactly like my brothers and sisters in the Host, with all the horror and tragedy that entails."

"Hold on," I said, aghast. "Brothers and—you and Kaira are *family*?"

Korbos frowned in irritation. "Do you want to hear this or not? No, we're not kin by blood. I use 'brothers' and 'sisters' loosely, although for a long, long while we were close enough to be. Now hush, and let me tell the story. You might not get it out of me another time.

"There were twelve of us in the beginning. Thankfully no more were ever made, but we were calamity enough for five worlds, sure. For nine hundred years, the Host have ruled this planet in some fashion. Sometimes with benevolence, but mostly through fear and destruction. They stamped out anyone who spoke against us. You've heard the legends, and even seen some of it for yourselves." He looked me in the eye. "But it's nothing even close to resembling the awful truth of what was done in those early years when we were learning our way around our abilities.

"I can't forget anything, and I don't age, but Order alight I wish I could forget how I was in those days." His voice grew soft. "We were *gods*, you see? Unaging, undying, immensely powerful. We only found out just how powerful because we rampaged our way across the continent unchecked. Those occasional skirmishes between themselves had done nothing to prepare any military unit, Imperial or not, for the likes of us. We scorched their forces like a fire blazing through a dry forest. The Thrane gave us our only spot of trouble, mostly because they could retreat under the waves. But within the first fifty years we'd subjugated the entirety of Elarin. Order only knows the scope of the destruction I was personally responsible for. How many lives I obliterated."

Korbos paused. Another small swig.

"We had purpose, you see?" he continued in a small voice. "Given to us by our creator and her cohort. We were saving mankind from the stagnation of peace, ushering them into a bright new dawn. It was our righteous cause to continue our creator's work and lift up the people, through force if necessary. A couple of us had our doubts in the beginning, but after a while it didn't matter. We couldn't have stopped if we'd tried."

The regret and self-admonishment in his tone nearly made my heart break, but I sat quietly, reserving any final judgement until the man's tale was done.

"Host powers are…addictive. The twelve of us had an energy reserve within us. A Well, we called it. It's really difficult to describe to normal folks, but it feels like having a small sun trapped in your belly that you can use to work what one might call magic. We could tap into that Well at will and create miracles or nightmares. Most Host could utilize all the different power sets to one degree or another, but we all have our certain areas of expertise. Kalos is a firemaker, for instance. Kaira uses telekinesis almost to a fault."

He shook his head.

"The thing is, the more we use Host powers, the more they corrupt. They—how can I explain this—remove our morality, if that makes any sense. Assuming of course that the Host in question has any morals to begin with. As you utilize the abilities more often, you care less about who gets hurt in the process, until you actively *want* to use them. You *want* to hurt the people around you. People, animals, random destruction, it doesn't matter. As long as that rush hits you. And Order knows we definitely enjoyed the rush.

"I once saw sister Kida tear down a 20-story studio building where she was doing a vizcast interview. She was unhappy with the *makeup* a studio assistant put on her. So she froze the assistant's blood in her veins and shattered her like a hammer hitting a pane of glass. Turned the bottom ten floors to ice, causing the entire building to collapse…with us still in it. She buried over nine hundred people without a second thought because of one person's perceived mistake. After we dug ourselves out of the rubble with our telekinesis, she invited me to lunch at a diner down the street. I ordered a beer, and we laughed as emergency crews raced to the scene. The common people just…didn't…matter."

I didn't understand what a vizcast interview was, but I got the concept. The selfishness and callousness were staggering. Plus, *ice powers*? That was the first I'd ever heard of such. What else could the Host do? It was fascinating, in a horrible sort of way.

"So, when I used my powers around the Strigori, the corruption crept into my mind. Just a little, but it was there. Enough that all I saw were enemies. Not sentient creatures with different values. Not people living their lives and protecting their home from an unknown intruder. Just attacking animals, to be put down."

Korbos scratched his jaw, where black and gray stubble was beginning to show. I mimicked the motion, feeling the rasp of three-day-old growth on my chin. We hadn't exactly brought shaving supplies on this trip.

"Firemaker?" I asked in wonder. "Ice manipulation? What other abilities are there? You can use all of them?"

He shook his head again. "I've got a touch in most of them, but some I can't wield at all. That's just how it was for us. Each of us had their particular strength. Kalos and Kida were amazing thermokinetics, able to manipulate fire and ice, respectively. Kaira almost exclusively uses telekinesis, like I said. Knossos could get into a person's mind and make them tear out their own heart. Kreiger could manipulate localized time. I mean, the technical abilities varied as much as we did."

"So," I continued, "the powers themselves turn you into a sociopath? You've never seemed particularly murderous to me, at least not until yesterday. How did you hold it off?"

Korbos winced at my bluntness. Mari shot me a dirty look and a swat to the leg. I felt bad for just throwing it out like that and hurting my friend, but he needed to know that I didn't approve of his actions, whatever the reasons behind them.

He groaned, rubbing his face in his hands. "I…met someone. He changed my way of looking at things. Let's just leave it at that."

"But…" I cut off abruptly as he jerked his head up, fixing me with a glare that dried my mouth and made my skin prickle.

"Leave. It. Alone." he growled, his eye sparking silver for a moment. I gave a hasty nod, holding my hands up in placation.

"Korbos," Mari interjected in a soft but firm voice, thankfully drawing his attention from me, "it's okay. We're your friends. For a long time, now."

The big man deflated. "You're right. Sorry, Pyk."

"It's all good, old man." I leaned forward and patted his arm, only a tiny bit rattled from him snapping at me. My hand definitely wasn't shaking as I tucked it under my leg.

He smirked, then took another small pull from the liquor. "Old man. How many times have you called me that, never knowing just how right you were?"

I gave a weak chuckle, acceding the point. Mari stood up and walked over to Korbos, throwing her tiny arms around his neck. Even with him seated, she still had to stand on her toes and reach up. His eye widened, then he leaned in, resting his chin on her shoulder and patting her back. She returned to her seat beside me as Korbos continued. He seemed closer to his normal self, if not terribly sober.

"After a while I learned that, if we spent time *not* using our powers, the hold they took on our minds lessened. I became more empathetic to those around me and finally internalized the level of destruction we'd caused. This was around sixty years after I first awakened, and by that point we'd come to control most of the world, and certainly the main continent. Our creator had driven us on a brutal campaign to take everything: overthrowing governments, destroying entire cities, and leaving the people looking for anyone to bring a sense of Order back to their lives. Even if it wound up being the ones who'd thrown it into Chaos in the first place.

"My…friend…made me realize, after so long, that we were in the wrong. Our rampage wasn't justified. Our cause wasn't noble. We were just conquerors, and particularly brutal ones at that. The people of Elarin never stood any sort of a chance against us, so why had our creator ordered us to wreak such havoc? We might as well have been fighting children armed with sticks. I didn't want to go back to that life. I didn't want to be who I was—a selfish, ego-driven butcher. I wanted to be the man *he* saw me to be. So I did the only thing I could think of; I turned against my creator, and my brothers and sisters.

"I fought back, and then I broke the world. I brought about the Ruin."

ELEVEN

"YOU *WHAT?*" I exclaimed.

Korbos sighed, taking a particularly long pull from the bottle. He wiped his eye as he set the nearly-empty container next to his leg.

"You heard me, Pyk. I caused the Ruin," he said. "Technically, it was several years of heavy warfare and a drekload of high-yield weapons, but I was the catalyst that started the entire process."

Cassidy's eyes widened. "Nulls," she muttered. Or at least that's what it sounded like. Korbos snapped his head around toward her, eye narrowed. He grunted, but she remained otherwise silent.

I sputtered, unable to form my thoughts into any sort of coherent sentence. Mariyana had her hands to her face, covering her mouth in shock. I didn't—couldn't—understand. The scope of it was too big. Korbos just sat there, a blank expression on his face. There wasn't an ounce of…well, anything. No remorse or regret. No emotion. He might as well have been talking about the specifics of forging a mooring cleat. It crossed my mind that maybe he was downplaying the toll that using his ability had taken on him.

"How…" I stammered, "how can you just *say* it like that? We've all heard the stories, Korbos, and they're *horrific*! The Ruin almost wiped out life on the entire frokking planet, and you sit there like it was nothing!" My fists clenched. I couldn't wrap my head around the magnitude of something so terrible, and it broke my heart and stoked a burning rage in turn.

Korbos shook his head, draining the last of the alcohol from the bottle in his hand. With a slight hiccup, he tossed it into a nearby waste receptor. My jaw worked as he reached into his long coat and pulled out *another* bottle from an inner pocket. I clenched my teeth, holding out my mechanical hand. He looked at me, wary, then unscrewed the cap and handed it over. I took a long swig, the warm burn lighting up my chest and soothing my nerves for a brief moment. Mari followed as I passed the bottle to her.

"It wasn't nothing, Pyk," Korbos stated, his eye narrowed with inner hurt. "Of course it was something! But you have to understand that it's been almost nine hundred years for me, and I've had to live with myself for all that time. I started a war that killed *billions* of thinking beings. Do you think that's something you could deal with, if you couldn't find a way to come to terms with it?"

His voice grew small. "It's a long time to have to carry so much pain. We were supposed to be the heroes."

Mari's eyes watered in sympathy. I remained still; quiet, thoughtful. He wasn't wrong. I couldn't fathom having to bear such a burden for so long. Were it me, wouldn't I try to be emotionless? Bury the guilt and pain deep down? My rage abruptly died away, leaving only aching sorrow for my friend. Whatever he said, for the past nine years he'd been nothing but kind to me and Mariyana; a father, almost, as neither of us had one of our own. I sighed, shoulders dropping in resignation.

"I'm sorry, old man," I said, and meant it. "Really. You've been good to us. The least I can do is hear you out, I guess."

Mari nodded in eager agreement. Order bless that girl and her forgiving ways.

"So," she began, "what was it like? Will you tell us?"

I could see Korbos's struggle. If it were me, would I continue the story, knowing that it would irrevocably change the perceptions of the only two people in the world that looked up to me? Would I feel like I needed to explain things, give my side of the tale? I couldn't answer that.

"I..." he started, then stopped, taking a pull from the fresh bottle. "I've never actually told this to anyone, not in all these long years. There's no way I can relate everything, so I...I don't know where to start."

It hurt to see the big man so unsure of himself.

"Just tell us what you can," Mari said, leaning over to place a comforting hand on the blacksmith's.

We sat in silence for a moment. The *Storm* shuddered, and I panicked, thinking we'd hit something mid-air. Mari and I clutched at each other, looking around wildly, although there were no viewports in the cargo hold for us to see from.

Korbos grunted. "It's fine, you two. Just the turbulence that Cassidy warned of."

"We're gonna fall out of the sky!" I wished my voice didn't sound like so much of a shriek. My stomach lurched as the skipship dropped suddenly, items not strapped down floating a few inches from the deck. I felt my bottom rise up from the crate. Mari let out a small scream.

"It's fine!" Cassidy snapped, raising her voice to be heard over my undignified clamor. "Order anyway, you keep saying that. We're not going to crash. This happens when a skipship passes through competing air currents. Think of it like a ship being hit with rolling waves from two sides. It'll jostle you around, but won't sink the vessel. The *Storm's* autopilot can handle a little turbulence."

That didn't comfort me. I'd seen ships capsized by just that. Cassidy gave me a reassuring pat on the back, her hand lingering for just a moment. I tried not to move, enjoying the feel even as my stomach tried to climb up my throat.

"Pyk, Mari," Korbos said, his tone softening, "trust me. I've ridden passenger on a few aerowings in my time. This is normal."

Indeed, the shuddering eased off, then stopped completely after a couple of minutes. My real hand was sweating, and Mari was pale, although Korbos himself seemed to pay it no mind. Suddenly, I very much wanted to be back on land. Even the heaving of a storm-tossed fishing junk was preferable to the possibility of careening out of the sky.

"Normal compared to what?" I muttered, shaken both literally and figuratively. I sat back down, bracing my hands against the crate, although it wasn't strictly necessary now that the turbulence had eased.

"Hmph," Korbos grunted. "That might actually be a good place to begin."

Another pull from his fresh bottle. A long one, this time. He exhaled, the harsh whiskey fumes riding the air.

"This technology—the aerowing tech—is thousands of years old. Oh, maybe not this particular ship, but the underlying principles have been around far longer than I have. There aren't many around these days, of course, but in the days prior to the Ruin they were everywhere; a primary means of transportation.

"I wish you could have seen it. There's been nothing like it since. Traffic patterns soaring over and through the cities of the Elarin Imperium, aeroracing competitions at the skytracks, suborbital flights across the entire planet. You could travel ten thousand miles in a matter of hours on one of the larger 'wings. We crossed the seas and skies with impunity. The people of Elarin were pocket gods, virtual masters of the world and elements."

"Larger?" Mari asked, looking at the ship around us. "Bigger than the *Storm*?"

Korbos chuckled. "Oh, yes, Mari. The *Storm* here is barely a mid-size aerowing. You could fit, what? Maybe fifteen or twenty in here, if we crammed in and didn't fight over the available bunks? The suborbital 'wings could fit *hundreds* of passengers. And they were just for mass transportation. You've seen some of the *big* orbital ships. You call them the Reef."

Cassidy leaned forward, intensely curious. This sort of knowledge must have been like a drug to her.

"I'd never even considered that they had been skipships," she said. "They seem way too massive."

"You're partly right. They weren't skipships, strictly speaking. Technically, they weren't even aerowings. They were space cruisers, designed to leave the planet's gravity well entirely. Some of them could house up to two thousand people, with living and work spaces." His face fell a little. "Yet another marvel I'm ultimately responsible for destroying. We had to ground them—all of them—to make sure the Host didn't attempt to get offworld.

"Back then, there were orbital stations ringing the planet, and if Kaira or Koliss or any of the others had been able to reach them we'd have never been able to root them out. It's honestly a miracle we were able to contain them to the planet at all. I wonder sometimes whatever happened to the stations and their crews, but even if they rationed supplies as long as possible, they've been dead for eight hundred years and more."

He shook his head.

"That's neither here nor there. I tell you this to give you some idea of the wonders of that age. Flying marvels. Cities larger than you can imagine, filled with a wider variety of people and species than you've ever seen, all living and working together and, for the most part, enjoying their small day-to-day lives. Devices in your pocket that could instantly communicate with kin on the other side of the planet. Machines that could access the collected knowledge of the world. Everyday science that folks nowadays would decry as sorcery. It was all commonplace, and utterly wondrous, and completely taken for granted.

"After I was awakened, Mother and I spent months testing and exploring my powers. While we bent the limits of what I could do, she busied herself with creating the other eleven Host. Kalos, Knossos, Kronus, Kaligos, Kneira, Kaina, Kaira, Kida, Koliss, Kreian, and Kreiger.

"My brothers and sisters."

His eye was distant, remembering.

"Considering what came later, it's ironic how quickly we bonded as a family. We all loved one another—an amazing feat if you've ever studied group dynamics. There's always friction between some members in any group, no matter how well they get along as a whole. But not with us. I wonder sometimes if Mother somehow engineered our bond. We were like clockwork, each gear slipping together perfectly to create a machine of utter devastation.

"Elarin didn't stand a chance when our creator unleashed us upon the continent."

I shuddered, feeling Mari do the same beside me. I slipped an arm around her shoulders, offering what comfort I could. Cassidy rubbed the side of her jaw.

"In those two years after our awakening, we'd mastered our powers and settled into our specialties, and we rampaged across the land like a wave crashing against a sand castle. It still took us forty-eight years to bring all the species under our thumb. There was *always* a resistance; a rebel group here, an uprising there. But eventually we created peace within the Imperium. The peace of strength. Of tyrants.

"My siblings and I were treated as gods, and we reveled in our power, in all its forms. I had my own palace, my pick of lovers. A kingdom over which to govern as I saw fit; I could build or destroy on a whim, and often did so. An infinite supply of men, women, and children to subjugate. Our absolute power corrupted absolutely. We each wanted for nothing, and our creator watched over all, keeping to herself and expanding her experiments further.

"It was during this period of rest that I met *him*, and had my second rebirth."

Korbos scratched the stubble on his chin. Ran a finger along the scars. A small smile creased his lips as he remembered.

"Rin was just a normal guy, one of the miscellaneous courtiers that hung around my home, ingratiating themselves to me and currying favor. They were a minor annoyance at best, but I put up with them and delegated everyday tasks that I couldn't be bothered to concern myself with. Rin handled my household staff. He was a beautiful man, in his early thirties, well-trimmed and lean, charismatic, and very good at his job. He personally foiled several attempts to poison me. Not that it would have been anything but a temporary inconvenience, but I appreciated his dedication and loyalty.

"I still don't know if he intuited what would happen or just guessed, but it was Rin who convinced me to live as a normal man would. It took him years of trying before I finally gave in, but the fact that I *did* give in to him should still give you some idea of how persuasive Rin could be. In any case, we came to realize that the mental corruption was connected to my use of Host powers. I was horrified by the sheer scope of the death and destruction I had caused. I realized the *wrongness* of our actions. That the Host needed to be stopped. That Mother had to come to justice.

"So many times I nearly gave in and returned to the power, but Rin—in his calm and loving way—helped me stay the course. We left my realm and went into hiding. It took us four years, but we raised an army to fight against the Host. Like I said, there was *always* a resistance somewhere."

"But," I said, confused, "if the powers were so tempting, how did you stay…sober, I guess?…for so long? How have you stayed away from them all this time?"

Korbos glanced at me. "Who says I have?"

My eyes widened. I knew he was in control of himself at the moment, but after that story it was hard not to be a little apprehensive. What would it take for him to snap and fall back into his old ways? My instincts told me that if he hadn't succumbed in nine hundred years, he wasn't likely to now, but, by Atia's bones, it still made me nervous.

A mischievous smirk twisted Korbos's mouth.

"I have Rin to thank for that as well, along with several clever machinists," he said. He leaned over, picking up his gun and holding it against his hip, inspecting it.

"He kept me from using my abilities for over a year after we ran, but eventually it became nearly unbearable. Like a deep-seated itch that you're not allowed to scratch, and it almost drove me mad. Well, again. Rin had been working with several brilliant technicians during that time, and one of them came up with a solution. This."

He shook the gun for emphasis. I cocked my head, not understanding.

"Bulwark here is a singular creation; a one-of-a-kind weapon that drains the Host power from my Well and filters it into plasma projectiles. That's why the blasts are blue, if you've noticed. I'm the one and only person on the planet that can fire this weapon. It acts as a buffer, utilizing the Host power without driving me to megalomania. I can still use the varying raw aspects of the Host—like telekinesis and cryokinesis—on occasion, but as long as the bulk of my efforts are filtered through the rifle, I'm okay. Sustained fire eventually tires me, but it keeps me sane at least."

"So," Mariyana began, "how often do you have to use it?"

"At minimum? About twice a month usually takes care of things," Korbos replied, staring at us in expectance.

Mari nodded, thoughtful. I sat in silence for several moments before perking up.

"Your 'hiking' weekends!" I exclaimed, snapping my fingers and pointing at him in triumph. "*That's* what you're up to when you take off!" I felt proud of myself for having figured it out.

"Of course that's what he was up to, you schmut," Mari said, rolling her eyes.

Korbos grunted. "Give the boy credit, Mariyana. I thought it'd take him longer, to be honest."

I bristled, offended. I raised a pointed finger, about to lay into them both, when I saw the corners of Korbos's mouth twitch. I sat there, mouth open and working, as Mari burst into gales of laughter. A broad grin split Cassidy's face, though she couldn't have had much idea of what we were talking about.

I chuckled—more at their mirth than my own slowness—although it felt sort of wrong to do so given the tale we'd heard so far. I had a gut feeling Korbos's story was only going to get worse.

"Then why don't the other Host use something like this...Bulwark?" I asked, gesturing to the rifle. "Wouldn't it make sense for them to have ways to control themselves? Or for your creator? Where was she in all this?"

"Mother went off-grid after setting us loose. I never saw her again after we began our conquest of Elarin. As for the other Host, they didn't actually know about this way of controlling oneself. Not that they'd have used it in any case. You have to remember, I *wanted* to make something better of myself. The period of time it took for me to realize the horror I'd caused changed me in many ways. Rin changed me. Order bless that man. The other Host wouldn't have wanted to become better. They considered themselves the pinnacle of evolution—gods, even—so why would they want to expose themselves to 'weaknesses' like guilt, remorse, regret? No, even if devices could have been crafted for each of them, they'd have never lowered themselves to actually use them."

He sighed.

"So, where were we? With my…problem…under control, Rin and I spent four years building an underground army across the entire continent. He turned out to be a logistical genius, I'll tell you. Probably the reason he was so effective as the head of my house. But as much as he was the mind behind the rebellion, I was the face. The Host Who Turned. I was known across the continent. I won't lie when I say that the adulation went a long way toward filling the void left by my self-imposed power restriction.

"We were a guerrilla army; never facing the Host directly, but proving an enormous thorn in their collective paws. We spent four years disrupting supply chains, raiding manufactories, overpowering the Hostguard occupying former Imperial bases and appropriating weapons and supplies, setting up storehouses across the countryside, and generally being the biggest nuisance we could possibly get away with.

"Perhaps it was my changed state of mind, but I felt we were doing more good than harm. We'd gone years without engaging my siblings, yet causing them no end of frustration. At least, so I assumed. Turned out, the Host just couldn't be bothered to care about us.

"I finally got their attention when I killed Knossos."

TWELVE

"Hunh?" I asked, at a loss for words. "*You* killed him? I didn't think you Host *could* be killed."

"How do you think there are only three of us left?" Korbos replied. "No, we don't age. We heal almost immediately from nearly any wound, and fast enough from situations that a normal person would have no chance of surviving. But we're flesh and bone, Pyk. We *can* be killed. It's just bloody damned difficult."

The big man ran a hand through his hair.

"I mentioned earlier that we took out every orbital vessel we could find. There was one we missed. The *Aesephine*. I got word through our intelligence network that Knossos was attempting to get offworld, and I couldn't allow that. Knossos was always the least stable among us, and I couldn't let him get to an orbital station where he could use the weapons systems to rain fire on the Imperium. He could—and would—have turned half the continent to glass, just so he could rule over the ashes.

"So we beat him to the ship. I lost two squads—some of the bravest beings I've ever fought beside—on the approach to the launch pad. Another squad as we battled our way up to the cockpit. By the end it was just me and him.

"I'll tell you this—the engineers of the day knew how to build a vessel. By all rights that ship should have been destroyed in the fight, but somehow it stayed functional. Knossos had already begun the launch sequence, and I ran out of time fast. I only won the fight because I managed to get close in and sock Bulwark's barrel right into the hollow of his throat. Blew his head clean off his body, although that was mostly an inconvenience to him. His torso was still crawling toward the navigation controls while I reprogrammed its trajectory to send him into deep space. I had to kick his head down two decks before I could scramble out of a hull breach prior to the self-repair systems sealing the damage.

"We were about two miles up at that point, and I'll just say that landing was probably the most painful thing I've ever experienced." Korbos pointed to his ruined face. "Even more than this, and this took two hundred years to carve."

Mari patted a little beat on her legs. "Did…did the ship blow up? Is that how you killed Knossos finally?"

Korbos looked down with a touch of chagrin. "Well…no. I say I killed him, but I don't think he was actually destroyed. I put a plasma burst through the guidance and control system before I jumped ship. Knossos probably got his head reattached eventually, but with no way to control his trajectory he's still screaming through the void at the moment. It's been eight hundred years, give or take. He should reach the next star system in another twelve thousand or so. For all practical intents and purposes, he's gone forever."

I shook my head in wonder. I barely understood the concepts behind what Korbos was describing, but the thought of an immortal life trapped inside a metal box gave me the shivers.

"When the rest of the Host found out what I'd done with our brother, they finally got angry enough to strike back. Our armies were completely at their mercy. They wiped out ten entire legions—ten thousand men—in less than an hour at the battle of Nagran Point.

"Then they actually got *started* fighting."

He paused, taking a swig from his bottle before passing it to the two of us. I welcomed the burning in my stomach as I took a big pull. Mari winced, but took two for herself. Cassidy took only a tiny sip before passing the bottle back to Korbos.

"Within four months," he resumed, "my brothers and sisters had gone a long way toward eradicating life on the continent." He shuddered, body wracked with memories. "The things they did...they didn't care who they were wiping out. *Everyone* in the Imperium was a rebel, to their minds. I don't know if Mother was driving them, though she did eventually resurface, given certain...things I've heard. I do know now that she still lives, pulling the strings behind Kaira and Kalos. That's why I need the signara. It contains the only records of her base of operations, according to some info Kaira let slip during one of our...encounters...a while back. She's stayed hidden for centuries, doing Chaos only knows what sort of foul science within her labs, protected by Kaira and Kalos."

His face hardened. "And by Order's light, I will see them all burn."

"How?" I asked, leaning forward in anticipation. This was the story I'd been waiting my whole life to hear. Cassidy was right there with me, fidgeting and eager. "How did you kill the other Host? What brought about the Ruin?"

Korbos exhaled a shuddering breath, face screwed up in horror at the memories. His jaw clenched as he forced the words through tight teeth. "We didn't have any other choice. My siblings were rampaging, wiping out entire populations. They just…didn't care. Us. Them. Civilians. Children. Didn't matter. But we had one thing that could wipe *them* out."

He looked up, locking a haunted eye with me, with Mari. "See, the only sure way to kill one of us is to annihilate the body, completely and utterly. Reduce it down to its component atoms, or destroy it so thoroughly that nothing remains but ash and a bad taste in the mouth. Very few weapons can accomplish this. Even burning our bodies down to the bone will leave enough for us to heal and recuperate. We needed a solution that could stop them for good."

He leaned forward. "So I 'secured' a stash of null bombs."

Cassidy inhaled sharply.

Mari and I looked at him blankly. Was that supposed to mean something to us? The tense silence was broken by a beep from the cockpit.

"Is that supposed to mean something to us?" Mari asked, echoing my thought. I suppressed a nervous chuckle. Cassidy just nodded, her topknot bobbing, as if Korbos were confirming some long-held theory. Did she know what these bombs were? Wait, she'd mentioned nulls earlier. Of course she knew what they were. For someone so young, she seemed to know an awful lot about ancient history.

Cassidy clenched a fist. "They were called world-killers. Explosives of such destructive power that just one could vaporize hundreds of miles. I learned about them while I was with the Seekers. It's been speculated for ages that null bombs caused the Ruin, but I never could believe someone would be *stupid* enough to actually use the frokking things."

Korbos nodded, a sickened twist to his mouth. "We had no other way, nothing I could consider worth a shot. I'd gotten lucky with Knossos, but I damn sure couldn't count on a similar situation happening again. The likelihood of true disaster was just too great.

"We spent the better part of six months in hiding, making our plans. We'd stage a multi-pronged attack, cutting across the path of the Host, then destroy them with the hidden null bombs. The whole time, my siblings laid waste to the cities, towns, and villages they thought were housing rebellion members and sympathizers. Which was to say everyone. They destroyed hundreds of thousands of people just to get to us. We had no other strategy but to hold them where they were and let the bombs do their job.

"The time came and our armies marched. I hated it. There was nothing those soldiers could do against the Host. Not directly. I put them in harm's way intentionally. Cannon fodder. Our armies had no idea what they actually carried to the fight. While I, their great general Korbos, The Host Who Turned, coordinated safely from our command center." Bitter sarcasm dripped from his words. "But it worked. Eight different locations, eight massive campaigns. We caught them. We had one shot, and we used it."

The smith's eye grew cold. He took a long drink.

"I waited as long as I could, to make sure we'd drawn my siblings out. They were cutting through our lines like a scythe through wheat. The sights I saw through the battlefield monitors have haunted me for so long. So long. But I triggered the bombs. Rin was by my side the entire way, helping me hold together. He helped me push the button. I loved him for that, and I can never forgive him."

His gaze grew distant as he shuddered, remembering.

"I destroyed it all. Our entire army. The cities they were fighting so hard to defend. All the civilians who couldn't get out in time. Two and a half million people under my command, who just wanted to fight for their lives and those of their loved ones. Two and a half million soldiers who trusted me to lead them to victory, even if it was a hopeless dream. Two-point-five *million* ghosts that I betrayed in order to save billions more. And I couldn't even do that right."

Korbos placed his face into his hands as an enormous sob wracked his body. I clutched at Mari, who had tears streaming down her face. After a long pause, Korbos sniffed and pulled himself together. I felt cold, unable to conceive of such a monstrous loss of life.

"All those lives, sacrificed—snuffed out in an instant. We didn't account for the aftereffects of so many null bombs, however. That much concentrated destructive energy was bound to have repercussions, but we were so desperate at that point that we never gave it due consideration. The shockwave alone laid waste to southern Elarin, creating a vast desert. It's called the Mohagan these days.

"The null pulses somehow reinforced one another—amplifying themselves as they crossed the globe—knocking out any technology and sending the entire planet back to a prehistoric age. Radiation crossed the globe, infected millions. Ash and dust clogged the sky for decades, destroying agricultural capacity. Starvation set in, pitting the survivors against one another for resources. Billions more died in the century after the Ruin."

Mari gasped, hands flying to her mouth. I rocked back and forth, hands on my knees. Each time I thought the worst had come, Korbos kept knocking my bearings from me. Cassidy—leaning against a bulkhead near the open hatch—looked unflappable, quietly absorbing the wealth of Korbos's tale.

"I've carried all those deaths on my shoulders for centuries, but we had no other choice. It was either destroy the Host or doom Elarin to an eternity of suffering and dying under their rule."

The big man sniffed, shaking himself and running a hand through his black and graying hair.

"We succeeded. And we failed. Obviously, we didn't get them all. Only seven of my siblings had come to meet the armies. Out of the remaining four, two held themselves back, protecting our creator in her laboratory. Fortress. Wherever it was that she holed up. The remaining two—Kaligos and Kaira—were monitoring the battles just as I was, and managed to capture and trace back the triggering signal I used on the bombs. Rin and I barely escaped as they annihilated our command post."

He sighed. Another beep came from the front of the *Storm*.

"We took out seven of the Host, and all but killed the planet in the process. Seven, at the cost of billions. You have no idea how many times I've wished for death—even tried to kill myself—to square that math. But my work's not done until they're all gone. Until the planet can progress on its own, without the threat and stagnation of the Host."

Cassidy stepped forward and placed a hand on his shoulder. "So many dead, but if it helps you any…I think you did the right thing at the time. How many billions more throughout the centuries would have lived their lives under subjugation and brutality if you hadn't pared down the Host's numbers? At least you gave the people not directly under their control a chance at true freedom."

Korbos looked at her hand, then up to Cassidy's freckled face. He nodded. "I appreciate the thought." He put his hands on his knees, heaving himself unsteadily to his feet, lurching ever so slightly as he brought the bottle to his lips. A burst of pity crowded the churning of my other emotions.

"It was a short-lived victory, in any case. Rin and I were on the run. We had stashes and storehouses and supplies all over Elarin, but no more armies to use them. My siblings hunted us without mercy, and within six months Rin was dead and I went into hiding. It took me a hundred miserable years to face them again."

He drew a shuddering breath, wiping a hand across his scarred face.

Mari raised a tentative hand. "I've got a question, Korbos," she began. "You mentioned your creator eventually reappeared, but who *was sh—*"

"What is that infernal *beeping*?" Korbos interrupted, spinning toward Cassidy. "Shouldn't you be checking on that?"

I shared a look with Mari. She took the hint and didn't finish her question. Korbos obviously didn't want to discuss that aspect of his life. Indeed, all told, he'd given us very little information regarding his mysterious progenitor.

Cassidy glanced toward the cockpit. "Proximity alarm. We'll be at Cortian in about half an hour."

I started. "Already?"

Cassidy threw me a wicked grin that made my pulse race. "Told you my girl makes good time. I've been burning the thrusters a little harder than usual, since we're full up on fuel now. Let's get prepped for landing. Korbos, I'll need you to scout a touchdown spot for me."

He grunted, slinging his rifle across a beefy shoulder and heading for the hatch. His step was surprisingly steady, given how much liquor he'd been slamming back.

I looked to Korbos. "Guess we'll have to come back to your story later. You said four of the Host survived the Ruin. Kaira and Kalos, of course, plus two others. I need to know what happened to the two that aren't around any more."

I didn't know how to process the feeling inside me. For years, I'd harbored a childish fantasy of revenge against Kaira for the loss of my village. The loss of my family. But that's all it really had been: a fantasy. I'd never truly believed that I'd be able to take her out. Deep down, I accepted that I'd probably die trying it now. I just wanted to look her in the eye and have her know that there were some that would always resist her. That not all worshipped her as a goddess, and indeed saw her for the vain, spoiled beast she was. To spit in her face as one final act of defiance.

But with Korbos's story, a new emotion had emerged. It felt like hope. The Host weren't invincible. There was a way to bring them down. And with one of them on my side, that childish fantasy suddenly seemed like it could become an actual reality. If we could get the signara to Cortian and pull whatever data from it that Korbos needed, we might have a chance to finally eradicate the Host forever. To avenge all those deaths. To avenge my family. I'd always thought I'd settle for killing Kaira, but in light of Korbos's story, I had a new drive. I wanted to destroy them all. And I'd do whatever it took to make that happen. My mouth settled into a grim line.

Now I just had to come to terms with the fact that my friend and mentor had nearly wiped out life on Elarin.

The smith gave me a long look, as if he could read the thoughts pouring through my mind. His head dropped a resigned nod. "Later."

THIRTEEN

"I never thought I'd actually visit this place," Cassidy said, leaning forward to stare out the cockpit window. The large glass sectionals provided a good view of the city before us, such as it was. We'd been lucky to find a clearing large enough to accommodate the *Storm,* which now rested on the edge of a high sloping hill overlooking the ruined city of Cortian. Thick-wooded forest stretched as far as we could see in every direction; the sheer size and variety of trees boggled my mind. Nobody would ever find this place—even as large as it was—unless they had a skipship or took a weeks-long trek through hostile wilderness. It was damn near completely cut off from the outside world.

The city, surprisingly preserved, lay in a wide but shallow bowl tucked into a jungle wilderness. An enormous circular wall surrounded a densely-packed variety of buildings. Tall multi-level edifices dominated the city center, with the average height of the buildings tapering off as they moved outward to the wall. From our perspective, Cortian looked vaguely triangular, like a pyramid of basalt.

I was blown away by the scale of the forest surrounding—and in many places, invading—the city; some of the trees towered as tall as the highest structures. No wonder the place looked abandoned. The high wall and what buildings I could see past it were completely covered in creeping vines and all manner of plants. The city was dead, but still teeming with life. Even the huge—markets? Offices? I didn't know what they were—lay patched in greenery, some nearly to their tops. I could see the occasional twinkle of reflected light from panels of unbroken glass that had weathered all the centuries this place must have lain dormant. No life moved that I could spot—aside from the odd flock of birds passing here and there across the dark metal and brick structures—yet the air was filled with the noise of the jungle. Hoots and howls and all manner of hollers.

The wall surrounding the city was higher than any I'd ever seen. The village where I'd grown up had boasted a wall of wooden logs, maybe twenty feet high. Being a coastal town, Hightide didn't even *have* a city wall, if one discounted the Reef.

This monstrosity appeared to be some sort of pitted stone at least two hundred feet tall. I couldn't tell with any certainty, as the height of the wall blocked out view of any nearby buildings to give it proper scale. It was rounded across the top and *thick*, with blocky towers jutting at regular intervals around the circumference. Otherwise it seemed to be unbroken, unseamed stone.

It was difficult to tell, but there seemed to be an outlying expansion to the city outside the wall, perhaps a mile wide, much shorter buildings completely overgrown by foliage. Little could be seen of the structures other than boxlike mounds, maybe two or three stories high, peeking through the gaps between enormous trees.

I couldn't see any roads leading into the city, although time and nature had surely reclaimed any such niceties. The odd twinkle of light reflected through the green from broken windows, and the vines and trees followed blocky patterns that might once have been streets and thoroughfares. Now, only thick swaths of undergrowth filled the spaces.

The lower fifty feet of the wall, in the couple of spots where it was visible through the trees, seemed to be covered in thick greenery. There was a sizable indentation in the coverage—slightly to our northwest—which might have once been a city gate, but we'd have no way of knowing until we hacked our way to it.

I had no idea how we'd even get into this fortress. If we had to chop our way through dense underbrush for the entire distance to the city wall, it would take us hours. Maybe days. I was glad we'd decided to wait out the night after landing and set out at first light. Masina Tamai, the broken moon, was visible above the treeline, on its way to setting for the day.

Cassidy turned to the big smith. "We're *actually* going to go through all this?" she asked, mirroring my thoughts. "This is gonna take forever."

"Yep," Korbos exhaled, resigned. He glanced at her. "I was surprised you even knew of this place, Cassidy. Not many do."

She raised an eyebrow, pointing a thumb to herself. "Seeker, remember? We've usually got enough sense to stay the hell away from Devoid cities, though."

Mari turned from pressing her face to the windscreen. "Devoid. You've mentioned them a few times before. What's a Devoid?"

Cassidy scratched the back of her neck, blowing out a long breath. "Whew. Um. Korbos, you wanna take this one?"

He snorted. "Better to explain after they've seen one. Words won't do it justice."

Cassidy snorted back. "True enough."

Korbos eyed her sidelong. "You've encountered Devoid before, then?" His tone was curious, but there was an edge to it.

"Well, actually…uh, no. But I've read plenty about them in the Searching Library."

Korbos snorted yet again. "Not the same, I promise." He sighed, giving me a quick wink. "This should be fun. You're all in for a real treat. Just keep your weapon handy."

This did not instill me with a great amount of confidence.

It took us an hour to prep our gear, loading up with blades, spare tents, and assorted gear that Cassidy had on-hand, along with water from the *Storm*'s recyclers. Mari, being the smallest of us, packed lightest, only bringing a few canteens and a pair of daggers sheathed at her hips. I did a double take. They were large kitchen knives, from the galley. Small as she was, they were still nearly the length of her forearm. Maybe a bit longer.

Our tents, along with the bedrolls and various other survival gear, rode fastened to a rather ingenious harness on Bastin's back. Cassidy had constructed the thing from scavenged cargo netting and tie straps to securely wrap his chest and haunches while leaving his forepaws and glide membranes free. The largest buckle, just below his chest, served as a rapid release in case he got hopelessly entangled or needed to move unencumbered for a while. Bastin's large eyes swiveled back and forth between us as he panted happily, eager to be out of the *Storm* and moving amongst the trees. I imagined it was like coming home for the arboreal native. Mari gave him a good scratch behind his ear and a treat from her belt pouch as his bushy tail swished a staccato rhythm against the bulkhead.

Korbos grunted as he gingerly settled the straps of his pack, as if he were carrying extra weight.

"Got something heavy there, big man?" I asked.

He eyed me. "Extra water," he said, then turned toward the cargo bay. I shrugged. Good thinking. I had a feeling we'd need it soon enough.

I strapped a thick, curved machete to my belt as the others shrugged their packs over their shoulders, and we set off.

Luckily, the hill upon which the skipship rested had a series of rudimentary steppes that served as natural switchbacks, so the downhill going was relatively easy at first. Things got much tougher when we hit flat land at the bottom.

As expected, the jungle growth was thick; tons of brush and hanging vines—some nearly as thick as my leg—with no naturally-occurring paths or animal trails that we could immediately discern. With a deep sigh, I pulled my blade and began the laborious task of hacking my way through. My real arm was going to get tired, fast. Not for the first time, I wished my mechanical hand had the manual dexterity of its flesh-and-blood counterpart. It was great for ripping vines and low branches out of the way, but not so dandy at swinging the machete, with its smallish hilt.

At least I could swap out with Korbos and Cassidy on occasion as we made our way into the woods. Which we did, frequently.

It took us three hours to travel a little over a mile. We finally came to the outskirts of the city expansion, and, as we'd guessed, nature had completely reclaimed what remained of the low buildings. Single-story homes crept by on either side of us, utterly devastated by green growth. Many had been destroyed by centuries-old trees bursting through their roofs and frames, collapsing the structures into unrecognizable green hillocks. Branches arced high overhead, their canopy framing the ruined, overgrown roads in perpetual shadow. I stumbled several times on hunks of a dark, stone-like material that reached up through the scrub and roots to trip and harry us.

"What *is* this stuff?" I asked, holding a chunk up to a thin beam of light spearing through the canopy.

"Quickcrete," Korbos murmured, pausing and wiping his brow after hacking through yet another thick copse of grasping thorns and branches. His eyes were unfocused, staring into a past only he could remember.

"They made roads out of the stuff, back before the Ruin. Millions of autocarts used these streets, throughout the years. Taking residents to work. Out shopping. To dinner with their families. See those low mounds to the side? Go take a look, and wonder at the marvels of ages past." His voice was laced with bitter irony.

I did as he bid, ignoring his sardonic tone and picking my way to the edge of the street before approaching a smaller mound of grass, moss, and vines. Korbos followed and stepped beside me, reaching out a hand and plunging it into the mound. There was a dull thump as he struck something solid and drug his hand down, pulling away the growth and revealing a dirty pane of cracked glass. I peered through, mouth open in wonder at the small piece of history before me. There were two seats, human-sized, and a wheel on one side, ostensibly for changing direction—like the yoke on Cassidy's skipship. I glanced up and down the ruined thoroughfare. I could see dozens of autocart remains, now that I knew what to look for. They were so *common*! A small part of me wept for the miracles of that distant past, now lost.

We caught glimpses of other relics. A child's doll—mostly buried in a patch of moss—made of some hard, glossy material that had weathered the elements far better than I would have expected. Other strange machines—Order only knew their purpose—poked here and there from the foliage; rusted, crumbling metal holding silent vigil for the lost. Slowly rejoining the earth.

I shook my head, thinking of the families that once called this place home. How long had this place been abandoned? What happened to those who lived here?

An hour later, we'd only progressed another quarter mile. The going was slowed significantly by increased growth, both in the ever-larger buildings around us and the woods bursting through the remains of the roadways. The buried autocarts were thick in this area, and some of the two- or three-story edifices had crumbled, blocking our path with overgrown debris which we were forced to either climb or blaze a new trail to avoid. We'd begun to encounter standing water, like miniature swamps coating us to our knees in muck. There were several nerve-wracking incidents where we were forced to crawl *through* the ancient wreckage, surrounded by crumbling bricks, steel beams, and trickling moisture. It was like spelunking through a tomb. Like being buried alive.

Tempers started to stretch thin, though we had to have been approaching the wall at last. Even Bastin was perturbed, snapping his jaws at the incessant swarms of bugs that buzzed around us.

"Watch it!" Mari exclaimed, after a particularly wild backswing from Cassidy almost took off her nose.

"Stop following so close then, short stuff! You got a problem, then *you* get up here and clear a path."

"*I* happen to think of others. Unless you stretches want to crawl through this mess again?"

"*Quiet*, you two!" Korbos snapped in a harsh whisper, interrupting the bickering. "No voices."

"No voices?" said Mari. "What does that even mean—"

She cut off, eyes going wide as…*something*…detached itself from a nearby tree and staggered toward us.

"Atia protect and preserve us…"

"*What the frok is that?*" I screamed. Which proved to not be the best idea. Six other *things* appeared from the scrub, drawn to the noise.

"That…is a Devoid," Korbos grunted.

FOURTEEN

I froze in sheer terror. The apparitions drew closer.

They were gray and green and brown—the colors of the forest around them—and blended in so well that I had trouble seeing them against the backdrop even when looking straight at one. Vaguely humanoid—in that I could make out two arms, two legs, and not much else—they were covered in vines, shelf-like fungus, and leaves; the detritus of the woods they occupied. One of the creatures, with a vine-encrusted, tail-like appendage, stood hunched like a Na'don, four oversized hands waving listlessly. They glistened, their bodies exuding some sort of thick black goo between the masses of tumorous growths. Or maybe it was sap.

The nearest one shambled yet closer, stretching out a bark- and moss-covered hand that ended in shredded, clawlike nails, dripping with that nasty black liquid. I couldn't make out a face. If it ever had one to begin, eons spent in the forest had left it completely obliterated by large swaths of fungal growth. I *could* just barely make out a mouth in the crush of irregular shapes, gnashing as the creature drew near, broken and pointed teeth chomping in anticipation of its meal.

The usual chatter of the forest had gone dead silent around us, making the stuttering shuffle-step and clack of the things' jaws that much louder. The splash as one staggered through a swampy stand of water. It was terrifying. There was a sense of *wrongness* about them; these creatures weren't natural, shouldn't exist.

I couldn't make myself move. I was far too busy attempting to not fill my pants. The nearest Devoid was only about three steps away, and still I couldn't make myself move.

Korbos brushed past me. "Go for the head. Stay quiet," he muttered, before swinging his blade in a wide arc and burying it in the Devoid's skull. The thing dropped like a rock, breaking my paralysis. They weren't invincible.

I tore my gaze from the one that had almost reached me and was shocked to see that we were surrounded by the creatures. At least twenty of them, each different from the one next to it. I squinted, eyes aching from the strain of trying to keep them from vanishing into the wooded backdrop. Mari had drawn her knives, her back pressed against Bastin, who was baring his fangs in a long hiss at the Devoid. Cassidy held her machete in one hand, and with the other pulled her extendable blade from its sheath at her spine. A muted *click-click* bounced off the trees as it locked into place.

We unconsciously formed a semi-circle to face the oncoming Devoid; Korbos on my left, Cassidy to my right, with Mari between her and Bastin. The creatures slogged forward, implacable.

All hell broke loose.

Cassidy glided forward—her soft boots making no noise on the mushy, springy ground—and took off a Devoid's head just above the shoulders. Bits of chopped fungus flew as she wheeled to take another. I bit back a scream as I ducked the wild swing of one's paw, spinning and burying my machete in the skull of another just beside it. A thrusting kick shoved back the first as my arm was dragged downward, pulling me off-balance; the blade was stuck in the thing's head. I wrenched it loose just in time and decapitated the first Devoid with an arcing backswing. Two more lurched closer as the body fell. Jagged teeth gnashed within their not-faces as they closed the gap far more rapidly than I would have anticipated. The way they faded into the surrounding forest made it incredibly difficult to judge their distance.

Cassidy vaulted past me, catching each with a kick to the chest and sending them staggering back. I whirled to the right as she came down and planted her feet. She had grabbed one of the Devoid *in a frokking headlock*, using its weight to balance against her own leap.

She bared her teeth at me a manic grin as she spun the thing away from her and stabbed it through the mouth with her machete, twirling gracefully and decapitating yet another with her flat-nosed blade. Movement registered in my peripheral and I swung, hacking the arm from a Devoid that was trying to slash her back with its ragged claws. I didn't want that black goo getting on any of us if I could help it. A quick thrust dropped the Devoid a moment later.

I glanced around just as Bastin took the head off a Devoid with a swipe of his massive paw. A loud *whop!* echoed through the trees as the creature's misshapen features went sailing away to splash down a few seconds later. Mari was finding it difficult to reach the creatures' heads for a killing blow, so she darted low, dodging swings and hamstringing the ones who got close enough for Bastin to finish off. The scuridai seemed to be handling the fight well, despite the gear wobbling around on his harness.

Korbos…well…

The man was a killing machine.

No less than ten of the Devoid lay crumpled at the big man's feet. Four more were closing on him. There were rents in his long coat, though none in his flesh that I could see. As I fended off yet another, flailing wildly, Korbos took a calm step forward and lopped the head from one, then rolled his feet and *punched* another square in the face. Its feet left the ground, and the mushy, fungal growths that substituted the Devoid's face folded around his forearm. There was an obscene splat as he withdrew his gore-coated fist, backhanding yet another creature before beheading it. Three Devoid down before I had time to draw as many breaths. A swift shoving kick, followed by a heavy overhanded chop, finished off the fourth.

More still approached, detaching themselves from the forest around us. We closed our circle, back to back, while Bastin romped around us, swiping at the Devoid who drew too close.

"That way," Korbos murmured, pointing with his machete. "Move steady. Don't stop." His eye flared silver for a brief moment, and Devoid flew, parted as if he'd swept his hand across an ant bed. The big man grimaced. A small opening appeared, the brush thinner and more easily maneuverable.

"Move it!"

We didn't hesitate, plunging through and hacking as rapidly as we could. Thick chopping sounds thudded behind us as Korbos held off the approaching Devoid. One made it close to Mari's position, and I buried my blade in its head.

We weren't making enough progress. Not fast enough.

"Chaos damn it all…*down!*"

We dropped, Mari grabbing Bastin by the harness and dragging him to the ground as thick bolts of blue energy screamed through the spot where our heads had been a moment before. The forest in our path disintegrated, the blasts clearing a rough tunnel through the thinner brush. Korbos wheeled and opened fire on the closest Devoid, blowing them apart. The *poom! poom!* of gunfire rattled across the woods like close thunder, vibrating in my chest.

My eyes widened in horrified realization. More would come, drawn by the noise. We'd eventually be overwhelmed.

Time to run.

I scrambled to my feet, snatching Cassidy up by the back of her shirt and pulling her along. We edged our way into the cleared path, moving as fast as we dared, heads swiveling as we kept an eye out for approaching Devoid. Twice I had to snatch Mari to the side as grasping, mucus-covered hands leapt out of the brush near her. I was just thankful the monsters went down so easy. Well, relatively easy. My real arm ached from repeated impacts as I pulled a head-sized leaf from a nearby tree to wipe down my blade. The black goo had etched splattery patterns into the metal, further reinforcing my instinct to not let it touch any of us.

Korbos backed in behind us, the shots from Bulwark coming with less frequency. Every so often, he would bark at us to move, then turn and shoot further along our path, the blasts extending the tunnel. We pressed on this way for about five minutes until a quiet moan from Mari snatched my attention. I'd been scanning the edges of the tunnel, keeping my head moving, eyes unfocused and watching for motion rather than the shapes of figures. As the surroundings came into clarity, my jaw dropped.

We'd made it to the wall.

It seemed to rise forever, blotting out everything in our field of vision. A narrow corridor of vine-covered ground, perhaps five feet wide, ran along the base of the wall to the east and west, as far as the eye could see. Which, admittedly, wasn't very far due to the masses of overhanging branches and foliage. It was like a tunnel had been carved along the wall's lower edge, framed by rustling windblown leaves and snaking, grasping vines that stretched the gap and clambered up the wall to some unknowable height.

Perhaps a hundred feet east of our position was an enormously thick, twisting tree that arced over and through the smaller branches, blocking the view before slamming into the wall itself and rising beyond sight. I goggled. I'd never actually seen a tree so large, and it made my estimate of the bigger specimens I saw within Cortian itself seem woefully inadequate.

From the west, motion caught my eye. The Devoid were coming—visible only as shifting green against the backdrop of the forest, like a heatwave made solid. I spun in a circle; that same wavering green peeked through every gap in the undergrowth. A terrible realization washed over me as I spun again, frantic.

There wasn't a single entryway visible along the wall.

We'd been backed into a corner.

Korbos stood solid as a stone, legs planted wide, his eye closed and hand outstretched. It swung side-to-side, slow and ponderous, before stopping. His eye snapped open and he raised Bulwark, and we all jumped backward as he triggered a massive blue blast at the ground ahead of him. Then another. And another. The vines criss-crossing the empty space shriveled and peeled away, revealing a small grate set into a patch of quickcrete. It looked wide enough to accommodate the big man.

His eye flashed silver, and he bared his teeth at the grate. With a wrenching snap, the bolts holding the rusted metal gave way, and the heavy lattice flew off into the dappled shadows of the woods.

Cassidy dropped to all fours, poking her head into the hole.

"Looks clear."

"Everyone in, *now*!"

At the same moment, a whining *yip* came from Bastin, and he thrashed about. He was stuck at the edge of vines and forest. He must have backed into a tree, tangling the harness amongst the branches. In moments, the scuridai had hopelessly entangled the webbing as Mari tried to calm him. She tried, frantic, to cut through the section of net.

"They're getting clooooose!" Cassidy mock-whispered in a sing-song voice.

"Chaos damn it anyway," Korbos growled. He reached over and slapped his hand against Bastin's chest, yanking at the release and freeing the scuridai. The packs and gear swung forlornly as Bastin wound his way around Mari, pushing her behind him and away from the approaching Devoid with a long hiss.

"Mari!" Korbos bellowed, the time for silence long past at that point. "Mount up and *get up that tree*!" He thrust a hand toward the giant specimen east of us. "We'll meet you on the other side. *Go!*"

Mari shook her head. "I'm not gonna le—"

She squeaked as Korbos grabbed the back of her mud-stained shirt, lifting her high and dropping her onto Bastin's back.

"*I said GO!* We'll find you, but Bastin *won't fit*! Get into the city, stay high, and watch for us!"

She hesitated.

"Damn it, Mari, they'll tear him apart and then *eat you both*!" Korbos screamed.

Her eyes went wide, then she nodded and wheeled Bastin about.

"Up, Bast, up!" she cried. He cleared the distance in several leaping bounds, then clambered up the tree in a flurry of claws.

I lost sight of them almost immediately. My heart constricted with worry, but a crunching sound close behind me turned my blood to ice. I whirled, barely ducking the sharp swipe of a Devoid. Cassidy took its head off with a sweep of her machete. She was panting from our exertions, but not a drop of fear touched her face.

"In! In! Gogogo!" Korbos cried, unleashing a blast from Bulwark and driving back the nearest group of Devoid.

I didn't have to be told again. Cassidy leapt into the opening with me close on her heels. I had a brief vision of hitting the bottom and breaking both my legs, but thankfully the drop wasn't very deep—only about eight or nine feet. Still, I hit hard, crumpling to the ground and rolling on my shoulder to absorb the fall. My pack and netanium arm took the brunt of the impact, saving me from any serious injury. I leapt to my feet, wheeling to take in a long circular tunnel that stretched to infinity in either direction. At least, as far as I could see, which wasn't all that far. Thick vines crawled down the walls of the tunnel, and the floor was covered in them much like the path surrounding the wall above. It made for uneasy footing.

From above us I heard the low bass rattle of Korbos's rifle, then he was dropping into the opening, briefly blocking the bright shaft of light. He landed wrong, and I saw his leg buckle on the uneven roots. A loud snap, followed by a grunt of pain. I winced. My earlier worry hadn't been too far off the mark.

A shadow above blotted out the sun as Korbos rose, favoring his injured foot. Bile rose in my throat as I saw the bright white of bone poking clean through his boot. With an agonized grimace the big man hobbled a few paces back and settled Bulwark to his shoulder as a Devoid dropped through the opening. Another followed.

"Back!" he cried. Cassidy and I scrambled backwards as he unleashed a barrage.

Blue energy lit the tunnel. Blast after blast collapsed a large section with a rumbling groan. Several tons of soil and quickcrete hurtled down, crushing and burying the Devoid threatening us. Blocking us in.

Trapping us.

FIFTEEN

My breath was coming too fast. Far too rapid. I was hyperventilating.

I was choking. Thick dust sucked into my lungs, bending me over in harsh coughs. I couldn't breathe. I was utterly disoriented.

After the cave-in, all light was gone. The tunnel was pitch black. I couldn't see my hand in front of my nose, and I staggered sideways, feeling blindly for something, *anything*, to give me a sense of grounding. I couldn't find anything. Shouldn't I have hit the wall of the tunnel? How was it that I hadn't, given the indisputable, all-encompassing fact that they were going to close in and crush me at any second?

For the first time ever, true panic hooked its tendrils into my brain. My whole life had been spent either on or near the open ocean. These tightening walls filled me with a terror I could have never anticipated, sending me thrashing about, utterly blind, unable to draw a complete breath. Heavy coughs wracked my body from all the dust and particulates in the air, and I couldn't frokking *breathe*. The animal part of me gibbered and quailed. I was trapped under the ground. I was never going to find a way out. I was going to die down here in the black. I cried out. I staggered.

I collided with Cassidy.

I knew it was Cassidy because my grasping, flailing hands wound up clutching particular parts of her anatomy they had no business clutching. Parts that Korbos assuredly didn't possess. And—of course—the realization cut through the consuming panic like a knife and cleared my brain in an instant. So I did what any self-respecting gentleman would do in such a situation. I froze. And—of course—my traitorous hands remained right where they shouldn't have been.

"Uhhhh…" her voice rang, inflection rising in anger. I—of course—was still frozen in mortified horror.

Whock! The darkness exploded into bright stars and whorls as she socked me across the temple. Of course.

That finally got me moving.

I clutched my head as I stumbled a few steps away, going down to one knee. I couldn't see a damned thing. I counted myself lucky that she hadn't stabbed me.

"I'm so sorry, I can't see. Sorry. Sorry…" I trailed off. *Lame*. Order anyway, I was a moron.

A faint snap sounded, and the tunnel flooded with a sudden green light. After the sheer black of before, it was blinding in its brilliance. I shuddered, scrabbling toward the illumination, throwing my arms around Cassidy's legs. Order above, I *really* didn't want to experience darkness like that again in my lifetime. She was holding a tube filled with some sort of glowing liquid. Any other time I'd have marveled at the light stick, but my lizard brain was too relieved at being able to *see* again. The light cut through the settling dust like a beacon through a thick fog.

"Get up, you idiot," Cassidy said, but a grin quirked her lips, softening the insult. The green glow threw weird, harsh shadows on her face and through the tunnel, though the illumination didn't extend too far.

"Up. Yeah. Sorry." I heaved myself from my knees, looking around. Korbos sat about ten feet behind us, close to the enormous pile of rubble from the collapsed ceiling. I shuddered to think of how close we'd come to being crushed by tons of fallen debris.

"You okay over there, big guy?" I asked Korbos. Ugh. What a dumb question. His *bone* was poking through his frokking *boot.*

He grunted. "Yeah, just give me a minute." His head cocked as he examined his broken left leg. My gorge rose at the sight of his shin poking from the large tear in his leather boot. How in Atia's name had he taken steps on that leg? The pain would have killed me. Or at least put me on my backside, screaming like a newborn babe who's missed a meal.

Korbos took several quick, shallow breaths and then—almost faster than I could follow—reached down and *wrenched* his leg, shoving the bone back through the boot. His agonized roar echoed down the tunnel. My stomach lurched, and I couldn't hold back.

I'd been a fisherman for most of my life. I knew how to gut and clean a catch. I was used to blood and viscera. But the *squelch* from Korbos's impromptu reset did me in. I did manage to avoid spewing my insides all over Cassidy's feet. Barely.

She laughed. "Steel arm, but not so much of a steel stomach, eh?"

Still bent double and heaving, I threw a rude gesture in the general direction of her voice.

Korbos took a long, long pull from his flask, then sat for several minutes—legs crossed, eyes closed, and breathing steady—as I wiped myself off and rinsed my mouth from the canteen at my hip. With an abrupt jerk, he climbed to his feet, bouncing a few times on his toes to test his weight. An approving nod followed, and he marched over to Cassidy, showing no signs that he'd ever been injured. I shook my head in wonder, placing my hands over my face and groaning softly. This day had already been full of surprises and terror enough for ten years, and though my mind was still wired, my body was beginning to feel the sluggishness of adrenaline crash.

"You brought a compass?" he asked Cassidy. "We need to head north. Now." His face was grim. I don't know how I could tell, but he was worried about Mari and Bastin being on their own. I guess I'd just been around him enough to know his moods. Concern tightened my chest as I thought of the two scrambling up the tree. Had they made it over the wall? Images flashed unbidden through my mind of them turning back to look for us… scouting the hole where the tunnel collapsed… the Devoid swarming out of the trees, overwhelming them, tearing into…

No. Stop it.

Cassidy held up a round device, fished from her satchel. It was unlike any directional tool I'd ever seen; exquisitely crafted, set in machined black metal with a thick glass face, numerous fine markings dotting the circumference. I raised an eyebrow, silently inquiring as to its origins.

"It's a compass, Guts," she smirked.

I grimaced. If that was going to be her new pet name for me, I couldn't say I was too crazy about it. Not like I could help my body's reaction.

"I know it is, *Cass*," I replied, deliberately using the shortened version I knew she hated. "Where'd you get it?"

"Same place I got these, Guts," she said, waving the green light stick under my nose. I cocked my head. "The storehouse? Where I found the *Storm*?"

"Ah..." I replied. It made sense. I was momentarily curious as to what other wonders she'd discovered in the Second Battalion depot.

"Are you two finished?" Korbos snarled. "Let's get moving."

"Why do we need a compass, anyway?" I asked. "This tunnel only runs in one direction, right?"

He looked at me like I'd grown a second head. "For now it does. This is a sewer outflow. When we get into the city proper, these pipes will branch in thousands of directions. I for one don't plan to spend the rest of my very, very long life wandering around down here."

He paused. "And those glowsticks won't last forever, you know..."

My eyes shot wide at the prospect of being trapped down here, meandering forever in the crushing darkness.

"Yeah, okay, let's go. What are we waiting for?"

Korbos took the lead, snapping another of Cassidy's light sticks and setting off down the seemingly endless tunnel, stepping over and around the thick roots that poked through the stonework. I stuck close to her as we followed, which wasn't entirely unpleasant.

Silence reigned as we progressed down the ancient sewage pipe. Though it was totally dry, I tried not to think about what sort of dust we were stirring up with our thumping footfalls. I held my breath as much as I could. The smell was dry and musty, centuries of uncirculated air wafting the funk of ages through our noses.

Quite a while later we were still walking, though we had to be well underneath the city by that point. We passed more than a few openings as we trekked, but Korbos kept us on a straight path.

I skipped a few steps ahead, pulling even with Cassidy. Stumbled over a large root. Closed my eyes and cursed myself for a clumsy idiot.

"Hey," I said, hesitant. She turned her head toward me, that disarming smile quirking and making my stomach flutter in a manner not too dissimilar from my earlier expulsion.

"Hey yourself, Guts." She flashed a beautiful grin, the horrid green light doing nothing to diminish its radiance. "What's up?"

"I just…" I paused, composing myself. I could feel the flush creeping up my face. "I'm sorry. About earlier? When I…grabbed you? I panicked. It wasn't intentional. So…sorry. Again. Won't happen. Again, y'know?" Order anyway, I *was* an idiot.

She laughed, the sound tinkling through the sewer and reverberating from the walls. Korbos threw a brief look back at us before redoubling his stalk through the tunnel.

"It's okay, Pyk." My chest beat faster hearing her use my name. "Next time, just be sure to ask a lady's permission first before you get all grabby." She grinned again, hopping a thick vine and pulling closer to Korbos.

I stopped dead. *Next time*?

Wait.

Was she *flirting* with me? I was thankful for the harsh green cast of the light sticks, because my flush felt like it'd turned me the color of a tomato.

I had no idea how to respond, so—true to form—I said nothing and fell back into my march through the Cortian underbelly. Cassidy glanced back and tossed another slow smile, turning my knees to custard.

Order above, was I really falling for her in a *sewer*, of all places? It felt true, and I was helpless to keep a ridiculous answering grin from my face.

"Hold up," Korbos barked. He raised his glowstick high, illuminating the dead end we'd come to. Tunnels stretched off to either side of us. Fewer roots climbed the walls here; they had faded the further beneath the city we'd travelled. Thoughts of Cassidy fled my mind. For the moment, at least.

"Which…which way do we go?" I asked, uneasy. I was still a bit freaked out by the possibility of never exiting the tunnels. We'd yet to see an egress of any kind. No ladders, no doors. Nothing.

"Cassidy?" Korbos looked to the skipship captain, who shrugged.

"Not like I have a map of the place," she replied. "East or west, one's just as good as the other to me."

Korbos grunted. "Fair enough." He took a right, heading down the eastern corridor. Cassidy and I glanced at each other, then adjusted our packs and followed.

We traveled for what felt like hours, turning this way and that as the tunnels branched and divided. Time had no meaning in this dark extended tomb. I yearned to see the sun again. Korbos had been right. It was a complete rat's maze down there, the further in we explored. Hundreds of large pipes and tributaries shot off to the sides—right angles, diagonally, even angling in from above in some instances—and *thousands* of smaller openings dotted the walls. In several places we had to pick our way around and over piles of rubble—detritus created where the sides of the tunnel had collapsed inward. As we made our cautious way over the stone and dirt, I kept sneaking nervous glances at the crumbling quickcrete. It didn't look like it would take much to send it tumbling down on our heads.

I was glad we had the compass to reference, because I quickly lost any sense of direction or bearing. Aside from numerous treks down side tunnels, Cassidy kept us pointed roughly north, deeper and deeper into the city. The silence, aside from the shuffle of our feet, was total.

After a while, however, perhaps half an hour, a sound intruded on the quiet; distant, but persistent. A hollow *poooong*, echoing through the pipes. Sometimes it would come in a burst, a rapid one-two-three, followed by minutes of silence. Then a heavier, louder strike—*BONG!*—as if a bell were being rung in a church across town. It definitely resembled the sound of a large piece of metal being struck by a hard object. I was reminded of the Reef and its giant starships. Every now and then you'd pass one where a hull plate had come loose, hanging by wires and getting tossed about by the waves. Whenever it would swing back and hit the ship, you'd hear a metallic gonging similar to the one currently assailing our ears.

The three of us looked at each other, and Korbos gave a shrug and continued walking. Cassidy checked her compass. The noise was coming from the direction we were heading, so we'd find out soon enough. It grew louder as we approached its location. Then louder still, until each strike was nearly deafening in the enclosed space. Just when I felt my ears couldn't bear the percussive assault any more, Korbos held up a fist to halt. We'd reached something new.

A ladder. The first we'd seen in what felt like hours spent in this maze.

A loud *pong* sounded from directly above it.

SIXTEEN

We exchanged another wordless glance, then proceeded to climb; me first, with Korbos second and Cassidy bringing up the rear. A short ascent later, and I was facing a circular metal plate set above the ladder. Just as I reached for it, another strike hit, causing the metal to vibrate against my fingers and my ears to nearly bleed. I cried out, the noise drowned in the metallic echo. Not wanting to endure another, I placed my artificial hand on the plate and shoved. It went up easy enough, and I got just enough purchase on the edge to slide it sideways with an ungodly harsh scraping. The light of a blue sky greeted me, and I closed my eyes as a breeze washed over my face. I'd never been so happy to stick my head out into the fresh air.

Where I almost had my brains bashed in by a chunk of stone the size of my fist.

I got lucky, opening my eyes just in time to see the rock descending and raise my netanium arm to deflect its course. My body rocked sideways with the impact, and I scrambled out of the hole and into a broad thoroughfare lined with multi-story constructions of steel and stone. Greenery climbed the walls, vines and leaves creeping toward the sun.

As I glanced at the street around us I noted quite a few hunks of stone, maybe masonry, lying near the sewer cover I'd just exited. I assumed those were what had caused the ruckus that led us out. Ruined twists of metal—the rusted, plant-strewn remains of autocarts—lined the street, many stretched across the lanes of shattered quickcrete. There were so many variations of size and shape! Tall grass poked through the broken avenue, and humongous, twisting trees occasionally dotted the landscape. Overall, though, the vegetation wasn't nearly so dense and all-encompassing as we'd encountered outside of the wall. The structures were surprisingly intact, and beneath the veneer of decay I could get a glimpse of the absolute majesty of this city in its prime.

A cheery whoop sounded above me, and I looked up to see Mari and Bastin, standing atop a nearby building. A huge smile creased my face as Korbos and Cassidy climbed out behind me, our pilot grinning ear to ear and waving—even Korbos had a relieved smirk beneath his large eyepatch. Mari disappeared for a moment, then Bastin launched them both from their rooftop perch. He circled twice above the wide thoroughfare before gliding to a halt near us. Mari threw herself off and hit the ground running before he'd even slid to a stop. The wind left me as she slammed into my stomach, arms clutching my waist. Bastin sauntered over and nuzzled Korbos's thick arm.

"Oh, man, you guys, I thought I was never gonna find you I looked all over for some kind of entrance below and never could find anything and then I happened across this big plate and thought y'know maybe it'd be a place you'd come out so I started chucking debris at it and gods what a racket it made but I guess it worked because you heard it and here you are and—"

She cut off her verbal barrage as Korbos laid a hand on her shoulder. The big man was looking around, head snapping as he searched for danger. He glanced down at Mari and gave a kind, heartfelt smile.

"It's good to see you, little one, and I'm glad you're okay. But let's keep the chatter to a minimum. There's not a chance that the Devoid we met outside are the only ones left."

"Oh!" she exclaimed, trying to keep her voice low. "Yeah, we definitely gotta watch out because the noise I made did draw a few of them but they look different and I had to space out my throws because they'd wander off but every time I hit the plate one or two would come back before losing interest and oh drek—"

Her large eyes went wide, and we wheeled as one to see what had cut off her tirade. Shambling down the street were nine or ten Devoid. Four more approached from the opposite direction, on our blind side. We had nowhere to run.

I hadn't quite parsed her words from a moment before, but Mari was right. These Devoid *were* different from the ones we'd fought before. For one, they were all thinner—little more than skin and bones—and way…well, *drier*…than the bloated creatures outside the wall. I could see far less of that black goo emanating from these, although their dark, cracked skin was smeared with even darker blotches that might have been dried excretion. For another, they were far more humanoid, without the encumbering vines and fungal growth that covered the previous Devoid. One even appeared to be a Thrane.

Jagged teeth gnashed as they approached with stuttering steps, and sharp, ragged nails swept the air before them. They were all in various states of undress, some completely naked while scraps of incredibly ancient-looking cloth clung to others. Most were male, but I could see the odd female interspersed. All were nearly bald, but the women seemed to have more patches of dirty, wispy hair floating around their heads.

Korbos unslung Bulwark, but set it gently on the ground beside him as he drew his machete. "We can handle these," he said. "Just keep it quiet. Don't draw in more."

Cassidy and I nodded, pulling our own blades and preparing to fight. "Good," she said, "I've got a few frustrations to take out. These'll do nicely."

Without acknowledging any sort of strategy, we all stepped toward the smaller group. Better to take them out first and then round on the larger cohort without the threat at our backs.

"I'll take left," I said, stepping to the side, and then we were engaged. I swung hard at a Devoid's exposed skull, and the thing actually *ducked.* I was so shocked that the thing almost got me, its claws raking furrows in my shirt as I leapt back. I managed to parry its other arm with my mechanical one before catching it in a rising swing, severing the head and sending it flying.

"Is it me…" I cried out, "or are these faster than the other ones?" I dodged a swing from a second Devoid. Looked like I'd drawn short straw on the first group. A return stroke buried my machete into the thing's head, dropping it. I turned just as Korbos dispatched his opponent, and

Bastin—out of all of us—took out the fourth by pinning it to the ground and pouncing on its head, squashing it flat. The sound was…unsettling.

Korbos turned to me. "Yeah, I think they're a bit quick-URK!"

He cut off as the vanguard of the second group—the massive Thrane—slammed into him from the side in a tangle of flailing limbs and gnashing teeth.

"Heads up!" Mariyana cried, a moment too late.

I froze for a split second. These Devoid *were* faster. They'd covered the distance between us far more quickly than we'd anticipated, and caught us off-guard. Cassidy and Mari were falling back, blades flashing, and Bastin turned in confused circles, swiping at the Devoid which threatened to surround him.

That half-second almost cost me everything. Another large Devoid plowed into me, nails tearing at my shoulders as its head darted straight for my face. We hit the ground hard, with me underneath a flailing dry corpse that felt staggeringly heavy and dense. Its broken, jagged teeth clacked shut less than an inch from my nose, and I shrieked. I managed to get my arm—the metal one, thank Order above—up just in time for the creature's next bite to scrape off the wide flat fingers. I heaved it upward and then took a page from Korbos's book, pistoning my mechanical arm forward and burying it in the thing's face. Its arms went limp as the skull crumpled inward, and it took a shocking amount of force to shove the dead weight off me. I rolled over to stare into the split face of the dead Thrane.

A deep roar came from my right, and I turned just in time to see a Devoid's teeth latch on to Korbos's shoulder from behind, into the thick muscle just above his collarbone. The big blacksmith spun wildly, dislodging the monster and crushing its face with a lightning-fast elbow.

Quick swipes of his machete dispatched two more Devoid, but blood sprayed from the wound in a torrent. The big man went to one knee, and then I lost sight as two more Devoid approached me.

I was better prepared this time, punching one and stunning it while beheading the female next to it. A clumsy backswing decapitated the first before it could recover. No more were near me, so I stepped sideways and turned to survey the rest of my crew. The street around us was silent. Cassidy and Mari stood panting, bodies laying at their feet. Mari was dabbing at Bastin's paws with a scrap of cloth, keeping him from licking away the black slime that stained his white and brown fur.

Korbos, however, was on his knees, face twisted in a grimace of pain. I ran forward, then pulled up short before him as I noticed the state of his wound. The Devoid had torn a chunk of flesh away, but the injury didn't seem to be healing. Black lines radiated from the mangled muscle, stretching up his neck and into the scarred portion of his face. The lines were even darker than the broad cloth of his eyepatch and writhed like diseased tentacles. I stretched out my hands, not quite daring to touch, as he kneeled with teeth bared and his fists clenched. He convulsed—a short, rapid jerk, quickly followed by another—then threw his head back and howled, the cords of his neck standing out. Every muscle tensed rock-hard as Mari and Cassidy joined me. I shot a glance at them, but they were as distraught as I was. None of us knew what to do.

Korbos's howl tapered off, and he lowered his head before slumping sideways.

"Pyk!" Mariyana cried, "Help him! We have to *do something*!"

"I…I…" I couldn't say anything. Couldn't think of anything other than standing there, stammering. Useless. I looked to Cassidy, who shook her head.

"No idea what's happening, Guts. I wouldn't know how to start even if I did. I fix machines, not people."

Korbos's back arched, and a high breathless scream issued from his mouth. He rolled over on to his stomach, and with a mountain of will began to push himself to his feet, staggering slightly. Shoulders hunched, he clenched his fists yet again and bore down, his eye searing silver-white. Almost blinding. Loose stones and bits of black liquid began to rise from the ground around him. I had to shield my eyes, until the flare died down. I could see that same silvery light emanating from the wound, which slowly—oh so slowly—began to close. A low rumble began in his chest, a growl which grew in intensity even as the light faded and the floating debris settled to the ground. Moments later, the black lines receded and the flesh of his shoulder knit itself solid. He quieted at last and fell backwards heavily to sit, panting as if he'd run miles.

"Damnation…" he huffed. "That was…awful."

I leapt forward, placing a hand on his broad shoulder and checking the whole, unblemished skin where he'd been bitten.

"Are you…okay, mate?"

He was silent for a beat, head drooping. "I'll live. Just tired. I haven't had to push it like that in a long time."

"You're sure…"

"I *said* I'm fine!" he snapped, eye glinting silver for an instant. I don't think the others saw it. I backed a step or two away, quick. He hadn't used Bulwark to offset the use of his powers, and I could see a bite of imperious contempt in his stare. I decided not to push the matter, holding my hands out in placation.

He climbed to his feet, gaining strength as he rose. He grunted, shaking his head and taking a deep, calming breath. "Sorry. Healing like that took more energy than I would have expected. I definitely wouldn't recommend any of you four try that any time soon. Mari, make sure you get all that drek off Bastin."

"Yeah, okay, on it," she replied in an awed whisper.

I realized that even though I'd told her of our fight in the Strigori village, this was the first time she'd actually seen Korbos heal himself. She muttered to herself, pulling a clean scrap of cloth from her pack and dumping her canteen over it, scrubbing industriously at Bastin's paws while trying at the same time not to touch any of the black excretions.

Korbos glanced around. "We're clear?" he asked.

"Yeah, good to go," Cassidy replied before hesitating. "For now." She quickly wiped off her blades using one of the ragged cloths recovered from a fallen Devoid. I nodded in approval and did the same, taking Korbos's machete from him and cleaning both as best I could. She held up her hand for a slap.

"Nice job there, Guts," she said to me. I quickly returned the gesture, marveling at the feel of her four-fingered palm against mine, however quick it was.

"Thanks. Good moves yourself, Cass." I smiled to show I was teasing.

She paused for a moment, giving me a shrewd side-eye, then threw a dazzling grin at me.

"Y'know, it doesn't sound so bad when you say it." She turned to Korbos. "So where are we headed, Patches?"

We might have earned some breathing room for a time, but she was right. The noise of the fight was bound to draw more Devoid. She had her compass out, checking our bearing.

Korbos bent down to pick up Bulwark and sling it across his shoulder. The bite appeared to be completely healed; he didn't flinch as the rifle's strap sank into the exposed skin. He took a deep breath, turning slowly as he surveyed our surroundings.

"There." He pointed to a building some distance away—taller than most, with a roof which narrowed at an angle before flattening out at the top. To the east, I determined, glancing over Cassidy's shoulder at the compass.

"That's our target."

We set off in the indicated direction, Korbos leading, followed by Cassidy, with Mari, Bastin, and I bringing up the rear together. Mari nudged me in the ribs with her elbow, which meant she had to jump a little to get it that high.

"Soooooo…" she began, "'Patches,' I understand, but 'Guts?'" A wide grin split her face, bright teeth shining from dark skin and her purple eyes glittering.

"Oh, shut up."

SEVENTEEN

We crept as quietly as possible through the wide roads of Cortian, three of us walking and Mari riding upon Bastin. The buildings grew larger and taller around us as we made our way downtown, pausing occasionally as a lone Devoid—sometimes two or three—shambled across the street ahead of us. I was a little disturbed by how relatively few there seemed to be in a city of this size. Lucky break for us, I guessed. We'd only had to dispatch another four thus far, and we were able to do so with little enough noise that we didn't draw others to our position. We weren't exactly silent, but our voices were kept low.

I was finding it really difficult to stay focused on our path. My eyes kept wandering to the ornate facades creeping past us, the likes of which I'd never seen. Hightide was built among the skeletons of a pre-Ruin coastal town, but over the centuries the structures had been stripped and weathered to the point that there was precious little left to indicate how they'd looked in the bygone days. The skybound towers of Cortian, however, were generally untouched.

You could still make out the ornate brickwork—crumbling though it was—that served as a decorative patio for an outdoor dining area. The glass and steel of what Korbos believed to be an office building, a place he described as a conglomeration of merchants. The lower corner of that one had a different aesthetic—more like a market, where workers could pick up goods on their way home. At one wide intersection there was a large grassy area, filled with high weeds and the rusted remains of structures so bizarre that I couldn't even begin to guess their function. Korbos said it had been a park. A place for city dwellers to relax and watch their children play.

I couldn't fathom the sheer number of people it would take to fill even one of these monstrous edifices, much less the multitude that filled downtown Cortian. Tens of thousands. Hundreds of thousands, most likely. More people than I'd ever seen in my lifetime, at any rate. As we walked, Korbos—taciturn at the best of times—became downright verbose, tossing out tidbits of information about the oddities we passed. Tall poles stood guard at the corners of every intersection, long cables sagging as they receded down the streets. They were used to help direct the ebb and flow of all the autocart and pedestrian traffic, he said.

Giant flat expanses where images once flickered, advertising such things as "plays" and "movers." Over there was a corner bakery, far larger than any baker's shop I'd ever seen, that sold breads and pastries to the passersby that frequented these streets. That one rented autocarts to visiting tourists. This one sold electronic gadgets.

Restaurants *everywhere.*

Squat bulbs situated every so often along the shattered sidewalks, which Korbos claimed held massive amounts of water to fight fires. They weren't very big, so I couldn't understand how they'd contain enough liquid to snuff a fire in one of these monstrous sky towers. At one massive intersection of five different roads, there was a gargantuan sign of glass tubes and strange unfamiliar letters hanging from the front of the central hub building. Korbos made special note of that one.

"Those tubes were once filled with a gas that glowed as bright as the sun at night," he explained in a quiet voice. "The city itself was never dark. Never slept. Even in the small hours of the morning you'd find hundreds—sometimes thousands—of people, heading to parties, heading to work the late shift, going out for entertainment or trysts."

"What does it say?" Mari whispered.

"'Deepcore: You never know what your depths may hold,'" he replied, the corners of his mouth twitching. "It's a beer ad."

My jaw dropped. It struck me again exactly how far removed from those times we actually were—how much had truly been lost in the Ruin. Sun-bright gases lighting up the night? Might as well have been magic, as far as I was concerned. But for it to have been so commonplace, back then? To sell *beer*? I couldn't wrap my brain around it.

Cassidy stared at everything in wonder.

"I bet I'm the only Seeker to ever see this place," she said. "Chaos burn me, what I wouldn't give to have seen this city in its prime."

"I thought you weren't actually with the Seekers any more," I mused.

"Hmmm? Oh, I'm not. But it's a lifestyle that you never really leave. Curiosity and a thirst for knowledge is a hard thing to just let go of, Guts."

I nodded, thoughtful. I could see her point, although I'd never been much of the inquisitive type. Knowledge for knowledge's sake had never much interested me. I liked more useful, practical facts.

"What language is all this, Korbos?" Cassidy asked. "There's no records of it in the Searching Library…no archives at all, but it shows up everywhere we turn."

"Hmmm? Oh, it's Imperial Standard. If memory serves, Coretongue was emerging as a popular alternative before the Ruin, but Imperial Standard was the common language for fifteen hundred years prior to that."

Cassidy shook her head. "What I wouldn't give for a translation key…"

The corner of the big man's mouth quirked upward. "If we have time when this is all over, I'll teach you. I'd imagine that would come in pretty handy for an ambitious Seeker." Her eyes lit up as she nodded enthusiastically.

Korbos's expression took on a strange quality as we journeyed on, and it was a long while before I finally realized what it was.

He was almost overcome by nostalgia.

"You knew this place, didn't you?" I asked, patting him on the back. He sighed.

"I did. This was one of the largest cities in the Imperium, back in its day. I spent time here quite often with my brothers and sisters in the Host. Enjoying the bustle, sampling the decadence of high society…" He shook his bowed head. "Terrorizing the people that annoyed me. Wreaking havoc at the slightest inconvenience."

Korbos pointed to a building at our left. "Do you remember my story of sister Kida destroying the vizcast studio? Turning the lower floors to ice and collapsing the entire thing? That's the one. Or, well, that's where it stood originally. It was built over in the years following, before the Ruin."

He sighed again. "Even after all these years, I still agonize over the destruction we caused. How many times did these people have to mourn their dead, then turn right around, rebuild and move on as if we were part of the natural order? Like a hurricane or an earthquake? More than I'd ever care to count, I fear. More than I'd care to count."

Cassidy crossed the street, walking over to the building and trying to peer through the opaque windows. Somehow, most of the lower windows were intact. They were crusted over with so much dirt and muck that they were impenetrable, no matter how hard she wiped at them. I was sort of glad. Several times I'd seen shadows moving behind the upper windows of structures we'd passed; undoubtedly Devoid that had been trapped in the buildings for Order only knew how long.

What I'd seen so far had filled me with melancholy, knowing that this city had once been a thriving metropolitan center. I didn't want to see the leavings of an era I'd never fully understand, although I couldn't begrudge Cassidy's curiosity. The Seeker in her was definitely showing.

I hadn't mentioned it, but I'd seen her picking up the occasional item here and there as we walked, stuffing it furtively into her satchel. An ancient fork from a passed restaurant, lying on the ruins of a table where some bygone couple might have had their first date. A tarnished necklace from the shattered window of a jewelry merchant, all pitted silver and sparkling gemstones. At one point she showed me a small, cardlike object, flat and thin, made out of some unknown material. Any paint or printing had long since faded, but fat markings were embossed into the scuffed surface. Korbos told her it had been used by many people instead of coin to pay for goods.

So much, lost.

A single Devoid, scrawny and emaciated, the size of a malnourished child, staggered from behind a squat structure near us, moaning softly and closing the distance with an eerie speed. Korbos strode toward it, not bothering to draw his machete. He paused before it, head cocked. The top of the creature's head barely reached his waist, and it carried itself with a mournful, pathetic aspect. His large hands reached up to almost caress the thing's face before grasping and wrenching violently sideways. There was a thin crack, and the big man caught the child's body, lowering it gently to the ground.

"Our destination isn't far from here," he said, turning back to us, his voice thick. "Maybe four or five blocks. Keep an open eye out." I was astounded to see him wipe a tear from his eye. It still surprised me to see the gruff bugger cry. This was twice now, in a short period.

"What *are* they, Korbos?" Cassidy asked, soft as a feather. "What are the Devoid, really?"

He actually *sniffled*.

"They're people, of course. The folk who lived here, nine hundred years ago."

I blinked. I mean, I *sort of* expected that, but wasn't really expecting it...you know? I understood the big man's flood of emotion. What he'd just done with the child was terrible, but it was also a mercy.

Korbos exhaled, lips vibrating as he blew out. "I told you once that my creator was a pioneer in biotechnology. That she lost all reason and experimented on civilian populations? Well, this was one of those experiments. She and her team dispersed an agent over the city—over several cities, actually—that killed the entire populace and turned them into...these. It was a version of the genetic process that created the Host. She was trying to improve the results on a mass scale.

"It failed, of course. In a way. The citizens were transformed into these soulless, shambling wretches, but they gained the Hosts' longevity. Thank Order above that they didn't get any of our powers. They can't die through natural aging, so what we've been encountering are the original citizens of Cortian. Ancient. Suffering. But unable to die."

Cassidy's mouth hung open. "Order anyway. That's...horrific."

"Oh, it's even worse. The reason she chose this city—all the cities she corrupted—was due to their walls."

"The wall?" Mari inquired. "What's special about the wall?"

"Not the wall itself, but the fact that it provided a perfect containment system. All she had to do was drop the agent from a skipship, and the city went into lockdown. All exits closed off automatically, trapping the people inside. Some outside were infected—you all saw the ones the jungle was trying to reclaim—but the Ruin happened soon enough after that they never materialized as a problem. The cities were forgotten and abandoned in short order. No one wanted to return to such places of death. The walls served to corral and keep them away from the world at large. For the most part. If they ever did get out en masse, they'd scour the land like a plague. But they were perfect for her purposes."

He tapped his shoulder. "The bite I received? That black drek the Devoid put off? It's infectious. Turns you into one of them if it gets into your bloodstream. I honestly wasn't sure if I could counteract it for a moment back there. It damn sure took some pushing of my healing."

I shuddered in revulsion. "That would have been nice to know before I punched several of them *in the face*, Korbos!"

"Yeah, apologies for that." His face was carefully placid. "I assumed you'd be smart enough to avoid getting black, sticky unknown substances on your skin. Guess I overestimated."

I shook my head in disbelief, aghast at his callousness. Then I noticed the small grin.

"Go frok yourself, mate." I snarked. That got a short laugh from everyone.

"Soooo..." Cassidy drawled, "why are we here, then? What's in *this* city that has anything to do with the signara? Why are we risking our lives in a dead city full of slightly less-dead people?"

Korbos scratched his unscarred cheek. "Well, because this is honestly the only place I could think to try. I need an Imperium alpha-level synthmind to access the signara, and even before the Ruin there were only ten or so on the whole continent."

"Who in the hells of Chaos records data on something you can only access in ten places?" I mused.

"Someone who doesn't want anyone to know her secrets, Pyk. Signaras were rare and generally used for extreme high-level Imperial data. Not for use by the general public. Since my creator and her partners were originally funded by the government, she had access to them.

"I've tried off and on for centuries to find a working synthmind, just in case a signara ever popped up. All of the others I know of are currently inoperable, and the only one I've not seen is here, in the Turris Imperialis Cortianis. Which is that tower. Which is where we need to go. Now, are we going to stand here waiting for more company, or can we get moving?" He turned and strode away without waiting for us.

The three of us—four, counting Bastin, who was nuzzling Mariyana's pockets and sniffing for treats—shared a look and set off after him.

Two blocks later, we heard the moaning.

EIGHTEEN

"Well, this is just frokking *great*," I griped, probably louder than I should have. Not that *anything* could be heard properly over the noise.

"Atia protect and preserve us," Mari whispered. Or shouted. Like I said, it was hard to hear anything. Korbos gave her a glare. Whether it was because of the noise, or her invocation of a goddess he didn't believe in, I couldn't tell.

The cacophony had first begun as a low susurrus, a whispering keen just at the edge of hearing, growing louder the closer we came to the tower. By the time we were only a block away, Mari was holding her hands over her ears and Bastin kept pawing at his, shaking his head as if to clear away a cloud of bothersome flies.

As we rounded the corner, we discovered what was causing the moaning, and I struggled to not soil my pants.

The streets surrounding the Turris Imperialis Cortian were swarming with Devoid. And I mean *packed.* We ducked behind the hulking remains of a long, dual-leveled autocart. I was nearly hyperventilating. There had to have been a hundred thousand of the things shuffling about the road, at the very least. Save a few scraps of what might conceivably be called cloth, they were all nude—the fabric they'd been wearing centuries ago had disintegrated from the crush and friction of bodies over the vast expanse of time.

I poked my head around the wreck, craning to see how far the mob extended. I couldn't see an end to them. The streets and avenues leading to our destination were straight as an arrow, extending for dozens of blocks in each direction until they hit the city's wall in the far distance, and near as I could tell the Devoid crowded every inch of them. I revised my estimate. There could have been as many as a million of them, an undulating carpet of desiccated, gnashing bodies bumping off one another as far as the eye could see. The smell, like dried spices, was overwhelming—our eyes were watering continuously—and the moan, as I mentioned, was nearly deafening.

Somehow, over the years, this was where the remnants of Cortian's population had gathered. I cursed our luck that it happened to be here. The Turris Imperialis was completely blocked off on all sides, the avenues saturated with shambling corpses. It would be suicide to even try to approach.

"Well, drek," Cassidy quipped. "No way we're getting in there. Now what?"

Korbos glared at us, frowning. "We didn't come all this way to be stopped by such as these."

He looked about, scanning the towers lining the road. He pointed to one directly across from our destination.

"That's it. That's our way in."

"I'm sorry, what?" Cassidy replied, incredulous. "How's sneaking into a completely different tower going to help us?"

Korbos gave her a flat stare. "Just trust me. Stay here."

He adjusted Bulwark's strap on his shoulder, then jogged back the way we'd come, taking a left at an intersection and disappearing from view. After another minute, I heard a faint chopping sound, barely audible over the ever-present moaning. Shortly after, Korbos rounded the corner again, winding a very long serpentine cable over his arm. I cocked my head, not sure what he was thinking. Was that…? Yeah, it was one of the cables from the traffic devices. He'd climbed one and hacked it down. How in the world was *that* going to help us? Order only knew how long the cable actually was. It bulged as he shrugged it over his shoulder and across his chest—the world's bulkiest bandolier.

"Come on," he said, heading for the building he'd pointed out.

"Korbos, what in all the hells, man?" The road between the towers was crawling with Devoid. Literally. I could see a number on all fours, or their bellies, unable to rise due to the crush of bodies around them. They moaned even as their comrades stomped on their backs, crawling over one other like greatsharks in a feeding frenzy.

"Follow," he said. Terse. No…determined. We didn't have any choice but to follow. I breathed a sigh of relief as he snuck away from the densely-packed street, away from the teeming horde. We kept low, putting the decaying autocarts between us and the Devoid as we backed away and cut down the same side street where Korbos had procured his cable. I could see the gap where he'd torn it from the poles lining the sidewalk. A block later, he stopped at a large set of double doors beneath a collapsed awning that sprawled almost to the street.

"This is us," he said. "Now we climb."

Mari, Cassidy and I all looked at each other. Bastin whimpered.

"Uhh...climb what, exactly?" Mari asked.

Korbos cocked his head. "Climb the stairs. What, you thought we were going to scale the building with a fiber cable?"

We all exhaled in relief. I didn't know about the others, but that's *exactly* what I thought he'd somehow had in mind.

He held the doors open, allowing us to pass under his outstretched arm as we entered the tower. Cassidy cracked one of her light sticks. Even cast in a horrible green glow and covered in centuries of dust and decay, I could tell the two-story lobby had once been a grand thing indeed. Ornate columns lined the vast circular room; an inner ring surrounding wide marble partitioned counters, with an outer ring supporting the upper level. A round mural high overhead dominated the view from the doors—although it was impossible to tell what the subject matter may have once been—and the walls and supporting arches were intricately carved with fanciful designs. Finely-wrought desks with thick, cushioned seats—now frayed and ratty—sat at intervals throughout the open floor. Along the walls were more marble counters, recessed beneath large glass windows through which we could just make out small offices. Two sweeping staircases wound their way to the balcony, and in the space between them was an enormous metal door with what appeared to be a steel captain's wheel centered within an explosion of gears and mechanisms. A vault. We were in an old bank.

"Pretty," said Cassidy as she entered the antechamber. "What's the plan?"

Bastin sniffed around one of the plush chairs, disturbing the dust. A massive sneeze followed, spewing clouds of particulate into the air.

"The plan is we go up," Korbos replied, hooking a thumb toward the decorative stairwells.

Without any opposing options, we followed. Korbos led the way, dust puffing around our feet, climbing until we reached an open landing on the second floor. Directly across, a plain, unassuming door stood alone, an embossed placard mounted at eye level. Unintelligible symbols were stamped into the metal.

"What does it say?"

Korbos glanced over his shoulder. "It says…'Stairs.' Let's go."

He shoved open the door, disturbing yet another cloud of dust, and revealed a narrow set of quickcrete steps leading upward. And then we climbed. For a year, it felt like.

My legs and lungs were on fire by the time we reached what Korbos claimed was the thirtieth floor. I shook my head. The tallest building in Hightide was only twelve stories, and it dominated the entire town. These behemoths of Cortian made it look like a Chek standing beside one of the Fingers of the Southern Reach. Another door led us into a large, open floor, studded with cube-like partitions and thick quickcrete blocks reaching from the floor to support the tiled ceiling. There were no outer walls that I could see, only the interrupted gleam of crusty glass windows. Overturned chairs and the sad remnants of a once-thriving office littered the floor.

Korbos didn't give the surroundings a second glance, stomping with purpose to one of the glass walls and peering out. He tapped the window with one meaty knuckle.

"Here we are."

A low, rattling groan echoed throughout the floor, and a dark figure rose from a cubicle just beside Mari. I cried a warning as the Devoid reached for her, and then Cassidy was there, swinging her flat-nosed blade and taking off the thing's head. She swung so hard that her followthrough passed mere inches above Mari's head, and the Chek yelped in surprise. Bastin hissed.

"That's twice, damn it!" she screamed before cutting off with a strangled "Eep!"

Two more Devoid rose from the depths of the workplace and lurched toward us with talons outstretched. They closed the distance with that surprising speed, one after the other, and I snagged the closest one by the throat with my artificial hand. The other hand flailed about my belt, struggling to free my machete. It was caught on something; I couldn't free it. The Devoid's face—it had been a man once, and a reasonably big one—pressed closer to me, its claws scrabbling at the metal of my arm. I couldn't get any leverage.

Korbos stepped behind the Devoid, wrapping one massive arm around the thing's neck and placing the opposite palm against its temple. A quick heave, and the former banker's spine snapped. Korbos let it slump to the ground, where it lay twitching. A few feet away, Cassidy finished off the second with a rather graceful pirouette.

I glanced around, panting, but no more Devoid emerged. My head dipped in a quick nod of thanks to my friend.

Korbos returned the nod and walked back to his previous spot at the cloudy glass. We were facing the Turris Imperialis, which sat maybe a hundred feet on the other side of the avenue. I settled beside him, staring down at the throng below. There was no way to make out any details through the dirty window, but a sea of muddled, distorted shapes writhed underneath us like the polluted waves of the Reef. Mari's nose was pressed against the glass as she craned her neck to see.

"You might want to stand back," Korbos intoned.

We took a step backward, curious. Without further warning, he shrugged Bulwark from his back, shouldered it in a smooth motion, and blew out the window with an ear-splitting *POOM!*. Shattered glass flew out into the street below, and several huge shards that hadn't been outright disintegrated popped loose and began their thirty-story fall. A second and third blast followed, aimed at the tower across the expanse. A large section of the building's glass facade simply vanished, directly across and about two floors down from our position.

I wiggled a finger in my ringing ear. "You could have given us a little more warning, you know."

"You could stay a bit more alert, you know. It's not like this whole day has been a pleasant stroll down the beach, Pyk."

Faint crashes sounded below as the window fragments impacted. The roaring moan of the Devoid was audible even this far up.

Korbos stepped to the edge of the floor and swept an open palm at the Turris Imperialis.

"Our way in, ladies and gentleman."

Cassidy leaned forward, staring at the gap. "*What?*"

Korbos shrugged off the bulky cable and gave a sharp whistle. "Bastin, come."

The scuridai trotted forward eagerly enough, and the big smith set about tying one end of the line in a loose knot around his chest. He sat on his hindquarters, placid and panting, as Korbos carried out his operation.

Mari's eyes widened in disbelief. "You're out of your frokking mind," she whispered. Unaccustomed language from the Chek notwithstanding, I was inclined to agree.

"It's the only way, Mari. We have to get into that building. That ocean of death down there means you're our only option to do so."

"Yeah, but did you hear the part about the whole *ocean of death*?!"

"You'll be fine, Mariyana. This is no different from the thousand other flights you two have taken."

"*Right, except for the whole* ocean of death *below us!*"

Cassidy remained silent, staring through narrow eyes at Korbos. She looked disturbed as I took Mari's shoulders.

"Hey," I said. "Hey! He's right. You can do this, Mari. I *know* you can."

The tiny woman's entire body was shaking. She was scared witless.

"I don't know, Pyk, this isn't anything we've done before trying to be so precise and what if Bastin's angle is off we'll just bounce off the side and fall and oh Order anyway there's so many of those things down there and what if there's not enough cable and we get yanked back when we're halfway there we'll fall and smash into the building then—"

"Mari!" I yelled, cutting her off. My tone softened. "When has Korbos let us down? He's got enough line, I promise you. Bastin can do this. *You* can do this. You *have* to do this. There's no other way."

Her eyes rolled wildly in their sockets before honing in on mine. She took two deep, shaky breaths. A third, slightly more steady. By the fourth, she'd stopped shaking. She gave a weary nod and turned to Bastin, hopping onto his back and settling herself. A steady hand held the reins, grim determination on her cherubic face. Bless that tiny woman's pure light soul.

"Here, Pyk."

I fumbled as Korbos tossed the other end of the cable to me. He busied himself sorting through the line for knots and kinks as I ran the cable around one of the thick quickcrete supports, tying it off with a quick clove hitch. He nodded in approval when I returned to Bastin's side. I gave the scuridai a good, solid scratch behind the ear, trying not to let my apprehension show. He picked up on things like that.

"I guess if we're going to do this, Bastin, we better get on with it," Mari said, patting his head.

"Be brave, Mariyana," said Korbos, "you've done this many times before. This is no different. Can you tie one of those knots like Pyk?"

She gave him a disdainful side-eye.

"Oh, please."

"Good. Time to go."

Mari exhaled, wheeling Bastin around. She took another deep, steadying breath, and kicked him into motion, crying "Up, Bastin!" Three bounds, and then they were out the window, Bastin's legs flailing outward, his gliding membranes catching the air as they sailed into the void, the line spooling out behind them.

I held my breath as they flew, releasing it only when Bastin shot into the open space within the Turris Imperialis, his claws scrabbling on the slick floor to gain purchase and bleed off speed. Mari dismounted and set about removing the cable, freeing it, then disappearing into the darkness beyond the shattered hole. The makeshift rope pulled taut as she took up the slack and secured it around the nearest support. She stepped back into line-of-sight and waved the all-clear to us.

Cassidy stepped to the edge of the broken window, holding the line and leaning out to peer down at the river of Devoid so far below us. Without realizing what I was doing, I reached out to put an arm around her waist. She looked down at my arm, then back up to me. That wry grin of hers was like the sun breaking through rainclouds.

"Thanks, Guts, but I got it."

I pulled back my hand like it had been burned.

"Oh, yeah, sure…sorry," I mumbled.

She laughed. "Just don't let it become a habit. Yet."

I stammered. Order anyway, she *was* flirting with me. I stepped back, rubbing my flushed neck, and she pulled a spare leather pouch from her pack. A couple of quick chops with her blade, and she held out two twelve-inch long strips to Korbos and me.

"And this is for…?" I asked. In my defense, I was still thinking of her grin.

She gave me a disbelieving look, as if I were the most stupidest dum-dum guy in the world, then turned and slung her leather thong over the line, wrapping it around her hands in two quick twists. Then she leapt out the window.

I mean, I *knew* that the plan was to slide down the cable, but I still couldn't help an involuntary cry as her feet left the floor and flailed into open air. She *zoomed* down the line, laughing merrily and whooping the entire way. As she reached the opposite end, she released her hold and hit the floor, tucking her shoulder and rolling before coming to a graceful halt.

"You're next, Pyk," Korbos grunted.

I swallowed. Chaos's fires, I was not prepared to do this. I settled my thong in the same manner Cassidy had, and closed my eyes.

That's when the screaming began.

NINETEEN

My eyes snapped open, immediately searching for Cassidy and Mari in the dark hole across the way. Fear burned through me as I saw them backing away from a dense group of Devoid. Cassidy slashed and hacked, and Bastin clawed at the oncoming threat. Mari stabbed at a few of the smaller Devoid, providing a distraction to them, running and dodging to try and draw them away from the larger group. The women were greatly outnumbered.

"Cassidy, no!" I screamed. I couldn't bear anything happening to either, but my thoughts immediately fixated on those green eyes and that wicked smile.

"I've got no shot!" Korbos yelled from right beside me. "Pyk, go!"

There was a hard shove and then I was sliding over the abyss, screaming my fool head off. I could feel Korbos's weight on the line, bouncing behind me as we picked up speed.

I'd never had a problem with heights. You can't on a boat, not if you have to climb the rigging or do your stint in the crow's nest. But this was something entirely different.

I made the mistake of looking down and screamed again, feeling like my throat was tearing loose. All thoughts fled my mind. My feet dangled three hundred feet above a river of Devoid, nothing between me and a splattery death but air. Only pure survival instinct kept my hands clenched tight; the rest of my body felt loose and liquid. I sincerely hoped I hadn't soiled myself.

Worse, my bellowing seemed to have caught the attention of the horrors below. Ten thousand faces were upturned, clawed hands stretching to the sky, reaching for me. Their blank eyes tracked my progress across the gap, and the ever-present moan grew even louder.

I prayed to Atia, to any gods above and below that might be listening. I vowed to never climb anything higher than my head in the future. I swore that if I ever got out of this hellhole of a city, I'd become a peaceful farmer somewhere out in the sticks where the land was completely flat. I…

…lost all breath as gravity suddenly asserted itself and I fell, slamming into the covey of Devoid advancing on Mari and Cassidy. They were bowled over as I frantically shook my hands loose of the leather strap, struggling to draw a lungful of air. I scrabbled at the machete at my hip, this time managing to pull it free. In my mind's eye, I charged the recovering creatures, laying about right and left as they rose to their feet.

In reality, I wobbled sideways as my legs, not yet recovered from their mid-air fright of a moment ago, turned to mush. This proved to be helpful, as the claws of the one Devoid I *hadn't* knocked over split the air where my head had been an instant before.

As my arm swung feebly, there was a sudden blur and then Bastin was hurtling past, claws raking gashes in the Devoid's face. Shouts echoed around me as the women attacked the fallen creatures with a startling savagery. Within a minute, there were fifteen corpses littering the floor around us. Bastin was merrily squashing the skull of the last. Aside from my impression of a rolling boulder, I hadn't actually touched a single one.

Wait.

Where was Korbos? He'd been right behind me on the cable. I turned to the ragged hole in the wall, and, to my horror, the wire was no longer stretched across the gap. It lay on the floor, pulled tight and wiggling gently. It had snapped behind me just as I was about to land.

"No!" I yelled, sprinting for the edge, Cass and Mari alongside me. We all three hit the ground, miraculously avoiding any cuts or scrapes from the shattered glass littering the floor, sliding on our bellies to peer over the side. There, about forty or fifty feet down, Korbos gripped the rope one-handed, feet braced against the glass exterior. The other held his rucksack. The straps were broken.

"What in all the hells happened?" I yelled.

He didn't respond, just shook his head.

"Drop the pack and climb up!"

Another shake.

I noticed that he didn't have Bulwark slung on his shoulder.

Korbos finally raised his head, looking supremely put-out by the situation. "Get your backsides to the top floor! I'll meet you there!" With that, he kicked off from the window, arcing back and smacking feet first into the glass. Cracks webbed outward. He pushed off again. And again.

On his fourth impact, the glass broke at last, and he swung into the Turris Imperialis. I exhaled a sigh of relief, even though I could no longer see him.

A beefy arm shot out into the space over the street and remained motionless for several seconds. I wondered what he was doing, then my mouth dropped open as Bulwark shot out of the mass of Devoid, flinging several aside and flying up into Korbos's outstretched hand. I'd watched him pull that same trick back at the Strigori village, but it was still amazing to see.

"You heard the man," Cassidy said, pushing herself to her feet. "Up we go."

It took a few minutes to find the entrance to the stairwell, during which we only encountered a single Devoid, a pitiful legless wretch dragging itself through the wispy remains of thousand-year-old carpet. Mari put it out of its misery with one of her galley knives.

Cassidy opened the stairwell door, then groaned softly. I completely sympathized. So, we climbed. Again.

There were two flights of stairs per floor. After sixteen flights, my legs were once again burning like the pits of Chaos. Thirty more, and I was cursing every ancient architect and engineer that might have had a hand in building this monstrosity of a tower. By the time we reached thirty *more*, I was literally crawling up the steps. What sort of masochists were the pre-Ruin ancients, to build sky towers this bloody tall?

"Let's…take…a break…" Mari panted. "Maybe…maybe Korbos can catch up."

The poor Chek, with her shorter legs, had suffered a much harder time than Cassidy and me. She'd taken a break for a few floors, riding on Bastin, but the scuridai was winded as well—saliva was pattering the floor—so she'd eventually reverted to her own leg power. Personally, I thought a pause was a grand idea indeed. Mari and Cassidy sat on the landing next to an entrance, panting heavily. I considered the seats littering the bank lobby and decided that a soft office chair would be a wonderful place to take a breather.

It should be noted that fatigue had, at that point, turned my brain to jelly. So, naturally, as one does, I pulled open the door—the rusted hinges gave off an eardrum-rupturing creak—and strolled through to the office beyond, looking for a nice comfy seat.

Where I came face to face with a veritable army of Devoid.

The floor wasn't packed like the streets below, but there had to have been at least a hundred of the things. The room was pungent with the centuries-old scent of dry decay. As one, they turned to see me standing framed in the doorway, lit from behind by Cassidy's glowstick, a sumptuous, juicy meal served up on a platter right to their doorstep. The closest one was only a few feet from me, and a wailing moan went up as it lurched in my direction, mouth open and jagged teeth gleaming in the grime-filtered daylight that saturated the room. I shrieked, kicking out and shoving the thing back with a foot to the chest. Then I turned and ran.

Mari and Cassidy leapt to their feet at my scream, and Bastin hissed as he smelled the Devoid. I slammed the door behind me as I entered the stairwell.

"Go go gogogo!" I wailed in a high voice that didn't at all sound like my normal bass. I cursed myself for a fool. I'd *known* there were Devoid in the tower, but my exhaustion had driven out any concept of checking for danger. And I'd just dived right into the greatshark's teeth. Order anyway, Korbos had even warned me about staying sharp.

We bolted up the stairs, and I looked down over the railing to the door, which opened inward to the stairwell and had no locks. Maybe we'd get lucky, and the Devoid couldn't figure out how to open—*reeeeeeeeek*! My hopes vanished as it swung open and a crush of Devoid began staggering onto the landing. They bottlenecked in the doorframe for a moment, then began spilling out, cloudy gazes turned toward mine.

I turned and ran, fatigue the furthest thing from my mind. I ignored the burning of my legs, looking back on occasion to see the Devoid gaining ground on me. They didn't suffer from sore muscles or low energy, and steadily closed the gap between us, banging between the rails and walls as they marched implacably up the tower.

Mari and Cassidy were a full floor above me, and I saw their faces peek over the railing, searching for me. Behind them, I noticed a wonderful thing. The roof of the building. It couldn't have been more than three floors above us. We'd been closer than I'd thought.

"Keep going! Almost there!" I huffed, unsure how long I'd be able to stay ahead of the creatures.

A few moments later and I burst through another door marked with strange and archaic signs, struggling for air. The others stood inside the room—bathed in the green light of glowsticks—at the top floor; it was much smaller and almost claustrophobic compared to the vast offices below. Large banks of electronics crowded the walls and desks of the center. The equipment looked very similar to the control stations of the *Storm*, but sadder somehow; centuries dead and lightless.

Cass and Mari's eyes were wide with fear—almost panic—and it took my slushy brain an abnormal amount of time to realize why.

I could see them from the landing.

There was no door here, other than the one we'd just come through.

Cold sweat ran down my back. We'd be completely exposed. I didn't even have time to think of any sort of strategy as the first of the Devoid crested the stairwell and lurched through the marked door. I backed into the room, machete drawn and at the ready. There were no windows, no glass on this floor, only quickcrete walls. The inside of the synthmind room was completely dark. Cassidy rapidly cracked a few more light sticks, throwing them to the sides and center, where they cast harsh shadows and lit our faces from below.

"They'll seize up at the door, like they did below," she said. "Try and stop them before they get into the room, and maybe we can barricade with the bodies."

I nodded. Good a plan as any, at this point.

We darted forward, dropping the first Devoid just inside the entrance, then the flood reached us. Time lost all meaning as we hacked and chopped, yet still they came, crawling over the corpses of their kin. The three of us were slowly but steadily pushed back among the crush of devices and consoles; Bastin growled and turned circles in frustration from the back of the room, where he was next to useless considering the tightness of space. He just had no room to maneuver or attack with us in the way.

Our swings and thrusts became wilder and panicked. Devoid began to crash into the synthminds as we felled them, knocking over stacks and damaging the shells with swipes of their clawed hands. I winced as a tower of electronics taller than myself collapsed and shattered, bits flying every which way. More were damaged as we shoved desks between us and the Devoid, who in turn just plowed them over with a crush of bodies.

Before long, we were at the back of the enclosed space, trapped. We barely had room to attack, our strikes coming dangerously close to one another. I looked at Cassidy, face grim. She shook her head. No grin for me this time. She knew it was hopeless. Tears ran down Mari's face, cutting tracks in the dirt and grime that coated her from the day's exertions. I patted her back quickly with my free hand. It was the only comfort I could give as I buried my blade into yet another Devoid's skull.

And still they came.

We had only a second of breathing room as another large group pressed through the door. My hand tightened on the blade, and my metallic fingers clenched as I prepared to go down fighting. Mari drew in a shaky breath, and Cassidy exhaled with a sigh. Bastin chirped his strange bark.

And then light erupted from the stairwell, backlighting the Devoid, who turned from us at the deafening *poom*! *poom*! *poom*! Rapid fire turned the entire floor blue. I could see Devoid outside the door disintegrating in bursts of blue plasma.

I nearly dropped my machete in relief. Korbos was here.

Gunfire blossomed within the room, blue fire shredding the last of the monsters as we took cover behind the final row of overturned desks. At last silence reasserted itself, and I peeked over to see Korbos stroll into the room, stepping over the smoldering remains, Bulwark leaning against a meaty shoulder.

He'd retied one of the straps on his pack, which hung on the opposite side. His face was grim as he took in the carnage around us. Without a word, he dropped the pack onto a desk with a heavy clunk, untying the laces and pulling out a dense brick-like object. Green lights glowed intermittently down its length.

"Uhhhh…" began Cassidy, "is that…?" Her face radiated outraged fury.

"Yes," he replied, terse. "You're welcome, by the way."

She planted her hands on her hips. "Yeah, thanks. Appreciated. Why do you have one of the *Storm*'s fuel capacitors in your pack? Why are you stealing batteries from *my frokking ship*?"

He didn't reply, hefting the battery into the cradle of his arm and stepping across downed creatures to open a panel in the wall. From within, he pulled a long cable with a box-like connector and fastened it to the capacitor. He flipped some sort of switch, and strong white light flickered on around us, both overhead and from the surviving electronics, cancelling out the green glow of the sticks.

"Korbos," I began, hesitantly, "I thought you said you'd brought extra water." My hands were shaking. "I'd wondered why you held onto the pack and not your gun when the cable snapped."

He grunted but said nothing.

"If you took one of the *Storm*'s batteries, how are we supposed to fly out of here?"

He sighed, turning his head to look me in the eye. "It's a spare, Pyk. The aerowing will fly just fine. As to why I took it," he continued, looking to Cassidy, "This city has been dead for nine hundred years. How did you think we were going to use a synthmind without power? I didn't mention it because there was no other choice. You've heard the saying, 'better to ask forgiveness than permission'? Well, I ask for neither. I'll do what needs to be done."

With that, he pulled the signara from the pack, its warm golden glow subdued by the harsh overhead lights. I was mesmerized by the fanciful patterns shifting under the crystalline surface.

Cassidy just stared at Korbos, mouth working but producing only disbelieving stutters. With a glare, she snapped her lips shut and crossed her arms, foot tapping in a rapid staccato. Mari swept her gaze between the two, concerned.

He glanced at the Chek, face softening at her worry, then sighed and turned to Cassidy.

"I apologize for taking it behind your back, but there really was no other way. The odds of finding a working power source in the city were virtually zero, so I did what I had to do. I would never do anything to harm the *Storm* or leave us exposed. You have my word on that."

The wiry captain made no reply for a moment, then finally uncrossed her arms and gave a terse nod.

"We're not finished with this conversation, Patches, but I'll go with it. For now."

He gave an unconcerned shrug, then turned to rummage through the wrecked devices strewn throughout the room, eye narrowed. Several minutes passed as he became more and more agitated, hurling pieces across the room. We had to duck several large bits, and Bastin hissed as one bounced off his flank.

Abruptly, Korbos stopped and stood ramrod-straight. A small groan escaped him. I moved forward, stepping to his side as he placed the signara to a square port on the top of a small gray machine hooked to a few of the flat image projector things. Blue lights stuttered dully in a distinct star-shaped pattern, and tiny clamps moved—sluggish and jerky—in an attempt to lock the signara into the cracked shell of the synthmind.

The obviously broken and non-functional synthmind.

TWENTY

Feeble lights flickered on the dusty gray box, and the projectors sizzled with multi-hued jumbles of lines. One sparked and hissed smoke that curled into the air above. But nothing else happened. The signara sat there, unchanged. Unread. With a *pop* of finality, a small jet of flame shot from the side of the synthmind and the lights blinked out for good.

Korbos's head dropped, wide shoulders slumping, before arcing backward and unleashing a fierce howl at the ceiling above us. It was extremely loud within the small enclosure, causing the three of us to clap hands to ears. His fists clenched so tight that—even over the bellowing—I could hear the grip of his rifle creak beneath his fingers. Thankfully, his finger was away from the trigger, or we might have all joined Order's light a bit earlier than planned.

With an abrupt clack of his jaw, the blacksmith cut off his yell, snatching the signara from the device with a snarl. He shoved the cube back into his satchel, taking out a large bottle in turn, pulling the stopper and taking a long slug. A strong smell of whiskey permeated the room, mixing horribly with the stench of the Devoid. I shook my head in disapproval as Korbos shouldered both the pack and his rifle.

He stomped from the room without another word, bottle in hand, pausing only to snatch the *Storm*'s fuel capacitor from its place in the wall. Brief sparks flared, then all the lights died out except for the glowsticks, which we picked up. We followed him to the stairwell, where—still silent—he flung a pile of Devoid corpses out of the way with a flare of his eye. Again, the bottle rose to his lips for several moments. Glug. Glugglug. Glug.

"Korbos, take it easy, man," I said. "We'll find something—"

His lip curled in a sneer, and he started down the steps without a word. I glanced at Cassidy, who shrugged.

We traveled down in silence, each of us lost in our own thoughts. The five of us—even Bastin—fell into an unconscious rhythm as our steps blended together, the cadence almost hypnotic, providing a backbeat to my racing mind.

What did this setback mean for us, if we couldn't access the signara? As much as I wanted revenge on Kaira and justice for the Host, I had no illusions that I was in any position to enact those daydreams on my own. And I was once again surprised to find how much I *really* wanted to bring those dreams to reality.

I mean, yes, I wanted Kaira dead for my own selfish reasons, but after all I'd learned about the Host's origins and my friend's part in them, I wasn't counting on the unexpected sense of duty I felt to make things *right* if I could. In my experience, duty was just a fee paid on fish coming into Hightide from foreign boats. I'd never given a second thought to civic pride, or even marginal concern for anyone other than myself and close friends, but the idea of my future children—Mari's future children, their grandchildren's children—suffering under the hands of Kaira and Kalos...well, that just ticked me off something awful. Action needed to be taken, but *how*?

Without the information on the signara, I worried that we would lose Korbos to whatever melancholy he currently found himself a slave. He was drinking steadily from his bottle as he walked. Without Korbos, we lost any advantage against the Host and their destructive powers. Without that advantage, we lost all hope of freeing Elarin from their grasp forever. And forever was a long time indeed when it came to the Host.

Could I trust that Korbos had actually visited and checked the other nine synthminds? That there even *were* nine synthminds? How would he have verified them without a signara to read? By his own words, he hadn't known any existed for sure until Cassidy crossed the threshold of his shop. But if we couldn't get to the data, then we ran the risk of losing Korbos. And if we lost Korbos, we lost our advantage—

The litany of thoughts circled in my brain as we descended. Forty-five minutes passed, and still no one spoke. Thankfully, we didn't encounter any more Devoid. My calves were on fire. So were the others', judging by Mari's increasing groans and Bastin's hissing. Order anyway, this building was too damned tall...how many more steps until we reached bottom?

As if my aching legs had banished them, the endless stairs disappeared at the next landing. We'd reached the bottom at last. I exhaled in relief as Korbos flung open the door and staggered through, bouncing off the doorframe. I wanted to chastise him, but didn't quite dare. Cassidy made a disgusted grunt behind me.

When I stepped through, I came to a dead stop, causing Cassidy to bump into me with a curse. Another thought had occurred to me, one my exhausted mind had been avoiding.

How in the fires of Chaos were we going to get out?

We stepped out into a lobby even larger than the one at the bank, though the general aesthetic was as different as could be. Sleek lines raced everywhere, framing the walls and windows at impossible angles. Low tables and chairs, whose sharp metal designs reminded me of Reef ships, spread across the wide space in evenly-distributed pockets. The only other structure was a massive U-shaped block of metal and granite situated dead center of the room, a path connecting it to the row of doors leading outside.

Muted illumination filtered through the dirty windows, backlighting the masses of Devoid teeming the streets outside. Their shadows undulated, giving the impression of deadly waves crashing against the Turris Imperialis.

I went cold. We hadn't even discussed how to exit the building. Just blindly followed the big smith, absorbed in our own troubled thoughts. The man himself stood just past the gigantic desk, swaying in time with the silhouettes. As I approached him, treading lightly, I was discouraged to see little more than dregs remaining in the flask flopping loosely at his hip. A little mad, too. We were all reeling from our failure upstairs, but you didn't see the rest of us retreating into the comfort of a bottle.

Especially not when we still needed to find a way past the monsters on the other side of that thick glass.

More than anything, I didn't want to draw their attention.

"Korbos, what's the plan on getting back to the shi—"

"*I DON'T KNOW, PYK!*" he roared, pointing the bottle at me and sloshing out a few drops. "You people seem to think I have all the answers, but I don't! I'm *old*, not omniscient!"

I reeled back, frightened by the fury in his eye. He took a step forward, off-balance, then lurched and stumbled to a knee as Cassidy stepped in and launched his head sideways with a rocketing slap. My jaw dropped in surprise as she got right in his face, finger stabbing at his nose.

"Get your frokking drek together, you child," she snarled. "I know *I* haven't known you very long, but these two are your friends. Given the way you're acting, I'll bet they're your *only* friends, and right now you're their only chance at surviving this Chaos-cursed place. If you want to drown yourself in whiskey, that's your business, but *do it on your own time!* Order knows you've got enough of it. Now sort yourself and help us figure out how to get out of here alive."

The big man raised his head slowly, a stunned expression on his face that gave way to a deep frown. His teeth bared in rage.

"You…" *WHACK!* I winced as Cassidy struck him on the other side. He went down again to one knee.

"You…"

Cassidy kicked him in the chest. Not a stabbing kick; nothing that would do damage. A flat-footed, shoving kick from the hip that sent the big man sliding backward across the smooth dusty tiles. I was amazed that she still had enough leg strength to do that, considering the effort of our climb and descent. Bulwark went flying from his shoulder, fetching up against the desk. Korbos immediately bounded to his feet, face a mask of anger as he screamed and threw the bottle, which shattered against the doors and sprayed liquor across them in a thin fan.

He stalked forward, not swaying at all now. Looming over Cassidy.

Who stood there, calm as anything, arms crossed and toe tapping. I was in awe. The man was almost twice her size, and she just stood there and stared him down. Korbos began to reach for her, and she exploded, thrashing his arm away and shoving him in the chest.

"*SOBER UP!*" she screamed.

He took a step back and stared, mouth open and working in anger and confusion. He looked to Mari, then me. The Chek had hands over her mouth and tears in her oversized eyes, and I could tell it nearly broke his heart by the chagrin that washed over his face. I felt my heart was breaking as well. Imposing as he was, in that moment Korbos looked pathetic, his eyepatch askew from the slaps and his cheeks and nose red from the drink. As old, wise, and powerful as he was, the turncoat Host was still just a man.

Korbos shook his head, as if trying to clear it, then adjusted his patch. A deep frown creased his face, sorrow-filled and remorseful.

"I...I'm sor—"

He was interrupted by a tinkling sound. We turned in time to watch cracks spiderweb the door where the bottle had struck. Murky shapes pressed against the glass, drawn by the commotion. My blood turned to ice. The cracks spread.

"Oh, frok me," I muttered.

The door shattered, and Devoid poured through.

I yanked my blade free, Cassidy and Mari doing the same from the corner of my eye as the creatures staggered toward us. At best, we had a few seconds to prepare while they crossed the lobby. Despair sank its claws into my chest. There was no escaping this, other than going back up, and I'd be Chaos-burned before I climbed those frokking steps again.

Korbos's arm shot to the side, and Bulwark flew to his outstretched hand. He shouldered the rifle and glanced at us.

"This is my doing," he growled. "I'll get us out. Stand back, and be ready to run."

The world turned blue as he opened fire, plasma bursts reflecting from the wall of glass. The Devoid clambering through the broken doors exploded in a burst of black goo and desiccated flesh. More approached, only to be blown aside by the powerful energy. Korbos took a step forward. Then another, and another, at a steady pace until he was to the doorframe. His firing arc widened, creating a small pocket within the Devoid nearest the Turris Imperialis.

"Come on!" he screamed, focusing fire in a direction where the crush of creatures appeared to be less dense. "Stay close, and keep them off our flanks! Quick, now!"

The blue pulse of the rifle increased. How long could he keep this up? I guessed we'd find out soon enough. Korbos began a light jog as we filed in close behind him, Bastin hissing and nearly throwing Mari from his back with a flurry of quick turns. His short fur bristled. The scuridai wheeled suddenly, leaping at the building and burying his claws in a column of quickcrete. He scrambled up the tower's exterior, Mari clutching to his back in desperation and screeching at the top of her tiny lungs.

I didn't have time to wonder what was going through Bastin's mind. As Cassidy and I struggled to keep the Devoid at bay with wide sweeps of our blades, the path that Korbos was plowing through was beginning to close in behind us. Cassidy's hand dipped to her thigh, drawing her gun and firing a shot point-blank into the skull of a Devoid who'd gotten too close. The roar of the two guns and the increasing moan of the Devoid was deafening. And the keening was growing even louder. More of the things were beginning to notice the commotion; the tide was beginning to surge toward us.

A shadow passed over us. I took a half-second to glance up, noting with pleasure that Bastin had reached an acceptable height and launched himself and Mari toward a nearby low-rise roof. At least one of my friends would be safe from the crush of bodies.

Our pace increased, faster and faster until we were sprinting through the crowded street and frantically trying to avoid corpses as we ran. It wasn't frokking easy, let me tell you. More than once I tripped, arms wheeling, thinking "*This is it, I'm going down for the last time...*" before catching my footing and pressing on. My arm was numb from the impacts of my blade slicing through skulls, necks, outstretched arms. My legs jelly from the abuse we'd just heaped upon them in the tower stairwells.

"Reloading!" Cassidy yelled for the fourth time. I slid sideways to cover her flank as she quickly chambered six more rounds into Jasmin. Her small ammunition pouch was almost empty. A claw nearly took off my nose before she snapped the firearm up and a magical fist-sized hole exploded from the back of the Devoid's head.

Korbos was sweating from the sustained fire he was unleashing. I saw him whip his head around, flinging droplets into the dried leather of a Devoid's face just before he blew the top of the thing's head into powder. He couldn't keep this up much longer, it seemed; the big rifle was draining his energy—his Well, as he called it—at a rapid clip. Yet he fired faster. We ran faster.

And then we were through, breaking out of the thick sea of monsters so abruptly that I nearly stopped in shock before realizing that would be a *really* bad idea. The Devoid were sparse on the outer fringe of the mob, and we began avoiding more than we had to put down. A stitch was forming in my side, but we still ran, the moaning crowd following behind. Order anyway, why couldn't these have been slow like the mushy ones?

Bastin and Mari glided above us, the scuridai leaping from walls and the lower rooftops.

"Mari, find us an exit!" Korbos yelled up to her. "We need a way out!"

"I thought there weren't any open gates!" she returned. "If all the exits were locked down how are we supposed to get out and I thought you said you collapsed the tunnel where you came in so how do you plan on clearing that and I *don't know what the frok I'm looking for!*"

"Just get us to the closest wall!"

"Why would you want to go to a wall those things are fifty feet thick and Bastin can't climb up them with anyone but me so oh wait maybe we could—"

"Mariyana!" he cut her off. "Just get us to the nearest one. And try to avoid any swarms!"

"Right, got it, yep, on it, *UP, Bastin*!"

The scuridai clambered several floors to perch on the nearest balcony, at a corner of the large intersection we'd travelled earlier. Mari's head wheeled as she stared down the avenues. Cassidy, Korbos and I panted as we slowed to catch a quick breather. We'd outpaced the Devoid, but the ocean of undead Cortians wasn't far off. The ever-present wailing was rapidly growing louder.

"This way!" Mari called out. "Nearest wall is this way!"

Korbos looked to us, swaying slightly. "Fast walk, you two. Quick and steady."

"What have you got in mind?" asked Cassidy.

"I'm…" I didn't like that look of uncertainty on his face. "I'm not exactly sure. These cities were designed to be airtight once they were locked down. The biggest priority right now is getting to the edge of the city and away from that—what did Mari call it?—ocean of death back there."

"You're…not exactly…inspiring confidence here, mate…" I huffed.

"Yeah, I know. Let's move."

We followed Mari and Bastin. I lost count of how many blocks we travelled, but eventually we turned a corner and saw the gargantuan wall rising into the air three or four streets away. Oddly—given how far we'd moved away from the main body of Devoid—the noise seemed to increase in volume.

As we approached the wall, my heart sank as we discovered why.

Only two streets over, another enormous crowd of Devoid milled about. It wasn't the flowing sea we'd encountered near the Turris Imperialis, but there were still thousands. Cassidy gasped and Korbos's face fell as one on the fringe turned and spotted us, letting out a howling rasp. More honed in on us and lurched into motion.

"Order *anyway*, go go go!" I screamed, and we burst toward the wall.

The two hundred-foot high, thirty-foot thick, rock-solid quickcrete wall. No doors, no windows, no visible exits of any kind as far down the avenue as we could see. Not that we could see far, given the army of Devoid headed straight for us.

"Hellfires and *Chaos*," I exclaimed, striking the quickcrete with my metal hand. "I'm done. It was nice knowing you."

"Don't just stand there!" Mari called from a nearby terrace. "Run!"

"I can't run any more, Mari," I called back. "I just can't. I'm done."

"I've got one more trick, Pyk." Korbos said, causing Cassidy and me to turn our focus to him. "Get behind that big autocart over there. Mari! Duck!"

We ran, not questioning. Behind me I could hear the *poom! poom!* of Bulwark firing. I turned at the autocart to see a sizable hole—about three feet wide and four feet deep—blasted into the wall. Korbos knelt, rummaging in his pack before coming up with the fuel capacitor he'd taken from the *Storm*.

"Gods of Order above and Chaos below, preserve and protect us," Cassidy murmured. "He's insane."

The big man heaved the dense capacitor into the hole he'd blasted, then turned and ran toward our hiding spot. He rounded and fired—his eye flaring silver—just as the Devoid came flooding into the intersections on either side of us. Cassidy yanked me behind the autocart, slamming me to the ground and covering me with her body. It wasn't entirely unpleas—

The entire world went white.

I screamed as the capacitor exploded. Ship-sized hunks of quickcrete flew and rained down around us, cratering the road as a roaring hurricane of dust and bullet-fast debris ripped through the narrow avenue and tore the roof from the decaying autocart that provided our shelter. Desiccated body parts soared past as the Devoid were pulverized. I raised my head to see Korbos bellowing laughter from his shelter behind the cart's wheel well. I couldn't hear a bit of it over the apocalypse he'd unleashed.

Order anyway, I was starting to agree with Cassidy. He *was* insane. But hope rose. He might have just saved us all.

Once the wind died out, we rose and stared at the wall of Cortian in disbelief. It was buckled and shattered as though struck by the hand of a vengeful god. Rubble framed a hole fully thirty feet high that punched through the entirety of the wall. Trees were visible through the opening, trunks and branches blown back and uprooted by the blast. I stood there, mouth agape, as Korbos strolled up beside me, brushing bits of gravel from his shoulder and grinning.

"Wasn't sure if I could pull that off," he quipped. "Had to put a shield in front of the hole and try to channel the blast through the wall."

I stammered. "You…*hunh*?"

His grin widened, drunken mirth twinkling in his eye. Of all the times for him to get giddy.

"Hey, it worked, didn't it?"

Cassidy joined us, looking very displeased. She punched Korbos in the arm. Not a light tap, either.

"You owe me a fuel capacitor, Patches."

The big man actually laughed. Cassidy's expression didn't change, and the humor on his face dried up in a hurry.

"Duly noted. Now let's get going. No time to stand about."

I jumped as that damned moan began again, climbing in volume. The immediate area had been cleared by the blast, but in the near distance I could see Devoid that hadn't been incinerated climbing to their feet. Or stumps. Or whatever they had left.

Turned out, I *could* run a bit further than I'd thought.

TWENTY ONE

We walked for hours through the dense woods, pursued by the horde. We'd escaped from Cortian proper, but the breach had allowed the Devoid to flee the city as well. The creatures were joined by their more…juicy…brethren. The same ones we'd encountered on our way into the city; all fungus and vine-covered, oozing with that black goo. They chased us into the forest, but we were outpacing them. Barely. They weren't as adept as us at navigating the grasping brush, thank Order's light. On the other hand, they never stopped, and we were all ragged to the point of exhaustion.

I had no idea how long it had been since we'd left the ship. Or where the ship even *was*, for that matter. Nobody had noticed it until much later, but Cassidy had somehow lost her pack in our flight from the Turris Imperialis. Her food, water…her compass, gone.

We were seriously lost.

All we knew was that we were traveling roughly east. There were several times where we tried to cut south to wheel back around, but the piercing cry of the Devoid drove us back to our original bearing in each instance. The two breaks we'd taken had been brief, unrestful things, cut short by the rising groan and stumbling crack and crash of our pursuers. Fatigue and adrenaline waged a constant war in my body each time I was forced to push myself yet again to my feet.

To make things worse, the sun was setting.

It was not easy going. The forest rapidly thickened; the leaves broader and heavier to push away, the ground giving way to peat swamp, the air humid and draining. More than once we had to sidetrack around wide stands of dark water, the unknown depths hiding Order only knew what manner of slithering creatures that rippled the surface debris as they swam.

I did *not* want to be stuck in this jungle at dark.

"P…Pyk," Mari panted from her seat on a fallen, rotting log. She was having a tougher time than the rest of us, even with Korbos and Cassidy doing most of the trailblazing. "We have to find a way around these things. Get back to the ship. Can't…can't do this much longer."

I wrapped an arm around her shoulders while Cassidy hacked through a thick patch of entwined vines.

"I know Mari, I know. We'll get out of this, we just gotta stay ahead. You saw how many Devoid came out of that city behind us. There's no way we can push through so many."

A thump sounded beside us as Bastin dropped to the ground and nuzzled Mari, chittering softly. He'd had spent the majority of the trek out of our way, climbing through the trees above and keeping watch for approaching predators. She smiled and scratched his ears, offering up a treat from her hip pouch, which he gobbled down.

Korbos stomped over, the swampy jungle detritus crunching and mushing under his huge feet. He placed a hand on Mari's shoulder.

"Sorry, little one," he said. "Can you maybe let Bastin take some of your burden? Rest for a while on his back?"

She shook her head and sighed. "I can't do that to him. He'd let me, but all this foliage is just too thick. He couldn't walk it, and I can't stay mounted while he's in the trees. It'd take more energy than just walking." As if to disagree, the scuridai nuzzled her neck, winning another smile from her.

"I know you would, wouldn't you Bastin? Yes, you would. You'd carry me all the way back to Hightide, wouldn't you buddy?" Another ear scratch, and Bastin chirped, thumping his back foot on the ground. She sighed and rose to her feet.

Just as a Devoid crawled over the log and swiped at the spot where she'd been sitting an instant before.

I screamed, scrabbling for my machete. Cassidy echoed it, falling back and swinging wildly at a creature struggling its way through the brush she'd just been hacking. We hadn't heard a thing. The ones from the city moved faster, but these others were eerily silent. No moan. No noise at all. Korbos slammed a boot onto the thing's arm, trapping it while I chopped its head off. We whipped around, searching the area, but it was too late.

We were surrounded.

Bastin hissed as Cassidy fell back and we formed a loose circle. I couldn't see a way out, and I was so exhausted I could barely lift my blade.

The others appeared much the same; shoulders slumped and weapons held no higher than waist level.

The Devoid lurched forward, claws outstretched. Korbos growled and raised Bulwark, his eye flickering a weak silver. He hadn't said anything, but I knew his Well was running dry. There was no way he had much energy left after blasting through so many of the Devoid during our escape. Not to mention directing the blast of that hellish explosion. Even as I had the thought, his eye returned to normal and he lowered his massive rifle.

"I'm…I'm sorry," he said. "I'm so sorry I got you into this." The Devoid moved in, only feet from us.

And halted.

Their heads cocked and turned, as if confused. Order knows I was. I could have stretched out and taken the hand of the nearest one. Why weren't they ripping us to shreds?

A dark figure hurtled out of the jungle and into the Devoid. They fell back under a flurry of blows; kicks from discolored bare feet snapped into fungal-encrusted necks, and rigid hands crushed skulls in sharp chops. Between the tendency of the Devoid to blend into their surroundings, and the disorienting sunset light spearing through the trees, it was all I could do to keep track of the fight.

Following the figure was a mass of pale animals, which swarmed over the Devoid like a flood. We all shouted in surprise as they ran through our legs and over our feet. Tiny claws tore and bit into the Devoids' flesh, staggering them under sheer weight of numbers. The undead creatures fell back, then turned and lurched away in a shambling approximation of a run. They never made a sound. What in all the fires of Chaos…?

The five of us stood motionless, mouths agape. The man—was it a man?—stood to its full height, a tattered cloak and hood silhouetting against the trees and fading sunlight. It was tall—taller even than Korbos. The figure turned, and I shouted again in surprise and no small amount of terror as it pulled back its hood.

It was a Devoid.

One unlike any we'd seen thus far.

For one thing, it was wearing well-made clothes under the shredded cloak—tight black trousers that ended mid-calf and a dark gray shirt with a fitted vest covering its midriff. Its legs, balanced on elongated feet, resembled a cat's. A strapped pair of opaque goggles obscured its eyes over a protruding muzzle dessicated and peeled back to reveal carnivorous teeth. The thing was completely hairless, with the dried skin of the Cortian Devoid. Four arms raised in a placating gesture as a long leathery tail swished behind it, disturbing the folds of the cloak.

A Na'don. A *Devoid* Na'don.

The smaller creatures curled and massed around its bare feet. I'd never seen anything like them. They were long, with six legs each—maybe some were arms; I couldn't tell—and were covered in a fine fur the pale white of a fish belly. Multiple pitch-black eyes regarded us from every fairylike face. They hissed as we dropped into defensive stances; Mari and I raised blades, and Cassidy and Korbos raised their guns. Bastin gave an answering growl.

We didn't know what to make of the strange Devoid, which just stood still, not making any threatening moves. The four hands patted the air again in a calming motion as the fuzzy white things circled its strange legs. Korbos took a step forward, raising Bulwark to his shoulder and pointing the barrel straight into the thing's face.

"Caaaalllllm..." the thing said.

Mari dropped her oversized kitchen knives from numb fingers.

"Atia protect and preserve us…" she whispered.

"Gunnnsss…" the Devoid continued. My heart was hammering. How in all the world could this thing speak? "It has been long and long since we have seen firearms."

Its voice was as odd as the rest of it, gravelly and multi-tiered, as if two voices were speaking at once—one high and pleasant, the other a rumbling bass. It was a layered, otherworldly sound, and it unnerved me something fierce. Not knowing what to do, I—of course—chose the path of greatest stupidity and charged it, my blade raised.

My feet immediately tangled on one of the small furry things and I went down in a skid, stopping face-to-face with the fae-looking creature, the wind knocked out of me. Its black eyes blinked as it plucked the machete from my limp hand and laid it at the Devoid's feet.

"Peace, traveler," it grated, "no harm is meant. Few and few travelers have we received these many years, and we would offer help where needed."

"It's right, Pyk," Korbos growled. He'd lowered his rifle, but held the gaze of the creature before him, his head cocked slightly. "It didn't have to interfere. The Devoid would have finished us off nicely without his rescue."

"Yesss, yes," it replied as I picked myself from the ground. It picked up my blade and returned it to me, hilt first. "We will help, my friends and I. Come. Come." The thing spoke Coretongue well enough, though with a weird accent and cadence I couldn't place. It waved with two arms, beckoning us to follow deeper into the swamp.

Korbos shouldered his rifle and turned to follow. I grabbed his arm.

"Do you *seriously* intend to just follow this thing?" I whispered. "What in the hells even *is* it?"

The creature turned to face me. At the same time, eight others like it, clothed in rather serviceable attire, stepped into view. Cassidy paled. We'd never heard these, either. The Na'don raised its four hands, slapping its own chest with an arrhythmic thump.

"Oben, I am," it said in its multi-layered voice. "Oben the Undying, called by some. Come, come. We will talk on the path to home." It beckoned again, then turned to join its fellows in hiking through the swampy scrub. Korbos shrugged, then followed. Cassidy and Mari did the same. The smaller white creatures swarmed past their legs and vanished into the trees and dense foliage.

"Well…" I muttered, "damn."

As we walked, Korbos eyed the creatures, intensely curious about them, judging by the tilt of his head and narrowed eye. We all were, I supposed. Mari bounced about with renewed vigor, her head swiveling back and forth to take in the strange Devoid and her mouth hanging open. I had to stifle a chuckle as a large bug rammed itself down her throat, causing her to cough and sputter. Cassidy was much the same. Her Seeker curiosity was definitely showing as she poked and prodded the nearest one. It seemed not to notice. Or care. Whichever.

Bastin just sniffed at the few white fuzzies that still marched with us, at least until one swatted at his muzzle. He snorted, then continued the trek with his nose turned up, as if to demonstrate his superiority and indifference to the much smaller creatures. I did see him smack one with a swipe of his bushy tail, throwing it into a stand of water.

These intelligent Devoid moved with a spooky silence, gliding through the swamp with no noticeable effort. To my relief, we found the going much easier by following their lead. None deigned to speak with us other than Oben, though I wouldn't have classified the quiet as uncomfortable. They *strolled*, as though they were enjoying a pleasant walk through a park, taking in the jungle and pointing to interesting landmarks; a bulky weed- and vine-choked autocart—nearly as large as a house—stood lonely sentinel among a copse of trees. A strange tubular contraption of pipes and vents, nearly obscured by thick moss, rose from a pool of brackish water. I couldn't begin to guess at its function.

At last, Korbos just couldn't handle his curiosity any more.

"Oben," he began. The Devoid turned its head with an audible creak of dry tendons. I shuddered. Korbos tilted his head even further.

"What *are* you?"

Cassidy perked up, sidling closer and listening intently.

Oben smiled, a singularly unpleasant expression. For a few minutes it continued on, saying nothing. We remained silent as well. I kept stealing glances at the Devoid surrounding us, growing increasingly nervous as we slogged through wet ground and dense vegetation. Why in Order's light were we following these things? Had we been saved from one awful fate just to fall to another even worse?

"Aka," it finally replied. "Aka is our name, among ourselves. I do not know if the outside world has a calling for us. We avoid most contact, do we."

"Aka?" I queried. "Aren't you Devoid? I mean, you're obviously different from those in the city, but…" I trailed off, not wanting to put my foot in my mouth and say something offensive.

The Aka made a strange noise, a sort of sharp, wheezing exhale resembling a scoff. Order anyway, did these things even breathe? It shook its head, eyes closed in what I interpreted as regret. Or maybe sorrow. It was difficult to tell in that desiccated Na'don face.

"The city Devoid, they are…cousins, one might say. Poor souls. Poor, unresting souls." Using its two upper arms, it pounded a fist into an open palm.

"When catastrophe came, many and many died in Cortianis. Many and many indeed. Friends. Family. Neighbors. Enemies. Employers. All in the city fell, turned, except the Aka. All fall to the weapon of our enemy. The *liaga*. Mother of Pain. Her, we hate above all others. We underwent great pain, great transformation, yet survived we did. Kept our minds, we did, though our bodies changed."

"That's extraordinary," Korbos said. "Cortianis. The old Imperium name. You've been around all these centuries since the Ruin? Why sequester yourselves?"

That wheezing snort again. "At first, we did not. We Aka tried to join survivors, join other communities. Feared, reviled, we were. Driven away. Hunted. Killed."

"You've survived all these years, but you can be killed?"

Oben shot a glance at Korbos and his rifle, its expression flat and unreadable behind the dark goggles. It paused for a moment before answering.

"Aye, killed we can be. We do not age, do not decay. Well…do not decay further. The centuries have been long and long, stranger. But we are Devoid, all the same. The world of men does not want or abide such as us, so we keep to our own, all this time. Best for all. Best for us."

"Fascinating. Why do you help us, then, if you have no use for others not of your kind?"

"Devoid, our bodies may be, but our minds remain our own, stranger—"

"Korbos. My name is Korbos."

"Master Korbos, then." Its mouth widened in a friendly grin, made grotesque by the exposed teeth. It extended a hand. "An…interesting name. Our pleasure it is to meet you."

Korbos shook, nodding his head.

"As I was saying, our minds remain our own. We understand the fear we evoke in…more normal folk. We do not blame them for their reaction, though of course we had no say in our condition. Best it is we remain to ourselves, but still we feel kinship to those who we once were like. We help when we are needed, although not often does man step into our domain."

"Fascinating," Korbos repeated.

We continued in silence. The sun set rapidly as we trekked, the shadows of the jungle growing deeper and darker. The moons were waning, and with little moonlight to trickle through the canopy, the night quickly became too dark. Twenty minutes later, my companions and I halted. The Aka turned as one, heads cocked in unspoken question.

"Why do you stop?" Oben asked.

"We…we can't see, Oben," Mari replied. Her hand stretched to the side, taking hold of mine.

"Ah!" it exclaimed. "Our apologies, friends. We forget, sometimes." A piercing, animalistic cry split the darkness, scaring us half to death.

"What the frok was that?!" I shrieked.

"Apologies, apologies," came Oben's layered tones. "A moment, friend."

A few seconds later, a pinpoint of light, soft and diffused, materialized between us and the Aka, bathing the area in a hazy blue glow. Several more of the glowing balls sprang into existence. The lights had an oblong shape—brightest in their centers, with blue wisps fading to the sides like small wings as they gracefully bobbed and swirled in the air. They reminded me a bit of the rays I'd see out in the ocean, swimming in their schools like swarms of angels.

I stared in wonder. The light reflected from all the nearby foliage. Some property of the huge leaves absorbed the illumination, casting it back out in spots and whorls and curves of bright blue and purple, further enhancing visibility. Flowers shone like small violet suns. Even the bugs flitting through the air cast their own yellow glow, turning the night into a dance of firelights.

It was one of the most beautiful sights I'd ever seen in my life.

"What in the…?" I murmured.

"Nightlings," said Cassidy in a low voice. "I've never actually seen one. Wow. This has been a day for firsts, Guts."

"An understanding we have with them, over these many years," intoned Oben. "They come to help, if we but call. Not that Aka have much need for them."

"What do you mean?"

Oben reached up with one pair of hands and lifted its goggles. Two dark, empty sockets stared out at us from the dry flesh. I felt Mari shudder beside me.

"Obvious on my part, it is, I think," it said. "But Aka have other senses to navigate the dark. Smell. Taste. Hearing. Among others. Very little light do we need. Apologies again, for the inconvenience. We do not deal with outsiders often."

"It's okay, Oben," I said, barely above a whisper. "This is worth the hassle." I ran my hand along a brilliantly-glowing fern.

We continued on, the nightlings leading the way, for almost an hour. I was fast getting sick of slogging through ankle-deep water and swatting biting flies from my neck. At least I could see them coming, as bright as they were. Our fatigue returned with a vengeance, and the five of us were soon staggering along, unsure of how much longer we could keep pace. My pack felt like a mountain upon my shoulders.

"Pyk," Mari said, tugging at my shirt. "Pyk!"

"What?" I grunted. I was almost sleepwalking.

"Do you see that?"

I looked up from my muck-covered feet and realized that the swamp around us was *brighter*. A yellow light shone through the trees. What in Order's name? No way the sun was coming up so soon. We hadn't been traveling *that* long.

The Aka led us through a thick copse, and my mouth dropped open.

Cassidy was right. This was a day for firsts.

Just past the scrub was a large clearing, perhaps six hundred feet across. The ground was covered in thick patches of grass and moss, with a wide stream arcing through one side. The yellow light gleamed from the fires of hundreds of tall torches, set into concentric rings around a massive central bonfire. Dozens of Aka milled about the area; some carried jugs of water from the stream, some tended the fire, others appeared to be sitting in a circle of wicker chairs and telling stories. Small log cabins dotted the clearing, several with fences containing pigs bedded down for the night. Others had fenced gardens, and there was one open-faced stall with an Aka hammering away at a forge. The small white fuzzy creatures roamed everywhere. A small isolated civilization, right here in the middle of undiscovered swamp.

But what really took one's breath away was the tree.

Set toward the rear of the clearing—at least as we were facing it—the tree dominated the view. Though not a great deal taller than the surrounding jungle, it was at least eighty feet thick, old gnarled branches twisting and turning out into a wide, thick-leaved canopy that covered almost the entire clearing. The leaves swayed in a light breeze, the bonfire's blaze casting creepy moving shadows. Small houses were built into the enormous limbs, with wood-and-rope bridges stretching across gaps.

Bastin chittered and danced around at the sight of it. I was surprised the scuridai had enough control to stay with us and not go bounding off to climb his heart out.

Light glimmered from the tree; both from torches set here and there among the branches as well as what appeared to be light emanating from *inside* the tree. I questioned the wisdom of having open flames around such an obviously ancient piece of timber, but I supposed the Aka knew better than I did.

The Aka themselves turned to stare with glassy, firelight-reflecting eyes as Oben led us through the small village. With the exception of their well-tailored hemp clothes, they seemed very similar in demographic to the Devoid we'd encountered in Cortian; mostly human, with a scattering of a few Thrane here and there. I saw two other Na'don, who raised hands in greeting to Oben. It hailed them with a cheery reply. I even spied what appeared to be a few children running about, chasing nightlings and lighted bugs, before realizing they were Cheks. Or used to be, at least. Mari seemed particularly interested in those.

Three Aka approached us as we neared the tree, long shadows trailing behind them as they raised torches in salute. I couldn't tell what they looked like.

To be fair, I wasn't focused on them. Now that we were closer, I could make out a recessed hollow at the base of the tree, framing what was unmistakably a door, carved with intricate patterns by a master's hand. That inner glow was coming from cunning windows set within the bark of the massive tree, spiraling upwards as if along an interior staircase. There was no chance this thing was hollow, was there?

Oben clasped forearms with all three Aka at the same time.

"Is he in?" it queried.

"When is he not?" responded the middle one. "You know he rarely leaves these days." The Aka gave a long-suffering sigh before turning and strolling over to knock on the door. Golden light flooded out as it opened, and a stooped silhouette filled the doorframe. The Aka exchanged several inaudible words, and the figure's head snapped up to look at us.

The fully human figure. A man, judging by his size.

"I'll be damned," he muttered in a deep but wavering baritone. "Outsiders!"

He hobbled forward, leaning on a staff collected from near the door, and firelight revealed an old man. A pleasant, somewhat surprised grin split his face.

"Welcome travelers! Welcome ye lost! Welcome to Lau Tuai! Come in, come in!" the old man exclaimed. He had a funny accent. I couldn't place it. Maybe Ahrimacian?

"Welcome to Lau Tuai, the Old Tree! Welcome to our home! All these years, and you're the first visitors I've had. Well, except for Oben and the other Aka, of course."

I didn't know what to make of him. He was huge, for certain—thick with muscle, sporting a rounded, not-quite-gone-to-fat belly—though stooped and leaning on his staff more than I would have expected from someone of such a powerful build. If unbent, I wagered he would still be several inches shy of my six feet. He was dark of skin—very dark—with a grandfatherly air, though it was impossible to determine his age. His mildly-lined yet grizzled face and powerful build, at odds with his frail walk and quavering voice, could have put him at any age between forty-five and eighty. The pure-white beard and matching thick mane of flyaway hair further added to the confusion. He held out a hand to us, a meaty paw with just the slightest of tremors to it.

"Eljin's the name. Eljin Dhovra, at your service, young masters and mistresses."

I snorted, quickly turning it into a cough at a sharp glance from the big blacksmith. I didn't think I'd be able to think of Korbos as *young* ever again.

"We appreciate your kind invitation," Korbos said. "My name is Korbos. This is Mariyana, Pyk, and Cassidy. And over there is Bastin." The scuridai chirped, though whether in greeting or hunger, I couldn't tell.

"Then we're well met!" the old man exclaimed with a beaming grin. It was infectious; I couldn't help but return it. I noticed Mari and Cassidy doing the same, although Korbos remained stoic as ever.

"Please, come in!" Eljin continued. "Have a seat, rest your rears! Hah! If my eyes don't deceive me, you've got the look of those who have had a rough evening."

I laughed—an involuntary reaction given the state of us. We were exhausted, mud-spattered, swaying on our feet, and shellshocked from our ordeal in Cortian. Rough evening was an understatement.

"Again, your kindness is appreciated, Master Dhovra," Korbos replied with a slight bow of his head.

"Not at all, not at all! You're doin' a kindness to me, sir! Heh! Why, I've not had a guest in many a year that wasn't a walking corpse!" He tipped an imaginary cap to Oben. "No offense to you and your kin, my friend."

"Mmmm...none taken, of course, Eljin," replied the Aka, its face inscrutable. "We are what we are."

"Truth! You are what you are, indeed. No changing what one is, that's for sure. Now. Come in, all! Welcome to our humble home!"

The old man moseyed through the elaborate door, and—Bastin excluded—we followed into a room from a dream. *Humble* wasn't the word I'd have used to describe it. Golden candle light, set within glass wall lanterns, bathed a wondrous two-story domicile that seemed to have been cut from the tree itself by the hand of a master craftsman. The enormous circular dwelling was more inviting than any home I'd ever experienced.

Everything was made of polished wood, intricately carved in curves and whorls. A massive table rested in the center of the room, surrounded by lush, high-backed chairs. Several thick sofas sat at angles in front of a wide fireplace, where a low-banked blaze warded off the chill of the tree's interior. Portions of the walls were carved with lifelike images depicting the story of Atia's creation of the world, broken here and there by small windows which looked out across the glade.

Where the reliefs ended, curved bookshelves hugged the walls from floor to high ceiling; a sliding ladder provided access to the upper shelves. I gaped. The entire Hightide public library didn't hold so many volumes. A wealth of knowledge, hidden within a gargantuan tree out in the middle of nowhere. Cassidy was staring at them like a drowning man who's spotted a passing ship.

Rugs covered the floor, and colorful plants and flowers bloomed in myriad boxes and vases, some cascading over planters hanging from the beams. Off to one side of the sofas was an artist's easel and work bench covered in paints, brushes, and tools—the floor around it littered with stretched canvases and half-finished drawings. Behind the easel, the wall was dominated by two large images of fantastical beasts that differed from the works strewn below; clearly they were painted by more masterful hands.

"Gods above and below," Cassidy breathed, "are those actual Najarian and Sully paintings?"

"Oho! You've a good eye, young mistress!" Eljin replied in delight. "I've always had a particular fancy for their direwyrms. I'll have to tell you the story sometime of how I came by them." He grinned wickedly. "Might even show you the Lockwood I've got stashed away."

Cassidy whistled in appreciation.

On the other end of the couches was a spiral of ornately-wrought stairs, curling upwards steeply to a higher floor. If the sleeping quarters were upstairs, how in the world did Eljin hobble up those every night?

The giant table at the center of the room was swamped with papers, quills, and all manner of open books and scientific devices. Clocks lay in various stages of disrepair. Beakers bubbled and churned on the large table in some incomprehensible alchemic labyrinth of glass and fluid.

Order anyway, how long had this old man lived here with the Aka? This was the centerpiece of an established home. A well-cared-for home, at that. I knew successful merchants back home that didn't live in this sort of luxury. The warmth of the fire and general coziness of the den set me staggering into the back of a plush settee, my exhaustion landing on me like a blackfin jumping the side of a boat.

"Master Dhovra..." Korbos began.

"Nawp! Nawp! Won't hear a thing of it, young sir! You people are dead on yer feet, so you are. Get rested, I insist! We can jaw with each other once yer brains have unfogged. Upstairs you go!"

Korbos opened his mouth to object, then looked to the rest of us and reconsidered. His eye narrowed at Eljin. "We won't surrender our weapons or packs."

"Wouldn't dream of it, sir! You'll find no harm here, on my hermit's word!" He held up his right hand in pledge. "Please, rest yerselves. Up the stairs and to the door on the right. You'll find beds enough for everyone. We'll talk soon enough once you can form a coherent thought."

"Will you be retiring soon as well, Master Dhovra?"

The old man laughed, deep from his belly. "Me? Oh no, young sir. I'm a creature of the night, so's I am! Just woke up at sundown, matter of fact! Why, you folks are the first conversation I've had today."

He chuckled, leaning in conspiratorially. "The heat of the jungle day doesn't jive well with these bones, understand? Order anyway, you'd think I was *old* or something!" He laughed again, long and loud. Even as loopy as I was, I smiled at his jocularity.

"Anyway, the Aka don't sleep, you see, so you'll have plenty of safety here. No boogums or darkterrors gonna get you in *my* house! Now, hup! Off to bed with you all! We'll talk tomorrow." He shooed us toward the spiral staircase.

Cassidy looked to me, a questioning eyebrow raised, but by that point I was near keeling over. I shrugged and nodded.

Korbos sighed. "Come on, everyone. Our gratitude to you, Master Dhovra."

"Atia's blessings on you, sir," Mari intoned, a serious look on her face. "You're a kind man." She held up her Atian medallion before him and brought it to her lips in benediction.

"Oho! And with you, my dear. It's absolutely my pleasure, young one." Eljin replied, smiling kindly down at her.

We piled up the stairs into a narrow but pleasantly-appointed hallway containing a door on either side and another spiral of stairs at the back end. Mari led the way through the right-hand entrance and squealed as she bounced into the room. It was made for guests, I could see, with two single beds and a double bunk, all covered with thick down mattresses and fluffy pillows that resembled nothing more than clouds.

My eyes watered at the sight of them, and I gave a soft groan of pleasure as I dropped my gear and flopped down onto the bottom bunk. I couldn't remember how many days it had been since I'd slept in a real bed. The crew bunks on the *Storm* weren't exactly suited for high living. Once I got off my feet, my entire body protested at its recent rough treatment.

"No, get up!" shouted Cassidy, kicking at my boot. My filthy, waterlogged, mud-covered boot.

"Oh drek," I muttered, heaving myself reluctantly from my feathered heaven and disrobing down to my underthings. In my exhaustion, I'd completely disregarded my utter filthiness. Luckily, the sheets didn't look any worse for the wear.

I wasn't particularly modest after so long spent in the cramped company of fishing vessels, but I was absolutely *not* expecting Cassidy to strip down right in front of me. I mean, it made sense; we were all disheveled and muck-covered. But I still wasn't expecting it. Korbos and Mari were disrobing as well, but I didn't even spare a thought for them as I quickly turned away and gave Cassidy a moment to slip under the covers. The little *bhuta* had stolen the bottom bunk from me. I frowned as I turned, then halted at the stunning lopsided grin she was giving me.

She was enjoying this. Making me uncomfortable.

I shook my head and climbed into the top bunk, trying not to drool at the thought of beautiful, wonderful, exquisite *rest.* Mari gave an ear-splitting yawn, then promptly fell asleep.

"Get some shuteye, you two," Korbos said. "I'll keep a watch." He began busying himself with wiping down his rifle.

I wasn't in any position to argue, but sleep turned out to be evasive. Jolly as he was, I didn't know if we could trust this Eljin. Maybe Korbos had the right idea by keeping one eye open. Well, the only eye, in his case. Maybe I was overtired. Too keyed up from the events of the last day. Had it only been one day? It felt like our adventures in Cortian had lasted a week or more.

Maybe I just couldn't stop thinking about that brief glimpse of Cassidy. I wondered what stories her scars would have told. The hard, ropy curves and freckled tan. That black hair spilling between her shoulders. Even her hands—the left with its missing ring finger—had their own beauty. But mostly those eyes. Those emerald, almond-shaped eyes and that grin that pierced my entire being.

I felt ridiculous. We'd known each other for mere days, but there was no denying that I was head over heels for her. I sighed, looking over to see Korbos stretched out on his bed, his hands behind his head and his eye locked on the door. In the few seconds it took me to roll over and adjust my covers, he was snoring lightly. So much for the watch. I chuckled, thinking that I'd never get any rest if he kept that up all nigh—

Sleep crashed over me like a tall wave.

TWENTY TWO

I woke, alone, to daylight pouring through the room's small window. I swung out of the bunk, muscles aching, and found a clean set of clothes set on the room's single nightstand. Gratitude washed through me; I really had no desire to dress in the nasty gear I'd been wearing through Cortian. My boots had even been scrubbed. Atia's bones, how long had I slept?

I stretched as I dressed, relishing the feel of the fine canvas pants and white hemp shirt as I laced them up. Faint voices came from downstairs as I exited the room and made my way down the spiral staircase. I followed the voices through a door I'd missed seeing the previous night, emerging into a small square kitchen set deeper within the great tree.

It was quaint, with a wood-burning stove and a metal sink scavenged from Order only knew where. Dishes and cups lined the walls on wooden racks, and a tiny door set into the wall opened on a well-stocked pantry. A short bistro-style table and chairs rested in one corner, where a small man sat staring at me as I entered.

"Morning sleepyhead!" cried Mari as she fried breakfast on the stove. She hopped up and down in excitement. "I didn't think you were ever going to get up did you get rested oh and say hello to Amadi, Amadi this is Pyk my oldest bestest friend and oh Pyk Amadi has been telling me the grandest—"

"Mari!" I barked, cutting her off as I rubbed my forehead. "It's way too early for all that. Can…can I have some of that food?" The smell of fried eggs was making my stomach grumble. I was famished, though I tried not to think about what sort of swamp creature had laid them.

"Coming right up!" she squealed. I smiled as I turned to the small man at the table. His chair scraped as he stood and extended a hand to me. Since he was a Chek, I had to stoop a bit to shake it. He was older, perhaps in his mid-forties. Deep bags settled under muddy yellow eyes, and his cheekbones stood out prominently against a razor-thin face. He had wan skin, rather pale and sickly-looking with a thin frame and stooped shoulders. All the Cheks I'd ever met were hearty and robust, so his appearance was a tad disconcerting.

"Amadi Omari, sir," he said. "Pleasure to meet you."

"The pleasure's all mine. Your…people…here saved our backsides last night." I winced, hoping the unintentional pause didn't come across as rude.

"We'd have done the same for anyone, but I'm glad we were able to provide assistance."

"I thought Eljin was the only living person here. We only saw him and the Aka when coming in."

Amadi nodded. "It's just me and him. My apologies that I wasn't around to greet your arrival last night."

"So how'd you wind up out here in the jungle with him?"

"That…that might be a story to tell later, sir. I'd prefer to let Eljin speak with you first, if you wouldn't mind."

I cocked an eyebrow but said nothing as I took a seat. Mari scampered over and plopped down a plate in front of us both, piled high with fried eggs, potatoes, and bacon. My mouth watered, and I didn't waste any time tucking in. Pure bliss. The plate was clean in less than three minutes, and I washed everything down with a glass of clear water. A resounding belch shook the air, and I grinned as Amadi blushed and covered his mouth.

"A fine meal, miss Naribi," he said. "My compliments."

She laughed. "Best praise a chef can receive, so thank *you*!"

I leaned back in my chair, lacing my hands behind my head. "So how long was I asleep? You all been up long?"

Mari took her seat and began laying into her breakfast, speaking around mouthfuls of food. "Mrrph…murbur thppt blargle."

"What?!" Amadi and I both said together, laughing.

She grinned and swallowed.

"You slept about eighteen hours. It's midday now, so I've only been up an hour or so myself. I've been having the nicest conversations with Amadi here, and he helped me prepare breakfast." She flashing a dazzling smile to the other Chek, who returned it with a bow of his head. "Turns out, he survived the Culls! First Chek I've ever met who's older than me, isn't that wonderful? He's been telling me all about his old village!"

Amadi nodded, though he looked somewhat embarrassed. A thick cough wracked his frail body, and he turned his mouth into the crook of his arm.

"It's been several decades since I've seen another of my kind," he explained to me. "It's been…nice, having someone to talk to about how life used to be."

Mari looked at him with a kind of worship in her eyes that worried me. I couldn't blame her, not really. The only others of her kind that she'd ever known were Rimple and Skot, our friends from Hightide. All three of them were orphans who'd grown up away from their kind, and not a one of them knew any of the history of their people. She'd always been borderline desperate to find out more of her race. To suddenly be face-to-face with what could be considered an elder member had to have been like grasping a life-ring while flailing in deep waters.

The only problem was that we didn't know these jungle-dwellers, and after the last few days my supply of trust was running shorter than the Cheks' bellybuttons. I gave Mari a warning glance, but she took no notice.

I turned to Amadi, who was staring at Mariyana with a strange, thoughtful expression.

"So," I began, "you were around for the culls? That must have been terrifying. We've had our experiences with the Hostguard as well."

The Chek coughed again. "Well…yes. It was…traumatic, to say the least. I was a young man at the time, but I've never forgotten the camps. Or the pits." He frowned and fell quiet, remembering. His features tightened, as if he'd come to a decision, and he reached forward to take Mari's hand.

"Mistress Naribi…"

"Oh, it's Mari, please, I insist!"

He coughed into his arm. "Mistress Mari, then. I realize we've only just met, but I wonder if I might speak with you about a matter of some importance? I fear I may not have another chance to address the matter, given my current…condition."

She leaned forward, one hand in his and her chin resting on the other. "Oh, please do!"

Amadi hesitated, then gave me a pointed look, eyebrows arched. I frowned. I wasn't about to leave Mari alone after a statement like that, but she rested a hand on my netanium one and nodded.

I sighed and decided to trust her judgement. She could handle herself against another Chek—especially one as sickly as Amadi—and I knew she'd just tell me what he said later, when we had a chance to confer.

"So where are the others?" I asked.

"I believe your friends are outside," replied Amadi, "enjoying our hospitality, sire Pyk."

I nodded and gave him a pointed look of my own. One that said "watch yourself." He gave a tilt—a very slight tilt—of his head in understanding.

I patted Mari's shoulder and left. I glanced at the library shelves in the den, half-expecting to see Cassidy poring over some old tome. As I emerged into the clearing, a wave of heat and sticky humidity washed over me, causing an instant sweat. I appreciated the thin hemp shirt even more as I crossed the crowded yard, seeking my friends. A shadow passed over me, and my head snapped up. Laughter bubbled in my chest as I saw Bastin gliding across the glade, chirping wildly. He went from one tree to the next, pausing long enough to redirect his momentum and send himself soaring on to the next. The scuridai was clearly enjoying himself.

Aka roamed the clearing, performing the various tasks of their daily lives. Several pulled carts filled with vegetables bound for storerooms. Others worked the wide gardens, hoeing rows and planting seedlings. One Aka tossed a potato high into the air, and I clapped as Bastin swooped past and snatched it to general laughter and applause. A loose line passed buckets to and from the stream, dumping the water into a series of spigoted barrels loaded onto a low wagon. Wild baghdas scuttled around the river banks, tentacles flailing as they dove in and out of the water.

I stared in wonder. Were the Aka vegetarians? Did they even *need* to eat? It occurred to me that we knew next to nothing about them. Barring their clothing, they looked exactly like the Devoid within Cortian, but their intelligence and humanity—for lack of a better term—set them apart. I saw many laughing with one another or greeting their fellows with cheer. Overall, there was an appealing sense of peace and normalcy that pervaded the community. These people had learned over the course of nine hundred long years to respect one another and band together for a collective good. It was impressive.

A squeal and bright laugh caught my attention, and I angled left to find Cassidy in a nearby pen giving merry chase after a piglet. I strolled over—nodding to several Aka mending clothes and gossiping—and propped my arms on a beam of the fence, chuckling as our pilot stumbled after the baby, bent over at the waist and arms outstretched. She managed to snag the critter, then held it up to me in triumph before walking over.

A broad grin split her freckled face, skin shining in the sweltering afternoon sun. She was wearing clothing very similar to mine, though of a much more feminine cut; hip-slung canvas pants, laced at the front and sides split to mid-calf, and a cream-colored hemp shirt, sleeveless and tied at the midriff. It was a very fetching look on her, and of course she noticed my appraising glance.

"Eljin says our clothes will be laundered and returned by tonight," she said with a laugh. "I will say these are pretty comfortable, though."

"Can't argue that," I replied. I nodded at the piglet. "Is that tomorrow's breakfast?"

"Pyk!" she cried in mock outrage, throwing half-hearted slaps in my direction. "As if we'd ever eat Pyk Junior!"

I ducked, arms raised to fend her off, laughing harder. "Okay, okay! I was only—wait…" I frowned. "Pyk Junior?"

"Well," she said, "Pyk Belloc the Second, if you want to be formal." She proceeded to cover the piglet's snout in kisses, making exaggerated smooching noises. "And no, we'd never eat Junior, now would we? Would we? No we wouldn't, he's such a good boy yes he is."

I groaned. I mean, the animal didn't even look anything like me. Well, except for the blue eyes. And maybe that shock of blond fuzz between its ears.

"So how's it been this morning?" I asked.

"I've only been awake a couple of hours, honestly. Order knows I needed the rest, given what we went through. Korbos got up pretty early, though, from what Juni here said."

I looked over to the Aka—presumably Juni—who was wrangling the other pigs. She raised a hand in greeting, which I returned. Order's light, it was going to take some getting used to, seeing Devoid walking about and working like normal folk.

"Where is he, anyway?"

"Open thine ears and listen, o' weary wanderer of the world." She cupped a hand to her ear.

Now that she pointed it out, I could hear the ringing of an anvil echoing across the clearing.

"Ah," I replied. "Should have known."

She shooed the piglet back to its family, and we stood in companionable silence for a while, leaning back against the fence and enjoying the sun. Well, *Cassidy* enjoyed the sun. *I* was trying not to drown in the waterfalls of sweat pouring from my body. Hightide was never this bloody humid. I tried not to move, however, as our shoulders were touching and her diminished hand was resting awful close to my flesh-and-blood one.

Eventually Cassidy raised her head and looked me in the eye.

"So," she began in a low voice, "this is nice and all, but how do we figure we're going to get back to the *Storm*? Not like we can stay here the rest of our lives, and I'm not going anywhere without my frokking ship."

"I honestly have no clue," I replied, glancing at Juni to make sure we were out of earshot. "I haven't had time to give it much thought, but now that you bring it up, I'm stumped. That was a drekload of Devoid following us out of the city. Even if we can get our bearings straight, they'll have spread through the jungle overnight, and that's going to be a shallow reef I don't want to sail."

"Mmmm…" she hummed in agreement. We lapsed back into silence.

"Wanna go see what Korbos is doing?" I asked. She nodded and waved goodbye to Juni as we strolled over to the smithy. A large Aka was affixing handles to a variety of farming implements; potato shovels, rakes, spades, and the like. I saw one or two ball peen hammers. Korbos stood at the anvil, putting the finishing touches to a four-pronged pitchfork. I was startled. He had a small smile on his face; he was obviously enjoying himself and the work. But his face was uncovered. He wasn't wearing his customary wide eyepatch.

I couldn't recall ever seeing him without it, and the effect was strange. Where his left eye should have been was a hollowed-out mass of scar tissue, as if he'd been born without one at all. The twisting, silvery scars traveled from his neck all the way to his hairline. He'd said it had taken two hundred years for Kaira to wear down his defenses and carve that ruin into his face. Given how fast he healed, I shuddered at the thought of that amount of sustained pain and suffering. How in Order's name had he endured it? My hatred for Kaira and the Host expanded just a tiny bit more.

"Having fun?" I quipped.

Korbos spotted us, raising his chin in greeting as he dunked the fork into a quenching barrel. He set it aside to be fitted for a handle, and nodded to the Aka sharing the workspace.

"My thanks to you, Ghein. You've a fine forge here. I appreciate you letting me assist today."

Ghein cocked his head and clasped the big man's forearm. "It's my honor, Master Korbos. Order above, the work you've produced this morning alone would have taken me a week! You're welcome in my smithy at any time."

Our friend removed his leather gloves and apron, then joined us. "Good to see you up and about, Pyk. Get rested?"

I nodded, trying not to stare at the ruin of his face. "Well as can be, I suppose. My legs feel like they've been pressed flat and stripped into pasta, but I'll live."

"Excellent. Now that you're here, I think it's time we held conference with Eljin. There are some things we need to work out." He pulled his patch from a pocket and fastened it around his face. It shouldn't have mattered, but the sight of his covered eye filled me with relief. Not that his scars made me uneasy, but the patch was...well, *right* for him. A part of who he was. Seeing him without it was like seeing him naked and exposed.

The three of us took our time getting back to the Lau Tuai, stopping here and there to converse with the Aka. I was struck again by how little difference there was to any random farming commune outside the expansive jungle. These were vibrant, communicative people—as different from their Cortian cousins as a blackfin was from a garwhale. Eventually, we came to the ornately-carved door, where Mari stood talking to Amadi. She seemed excited—wide-eyed and bouncy. I wondered what it was that they'd discussed.

"Korbos!" she exclaimed as we approached, throwing her arms around his legs. He patted her back with a hand nearly as wide as she was.

"Good to see you too, little one."

"Oh Pyk," Mari said, "we need to talk, Amadi and I had one heck of a conversation and he told me about some things that you and I need to—"

Amadi laid a hand on her shoulder, cutting her off before nearly doubling over with a wracking cough.

"Oh, right. We'll talk later. By the way, Korbos, this is—"

"We met earlier. Amadi, we need to speak with Eljin."

"Yes, we assumed you'd request as much. We can all converse when he'll be awake later in the even—"

"Or, we can go ahead and get our jawing done," came a voice from the doorway. "Heh. No better time than now."

"Eljin," said Amadi, bowing at the waist in respect, "Wasn't expecting to see you up so soon. Can't say I'm surprised, though."

"Yeah, well, I've slept enough," the older man said. "Don't you badger me none."

"As you say," replied the Chek, bowing again.

"Ah, don't mind him!" barked Eljin, pounding Amadi on the back. The small man stumbled forward a step and shook his head, as if it were a common occurrence. "He's the one I need to be worrying about, with that cough, but he frets about me like an old mother sow!" Eljin put his arm around the Chek's shoulders and hugged him in close. Amadi gave the long-suffering sigh of an introvert who's forced to deal with the boisterous outgoings of an old friend, slumping further and looking even more frail than usual. I couldn't help but glance at Mari, who wore her concern on her sleeve.

Korbos nodded his head to Amadi. "We hope your health recovers swiftly, Renti Omari." The Chek's eyes widened, and he stood up straighter to return the nod with a bit more formality than I'd seen thus far. I glanced at Cassidy, confused.

"Renti is an honorific," she leaned in and whispered. "Used in respect to clan elders. Strange to hear it from a non-Chek."

"*Oho*!" boomed Eljin. "A well-traveled man, I see! Well-traveled indeed! And do I see someone before me who's involved with the Seekers?"

I looked at Cassidy, who stared with wide eyes. There was no possible way the old man could have known she was a Seeker. My muscles tensed, body on high alert, when he stepped forward and rapped his knuckles on my metal shoulder.

Oh, right. My arm was Seeker-made. I let out a held breath.

"Not trynna be nosy, son, promise. But I know a good piece of work when I sees one, so I do! Hah! Mind if I look closer?"

I shook my head, still not sure what to make of his interest, and rolled up the short sleeve over my shoulder to better show the entire piece of machinery. He stepped closer, peering in at the metalwork and plate joins. He ran a wizened—though large—finger from metal bicep to forearm.

"Very nice fittings…very nice," he hummed before looking up. "And how long since it was bonded?"

"Nine years. Well, four, for this iteration."

"Yessss, very nice craftsmanship. Hah! And nary a day it's gone wrong on you, I'd bet! They've got their faults, the Seekers, don't let it be said they don't! But they sure can make a limb. Got to give 'em that! Now, you take this old thing…"

I gaped as he pulled up his left pant leg, revealing a netanium leg from the thigh down. It was obviously older, with heavier plating around the quad and calf, but every bit as well-made as my arm. The oiled plates and pistons hissed softly as he shifted his weight. I couldn't help my smile.

"Got this bad *bhaka*, oh, going on forty years ago now. I'us a younger man back then, without quite so many wrinkles and aches, but it's served me well all these years." He poked my shoulder. "Even without the tuneups! Hah! Damned if the knee doesn't grind every now and again, though."

My grin widened. It was rare that I crossed paths with another person gifted with a Seeker limb. My friends never paid my arm any mind, but I sometimes resented the looks I got on the Hightide streets. Seeker limbs weren't *rare*, exactly, but there were enough unmodified disabled folk roaming about that those of us with enhancements were still considered an oddity. It was nice to be able to commiserate with another like me, even if only for a little while.

Eljin leaned in. "Let you in on a little secret, son…got me a Seeker heart, too! Hah! Big old clockwork ticker, just a'jammin' away in there! Buh-*BUMP*! Heh."

My eyebrows rose. Now *that* was unusual. Artificial internal organs were much more rare, and select, than limbs. They were insanely difficult to integrate. Insanely expensive, as well. Maybe half of the recipients even survived the process, so they were usually reserved for the direst of needs, the exorbitantly rich or the well-connected. I'd heard of minor royalty that weren't able to get Seeker organs. My curiosity level spiked. Who in the world *was* this old man? Korbos and Cassidy stared at him with heads tilted. Mari was hunkered over her heels, tapping a nail on Eljin's leg. He didn't seem to care.

"That's very impressive, Master Dhovra," Korbos said in a dry tone. "But we need to get to the matter at hand."

"Of course! Heh. Come, come," Eljin barked. "Let's get out of this blasted sun. I'd sure be interested to hear yer stories. Then maybe we can figure out what's to be done with ya! Let me just get…now where is that blasted…"

He trailed off and craned his neck, looking about the clearing and letting out a loud whistle when he finally spotted Oben. The old man waved the Aka over. We filed our way into the Lau Tuai and took up seats in the plush seats surrounding the fireplace. Eljin and Oben took a rest directly across from Korbos, Cassidy, and me. Amadi and Mari sat in the middle couch. She had her hand on Amadi's knee in a manner I didn't much care for. It took a lot of effort to not frown at the way she was staring at him. The pale Chek sighed and smiled as he glanced at her. He looked uncomfortable, so maybe there wasn't anything for me to worry over. I mean, he was twice her age, at least.

"Now, tell me yer tale, if you wouldn't mind," Eljin said, "and let's see what us old recluses can do to help you along yer way." He and Oben leaned forward, attentive.

My friends and I looked at each other. An understanding flew on silent winds between us. Order only knew if we could trust these folk, but I liked them. It felt right. Their kindness and hospitality went a long way, in my book. No need to tell them everything, of course, but I couldn't see any reason to keep our story from them. The others nodded to me, so I took a deep breath.

And so we began.

TWENTY THREE

By unspoken agreement, I did the talking, beginning with the *Quay* racing home ahead of the storm. I hesitated when I got to the part of Kaira invading Korbos's shop—leaving out the fact that she was looking for the signara; they didn't need to know about that—and looked to the big smith. He exhaled and nodded, so I explained his abilities. His nature as one of the Host. I was prepared for incredulity. He was prepared to demonstrate.

In no way were we prepared for Oben to go berserk.

I didn't even have time to shout as the Aka snarled and launched itself across the gap, four arms enveloping Korbos and tumbling the couch head over heels. I went flying, rolling backwards as I hit the rug. Oben threw punch after punch at Korbos, who covered with his forearms and reeled, a stunned expression on his face.

"You are one of them!" Oben was screaming. "You are *hers*! The *liaga* Vestan! You dare enter this place?! You dare show yourself to the Aka?!"

Before I could enter the fray, Eljin was there, grabbing the Na'don and dragging it off Korbos. No easy feat, given that he had four flailing fists to contend with. Oben was still lashing out at my friend, who rose to his feet with shocked incredulity. His eye flared silver, and Eljin stumbled back as the Aka's limbs snapped outward and it shot into the air, slamming into the ceiling before floating back down to hover a few feet off the ground.

"Korbos, no!" I shouted. Memories of the Strigori village flashed through my head.

"I'm not going to hurt it, Pyk," he replied with more calm than I would have had after being attacked out of nowhere. He held a steady gaze to the sightless Aka. "What in the fires of Chaos was that all about?"

It spat and sputtered, pointed teeth gnashing. "You are Host. Spent years fighting you and your kin, I did. Fighting *her*. The Mother of Pain. Creator of the Aka. I will not rest until we dance upon your bones, abomination!" Its limbs thrashed against invisible bonds.

"Fascinating." Korbos's eye widened in realization. "You...were a member of the Resurgence? *Sa etau?*"

Oben fell immediately still, mouth dropping open and working soundlessly.

"*Sa ave auma sefusu*," it replied softly. "*Sola teteen.*"

I glanced at Cassidy, who shrugged her shoulders. No idea what language they were speaking.

The Aka floated down to the floor, expression wary. Its arm reached toward Korbos, all the fight seemingly gone from it. If it had eyes, I'd have said it was staring at my friend in...awe.

"You...you are..." it stammered, "you are *Seta Sietau*?"

"The One Who Fights," Korbos said with a small, sad smile. "Yes, I am. I was, in any case. Guess I still am."

Oben dropped to its knees, hands raised palm-up in supplication. The rapid turnabout left me confused and uneasy.

"Forgive me, old one. Shamed myself and my comrades, have I so done. Never in all our long years would we have known you still walked this world, *Seta Sietau*."

"Get up, please," Korbos said, waving the Aka to rise. "We are met as equals here, Oben *ta'ita mula*. I'll have no bowing or scraping from an ally of old."

Old ally? I was dumbfounded, had no idea what in the world was happening. The Aka was every bit as ancient as Korbos himself. Had they actually known each other in the days of the Ruin?

My friend turned to the rest of us. "It's okay. Just a misunderstanding, and a justifiable one at that. Oben here was a soldier of the Na'don armies that fought against the Host prior to the Ruin. We can trust in it."

"Oooookay," I drawled. "But what's with the *Seeta Seetow* thing?"

"*Seta Sietau*," he said, correcting my pronunciation with a slight chuckle. "It's a little embarrassing. That was their name for me. I told you once that I was the face of the Elarin resistance, but most of the fighters only knew of me through reputation. Not what I actually looked like. Everyone knew of the Host Who Fought, though. A legend in my own time, so I'm told, although I didn't exactly want to be. The Na'don were our allies then, though they weren't part of our formal military. More guerrilla fighters than anything."

I shook my head in wonder. They were talking about an era so far gone into history that my brain couldn't process it.

"So how did you become an Aka, if his creator bombed the Devoid cities *before* creating the Host?" I thought I had that right.

The Na'don turned its head to me, a pained expression flickering across its face. "Cortianis was last of the cities to fall, during the war against the *liaga*. On a detachment, I was, within the city when the gas fell and the people began to die."

I shuddered, picturing it in my mind. A rain of Order-knew-what substance, then everyone around you dropping like flies as you screamed in agony. Horrible.

"Correct," Korbos clarified. "Mother continued her atrocities, however infrequently, up until the day she disappeared. I know of two cities at least that were annihilated before the Ruin shut her down."

Korbos extended a hand to Oben, who rose and took it in three of its own. "My apologies to you, Korbos of the Host. I attacked without thought, and my shame is great and great. Had I but known—"

"You hold no shame, Oben *ta'ita mula*," Korbos replied in a formal tone. "There is no way you *could* have known me. The shame is Mother's, and the Host's, for what happened to you in Cortianis. You and yours have suffered much and long at the hands of my kin, and your response was not unreasonable. Let us continue as brothers, and lay on with the battle we began so long ago."

Eljin looked around at all of us. "Well. Heh. If that's out of everyone's system, can we get back to the story? If it gets any better than this, I'll have to have new furniture made. Hah!"

Mari and Amadi nodded with enthusiasm. The Na'don's simian muzzle curved in a grin, and it bowed before stepping over to upright the couch on which we'd been sitting. Everyone returned to their seats.

The rest of the story went without quite so much uproar. I spoke for hours, until my throat was dry and sore. Amadi trekked to the kitchen twice to bring back water, which I accepted with thanks. On occasion my friends would interject a point or bit of information I'd missed, but for the most part I got through the recitation alone. I glossed over the parts regarding the signara, saying only that Korbos was on a quest to find information to bring down the Host. The jungle-dwellers ooo'd and ahh'd and sat on the edge of their seats at the exciting parts.

By the time I finished with Oben and the Aka saving us from the mushier Devoid, the sun was well on its way to setting. An unfamiliar Aka circled through the den of the Lau Tuai, lighting lamps. We sat in silence, me sipping my third glass of water while Eljin prodded the fireplace ashes with a poker.

"Well," the old man began, "that was, uh, quite the tale. Heh. Far longer than my own, and ten times more interesting. But I do believe we have a few things in common between us all. Yes, indeed."

He sighed. "The biggest of which is that we've all got our reasons for hating the Host. Kaira in particular. Heh. Frokking *bhuta* that she is."

He spat this last with venom. I was under the impression that he'd been in this jungle for quite a long time, so I was curious as to what would cause such animosity toward the High Lady. I had my guesses. Everyone's reasons were usually the same.

Cassidy scoffed beside me. "Speak for yourselves. I want nothing to do with the Host. I just want my money. Chaos burn me if I want to go against them. Our little encounter in Hightide convinced me of *that*."

Korbos glanced at her, frowning, but said nothing. He turned to Eljin. "Master Dhovra, the point to be made is that we need to return to our skipship—"

"*My* skipship, thank you," interjected Cassidy.

"*The* skipship. We cannot thank you enough for your aid so far, but—being perfectly honest—I can't see a way to get back that doesn't end… badly. Any assistance you'd be able to provide would be most appreciated."

The old man swung the poker in a mock slash, swiping as if he were fencing an invisible opponent. The movement looked practiced and familiar, and I wondered what sort of training he'd had. Military? Gladiatorial?

"Hmmm," he said. "I think we might be able to help one another, Master Korbos, but would you indulge an old fellow for a while and let me share my story?" He looked to Amadi. "Our story, such as it is? It might give you a little insight and balance yer decision as to the favor I plan to ask of you. Heh. Besides, it's not like you're going to get going back to your ship tonight. Not with the sun setting out there. Hah!"

Korbos arched a skeptical eyebrow. I was in agreement. What favor? We owed these people our lives, true, but I didn't exactly feel comfortable being in that debt.

"We…" he began slowly, dragging the word out, "can probably come to some sort of mutual accommodation, sir. And I for one would be very interested to hear your tale."

"Heh! Excellent! It won't be so long as yers, as I've said, but you might find it enlightening to a few things. Now! Oben, would you be so kind as to grab that bottle of moss whiskey over there? I find that telling a story goes much smoother with a dram or two."

I closed my eyes and let out a soft groan. I didn't like the way Korbos's eyes lit up at the mention of whiskey. Indeed, he held out his hand to pour when Oben returned to the couches with a tray of glasses. Eljin and Amadi both accepted a tumbler, though Mari, Cassidy and I abstained.

Korbos slugged back his glass. "Good stuff. You make it here?"

"Oh, yes!" cried Amadi. "Very proud of their whiskey, the Aka. I believe they see it as a point of pride. Distilled from their potatoes and flavored with local mosses. The recipe's over nine hundred years old!" He spoke like a proud parent, and from the way he knocked back his glass, I gathered the Chek was the primary imbiber around here. Wouldn't have figured it, as tightly wound as he normally seemed. Thing was, it actually seemed to help his cough. He exhaled in satisfaction. "And let me tell you…you haven't seen anything half so funny as a bunch of drunk Devoid after a harvest celebration."

"I…guess I could try a glass as well," said Mari, smiling. I raised an eyebrow at her.

"What?" she spat. "You're not my father, so shove off, Pyk." She took a big gulp and doubled over in a fit of coughing. Amadi chuckled and pounded on her back.

"Whoooo, that's got a kick," she wheezed before sitting back and continuing with much more delicate sips. Korbos sloshed back his second. I was going to have to keep an eye on that.

"So!" began Eljin, crossing his legs and leaning back, "The short version of my tale is that Her High Ladyship ruined my life, and I'll see her burn for it."

His face darkened, white eyebrows furrowing so much they nearly touched in the middle. The edge in his voice could have cut firewood.

"I actually worked for her, once, you know. Heh. When I was younger."

I sat forward.

"My wife—Order's light shine upon her—and I were thralls in Kaira's great temple. The Temple of Kol. Hah! Temple of Carnal, more like. The things that…woman…gets up to in there would curl your toes, make no mistake of it. Heh.

"I was just a lowly custodian. Kept the halls swept, the privies clean and orderly, that sort of thing. But my wife, ahhhh. Hethera was handmaiden to the High Lady herself. And a damned good one, too! She lived to serve that...woman. Preparing her hair, applying her makeup, procuring the latest fashions. Heh. The Host tend to go through servants like a scythe through wheat, I'll tell you, but Hethera performed her duties for near on thirty years. Since we was young teens. Long enough for us to get complacent, in any case. To think we actually mattered to Kaira.

"Like I said, I was pretty much a nobody in the Temple of Kol. Just another faceless minion tooling about in the shadows and avoiding the attention of the higher-ups. The courtesans. The Inori priests. The Hostguard. Hundreds of folk always coming and going at all hours of the day. They all tended to overlook me, and that was the way I liked it. Heh. Let my wife have all the glory, I thought. I was perfectly happy to do my job well enough and then fade into the background.

"Hethera, though, she loved the attention she received as one of Kaira's subordinates. We had a pretty lush set of apartments in the upper-mid levels of the temple, and we didn't want for anything while in Kaira's care. Compared to most people in Elarin, we lived like kings. Hethera called me her Royal Janitor. Hah. But when all was said and done, we were no more than pampered slaves with a puffed-up sense of importance."

He leaned his head back, staring at the ceiling.

"Which we were...forcefully reminded of, one day. Thirty years of service, and all it took was one mistake. One big mistake."

He leaned forward and rubbed his face.

"The temple is enormous, you know. I spent a big chunk of my life cleaning and caretaking that palace, and there were entire wings I never entered. Custodial staff was rotated throughout different sections, but as my wife's husband, I was afforded the slight privilege of keeping to my preferred zone throughout the years. I liked to stay where I could see and be around my love, you understand.

"There was one level, however, where *nobody* was allowed. Host only. Maybe the Guard-Captain, on occasion. Most folks in the place didn't even know about it. And of course that's where my wife's mistake comes into play. I guess, after so many years, the temptation just grew too much for her. She snuck in, and whatever she saw in that floor scared her badly enough that she couldn't stay in the temple any longer.

"I mean, we knew the sorts of things that Kaira and her brother Kalos got up to. I personally saw her lose her temper with some sort of envoy once. Fattest man I ever saw in my life, and she rendered him into his basic components like a block of cheese thrown into an oven. Order anyway, the mess I had to clean. Heh. We knew what they were, but better to serve than be subjugated, am I right?

"So, what Hethera encountered scared her worse than thirty years of combined luxury and atrocities put together. She wanted to leave, *right then*, and if she was that terrified then I wanted no part of it any longer. I left her alone in our apartments and went to gather up some traveling supplies. It was stupid, and by the time I got back, it was all over."

He shuddered, a disconcerting thing to see from such a swarthy man. Mari gasped and drained the last of her glass.

"At first, I thought the rooms had been repainted while I was gone. It just...didn't register. That the red coating everything in that den was the only bit left of the woman I loved. There wasn't even anything left to bury. Just the shredded clothes she'd been wearing, and this."

He pulled a fine-linked chain from under his shirt, upon which hung a silver ring, before tucking it back. Amadi leaned over and handed Eljin a tumbler of whiskey, which he drained at a gulp.

"Ahhh," he sighed, wiping his eye. "Thank you, sir. So! I passed out and came to hours later soaked in my wife's remains. Kaira hadn't even sent someone to clean up. Heh. I gathered up what supplies I'd dropped, grabbed a stash of money and jewels we'd set aside, covered up with a big cloak, and got out of there as quick as I could. Didn't even bother to change clothes.

"I can't say I was thinking straight, but my natural reclusiveness did me a favor that day. Nobody paid me any mind as I slunk out. I don't believe anyone ever realized I was gone. Still think it's a miracle nobody noticed the bloody clothes under my cloak. Maybe they did, and the look on my face warned 'em off.

"I spent nearly a year traveling place to place, always staying away from population centers. I wanted nothing to do with people, you understand. People meant unwanted attention, and unwanted attention could have gotten back to Kaira. I felt like she was hunting me. Pfah! She barely even knew I existed, but it was a hard feeling to shake.

"Came the day when I had no other choice. I'd been living in a cave for months, and I was starving. Game had dried up over the winter, and I'd not stored enough aside. Heh. I'd been surviving, but what did I really know of foraging and survival? I'd spent twenty years inside a Chaos-damned *palace*, for the love of Order. So, I didn't have a choice. I had to go to town."

Amadi grunted and closed his eyes.

"It couldn't even rightly be called a town. Just some dusty crossroads at the edge of a big jungle, with a couple of mercantiles, an inn, and a rowdy tavern. I used a few of the jewels and stocked up on food, new clothing, and a deck of cards to keep myself entertained. Heh. That *bhaka* of a shopkeep ripped me off something fierce.

"It was there, as I was leaving that crossroads, that my worst fear came true. Outside the bar was a small regiment of Hostguard. Four of 'em. They were gathered around a small figure—looked like a child—huddled on the ground. A few were kicking it, and those tiny cries of anguish were the worst assault on my ears.

"Something in me just snapped. In my head, all I could see were Hostguard strutting around Kaira's palace. The embodiment of the Host's will. Their enforcers. Good enough stand-in for the real thing, I figured, and I. Just. Snapped.

"Alls I had for weapons were a belt knife I'd taken with me from the Temple of Kol and a long walking staff I'd carved to stay busy. I didn't even think as I started laying into those bug-armored bastards. Hah! Dropped two of 'em before the rest even knew what was happening. Took down a third while the last was turning to raise that bloody pike of theirs. I was facing him down when the small person on the ground hopped up and buried a knife where that armor of theirs don't protect. He dropped, and there I was face to face with a young Chek. Bravest little bugger I know."

He tipped his empty glass to Amadi, who returned the gesture. Mari graced the Chek with a beautiful smile and a pat on the leg. A tear was running down her cheek, bless her soul.

"So there we were, dusting ourselves off, when out of the tavern bursts the *rest* of the regiment. They see us standing there over the bodies of their mates, and they start coming.

"I ain't been that scared since, I'll tell you that. I knew if they didn't just kill me outright, they'd eventually take me back to Kaira. Heh. And that just wasn't gonna happen, if I had any say in the matter."

Eljin reached out his glass for a refill, taking a milder sip this time. He licked his lips.

"Two or three, I might could have taken. Dunno if you've noticed, but I'm a fair-sized fellow. Back then, I could have stood a chance against two or three. But not five. Not without the element of surprise.

"Me and the Chek, we look at each other, then turn and take off down the road with Chaos itself on our heels. I figured there was no way they'd be able to get through the jungle with all that armor on, so I steered us off-road and into the mess.

"Turned out they're perfectly capable of storming through the jungle. There was several times I just knew we were frokked. I dunno how long we led them on that chase, but my ribs were fit to bust and we were completely lost. Even if we'd been able to lose 'em, I dunno if we'd have ever found our way out of that jungle.

"But of course, we didn't lose 'em. Got cornered at the edge of this pretty lagoon. The waterfall was beautiful, but all I could see was our place of dyin'. There was no way out; no way we'd have been able to climb those rock faces. We turned and readied ourselves to fight when out of the jungle step these things out of a nightmare. Crusty, scary, well…you understand. Not like I had any idea at the time what the Devoid were, much less the Aka. Please don't take any offense, Oben."

"None at all, Eljin," Oben replied. It crossed its legs, resting its hands on knee, shin, and ankle.

"Well, they take one look at the Hostguard and just obliterate them in less time than it takes me to tell it."

"Servants of the *liaga* will ever be our foes," Oben stated in a dire chorus that made the hair on my neck stand up. Korbos slugged back another shot of whiskey.

"The Chek and I—we hadn't even had the chance to exchange names—were about to mess our pants at this point, all huddled together at the water's edge and terrified beyond reason. Then, you know what happens? Old Oben here walks right up to me and asks if it can be of assistance! Hah!

"You can guess the rest after that. They led us here, and we set up shop. Been here ever since, staying away from the outer world and living the best we can. That's been, ohhh...twenty-two years?" He looked to Amadi, who confirmed with a nod. "Yeah, twenty-two years ago now."

Eljin took another long sip from his drink as Korbos refilled his own glass.

"So that's our story," the old man continued. "Now you know we've got just as much reason as anyone to hate the Host and their ilk."

Cassidy frowned. "And a rousing tale it was, Master Eljin, but I don't see what that has to do with our current situation."

"Hah! To the point, I like that, lass! I tell you our story to say this: The Aka don't lie when they say they're happy to offer help. Especially to those who'd defy the Host. I believe, if you'll let me spread yer troubles around the glen, that we can help you get back to your *Storm* and on your way to do whatever it is you need to do. If you'd go against Kaira, we'll get you back on yer path."

"Hmmm..." muttered Korbos. "That assistance would be greatly appreciated, Master Dhovra. And what of your...favor? In return?"

"Heh. Well...we'll get to that. We'll get to that in time, indeed."

TWENTY FOUR

With our story time wound down, the group broke apart. Oben and Eljin left to spread word of our need throughout the Aka. Telling his tale seemed to have invigorated the old man. He walked taller and with purpose as they exited the Lau Tuai. His steps seemed less frail.

Mari, Cassidy, and Amadi adjourned to the kitchen to begin dinner preparations. I was on my way to join them when a large hand dropped onto my shoulder.

"Pyk," Korbos intoned, "can I have a word?"

"Sure," I replied. "What's up?"

"Let's get out of everyone's way for a minute." He started up the spiral staircase. I shrugged and followed, stretching out on Mari's bed and lacing my hands behind my head once we reached the room.

"So what's the deal?" I asked.

"We need to talk about Cassidy."

I sat up, cautious. "What about her?"

Korbos hesitated for a long moment, running his finger along the edge of his bed. At least he'd left the whiskey downstairs.

"She's been a help, but I don't know that we can trust her, Pyk," he said at last. "Parts of her story don't make sense, and the further we get into this debacle, the harder it's going to become to have her entangled with us. If we can't depend on her, I'd prefer we cut her loose now, before it gets too difficult to let her go."

I gawked, unable to gather my thoughts. "What possible reason could you have to not trust her after what we've been through?" I finally blurted.

"Don't get me wrong, Pyk. She's been a good companion thus far, but don't forget that she's in this for the money. We haven't known her that long. And she's not telling us the entire truth when it comes to certain things."

"What things? Where do you get off calling her a liar, Korbos?" I was getting angry and defensive, I knew, but I couldn't help it. I didn't want to hear anything against Cassidy, not when I was still trying to sort out my feelings toward her.

The big man eyed me, then gave a tired sigh. "This is why I didn't want to bring it up," he muttered, "but it needs to be done. She's had the *Storm* a couple of months, right? That's what she told us on the way to the Southern Reach. That Hightide was her first port of call after teaching herself to fly it?"

"Yeah? So?"

"So, how did she already have an agreement with the Strigori for fuel? How did she already know their language? The impression I got was that she had a long-term partnership with them. She knew exactly how much fuel to bring back to the *Storm*. She *knew where to steal it* while we distracted the village. Where it was stockpiled. That's not the sort of thing you just set up in a few weeks."

"You can't know that, Korbos. Maybe she'd visited the place when she was with the Seekers and learned the language then. Way easier to set up a business partnership with folk you're already familiar with, right?"

"I suppose it's possible, but not very likely. You saw the primitiveness of that village. Strigori don't normally make money off tarbrine. They'd trade for food and necessities, when they can even trade at all. Most skipship owners are insanely rich and just take what they need. Or have people take it for them.

"At best, they import it and give payment to the sort of unscrupulous characters who raid the islands. For Cassidy to have a direct line to the tarbrine, that's a relationship that requires time and effort to establish. So what she told us makes no sense."

"I...uhhh..." I didn't know what to say. He had a point.

"Consider this as well," he continued. "Cassidy said she found the signara in that Second Battalion storehouse of hers. Which I know for a fact is a lie. Imperial military were absolutely not allowed access to signara, ever. Or their synthminds. The Imperium kept it that way to protect against a coup. High-level governmental administrative access only. All the signara were destroyed in the Ruin, aside from the one we now carry. The one my creator possessed. So there's no possible way she found it in that depot."

"You're just guessing now, Korbos. There's no way you can know that for sure."

"I'm not guessing, Pyk, I *know*!" he exclaimed, pulling the signara from his belt pouch beside the bed and holding it in front of my face. "Please, trust me on this. I've spent an untold amount of time searching for this device. I've travelled the entire continent, and this is the only one left! And...*and*...!"

He paused, eye locking on mine.

"Think back to when we met her. When she burst into my shop. She said, 'I was told you'd pay me good money for this thing.' *So who told her I'd take it from her?*"

My jaw dropped. I was silent. I'd forgotten all about that.

"Kalos and Kaira are the only two people on this planet who knew what I am. So who in Order's light would have sent her to me? Who else would know that I was searching for a signara? And why send it with Cassidy as an intermediary?"

I had no idea how to respond. Just sat there, hands on my knees, quiet and thoughtful.

"Pyk, I know this is difficult. I know you're becoming...well, I know it's difficult. But we need to figure out how far we can trust her before it's too late."

"Oh," came a furious voice from the door. "I think it might be too late already."

Cassidy stood in the door frame, face flushed and clenched fists shaking at her sides. My stomach flip-flopped. How much had she heard?

"Eavesdropping, now?" asked Korbos in a cool tone.

"I was *going* to let you guys know what's for dinner," she said, voice rising, "and here you sit talking drek about me? About whether you can *trust* me? Don't worry, you won't have to wonder much longer. When we get back to *my* ship, you're going to pay me the money you owe, and then I'm *gone*."

She turned and strode away. I could hear her stomping down the staircase, the metal rattling with each heavy step. I looked to Korbos, who was frowning.

"Thanks, mate," I spat. "Good job." Then I ran after Cassidy.

She made it out to the clearing before I caught up with her, spinning in fury as I laid a hand on her shoulder.

"Don't!" she screamed, pointing a finger to my nose. "My business is my own, Pyk! You'll know what *I* decide to tell you about me, and not a frokking thing more. Don't forget, I don't know you, either. How can I trust people that drag me into danger and then talk drek about me behind my back?"

She threw her hands up.

"Since I joined up with you *bhakas*, I've been chased, fought Hostguard, had ships thrown at me, stabbed at, almost been bitten by monsters, nearly fell off a mountain-sized building, and dragged through a frokking jungle! It's almost not worth the money!" With each point she stomped forward, stabbing her finger into my chest and driving me back a corresponding step.

I raised my hands in surrender. "You're right! You're right. I'm so sorry. I didn't mean to hurt you, I swear. You've saved my backside several times now, and you don't deserve this sort of treatment. I know that, but… you've gotta understand that Korbos has his own issues."

"Damn right he does," she said, sighing and resting her hands on her hips. "Look, Pyk, he caught me off-guard. I've been wanting to talk to you about *him*, and I thought I'd missed my chance. That he'd turned you against me."

I cocked my head. Why would Korbos want to turn me against her? I understood the reasoning behind his apprehensions, but I hadn't gotten any sense of malice from the conversation.

"That's not his style, Cassidy," I said. "And you have to admit, his concerns are valid. He raised some interesting questions."

She huffed, face going red again. "Well if that's how it's going to be..." She turned to stomp off.

"Chaos damn it all, will you stop and talk to me?" I spun her around, grasping both shoulders. A moment later I let go in a hurry, mainly due to the razor-sharp blade that pressed against my throat. At least she hadn't pulled the gun.

"Okay, okay, cool down," I murmured, not wanting to move my jaw or throat any more than necessary. My eyes darted; the Aka passing by were beginning to stare at us. "We're, uh, we're attracting attention."

She sheathed the blade at the small of her back, and I exhaled in relief.

"Cassidy, I'm on your side here," I said, anguished. I tried to put every ounce of my emotions into my statement. "I...I don't want to lose you. Don't leave us. Not a single person in this group makes friends with any sort of ease, and you just...you just click. You *fit* with us. We all make a good team. You belong with us. You...well..."

I stared into her eyes, unable to continue. Those beautiful green eyes, locked on to my sea blues.

"Yes?"

"Order anyway," I whispered. "You belong with me." I squeezed my eyes shut, waiting for the inevitable punch to the nose.

When one didn't land, I cracked an eyelid to see her standing there, staring at me with furrowed brows. I actually flinched as she raised a hand, and she hesitated for a second before cupping my face. I felt myself flush, and she gave a tiny laugh.

At first I was encouraged. That had to be good, right? But there was a deprecating current underneath her mirth. Was she laughing at me or herself? She gave a brief shake of her head and tossed me a smile that made my knees wobble.

"Oh, Pyk," she said. "You beautiful idiot. Your timing is unbelievable. So, so bad."

My heart dropped. That definitely *wasn't* good.

She sighed again. "I…I like you. I really do." My heart shot back up into my throat. "But I've got my own issues to deal with, Guts. There's way too much happening to get involved with someone and drag them into my own mess. Maybe…maybe if things were different…" she trailed off.

"Have you *seen* the state of my life lately?" I pleaded. "I can handle a little bit of mess."

Cassidy laughed, bright and clear in the meadow. Masina Atoa, the full moon, shone overhead as nightlings danced around us. She looked beautiful. I froze as she leaned forward, stretching up to brush her lips against my cheek. The skin there burned as she pulled away. It was the closest thing to a perfect moment that I'd ever experienced.

"I like being around all of you," she said. "You all feel like family—even Bastin—and that's something I haven't had in a long, long time. But that's precisely why I'm not going to drag you into my problems. Once we get back to the ship, we're going to have to part ways. I just hope you know that I'd never do anything to hurt any of you."

That was not so perfect, but I nodded. Funny thing was, I *did* know she meant it, somehow. I didn't understand, but I knew she was being honest.

"So," I croaked. Gods, my voice was hoarse. I cleared my throat. "What did you want to say about Korbos?"

A troubled look crossed her face. "Just...watch out for him, Pyk. I know he loves you and Mari, maybe even thinks of you as his own family, but he's been...erratic about this quest of his. Putting you two in danger. You almost got killed in that Strigori village. He sent Mari across that sea of Devoid without a second thought."

A squealing piglet ripped past us, chased by a torch-wielding Aka. Another small group followed, herded along to bed down for the night.

"He also saved all our bacon a dozen times," I said.

Pyk Belloc, ladies and gentlebeings, master of comedic timing.

"True, but I worry about you two when you're with him. He's been single-minded about this whole thing with the signara, and I don't want you getting killed due to his obsession. Not to mention the issue of his drinking. I'm not too proud to admit his little outburst in the Turris Imperialis scared me out of my mind. That business with the *Storm*'s fuel capacitor could have given us all a bad case of death. Who in the fires of Chaos gets drunk when surrounded by a city full of monsters?"

"Yeah, I'm keeping an eye on that. But don't you see? That's another reason we need you around! You know he'll only get worse the longer this goes on. What happens when we don't have the *Storm* to get about?"

I threw my arms wide. "Moreover, what are we supposed to do now with the signara? No Imperium synthmind, no way to get at that information, no way to use it to bring down the Host!"

"I know, Guts, but—"

"Excuse us," came a grating, multilayered voice. I turned to see Oben and Eljin standing right behind us, both wearing identical puzzled expressions.

"Apologies, friend Pyk. We do not mean to eavesdrop, but did I overhear you mention a signara?"

Chaos burn my loud mouth.

"I think you might have misheard me, Oben *tita moolah*." The Na'don's shrunken lips flattened at my butchery of its language. "We were just discussing—"

Hold up.

Oben was just as old as the Host themselves. Didn't it stand to reason that it'd know about the signara? Could it know where…? I quickly weighed the risks in my mind and came to a decision.

I turned to Cassidy, taking her hand in mine. "Can we please finish this later? I absolutely want to continue, but we need to talk to Korbos *now*."

She nodded, confused.

I sighed. "Thank you. I promise we'll talk." I turned to Oben and Eljin. "Please, come with me, you need to see something."

I led the group back to the Lau Tuai at a brisk walk, just shy of a jog, my mind racing. Several Aka waved to me from the rope bridges above, and I returned it half-heartedly, distracted. Behind me I heard Eljin's loud whisper to Oben. "What the frok is a signara?"

We filed through the door to find Korbos, Mari and Amadi on the couches, staring at the fire. Korbos was sipping a whiskey.

"Hey," I began. "Oben needs to see the cube."

"Order above, Pyk," Korbos groaned, throwing his hands in the air. "What else did you tell them? My boot size?"

I had the decency to blush. "They, uh, sort of overheard me talking. Loudly. About it. The signara. But Oben knows what they are! It's your age, right? Maybe it…?" I finished in a rush.

Korbos's eyebrows shot up, then furrowed in consideration. It was plain the thought hadn't yet occurred to him. "One second," he said, setting down his drink and heading up the staircase. A few moments later he returned with his belt, and we started the laborious process of clearing a spot on the humongous table at the center of the room.

It wasn't easy, what with all the books, papers, and apparatus strewn about.

The seven of us crowded around the table as Korbos removed the signara from its pouch and set it in the center of the cleared area. An atonal hum of surprise came from Oben as its warm glow shone outward, reflecting from the glass beakers and tubes still on the table.

"Near on a millennia has passed since I last saw one of the signara," it said. "Gone, I thought they all were. Where in Order's name did you find it?"

Korbos looked at me. "You unfurled this sail. You trim it."

I nodded and began to fill in the missing parts of my earlier story, beginning with Cassidy's revelation of the cube and ending with a description of the trashed synthmind we'd found in Cortian.

"So I was thinking," I said, "that maybe Oben might know of a drive somewhere. A synthmind Korbos might have missed in his search? We're sailing a windless sea without one, so it can't hurt to ask."

"Hmmmm…" Oben's chest rumbled in layered notes. "Help you I cannot, sire Pyk, though I wish with all my being that I could. Only one signara drive did the Na'don possess, and it was destroyed in the Ruin nine hundred years gone."

My shoulders dropped, defeated. That was it. I was out of ideas.

Korbos scoffed and tossed back his whiskey at a gulp. Mari and Amadi conferred softly, and the rest remained silent, staring down at the glowing cube.

Long moments passed.

"The Aka have agreed to get you back to your skipship," Eljin stated. "So there's that. Whenever you're ready to continue yer journey, they'll be there to help."

"Eljin," piped Amadi, laying a hand on his friend's arm. "You have to tell them."

I looked up. "Tell us what?"

"I was getting to that, eh? Heh," the old man replied, placing a hand on the Chek's shoulder with a fond smile. Amadi returned it before he was wracked with a fit of coughing.

Eljin stood up a little straighter. "First off, describe to me again that smashed thing you found in Cortian. Synthmind, wasn't it?"

Korbos crossed his arms, tilting his head in curiosity. "Dark gray box, about the size of a small crate and the color of charcoal, with bright blue lights in a starlike pattern on the front panel." He poked his fingers in the air to illustrate. "One, two-two-two, one, one. The star symbol of the old Imperium. It was hooked to a single—or maybe a pair, I don't recall—of monitors. Flat screens that project images on their surface. A clamp-like device on top, big enough to hold the cube."

Eljin exhaled through his nose, hard.

"Order's light blind me," he murmured. "That's the one."

I leaned forward, palms on the table, excitement racing through me. Korbos's eye widened a fraction, and he raised his chin in a sharp inhale.

"I didn't quite tell you the whole story earlier. Heh. About my wife and what she saw in that lower level of the temple." He picked up the signara, and I felt Korbos tense beside me. Cassidy, trying to be as casual as possible, rested her hand on the butt of her gun. "Didn't wanna send anyone to bed with nightmares, you understand."

He set the cube back on the table, and a soft sigh escaped me before I could stop it. Eljin looked to me and winked, the wrinkles around his eye creasing deep.

"I may have implied that I didn't know what was down there, but that's not the truth. Hethera told me. Before…well, you know. Heh. She told me, she did, and by Chaos that's what got my backside a'movin.

"That bottom floor weren't nothing but a big warehouse, she said. A big, long, wide hallway with glass-walled rooms lining each side. All manner of crazy metal tables and sharp instruments in each one. Huge containers full of bubbling liquids.

"But what scared her so bad was the tanks, see. Going down the length of that hallway, she said, was these tall tubes, filled to the brim with bodies. Horrible, monstrous things, she said, so she did, all black claws and eyes and rending teeth. She swore up and down that they was looking at her as she passed through. Heh. Terrified her something fierce, but she kept going. Drawn in further, Order bless her curious soul.

"At the end of the hall, see, there was this massive wall of boxes and these 'screens' you mentioned. Dozens of 'em. Hundreds of flashing lights, and the pictures moving on the screens showed different rooms throughout the temple. Heh. Hethera swore she could see everyone in the place all at once.

"She was entranced by them pictures. By the thought that the High Lady could watch the moves of every being in that temple at any time. I've no idea how long she was down there, just staring, but she caught a peculiar movement out of the biggest monitor in front of her. It was Kaira herself, sittin' on her throne, staring straight at Hethera. Like the High Lady knew she was there.

"Well, the missus shrieked her fool head off and dropped the handbag she'd been clutching, where it banged off one of them flashy boxes. She remembered it, 'cause she said it didn't look like any of the others. It stuck in her mind as she was scrambling out of there like the fires of Chaos itself were roasting her feet."

Eljin leaned in conspiratorially, arching an eyebrow.

"A charcoal gray box with a clamp on the top, bright blue lights in a star down the front."

Mari and Cassidy looked to each other in wonder.

Korbos dropped his hands to his side and clenched his fists as he took an involuntary half-step forward, his expression triumphant.

"That's it!" he exclaimed. "Kaira has one! Where?! Where is this Temple of Kol, Eljin?"

The old man sighed. "If you must know, then this is where I'll ask my favor of you."

"Yes, yes, anything. Don't draw it out, man. I *have* to know where that synthmind is."

"The favor I request is that I go with you. I owe that *bhuta* for twenty-two years of pain and hurt, and if you're heading into a confrontation, then…well, I want a piece of it."

Korbos reined in his excitement, giving the old man a shrewd look. "You're not leaving me much of a choice in the matter, Master Dhovra."

"Hah! Nope. Nope, I'm not."

"Very well, then. Now *where*?"

"The Temple of Kol is about a month's hard ride south of Jipar, right on the edge of the Mohagan desert. Heh. It's all nestled in amongst a bunch of flat-top hills, with a long approach and nothing but sand and slopes stretching off behind it."

Korbos grunted as if he'd been gut-punched. He stumbled back a step, off balance, swiping the bottle of moss whiskey from the table. He staggered to a chair, plopping down and missing the seat entirely, winding up on the floor with the bottle in his mouth and turned straight up to the heavens.

"Korbos? Korbos!" I yelled, alarmed at his reaction. Cassidy and Mari rushed to his side as he lowered the bottle and stared into nothingness.

"Mate, what's going on?" I asked, shaking him by the arm. "You're scaring me, buddy."

He just stared, expression blank. A long moment went by, then he took another quick shot from the bottle before climbing to wobbly feet.

"The temple wasn't always there," he said in a shaky voice completely unlike his usual booming baritone. "It was built later."

"Aye," said Eljin, looking to my friend with concern. "Took near on a hundred-fifty years to build, so I was told, and wasn't completed until around two hundred ago."

Korbos burst out in a gale of bitter laughter. There was an edge of hysteria to it that I didn't care for, and my friends and I exchanged nervous glances.

"Figures," Korbos said before slamming another gulp. "It figures."

"Korbos, what the frok is going on, mate?" I asked. "Do you know the spot or something?"

He scrubbed a hand across his mouth. "Yeah. Yeah, I know it. It was a laboratory once. Mother's bunker laboratory. Kaira built her temple on top of the lab where Mother created the Host."

He shuddered. "The lab where I was made."

TWENTY FIVE

Light bloomed through the dense foliage surrounding the clearing, and we stumbled about, packing away gear and supplies, eyes still bleary from too little sleep. Just past dawn and we were ready to go, our clothing cleaned and mended, our packs refilled and shouldered. We decided against another harness for Bastin, and Mari perched between his shoulders, freshly-fitted reins in hand.

I stared at Eljin as he strode out to meet us. The old man's bearing had changed dramatically since we first arrived. Where he at first seemed frail and weakened—despite his large size—he now walked with a straight back, head high, and a spring in his step. He wasn't leaning on his walking stick nearly so much, though he carried it with him still. The prospect of adventure—or maybe just good old-fashioned revenge—had infused him with a renewed vigor.

Amadi, on the other hand, worried me. He seemed more fragile than ever, stifling a near-constant cough and moving with a hunch that gave him the appearance of being smaller than even Mari.

"Will he be able to make the trek?" I asked Eljin in a low whisper. Not low enough, apparently.

"I'll be fine, sire Pyk," replied the Chek with some pique. "Where Eljin goes, I go." I nodded to him, somewhat ashamed, and he barked out a few rough hacks.

"Ah, he's got the way of it, boy!" said Eljin, wrapping a thick arm around Amadi's tiny shoulders and setting off another round of coughing. "We'll get some warm tincture in him a'fore we set off and he'll be right as rain. Heh."

"Fair enough." I sighed, not looking forward to another hike through the jungle, even considering the added benefit of our Aka escort.

Eljin had persuaded twelve to accompany us—Oben leading them, an enormous long-handled blade strapped to its back—and they milled about us, talking amongst themselves and double-checking supplies. Each carried a six-foot spear. Something felt a bit off; the Aka kept giving us strange looks, and the few I tried to make conversation with were a little more brusque than I would have expected. A bit unnerving, given their overall resemblance to the creatures we were hoping to avoid.

I mentioned it to Oben, and all I got in return was a cryptic "Concerned are the Aka, friend Pyk. Events proceed quickly." Nothing more.

At last, everyone's gear was stowed, farewells were said, and we headed into the jungle. I paused for a moment at the treeline, taking a long final look at the Lau Tuai and the surrounding quiet village. I sort of envied the Aka their life here. Simple. Away from the chaos and stress of the outside world. There was a definite appeal. I had a harder time turning away from it than I would have expected.

"Come on, Guts," Cassidy said, putting a hand on my arm and steering me toward our future, whatever may come.

We took a western heading, angled slightly to the south, which Oben explained to me would bypass Cortian itself and take us almost directly to the *Storm*. As we moved further and further from the Lau Tuai, we passed the occasional overgrown ruin of some ancient building or another, lone sentinels standing sparse vigil throughout the jungle. I wondered what sort of people had lived or worked so far removed from the city center.

"So," I asked the Na'don as we walked, "you were in Cortian when the *laigan* dropped her stuff over the city, right? Did you live there?"

"*Liaga*," it corrected me. Order anyway, I was never going to pronounce those words correctly. "Yes, my unit was assigned to Cortianis."

It fell silent.

"Soooo," I continued, "can you tell me what the city was like?"

"Crowded."

I blinked. Nothing else was forthcoming. Why was Oben being so short with me? Had I done something to offend? Puzzled, I drew back a few paces, falling in with my human and Chek companions. All the Aka walked ahead of my group, alert and scanning the jungle around us. I remembered how relaxed they'd been after first rescuing us, and I wondered what had changed.

"I'm worried about Korbos," Cassidy said in a low voice. "He hasn't been right since last night."

I knew what she meant. The big man had fallen almost completely silent since his revelation. He walked alone, away from either group, nursing a bottle of Eljin's whiskey. Bulwark thumped against his back as he trudged heavily through the brush.

I hadn't known he'd brought the liquor with him.

"Give me a minute," I said, steeling myself and stomping over to him, sticks and downed foliage crunching under my boots. He said nothing as I approached, just giving me a quick side eye before turning the bottle up in a pull.

"You really think that's a good idea right now?" I asked, keeping my voice down.

He didn't respond.

"Korbos. Mate. You've got to pull it together, man. This isn't the best time to be knocking it back like that. Remember what happened in Cortian?"

I reached for the bottle, then squawked as he snatched me off the ground by my shirt. Literally off the ground. My feet hung several inches in the air as he pulled me close at eye level. His good eye shimmered silver.

"Keep your hands to yourself, Pyk. And leave me be."

Each time he'd directed that silver sheen at me before, I'd cowered in bowel-loosening fear, but at that moment it was only making me angry. Really angry. What in Chaos's fires was *wrong* with him?

"Frok you, man! Order only knows how many Devoid are around here, and you're drowning yourself in spirits and pushing away the only people who actually give a damn about you! Get your head right!"

I punctuated the statement by shoving his chest, causing him to drop me in surprise. His eye, nearly obscured by his furrowed brow, looked down at me with frustration.

"What's the point?" he hissed. "We can't go there. That lab is death—at best—for all of you. Don't you get it, Pyk? I swore *I'd never go back there*!"

I sneered at him in disgust. "So that's it? You're just going to crawl into a bottle and quit because you're scared?"

"Yes, damn it! I can't lose you like I lost Rin!" His shoulders sagged. "I…I can't take that. Not again. You're damn right I'm scared."

"Kor, we came of our own choice, remember? We're with you 'til the end."

"Not Cassidy," he said, looking over to where she was laughing with Mari and Amadi.

My chest tightened. I had no response to that. He had a point.

"Besides, 'the end' is what I'm worried about, Pyk. Go away." His tone brooked no argument.

That hurt. Hurt more than I would have expected. It wasn't like the big man to be so dismissive toward me. I shook my head and left him to his drink, returning to the others.

Mari took my hand. "Everything okay?"

"No. Not really."

She patted my arm, throwing a quick glance at our big friend.

"He'll come around," she said. I wasn't so sure.

"Amadi," said Cassidy, "I've been meaning to ask. What's with the little fuzzy guys here?"

The furry white cat-things were all around us, keeping pace with the company and darting in and out of the brush in random intervals. They'd followed us from the moment we left the Lau Tuai clearing.

Amadi laughed, which turned into a choked cough. "The felis? Cute, aren't they?"

I couldn't attest to their cuteness. Not when the one near my foot looked up and hissed, black eyes glittering over a tiny maw of shark's teeth.

"They have an affinity for the Aka," the Chek continued. "No idea why, but they're almost domesticated. Felis will follow the Aka whenever they travel and even fight for them if need arises. I'd never even heard of the things before I wound up here with Eljin, but I've come to enjoy them."

"I'll say!" cried Mari. One of the furballs, with a star-like blond marking on its forehead, had leapt into her arms to be petted. "Oh I just think they're so cute and hey Pyk we should take one back to Hightide with us if we ever go back do you think we'll ever go back I guess it's possible we might not for a while if we have to go to this temple thing and—"

She cut off as the felis she was holding arched its back in alarm at her tirade. It didn't scratch her, thankfully, but hurled itself to the ground, landing on six nimble, claw-tipped feet. It stretched and yawned, mouth gaping, and took up its pace alongside us again.

Cassidy grinned. "I don't think they like chatterboxes, Mari."

I afforded a small smirk, but my mind was elsewhere. I couldn't get Korbos's behavior out of my head. How in Order's light was I going to get through to him?

Three hours later we were still continuing on the same southwestern heading, busying ourselves with small talk as we followed some sort of game trail. I could hear the gurgle of a nearby stream, or maybe a small river.

Korbos still hadn't joined the group. The Aka were still being standoffish. I'd been able to have a few small conversations with Oben, but the rest hadn't said so much as a word to us. I didn't get a sense of dismissal from them, or even disinterest. Just disapproval. The jumble of emotions and attitudes from all sides made for a very tense hike.

The convoy made its way down a sloping hill to an impossibly blue stream pool at the base of a small cascading waterfall. We took a short rest, and Mariyana tiptoed across the stream to begin climbing the steplike rocks on the other side.

"I can see Cortian!" she cried down. "Well, the wall and some buildings at least, it's way closer than I thought it would be so hey maybe we're close to the *Storm* oh this is so exciting and—"

It went on like that for a while.

I was kneeling down to refill my canteen when Oben placed two of its hands on my shoulder.

"Soon we will be reaching the old suburbs of Outer Cortianis," it said in its dire, layered tones. "Much more dangerous. Devoid have stayed away from us thus far. They fear the Aka and keep their distance. But as the old city grows around us, braver and more numerous will they become. More difficult it will be for Aka to keep them away."

I nodded in understanding. I knew it only meant to warn me, but that didn't bode well for the Aka's ability to keep us as safe as promised.

Oben's prediction turned out to be correct. Within thirty minutes we stepped out of the thick jungle into a familiar vista of shattered and overgrown quickcrete roads. Foliage-shrouded structures loomed on either side of us, sparse at first but quickly condensing to green walls boxing us in as we proceeded on our course. The Aka spread out into a wide circle around the living, necks craning in all directions as they kept watch. Houses gave way to taller shops and offices, all nearly obliterated by plant growth. Retailers of the Ruin, I decided to call them.

I stepped closer to the Na'don. Good a time as any.

"Oben," I started, hesitant, "why do the Aka avoid us? Have we done something to offend you?"

It let out a heavy sigh. "No, friend Pyk. Not offend. Aka are concerned because you and your friends have released our cousins from Cortianis. Spread, they now will, and this could cause much and much distress for the Aka. We…do not begrudge your survival methods, but undone hundreds of years of our containment work, you have. Difficult it is to reconcile our assistance with the consequences of your actions.

"We do not begrudge, but neither can we ignore. So, we distance from you."

I opened my mouth to reply, then shut it. There was nothing I could say to that; by that justification, they had every right to be upset with us.

"Contact right!" came a cry.

We wheeled to see a Devoid stagger from a verdant alley. The nearest Aka stepped directly in front of it. The creature paused, its fungal mass of a head craning and sniffing. The Aka—I thought her name was Raline—reached out and turned the Devoid to face the opposite direction, then pushed it along. Raline stayed close and followed it a few steps into the alley, blocking its view of us, and then the Devoid was gone, stumbling away in pursuit of other prey. I exhaled a sigh of relief.

"More behind!" another voice cried.

Damn it all to Chaos.

A line of Devoid, jerky and oozing, moved into the street a block or two behind our company. Only five or six to begin, but quickly followed by more. And more. Soon there were twenty-five staggering toward us. Then thirty-five. Forty. The felis that had been following our trail scattered, unwilling to deal with superior numbers.

"Contact ahead!" I spun around in terror as even more began creeping from the alleys on all sides. We'd be surrounded in moments.

"Oben, we need to go!" I shouted.

"Quickly now, move we must!" it cried, waving us to stay in the center of their circle, which launched into sudden motion. The Devoid were reluctant to approach the Aka, but they began to press closer as their numbers piled up. Fungus-hidden teeth gnashed, and black-dripping claws swiped the air around our perimeter. The crush of bodies pushed closer to the Aka with each passing second.

"For Order's light, go, go!" Cassidy was screaming. She had her blade out and extended. Korbos, still silent and grim, had stowed the bottle and had Bulwark out and shouldered, though he wobbled slightly as we picked up our pace to a light jog. Eljin limped in an unsteady gait caused by his artificial leg, his hand prodding Amadi along. The poor Chek was having a tough time of it, hunched over in a teetering jog, a steady cough making it difficult for him to catch a breath. Mari was—

Wait.

"Mariyana!" I cried. "Where are Mari and Bastin? Anyone have eyes on them?"

A loud chirp sounded from a two-story office to my right. Relief washed over me upon seeing the two scurrying along the ledge of the roof, Mari waving for us to hurry. Bastin must have bolted for higher ground at the first appearance of the Devoid. Fine by me. Two less to worry about within the tightening circle in which we found ourselves. It had worked for them before, in Cortian proper, so I was glad they were out of harm's way for the moment. They bounded from rooftop to shattered rooftop, scouting ahead.

We kept up our speed, the Aka pushing through the growing mass of Devoid. They were no longer attempting to turn them away and had resorted to cutting down those impeding our path. Oben laid about with its long-handled blade, shearing what could loosely be construed as skulls from necks. I prayed to Atia and all the gods of Order above that we weren't too far from the *Storm.*

The crowd of Devoid fell behind as we made our way down the thoroughfare, dodging the soil-and-grass-covered ruins of autocarts big and small. They harried us, backing us inexorably away, though we were able to slow our pace. It felt like Amadi's wheezing could be heard for miles.

A muffled thump sounded behind me as Bastin landed nearby.

"We've got a big problem guys there's about a million Devoid ahead of us and the way is blocked off it's just a big giant building with water around it and these tall round stacks sticking out of the top but the Devoid are coming all around the sides of it and—"

"Mari!"

She stopped. Took a deep breath. "We're cut off, Pyk. The last street up the way is blocked on either side, and there's like a small lake or something along the outside edge of the road. It's not deep, but there are hundreds of Devoid coming this way."

"Drek!" I muttered under my breath. "Cassidy, can you hold things for a moment?"

She looked around, then shrugged her shoulders. We were moving at a walking speed, the Aka having reconfigured in a semicircle between us and the Devoid, their spears held out before them in an interlocked makeshift barrier. They shoved and kicked the creatures, keeping them at bay for the time being. Korbos swayed, finger twitching near his rifle's trigger.

"Show me," I said to Mariyana, then took off at a run as she spun Bastin and led the way to where the wide street we were on dead-ended—sort of—into a low quickcrete wall that stretched off in either direction. The cross-street was blocked both ways, covered by collapsed buildings and centuries of vegetation. Beyond the short wall was an expanse of dark, brackish water that looked to be maybe waist-deep.

A large white bird squawked in annoyance and flew from the branches of a mostly-dead tree growing through the center of a half-submerged autocart. I could just make out the wheels below the murky algae and oragi pads.

The only egress I could see was a passage, about seven feet wide, that continued through the low wall and across the water to a huge, blocky compound—several buildings jutting off at odd angles from each other. Large tubular chimneys, some collapsed from age, adorned the tallest central structure.

The passage—it could be barely be termed a bridge—led directly into a covered quickcrete and glass tunnel connected to the middle building, which looked to have weathered the centuries better than the others. Around the cluster of structures was a wide flat campus, dotted here and there with thick trees, utterly crawling with Devoid. Mari was right; there had to have been a thousand, maybe more. The kind from inside the city, desiccated and thin; they wandered, aimless, having not spotted us yet. That wouldn't last long, I feared.

"Oh, Pyk, look!" Mari cried, pointing. I followed her finger and lit up with hope. About a mile away—past the complex, just over the tops of the treeline—stood a tall jungle hill, switchbacks sloping up. At the crest gleamed a tiny pinpoint of reflected sunlight. The *Storm*. Right where we'd left her, what felt like a hundred years ago.

"Mmmm…" Oben hummed, coming to stand beside the group. "Long ago, this was factory land. Made aerowings here, they did. We are close, friend Pyk. Is that your ship I see reflecting the sun?"

"It is! Ha-haaaa!" I punched the air and gave Mari a jubilant hug. She leaned over from her mount and pounded me on the back.

"Would not celebrate too early, my friend," said Oben.

My excitement turned to ash as a low moan rolled across the water. The Devoid had seen us. As one, they began their stagger across the high grass of the campus.

We were in trouble. That central factory was our only option of escape, but as soon as we crossed the water the Devoid on the other side of the lake would launch themselves at the tunnel, with us in it. Order alive, though, *we were so close*!

I wheeled around. "Cassid—" I began, cutting off in shock as I realized how close the group had advanced. Our pilot and Korbos were mere steps away, the Aka stretched across the avenue and shoving back the Devoid for all they were worth. We were out of time.

"This way!" I cried, pointing to the pathway. Cassidy, Korbos, Eljin, and Amadi charged past me, following Bastin onto the bridge. Korbos was carrying the Chek, who was wracked with barking coughs. "Aka, come on!" I snapped.

Oben rushed by, and the Aka released their barricade, turning to flee. The Devoid surged forward, and I leapt into motion, catching up as best I could. Wet slaps sounded behind us as oozing feet marched onto the flat quickcrete.

We ran faster.

TWENTY SIX

Ahead, the wailing of the city Devoid rose in volume as they staggered toward us—hurling themselves over the low wall on the opposite shore—and splashed into the shallow water. Dozens emerged at once and reached out, slogging through the waist-deep liquid in an attempt to cut us off. By the time we reached the end of the bridge, arms flailed over the sides of the quickcrete barricade at left and right.

Bastin snarled as one brushed his flank, then edged toward the middle before bursting into the glass and stone tunnel. I whipped my leg up in an arcing kick, catching the face of a Devoid that had nearly climbed over the wall. My knee rang with the shock of impact, but I didn't slow. We hurtled down the tunnel, Devoid on either side of us bouncing off the thick glass plates as they threw themselves at us.

More than one began to crack as we flew past.

Mari and the others stopped before a great metal door, ribbed and rusted. There were no visible hinges. To our right was a quickcrete staircase, wide enough for two people, curving upward out of sight.

"Up, friend Pyk!"

Oben and the rest of the Aka hurried to our position, and three of them slammed their spears under the bottom of the great door. To my surprise, they levered it up several inches, and I realized that it was designed to slide upwards on tracks set into the frame.

"Up, you must go up now!" Oben cried, pointing at the stairwell. From a ways behind us came the crashing tinkle of the tunnel glass giving way. The moan increased.

I cursed. I'd had just about enough of bloody Cortian stairs.

"Go, go!" I yelled, slapping Bastin's rump to get him moving. He shot up the stairs like his tail was on fire, followed by the others. Korbos held Bulwark in one hand, using a rusty handrail to steady his steps, Amadi straddling his back with arms around the big man's neck. Eljin was panting, but otherwise seemed no worse for our mad dash. I turned to Oben.

"Let's go, Oben, c'mon!" I pleaded. Five of the Aka had gotten their fingers under the door and lifted it several feet. The others rushed in to boost it higher, until the opening rose higher than their heads.

"Go, friend Pyk, we will try and lead our cousins away from you. Make your way through, and we will meet you on the other side, Order willing." It pushed me, none too gently, toward the staircase. I had time for one quick glance down the tunnel, then I was barreling my way up.

Behind me I heard the yelling and banging of the Aka attempting to get the Devoid's attention and lead them into the lower level of the factory. Before the curve of the stairwell hid them from view, I saw the horde begin their stagger through the raised door.

I was gasping for air by the time I reached the others, who stood on the third floor platform, gathered around a more standardized metal door. This one had no knob or handle, just a flat piece of metal set into the wall. I groaned. Was *any* of this going to go our way?

"Back up," Korbos snarled. His eye flared, and the door *exploded* away from the hinges, banging off the stairs with an almighty clamor. I winced, thinking of the flood of Devoid we'd only just evaded.

"Think they heard you back in Hightide?" I hissed.

He gave me a flat stare. "In."

We filed through the doorway and into a narrow hall. A few long paces and I stopped short, flabbergasted by the vista before me.

"Atia's bits and bobs," Cassidy murmured. She wasn't wrong.

The factory floor was *enormous*, the entire space filled with strange machinery of which I couldn't even begin to guess the purpose, all in various states of ruin and disrepair. Hulking, unfinished skipships occupied bays, their rusted chassis poking from among robotic construction arms like skeletal ribs.

The center of the cavernous area was home to an aerowing maybe five or six times the size of the *Storm*, its bulk extending vertically far past our view from the third floor. I could see at least five decks through the open spaces where hull plates waited forever for a welding that would never come. Catwalks and construction gantries grew around it in crystalline patterns, extending throughout the length and depth of the factory.

The floor itself writhed with Devoid—of course it did—with more flooding in through the open door below us. Oben and the Aka shoved their way through the crowd, pounding spear butts into the quickcrete floor for noise, drawing their pursuers deeper into the undulating mass.

As we stared, the rising moan of the creatures filled the air. A group of ten or fifteen rounded the corner at the end of the hall we were crowding, and a second cry rose from behind us. From the door. Some of the Devoid had followed me up the stairs. We were trapped between two flavors of creeping death.

"Frok it," snarled Korbos—Amadi still clinging to his back—as he shouldered his gun.

"Korbos, no!" Cassidy and I screamed in unison. The hall flared blue as the big man fired off a volley, disintegrating the heads of the group to our right. The noise was apocalyptic, and we all clapped hands to our ears, deafened by the blasts.

"Atia's bones, man, have you lost your mind?!" I could barely hear myself scream.

The Devoid behind us drew closer, and more rounded the corner to take the place of those that had just been dropped.

Korbos's face fell, a complex mixture of fear, anger, and frustration running over it like a swell across a deck. He settled on anger and whipped his gun around, smashing the large plate of glass closest to him. It shattered into ten thousand tiny pieces—I'd never seen glass break like that—before he brushed away the clinging fragments and climbed over, Amadi hanging on for dear life.

"Come on," he said. At least, that's what I assumed. It was like trying to hear someone speak through a thick down pillow. We got the idea, though, and scrambled through to land on a precarious section of gantry.

Korbos stayed off to one side, covering the window and allowing everyone time to get through. Amadi climbed down from his back.

I worried for a moment that Bastin wouldn't fit, but the scuridai managed to squeeze his bulk through the shattered window with little effort. He was a lot skinnier under all that fur than I would have guessed.

I banged my metal hand on the railing to get everyone's attention, then pointed in the direction of the factory's opposite wall. They took off, Eljin in the lead, followed by Cassidy, Mari, and Bastin.

I followed the scuridai, waving for Korbos and Amadi to come just as the Devoid reached the missing pane. The Chek ducked under the grasping arms. Korbos just punched the nearest Devoid in the face and brushed off the flailing claws as he stumbled forward. Once he cleared the broken section of window, he paused, taking the whiskey bottle from inside his coat and raising it to his lips.

Unbelievable. "Again, not the best time, man!" I yelled.

The gantry shuddered as Devoid dropped over the wall in pursuit. The other windows collapsed inward from the weight of bodies pressing against them, and then the chase was on. Dozens of the creatures ambulated across the metal walkway, teeth gnashing. We made our way around to a short metal staircase leading up to a long suspended catwalk that looked to run the entire length of the factory.

The group managed to stay ahead of them, barely. Though it had weathered its time well since the Ruin, the catwalk wasn't wide, and parts of it were nearly rusted through, causing uneven footing and soft spots we had to slow to avoid. The clomping of footfalls and rattling metal had reached the sea of Devoid covering the factory floor, and the answering moan was horrendous. I supposed I should have been grateful to hear it; my hearing was coming back, at least. Thousands of arms reached up to us, as though they sought to pull us from our height by sheer force of undead will. If they even had wills.

I was looking back to check on Korbos and Amadi when I slammed into Bastin's rump. I craned my neck around his bulky fluff, and fear spiked at the sight of Mariyana and Cassidy yanking at Eljin's artificial leg. It had broken through a soft spot in the metal and gotten entangled. The Devoid marched on us, staggering and bouncing off the rails. One disappeared as it hit a rusty patch and the metal gave way, sending the creature plunging down into the hungry mass below. The other Devoid never slowed, even as more fell through the hole.

"Cassidy, we gotta move!" I screamed, not taking my eyes from the wall of creatures now only about fifteen paces away.

"Working…on…it," she grunted.

"Pull harder!"

"You could come help, you know!"

I squeezed around Bastin as quickly as I could and took a look. The metal of the catwalk had bent inward but not broken, and gotten lodged in between plates of Eljin's leg.

"Push his leg down just a bit," I ordered. They complied, shoving the limb just far enough to pop the entangled bits loose. I reached down with my netanium hand and bent them further inward. Eljin yanked himself free with a ripping tear as his pants leg hung on the jutting spikes.

I rose just in time to see Korbos—Amadi at his side—shoulder his rifle and open fire on the Devoid, who had nearly reached us. Those directly in front of him went down in a spray of plasma and organic matter, and he swayed slightly as he began to sweep outward, targeting those at the edge of the walk.

The edge of the walk. Where the age-frayed suspension cables connected via rusty bolts and flaking clamps.

"NO!" I screamed. "Korbos, don't—"

Two of the cables disintegrated, letting go with a sharp *twang!* as a section of the catwalk plunged, spilling Devoid over the side and twisting free to smash into the ground beneath. I grabbed a rail and hung on for dear life, expecting the whole shimmying thing to break loose and send us to our doom.

A low creak echoed through the factory as the portion of the walk upon which Amadi and Korbos stood dropped a few inches. The big man had just enough time to lock eyes with me, then the cables snapped and it fell away, hinging downward at a sectional joint just in front of me. The two vanished.

Cass and Mari screamed behind me, and I immediately dropped to my belly. They started toward me, and I flung out a hand.

"Stay back! Get Bastin back, we don't want this one to go too!" I scooted forward, peering over the edge.

Korbos hung by one hand from the swinging catwalk. His other held onto Bulwark's strap, which was straining under the weight of Amadi, who was gripping the rifle itself.

"Pyk!" Korbos bellowed, "I'm going to swing him up to you, get ready!"

"No, don't!" replied Amadi. "I can't hold on!" The Chek's arms were trembling with the effort of gripping the massive gun's frame.

"You're going to have to climb up, then!"

"I can't, I'm too…too weak!"

"If you can yell that loudly, you can climb up. Now move it, Chek!" The big man barked orders like a peg-legged captain. "Hand over hand, that's it! Now grab the grip and put your foot on that part, yes! Now reach up and take my—"

When I looked back on events later, it was remarkable how everything seemed to slow down. You always hear folks tell stories about time distorting during traumatic moments, though I always discounted the phenomena as an old maid's tale. But it wasn't. Not this time.

Everything dropped to a crawl as Amadi reached up to take hold of Korbos's arm, a splash of excited hope washing across his face. Followed by a tiny moment of confusion. Followed by a rattling inhaled breath and eyes widening with fearful realization. His trembling hands loosened, and his torso contorted itself inward as a fierce series of coughs wracked his body. His small hand reached out as he fell, the coughs turning into a soundless scream.

Korbos's eye flared silver as he stretched out toward Amadi. The Chek's descent slowed; hope flashed across the small man's face.

And then the soft metal tore away beneath Korbos's hand.

He flung both hands toward the swaying catwalk, just managing to reset his grip as he jolted to a clanging stop.

Amadi fell, and time resumed its normal pace with a sickening thump.

Somewhere, far away, I could hear Mari wailing. I couldn't stop staring at the place where the Chek had hit, swarming now with frenzied Devoid. I tried to tell myself I didn't hear a tiny scream from below. I wasn't very successful.

"Pyk!"

I looked back to Korbos, who was hanging on for dear life. The bolts holding the section of catwalk groaned and pinged beside my head.

"Bastin, come!" I screamed. The scuridai bouldered his way up to me, and I gave a quick thanks to both Atia and Order above that the walkway didn't collapse beneath us. Moving as rapidly as I dared, I unwound and removed the reins from Bastin's horns and wrapped it twice around my metal arm before lowering it down to Korbos.

"I'm gonna need help here!" I managed to get out before Korbos's weight almost yanked me off the platform.

Two arms—one large and brown, one tan and muscular—enveloped my waist as Eljin and Cassidy grabbed hold of me. We heaved, step by step, and slowly Korbos appeared over the lip. He lay there for a moment, panting, before crawling to his feet and pointing toward the opposite end of the factory. His face was a mask of anger and sorrow.

"Let's go," he said in a shaking voice, pausing for a moment to put a hand on Mari's shoulder as she sobbed over the rail, staring at the Devoid below. Eljin approached, and she flung her arms around the old man, who returned the fierce embrace with head hung and tears dripping from the tip of his nose.

"We can't stay," said Korbos as he slung Bulwark over his shoulder.

"Order anyway, man, just give them a moment!" Cassidy spat. "We don't have those things breathing down our neck any more, so just…give 'em a moment."

She was right. Our side of the catwalk was clear, and seemed relatively stable. Sunlight beckoned through a door at the far wall. The sea of monsters that had taken Amadi boiled below us.

We gave Eljin and Mari a short time, until her sobs subsided, then set off toward that brilliant patch of light. It turned out to be another hall, this one with windows that looked out onto a wide landing set with ancient, ruined furniture. An outdoor break area for the workers here, perhaps. Heavy, vegetation-bare stone planters rested against another low quickcrete wall.

Cassidy forced open the door and we stepped out into air that didn't smell like centuries-old decay and machine oil. I stepped to the wall and looked down three stories to the tall grasses below, where Oben and the other Aka stood, waving up at us. There were no Devoid around that I could see, and none left on the floor with us.

We were clear. For now.

A shuddering sigh passed my lips as events caught up with me. I leaned against the wall and hung my head. Poor Amadi. No one deserved to go out like that, much less the polite little Chek.

Oben's four arms beckoned us down. I stuck my head over the ledge, looking for a pipe or trellis or some other means of climbing down, but found nothing.

"Korbos," I called, waving him over and motioning for him to take a look. "You got any ideas here? Mari and Bastin can get down easy enough, but the rest of us might have an issue."

He said nothing, just grunted. There was a look in his eye that I didn't like, distant and slightly glazed from the alcohol. I found myself hoping he'd dropped the bottle in the fall.

Korbos shrugged off his backpack and unlaced the threads, rummaging around for a moment before pulling out a somehow familiar thick length of coiled cable.

"Is that…is that the cable we used to cross into the Turris Imperialis?"

Grunt.

"It snapped, though. You rolled up the section that was left and have been carrying it around since? Like…just in case?"

Grunt.

"Order above, mate, *talk* to me!"

He said nothing, merely turning his thick neck to glare at me. It was like looking into a doll's dead button eyes. I shivered.

The big man fastened a running knot around one of the giant stone planters, still full of moist soil. I tried an experimental push and couldn't get the thing to budge. Should hold us. The loops of cable went over the side, just long enough that a short drop would get us to ground.

"Here we go, gang," I said, ushering Cassidy and Eljin to descend first. Once Eljin began his climb down, Mari hopped onto Bastin's back and launched in a smooth glide. I followed, with Korbos again bringing up the rear.

After dropping the final few feet—and immediately slipping on the damp grass—I brushed myself off as Oben walked over to clasp my shoulder.

"Good to see you alive, it is, friend Pyk. And all of you," it said. "But where is Master Omari?"

Mari burst into tears again from Bastin's back. The scuridai, sensing her distress, chirruped in an attempt to sooth her. Eljin patted her knee with a meaty hand.

"Amadi, he…" the old man said, voice breaking, "There was an accident, Oben. Amadi didn't make it out."

The Aka all bowed their heads as one and made a strange gesture, touching their chest, lips and foreheads. Spears thumped against the ground.

"May he shine in Order's light for eternity," Oben intoned in its multiple voices. "Sorry I am to hear this, Master Dhovra. He was well-liked among the Aka. A time for mourning, this is, but we must leave, I fear. There is still ground to cover before Masinas Tamai and Atoa begin their climb. The bulk of our cousins are not near, but I still would not have you journeying at night, friends."

I, for one, agreed with that assessment.

"Thank you, Oben," Eljin said. "He appreciated all of you."

As one, we all shouldered our packs, turned to the hill, and set off toward the *Storm*.

Silent. Somber. I turned to look at the blocky building that had taken Eljin's friend and companion, and murmured a silent farewell. I hadn't known Amadi long at all, but it felt like a part of us had been irrevocably ripped away.

I repeated the respectful gesture the Aka had made—chest, lips, forehead—and wished Amadi's spirit to a better world.

Then we walked.

Masina Atoa was already beginning its great arc through the sky as we reached the skipship. Cassidy tapped a few buttons on the rear left landing strut, then spread her arms wide as the ship powered up and the ramp began to ratchet its way down. She looked like a proud parent awaiting a hug from their precious child.

We milled about the ramp for a few moments until Oben cleared its throat, drawing our attention. Only Korbos didn't turn; the blacksmith stood off to the side of the ledge, looking out over the ruins of Cortian.

"It was our pleasure to meet you, new friends," it said, its lower tone dominating with a sense of…sadness? I didn't know the Na'don well enough yet to tell for certain, but it sounded that way. "We wish you well on your journey, but the Aka cannot accompany you."

"What?" asked Eljin, surprise plain on his grizzled face. "You stand to gain as much as anyone by bringing down Kaira, Oben…I thought we had an understanding."

"An understanding we had, Master Dhovra, but new complications have arisen. Many more of our cousins have broken free of Cortianis than anticipated. Repair the containment and corral our kin, we must, and it will take many and many Aka. Much work to do, in little time. We cannot accompany you."

"All hands on deck," I murmured.

"Just so, friend Pyk," it rumbled.

I hesitated, then stuck out my hand. "It's been a…well, not exactly a pleasure, Oben *ta'ita mula*, but I'm glad to have met you and your people. I will forever be indebted to you for the gift of our lives. You're an honorable being, and you'll always have a friend in Pyk Belloc."

The blind Na'don raised its head, neck stretching long in what could be interpreted as surprise, then gently took my hand in two of its own. It bowed low, putting its head roughly on a level with my own. "The honor was ours, Master Belloc."

Cassidy gave me a long look, as if she were sizing me up in a new light, then stepped forward to give her own thanks. Mariyana followed, sniffling, and Bastin gave the Aka a quick swipe of his tongue, to which Oben laughed.

Eljin was distraught, but he wiped a strong hand across his eyes and clasped forearms with the Na'don. Oben leaned in, and the two exchanged words, though I couldn't make out what was said.

Oben strolled over to Korbos, who hadn't yet moved, laying a hand on the blacksmith's shoulder.

"A doubtful mind weighs heaviest on a man's shoulders, friend Korbos," it said. "Many and many years you have carried burdens not meant for mortal man, *Seta Sietau*."

"I'm not a mortal man, though, Oben," growled Korbos, the first words he'd spoken since leaving the factory.

"No. No you are not, *Seta Sietau*. This weight you bear…let it crush you beneath it, you must not." It swept an arm to encompass the whole group. "You have loved ones to help ease the burden, now. Do not retreat from them. This I speak from long and long experience."

Korbos turned his head away.

Oben rounded on the rest of us. "Difficult your quest will be, friends. It is no easy task to defy the Host and their *liaga*. Wish you all the best in it, the Aka do. Stand. Fight. Be true and you will find the victory you desire, I have no doubt. In the future, if the Aka you need, there we will be." It spread its arms wide and bowed again, to all of us this time. A sharp motion, and the rest of the Aka joined it near the treeline at the side of the hill.

And then it was time for them to leave. The first outriders of the broken moon Masina Tamai had begun to crest the trees, cleaving a path for their shattered mother to follow.

"Bye, Juni!" yelled Cassidy. "Take care of Pyk Junior for me!"

I groaned, loud enough for everyone to hear.

The Aka turned and raised her spear, surprisingly white teeth shining from her desiccated features.

We watched as they melted into the jungle, not bothering with the switchbacks. Bastin chirruped in farewell.

TWENTY SEVEN

Things were not going well.

I stared into a bleary brown eye as I faced down Korbos. Well, faced up. Order anyway, he was tall. A beefy finger poked into my chest.

"*You* don't get ta tell me what to do, you little drekface," the big man slurred. In the two hours we'd been back aboard ship, he'd shut himself in the cargo hold and proceeded to get blisteringly drunk.

Empty wine bottles lay about the hold. I counted at least five—thanking all the gods above and below he wasn't drinking anything harder. Even so, his healing had to be working overtime, with all that on top of the moss whiskey. I couldn't fathom how he was still conscious and breathing, much less standing on his own two feet.

Worse still, he was being super belligerent.

I'd never seen him like this.

But something had to be done. Now.

"You people drag me out of my home, my shop, and my life, and you expect me to jush…what? Shave you? Go along like a good little hero and shave the day? Oh shure, let's jush go blow up the frokking Hosht and heal the planet or whatever! Eashy walk on the beach, that ish."

I fought to keep my voice even and calm. "Korbos, mate…"

He pushed my shoulder. "Don't you 'mate' me, Pyk. I…"

"Keep your hands off him, *bhaka*," growled Cassidy from beside me.

"Or what? You gonna shoot me up with your little pishtol? Go ahead and try." He gave her a wicked smile, teeth bared, daring her to draw on him.

"Kor!" I yelled, drawing his attention back to me. Order above, this was terrifying. Rage and sorrow vied for dominance upon his face, one flickering to the next.

"*I don't know what to do, Pyk*!" he screamed. "That Chek Amadi is dead becaushe of me! I get everyone around me killed, and that'sh just how it ish, for *nine hundred frokking yearsh!* Now you *bhutas* want to march yourselves right into the cragcatsh' lair without any idea about what you'd be facing. I…I can't handle that. I don't have the shtrength to handle it if any of you getsh killed becaushe of *me*."

He sat down hard on a loose crate, despair washing over him. Despair or self-pity? It was a tough call.

"Are you more worried about what happens to us?" I asked softly, "or how *you'll* feel if something *does* happen to us?"

His head snapped up, and he lurched back to his feet, taking a staggering step toward me and pointing his finger into my face.

"Don't you shay that. You don't know what it'sh like, with your entire nineteen yearsh of worldly experience." His sarcasm was dripping, but I held his gaze. "I'm reshponshible for the deathsh of more people than you can ever hope to meet in your entire frokking lifetime, so you don't get to lecshure me on guilt."

He spat to the side. "I will *not* be reshponshible for Kaira turning your insidesh to your outsidesh!"

"Nobody ever said you would be, mate. I've told you before, we're involved in this of our own choice. We *are* going to this temple, we *are* going to deal with the signara, and you *are* going to do your part, so we need you to get your drek sorted and get on board with us. That means putting down the frokking bottle."

He scoffed. "Put down the…" He drew himself up straight, with only a slight wobble, glaring at the two of us. "I'm *fine*, thank you very mush. Matter of fact, I don't even need you. You can jusht drop me near the temple, and I'll take care of thingsh by myshelf."

"And we're not going to let you go off and do this by yourself, man. You're our friend, whether you like it or not, so we'll be sticking with you. But you have to realize that you're not just hurting yourself here. You're hurting others. You're hurting us."

His eye narrowed. "And what makesh you think I don't know that? What makesh you think I *need* you? The whole…whole point of my going alone ish to keep you out of rishk."

"Life is risk, Korbos. We have a chance to do a great thing here, and we're going to take it. I'm with you. Mari's with you. Cassidy's with you."

I ignored her raised eyebrow. "But we need *you* to be with *us*. And that means getting off the drink."

He scoffed again. "Shure. Shure. Let me do jush that. Be done in jusht a moment." He reached into his coat, pulling yet another wine bottle—wait, no, it was the remnants of the whiskey he'd gotten from Eljin—and popped the cork.

I couldn't help it.

Rage bubbled up inside of me, though I was outwardly calm. I swung my mechanical left arm in a vicious backhand, shattering the bottle as he raised it to his lips. Liquid splashed across the deck, my hand, his face. He wiped a slow hand across his mouth before snarling at me.

Probably not the best way for me to handle the situation.

His eye flared, and suddenly I was flying across the hold to slam into the bulkhead. I struggled to get air into my lungs, which didn't work too well considering the massive paw that wrapped around my neck an instant later.

"Gak!" I honked out. It was the best rebuttal I could manage under the circumstances. Korbos's face was pressed nose-to-nose with mine, and Cassidy was beating at his back, nearly hitting me with her wild swings. The big man didn't appear to even notice her. His eye burned silver as the molten steel in one of his crucibles.

He didn't appear drunk at all any more.

Cassidy drew her gun and jammed it to the back of his head. Which was doubly terrifying, given that my face was on the direct opposite side of said head. It would be a bit counterproductive if she put a bullet through both of our skulls in an attempt to save my life.

My vision began to darken around the edges.

Then the pressure eased. Korbos's eye returned to its normal dirty brown, focused on me, and abject horror crept over his face. He dropped me to the deck, which is when I realized he'd been holding me nearly a foot above it. A step back, then two, and Korbos dropped to his knees, slapping his forehead with the heel of his palm.

"Stupid! Stupid! Frokking! Idiot!" he cried, punctuating each outburst with a smack of his palm.

"Guh," I replied, unable to force a more coherent sound through my windpipe. Blessed air filled my lungs as I sucked it in like water through a bilge.

Cassidy kept her gun trained on him. I waved it down, putting myself between the two. She eyed me, then with a low groan of reluctance returned Jasmin to her holster.

"Kor," I croaked, "are you…better?"

The big man remained on his knees, head bowed. "Well, I'm not drunk any more, if that's what you're asking. Power burned off the inebriation. I can't say anything about 'better,' though. Chaos burn me, Pyk, I'm so sorry!" He looked up to me, and the pure anguish in his face made my chest tighten. He reached out, clutching, desperate for forgiveness. "I'm so, so frokking sorry!"

I hesitated only a moment, then stepped forward and put my arms around him. I jumped, shocked, as he burst into great, heaving sobs against my stomach. Cassidy was wide-eyed as well.

This whole thing could have gone better.

When the crying jag wore off, Korbos stood, wiping his eye and making a concerted effort to pull himself together.

"There's…I have no excuse for my behavior, Pyk. I am so very sorry, and I can't expect your forgiveness. Just…I…it…it won't happen again, I swear to you."

I had no idea what to say. I didn't know what to feel, given the fact that my friend had just tried to choke me out. But I was the one who started this intervention, so I couldn't bloody well let it go without trying to see it through.

"Mate, I've been in worse scraps fighting over whose turn it was to use the head on the *Quay*. Nothing to forgive. But do I need to repeat what I said earlier? Now that you're thinking clearly? You've got. To stop. With the drink."

He sucked in a deep breath. "I know," he whispered.

"I know you know. But I want to know that you're going to *do* something about it. You have a problem. And *you're* the only solution."

His face twitched in a tormented spasm. "I'll try, Pyk. Order above witness my words, I swear I'll try. I…I can't do this any more. After all the years and all the death I've caused, something inside me is broken. But I'll try. I promise you that."

"Then that's all I can ask from you, mate." I put my hand on his shoulder, jostling him.

He coughed a bitter laugh, returning the gesture. "When did you get wiser than me, boy?"

"Pshah! I just backslapped a frokking member of the Host. I'm about to try and sneak into the temple of another and then get back out alive. I don't think wisdom has a thing to do with it."

He chuckled, then looked around the deck and back up to Cassidy. "I apologize to you as well, Cassidy Ninefingers. Both for my poor companionship…and for the mess." He bowed to her, remaining bent over to pick up the bottles strewn about before dumping them in a bin.

"It's fine. Just don't forget what you owe me."

"Never in my life," he replied, bowing his head. "If you'll excuse me, I'll…I think I'll take my leave for a while. There's a lot to mull over."

It hurt worse than being slammed against the bulkhead to see my friend at such a low point. So unsure of himself. He gathered up his pack and rifle, then spun the wheel to open the cargo bay door and headed to his bunk. I was somewhat surprised at how quickly my anger had faded, replaced by pity that I'd never, ever embarrass him by showing. Cassidy and I remained in the hold for another minute, just looking down the passageway after him.

"So yeah," she said at last, "we're gonna need to keep an eye on him."

"Yup."

She turned and threw a punch at me. "What the frok was *that*? Do you *have* a death wish?!"

I sighed, rubbing my arm where she'd connected. "First off…ow. Secondly, nah. He had me worried for a minute, but I didn't think he'd actually hurt me. A few more seconds, though, and I might have been waving for you to put one in the back of his head."

She cocked her head. "Then either you're a complete fool, or you've got bigger balls than I do."

"I should hope so!" I laughed, still too relieved to even be properly embarrassed by her crudity. She cupped my face with her four-fingered hand and gave me that beautiful wry grin.

"Well, at least Mari and Eljin didn't have to see that," I said. The two had holed up in Mari's small cabin, stretching out on the bunks, playing soft music through that contraption on the wall and consoling each other over the loss of Amadi.

"I don't…think they need to know about that whole incident, do you?" Cassidy asked.

I thought about what Mari's reaction to the scene would have been, so close on the heels of losing her new friend, and shuddered.

"Definitely not. Probably for the best if we just kept the whole thing between us."

"Right."

Mari stuck her head out the door as we made our way to the flight deck. "Is Korbos…okay? He actually looked a little better when he walked past just now."

"I *hope* he'll be okay. We just…had a little chat. He seemed receptive. To a degree." I rubbed my sore throat.

"Ah. Well that's good hey I've got one bit of good news for us we might just happen to have a new traveling companion please Cassidy just don't freak out I think he'll be a good pet I just need to learn how to train and take care of—"

"Mariyana…" Cassidy interrupted, "what is that noise?"

A low humming sound was coming from inside the cabin, almost a purring. Mari backed her way in, followed by the two of us.

Turned out, it *was* purring. Bastin lay curled up on the floor, head aloft and looking up to Eljin, who sat crosslegged on the bottom bunk. In his lap was one of the felis, stretched out long and enjoying a good back rub.

"What in the…" Cassidy began. "Mari!"

"What? I promise I didn't bring him on board he must have snuck on while we were all saying goodbye to the Aka and Oben and he's just so darn cute Pyk look it's the one that was following us earlier see the markings and can we keep it I'll feed him and—"

"Mari!" Cassidy and I said in unison.

She was right. It was the same felis that had jumped into her arms for petting, the one with the blond star-shaped mark on its head. It had tracked us all the way here? I thought they'd all run off when the horde of Devoid appeared. Its multiple black eyes pivoted to stare at us, and it purred even louder as Eljin hit a sweet spot between its shoulder blades.

"I don't know if a skipship would be a good home for this little guy, Mari," Cassidy began, trying to let her down easy.

"But...but...I've already named him..."

Mari's oversized eyes went wider than I'd ever seen. Her bottom lip trembled, and she brought her hands together in pleading. A little hop sent her puffball hair bouncing.

I couldn't help but laugh. Partly it was nerves. I was still on edge from the events of the day, trying to come down from the near-constant flood of adrenaline. But mostly I laughed at the Chek's blatant manipulation tactics. It was impossible to say no to her.

"I...suppose," said Cassidy. She didn't look too pleased with the situation, but she didn't offer any further argument. "But *you're* cleaning up the thing's drek."

Mari actually squealed, giving Cassidy a crushing hug then running over to plop down beside Eljin. The felis gave a languid stretch and hopped into her lap, where she resumed its pampering.

"So what'd you name it?" I asked. "Pyk the Third? That'd be a good strong name. And at least it wouldn't be a pig." I shot Cassidy a glare. She flashed a grin, then snapped her fingers.

"Oh man, I just thought of a way better name. *Pig* Belloc! Junior, of course."

I rolled my eyes so hard they ached.

Mari cuddled the felis. "His name is Omari."

That sobered me up. "After Amadi, of course," I muttered. I looked over to Eljin. "You're okay with that?"

"Okay with it?" he replied. "I think it's a grand idea. Hah! A good way to honor my friend, Order's light embrace him. Heh." He reached over to scratch the felis's ears.

"Omari it is, then. You realize that's going to confuse the hells out of me?" I seesawed my hands up and down. "Mari? OH-mari? Way too similar."

"I think you'll be okay, Pyk," Mari responded, sticking her tongue out at me in mock anger. "Come on, Omari, let's get you some food."

The felis hopped down as she stood up, and walked on its six legs to where Bastin lay, curling up next to the scuridai.

"Well, at least they get along," I noted.

Cassidy turned to me. "Speaking of getting along, we need to finish our conversation."

It took me a minute to realize what she was referring to. My chest constricted as I recalled our chat at the Lau Tuai, where she'd told me she wanted to go her own way. I gulped and nodded before backing out of the room.

"You two might want to come," Cassidy said to the others.

We all filed down the passage to the cockpit, Cassidy poking her head into Korbos's berth and beckoning him to follow. All hands on deck, indeed. Lovely.

The four of us took our seats, rotating the couches so that we could see one another. Omari followed and jumped into Mariyana's lap, curling up and purring softly.

Korbos stepped in, ducking his head and leaning against the bulkhead as he straightened and stood at the rear of the cabin. He looked haggard, an unsettling sight. The signara was in his hand, and he stared at its soft glow before putting it away.

"Pyk and I had the beginnings of a conversation back at the big tree," Cassidy began, "but I felt you all needed to be involved, since it concerns everyone."

She took a deep breath. "I'm out. I didn't sign on to fight a suicidal war against the bloody Host themselves." She raised her chin to Korbos, who didn't meet her eye. "You hired me to get you to Cortian, and that's what I did. You owe me for the cube. Forty thousand, payable on completion of the job.

"Well, the job's been completed, and then some."

"Cass…" I began.

"Pyk, I told you already, I can't afford to drag all of you into my personal messes. It's best this way, for everyone. Pay me what I'm owed, and I'll drop you off wherever you'd like—anywhere that's *not* on Kaira's doorstep. But then it's time to part ways. I've got no desire to get myself killed chasing an old man's dreams. No offense, Korbos."

The big man grunted but said nothing. He was still staring at his feet. Order above, had Amadi's fall dealt that much hurt to him? The confrontation we'd had? He didn't seem the stalwart, decisive man I'd known most of my life. The years and heartbreak weighed upon his soul, just as Oben had said. He seemed…lost.

Like I'd be without Cassidy around.

"Look," I said, "we can't get to Kaira without you and the *Storm*. You can fly, you can fight. You fit with us. I meant it when I said it earlier. We're here for you, no strings. You can have a family."

Mari clapped in approval. Even Korbos was nodding his head. Eljin remained silent, remaining apart as the newcomer.

"You see? We all want you to stay. We *need* you with us. I…I need you with us. How could you leave, with all we've been through in the last weeks? As a Seeker, you know better than anyone except the Host themselves how much damage they've caused the world.

"How can you walk away, knowing that we have a chance to end them, to make things *right* again?"

I left my couch, dropping to my knees before her and taking her hands in mine.

"Please, stay."

The others might as well not have existed. This was between me and her now.

She bit her lip, leaning forward until her forehead was almost touching mine.

"You…you could maybe come with me?" she asked, soft as Omari's fur.

I shook my head. "You know I couldn't do that. I can't leave Mari, not in the middle of this. And I won't leave Korbos to fight his battle alone. I don't know what help I'll be—I'm just a bloody fisherman—but I have to do whatever I can."

My voice dropped to a whisper.

"I'd give up my own revenge to go with you, but I won't abandon my friends. My family. You're a part of that now, so please don't make me abandon you. Don't abandon us, I'm begging you."

Her eyes stared into mine; all else faded.

She released my hands, biting her lip. A look of pained indecision warred with desire on her face. Whatever sense of belonging she'd received from us in our short time together, Cassidy was obviously reluctant to let it go.

She leaned back in her couch.

She smiled.

"Ahhhhhhhh all *right*!" she exclaimed, throwing her hands in the air. She spun the pilot's couch in a fast circle. "Frok me frok me frok me you're an *idiot*, Cassidy Ryker!"

She stabbed a finger at Korbos. "You! Big guy!" He finally looked up, eyebrow arched. "Double or nothin'. You get your ride, you get me, you get the whole package. But once this is done, I'm set up for *life*, you hear me? Life! I never want to worry about anything, ever again!"

Set her up for life? How in the world was Korbos supposed to do that? I mean, he was immortal—a Host and all—but he worked as a *blacksmith*, for Order's sake. Why would he be doing that if he had riches stashed away somewhere? I was again reminded of just how little I knew about the big man.

He tilted his head and nodded, just once, stepping forward between the rear seats to take her small hand in his massive one. They shook.

"Our bond is made, the bargain struck, captain." I shivered, remembering the words that had brought us to Cortian in the first place.

Mari cheered, scaring the jeebers out of Omari, who shot off into the rear of the ship. Eljin gave a slow clap.

Tension drained away from me in a rush, and I leaned forward, placing my face next to hers, cheek to cheek.

"Thank you," I whispered into her ear. She gave a little shudder before quickly rotating the chair back to ready position and firing up the *Storm*'s engines.

"Order anyway, don't you people get all mushy on me," she said, but I saw her wipe a small tear from the corner of her eye. "So where to? I'm getting awful tired of staring at that Chaos-cursed city."

Korbos scratched his chin. "We'll need supplies."

"We'll need food!" cried Mari. "And weapons! And temple-break-in tools and disguises and hey I should probably stock up on boompowder like I said I was going to and it wouldn't hurt to fashion some new reins for Bastin and—"

"Yes, little one," said Eljin, patting her arm. "That's generally what 'supplies' means. Heh. Question is, where are we going to *get* said provisions?"

Cassidy spun her chair, smiling that wicked grin I was fast coming to love.

"Well, I *might* have an idea for that."

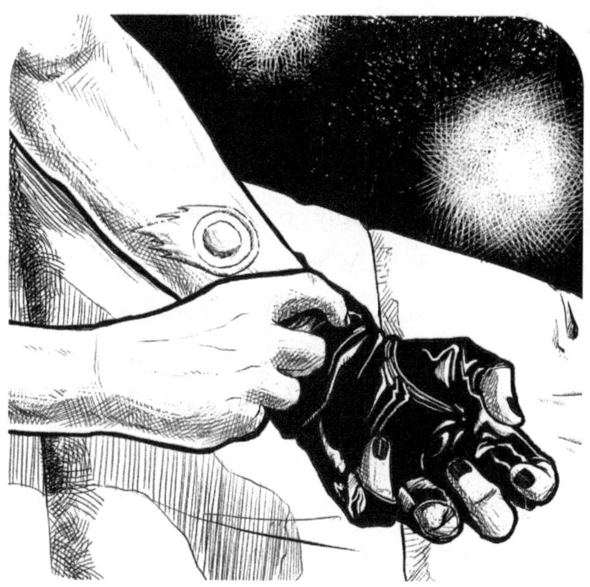

TWENTY EIGHT

"This...is unreal," I said, slack-jawed and staring around in wonder.

The place was gigantic, bigger even than the aerowing factory. And completely hidden, concealed within a high cliffside overlooking a dry lake bed a half-day's flight southeast from Cortian. There had been no indication whatsoever that anything was amiss until Cassidy punched a few buttons on the *Storm*'s console and a portion of the ragged cliff face slid open like the pocket door on Ardis's pantry, allowing the skipship entry to set down on a gantried landing platform.

I may or may not have wet myself a little, given that the ship had been barreling straight toward said cliff at the time.

We stood in the center of an immense military bunker. Cold white lights shone far overhead, bathing the area in harsh light. It was a mess. Stuff lay everywhere in disarray. Collapsed shelves rested atop strewn containers, contents spewed out across the quickcrete floor. Crates of every size were stacked haphazardly everywhere, many knocked over in some catastrophic upheaval. What looked like miles of warehouse shelving receded to the distance in parallel rows. Bits of paper, markings almost completely faded with age, fluttered about in the cool dry air blowing from large vents set into the walls. I picked up a sheet and marveled as it crumbled to dust in my hand.

Off to my left was a wide area packed tight with large, blocky autocarts, metal rims on the rotted remnants of strange wheels. Some of the vehicles had more crates stacked in the long beds behind the driver's compartment. Others were covered by thick canvas tarps.

Mari looked interested in anything and everything, but didn't seem especially manic about the place as Omari wound around her feet. The felis scampered away to explore, followed by echoing thuds as Bastin chased him.

Eljin was utterly dumbfounded. His mouth hung open, working soundlessly as he whipped his head around to take in the sight. One large hand idly rubbed the back of his head, sending his white hair streaming about like a waterfall. He'd obviously never seen anything like the storehouse, which answered my unspoken question about whether he'd ever ventured into Cortian proper during his time at the Lau Tuai.

"Something, ain't it?" asked Cassidy, spreading her hands wide and grinning ear to ear.

"Something, all right," mumbled Korbos, who stood looking at the bunker with a stony expression. He stared at a large placard mounted on a wall near the autocarts.

"What's it say, mate?" I asked.

He was silent for a moment, then replied, "Gold Base, Second Battalion, Third Division. 'All hail the Imperium,' along the bottom there."

I whistled softly. We were actually standing in yet another piece of history. I wondered how many of these storehouses could be left across the continent.

"Want the tour?" Cassidy grinned.

She led us into the base, working her way through the toppled crates and pointing out hallways and rooms that branched out from the main bay.

"You already saw the vehicle depot over there..."

"Motor pool," corrected Korbos.

"Sure, what he said. Not that they're motoring anywhere these days. There's a lot of this place I never checked out. Might be some stuff in those crates we can use."

Korbos nodded, as if to himself. "I can help with that. Translating the contents, at least. Everything should be inventoried and labeled."

"Over there are the kitchens, down that hall. No perishable food, of course, but there's a bunch of tight-sealed packages that are actually still edible. Kept me alive when I found the place, at least. Bunks and living quarters through that next passage."

"Where are the weapons?" I asked.

"We'll get to those soon enough, Pyk," said Korbos. "I'd like to take a look around and see what sort of usable resources are available first."

"Right on." I looked up at the high ceiling and the bright lights shining overhead. "So what's making these lights work?"

"If I had to guess, geothermal power. I didn't see any solar collective panels anywhere. They'd be a little too obvious for a secret base."

"So geo-whatsis, then. And that is?"

Korbos snorted. "Somewhere in this place is a reactor that generates power. It uses the heat from the planet's core and makes energy to spark the lights, kind of like the fuel capacitors from the *Storm*. If we're lucky, there's battery storage somewhere that we can maybe use."

"Oooookay. That's…kinda cool," I replied.

"I don't know about you guys," said Cassidy, "but the first thing I plan on using are the showers. There's a big communal room over that way that has private stalls with hot water, privies, the works."

"Atia's blessings and benevolence," moaned Mari, "a bath would be wonderful."

"I agree," said Korbos. "Let's get cleaned up and meet back here."

Thirty minutes later, we all stood around the kitchens, scrubbed and munching on nine-hundred-year-old packaged nutrition bars Cassidy pulled from an air-tight container. There were more of those around than I expected.

They weren't bad, even if I had to force myself to take that first tentative bite. Cassidy grinned as she chewed hers, mumbling around a mouthful as she showed off the area. Bastin crunched on some of Mari's kibble from a metal bowl she'd found and rinsed in the bathtub-sized sink.

We drank clear, cold water, processed through something that Korbos dubbed a "refrigerator" that kept food and drink cold without the benefit of ice. A true miracle of forgotten technology, I felt.

I rummaged around the cabinets, digging through the detritus of centuries past. They were filled with many boxes, the printing washed out, the writing illegible. Most had faded images of whatever they'd contained; I found boxes of tea, tiny cakes, shiny bags full of rotted crispy chips, and all manner of other inedible foods. The entire room had a dry, dusty smell, which was preferable to the scent of decay I'd expected.

One tall cabinet, made of hammered steel, stood to the side of the pantry. There was an ancient lock hanging from a clasp, which snapped and skittered across the tile floor upon judicial application of force. Which is to say, I whacked the drek out of it with a mallet found hanging from a row of cooking utensils.

My heart fell as I opened the door to a riot of colored glass bottles, the ink upon their labels much clearer than the boxes which had been exposed to light. I couldn't read them, but I knew what this was.

A liquor cabinet.

I stole a glance at Korbos, who exhaled hard and strode over to my side. I said nothing as he stretched out a hand, caressing one of the bottles. He hefted it, a soft smile on his face.

"Kikasini," he said, reading the label. "Good whiskey. This was one of my favorites, lifetimes ago."

He sighed, gently placing the bottle back on the shelf and easing the door shut. His fist clenched and trembled a bit as he patted the twisted handle. I couldn't help my wide smile as I placed a hand on his shoulder.

"Good for you, mate," I whispered. "Way to be strong."

He gave a curt nod, then turned to the others.

"Now that our bellies are full, the first order of business remains." He looked to Cassidy. Unease gripped me. I had an idea of where this was going to lead.

"Cassidy Ryker," he began, a formal note creeping into his voice, "the air needs to be cleared between us. I cannot lead a team into danger such as this if I cannot trust them. And the trust between us has been broken by your…omissions. If you'd continue on with us, and I sincerely hope you will, we must have the truth."

Cassidy stared daggers at the big man. "And what if I don't feel like telling you the truth? What gives you the right to pry into my life?"

He stared back, unblinking. Unfazed. "The right of bond. In our short time together, we've suffered much. Conquered obstacles most living people never experience. We offer you the opportunity to join our little family, to do something meaningful, but I cannot spend my time watching my back against someone I do not feel is completely honest with us. You know our stories, so it's time we heard yours. The true story."

Cassidy looked to Eljin. "You trust *him*? He's been with us all of two days! What makes you so sure he won't knife us in the back at the first opportunity? For Order's sake, he used to frokking *work* for the Host! No offense intended, Eljin."

"None taken. Heh."

"I trust Eljin insomuch as he has sufficient reason to strike against the Host. Revenge is a powerful motivator, mistress Ryker, as Pyk can well tell you."

"Hey, don't bring me into this!"

"The fact is, Cassidy," Korbos continued, "that you are the wild card in this hand. Now please, tell your tale and make me believe."

"I'm sensing an 'or…' here," she replied.

"We'll get to the 'or' if necessary, but I'm hoping it won't be."

Cassidy bristled, then relented with an angry sigh. "Fine! Fine." She sipped her water. "But not here. Let's go to the common room. There's at least some comfortable chairs there."

We followed her from the sterile kitchen into a wide room filled with semicircular couches. Thin screens were mounted here and there, with a particularly large one situated in the middle of the longest wall. A blocky table sat to one side, hosting a number of colored balls and stitched markings. Some sort of gaming and recreation room, I assumed, undoubtedly for the soldiers' relaxation.

Each of us took a seat on the plush couches, which were surprisingly comfortable. Omari, who had rejoined us, stretched himself out, plucked at the fabric, and curled up to nap. If we were to stay, I hoped the bunks were so plush.

"Where do you want me to start?" asked Cassidy.

"I heard the story you told Pyk," Korbos replied, "so why don't you start there and tell us the rest...the parts we don't know."

I blinked. He'd been listening to our conversation on the *Storm*? That talk felt like a million years ago.

"Okay, then," Cassidy began, whistling low through her teeth. "I told Pyk the truth. It's just the...the timeframes were a little off. Well, let me back up a bit."

She sighed. "I grew up in Nordinaar, and left when I was thirteen for... reasons. Moved around for a little while, then wound up in Newsome, where I took up the mechanic trade. Learned that I loved working around machinery and equipment and that I was good at it. Spent two years doing that with my master, then he died of wetlung. After he passed, I wound up with the Quicks Guild.

"Now here's where it gets hinky. I think I implied to Pyk that I wasn't with Quicks too long, but I spent three frokking years stuck under Javi Quicks's thumb. I was fifteen when he found me and took me in. I knew they weren't exactly on the straight and narrow path, but the Guild offered good protection, and Javi made sure nobody ever bothered me in...certain ways. Fifteen year old girl in a gang full of thugs and bandits... well, you get the idea.

"Three years I spent arming those *bhakas* with stunpikes, crossbolts, a few steamcarts to overtake the horses—whatever tools they needed to carry out their raids. What did I care? The money was good, and I was treated with respect. I never had to see the results of my work."

She inhaled a shuddering breath. "Until they robbed old Tommas Merin."

Cassidy turned to me, pain in her eyes. "I was there. Javi thought it was time for me to be part of the Guild proper-like; to get my hands dirty. We rode down the caravan in steamcarts that I built. Shot the guards with crossbolts that I designed. They made me watch as they killed Merin's family. They lined up his wife and kids against a wagon and shot them with weapons *I made*."

She rocked forward, arms wrapped around her body. Her eyes welled. "I was the one who took Merin's head."

She buried her face in her hands, the tears finally spilling over. My jaw dropped in shocked surprise.

"Javi himself made me do it. He put my own sword to my throat and told me it was my neck or the merchant's." She touched the collapsed blade at her lower back. "The Guild was in a blood frenzy. I didn't have a choice. I wanted to live."

I reached over to offer a comforting hand. She took it, squeezing tight. "You did what you had to do," I said. Hatred for this Javi Quicks person set its hooks into me.

"But I didn't!" she cried. "I could have refused! I still don't know if Javi would have killed me or not. He needed me to make his frokking weapons. It's been almost four years, and I still cry myself to sleep some nights thinking about what I could have done differently.

"I tried. I tried to get out. I refused to make anything more for the Guild when we got back from that damnable raid. They beat me for two days. Javi finally had enough, took my finger, and I caved in and went back to work."

She held up her left hand, wiggling the stump of her maimed ring finger.

Mari gasped and covered her mouth in horror.

"I couldn't just leave after that. Javi would have hunted me down. Order knows his people are still trying. So on a supply run—a snatch-and-grab spree, more like it—I knocked out my escort and ran and turned myself in to the Newsome constabulary. Told them where the Guild was holed up. They'd been looking for years, so it didn't take long for the sheriff to round up his posse and burn the place out. That did the trick on ending the Guild. I haven't seen him since, but I know Javi Quicks is still out there. I've had to fight off six of his hunters over the years."

Cassidy rolled down her glove, running a thumb over the flaming comet branded into the flesh of her wrist. Traced a scar across her forearm.

"The sheriff granted me clemency for giving up the Guild. I hooked up with a Seeker Ashlar two days later."

"How long did you actually stay with the Seekers?" Korbos asked.

Cassidy gave him a strange look. "About nineteen months, why?"

"Just curious. You weren't with them all that long, then."

"Yeah, about five months past my eighteenth birthday is when I joined. Left them just after my twentieth. So I've been alone on the *Storm* nearly two years now."

"So that's how you've had time to build trade with the Strigori. Among others, I assume?"

Cassidy sighed. "Yeah."

"Sooooo…what happened with the Seekers?" I asked. "You told me you'd only left them recently, but it's been two years?"

"Almost two. Give or take a month. It wasn't entirely pleasant." She rubbed a hand across the back of her neck. "I *loved* my work with the Seekers, understand? I wanted nothing to do with mechanics or weapons after the Quicks Guild, so I developed a real passion for history and exploration and discovery with them. It's insane how much knowledge I gained during my time with them. But after about year and a half it got… problematic.

"I'd fallen in with a boy from my Ashlar—that's what the Seeker sects are called—and it had gotten kind of serious. I mean, I'd messed around with boys here and there before, but Luc was something special. A musician, on top of being one of our top preservationists. Order anyway, the things that boy could do with his hands…"

I wriggled, more than a little uncomfortable with this line of conversation, but I said nothing. Couldn't help making a hurry-up twirl with my fingers, though. Cassidy grinned, causing me to blush. Order anyway, the woman enjoyed making me do that a little too much.

"The Architect of our Ashlar was a man named Nicson. He was good-looking enough, I suppose, but he was a pushy *bhaka.* Thought far too highly of himself and wouldn't take no for an answer. I had to start fending him off almost from the moment I joined the Seekers, but I never really paid him much mind other than as an annoyance.

"When Luc and I began courting, it drove Nicson crazy. Months of snide comments, drek assignments, little sabotages. We just tried to ignore it and move on. Even put in a request to switch to another Ashlar across the continent, although I'm pretty sure that never got filed properly. The clerks were Nicson's creatures to a man."

She turned to me.

"Pyk, you remember me telling you about that mechanical man the Seekers found? The giant outside of Qirim?"

Korbos leaned forward, but stayed silent.

I nodded. Still didn't believe it, but I remembered.

"When that was discovered, they also unearthed a compound a lot like this one we're in now. Some sort of central control building or something, though it was a lot smaller than this place. Luc and I were the ones assigned to investigate and catalog.

"I should have known something was up just from that. We never got the good assignments by that point. Nicson sabotaged us every way he could in terms of advancement.

"We took a team into the ruins. Took us a full day to dig our way through the sand in the outer structure, but once we got inside? Oh, man. Old synthminds like the ones we tore up in that room in Cortian. Giant devices we'd never seen before, with no indication as to what they were made to do. Faded books, manuals, the works. It was a treasure trove. Most of it was absolutely useless, of course, but from a historical perspective we were bathing in Order's light.

"It was in one of the side offices where I found the map that led me to this storehouse, you know. Luc and I kept it from the team, because we knew Nicson would never let us be the ones to investigate.

"Parts of the building were in bad shape. Weak structural integrity, you know? Luc was checking out this one large room with another member of the team, an engineer named Shad. We'd poked our heads in earlier, and the entire place was held together by spit and a few shaky struts. I was on my way back to join them when the whole thing came crashing down.

"Shad *somehow* managed to avoid being crushed, but I lost my Luc. He was on the far side of the room. We had no way to dig him out. I lost it. It took three other team members—big men, mind you—to drag me out of the rubble where I was digging with my bare fingernails.

"It was ruled an accident by the Architect, but I knew better. I saw Shad's face when he stood there looking at the carnage. He was the

Architect's man to the core, and he was frokking smiling. Just a tiny grin, but it was there."

Cassidy paused, inhaling a shaky breath.

"Two days after we got back, Shad met with an unfortunate accident. I ambushed the scrawny *bhaka* in his room and beat a confession out of him."

Her face drew into a frown of remembrance, eyes haunted.

"He admitted the Architect had ordered him to get Luc out of the way if there was an opportunity. I was stuck. There was nothing I could do to Nicson himself at the time. He was always surrounded by sycophants and his harem.

"But I could and did do something about Shad. He'd taken my man from me, so I took his manhood from him before I gave him a second red smile."

She drew her thumb across her throat, still staring out into nothing. I shuddered at her empty tone, unsure of how to process this new information about the woman I was falling for. She was justified in her actions, I felt, but how could she be so callous about them?

Cassidy looked up, eyes meeting mine, and I knew I was dead wrong. It wasn't callousness, it was dissociation, and telling her story was dredging up feelings she'd kept hidden for years. A tear crept a trail over her freckles to her chin, and agony filled her voice. She clutched at me, imploring me to understand and forgive.

"I'm not proud of it, Pyk, but some things just need doing. Some men just need killing. Shad had murdered the first man I'd loved, all because another man thought he was entitled to me. That I should be his just because he wanted it. Some things can't be allowed to stand."

I wrapped an arm around her, and she laid her head on my shoulder.

"What happened after?" asked Korbos.

I raised an eyebrow at him. "For Order's sake, man, give her a moment."

He grunted, then mimicked the same hurry-up gesture I'd made earlier, twirling his fingers in the air.

Cassidy sat up, staring daggers at the big man. I took her hand in mine, wincing as her fingers twined in a crushing grip. I kept forgetting how strong she was.

"What happened after is I ran. Ran like the fires of Chaos itself were nipping my heels. I still had some money stashed from my time with the Quicks, and I put distance between myself and that Ashlar. I kept the map that Luc and I found and eventually found my way here. Found the *Storm*. Been fixing her up and finding out what makes her tick ever since. Once I sussed out how she ran on tarbrine, I set up with the Strigori. Been trying to stay low-key, taking the odd cargo job here and there across Elarin to raise money."

"Money for what?" Eljin asked.

"For *freedom*!" she cried, clenching her fists to her chest. "I've been on my own for two years because that's how I like it! You think I *want* to be around everyone else after what's happened to me? But then I wind up in this little hick coastal town and end up in some crazy adventure with a bunch of *bhakas* that want to take on the frokkin' *Host*!"

She ran a hand across her topknot. "I…I just wanted to score enough that I could find some out-of-the-way place, maybe build a little house, and never have to deal with people in general again. I wanted *away*. Away from groups, away from power structures, away from all the petty drek that folk concern themselves with that doesn't frokking *matter*."

"And instead you've stayed with us," rumbled Korbos.

She eyed the big man. "Yeah. And then I found myself caring about you guys. About what you're trying to do. Why do you think I keep upping your fee? I mean, it's not like you're walking around with eighty thousand karani actually on you. I know that. But I'm *scared*, Korbos. This is all way bigger than me. If I can tell myself that I'll be set after it's done, that gives me a reason to stay. To be involved in something I promised myself I'd never be a part of again."

Those green eyes flickered to meet mine. "Well, *another* reason."

My pulse quickened.

She looked around at all of us, defiance on her face.

"Now, can we stop with this frokking inquisition?" she spat. "Can you *trust me* to not frok you over? Because I won't. Haven't so far. Don't plan to."

Mari and I nodded, ready to be done and get moving on our plan for the Temple of Kol. Eljin just shrugged, ambivalent.

Korbos, however, fixed Cassidy with a stony gaze. His muscles tensed, and he leaned forward, large and threatening. I felt Cassidy recoil and felt like doing the same myself. I shifted, putting myself slightly between her and the blacksmith.

"Just two more questions, mistress Ryker, and it would be in your best interest to answer truthfully. Where did you *really* get the signara? And who in the blazes of Chaos told you where to find *me*?"

TWENTY NINE

Cassidy cringed, sinking back into the plush fabric of our couch. I thought back to Korbos's assertion that there was no way she'd found the signara in the storehouse. Looked like he might have been right after all.

"I…I…" she stammered. "I don't want to tell you that. It touches on parts of my past I don't really care to talk about." She looked to me for help. I looked to Korbos, looming over us like a mountain.

"No more lies or half-truths, Cass," I whispered, leaning in and placing my lips close to her ear. "Put it out there and let's get past all this."

Her shoulders slumped. "Chaos damn it all," she mumbled, before lunging up from her seat and pacing, eventually coming to a rest against the weird gaming table.

"I don't like talking about this part of my life," she repeated, frustration visible, "but if it'll do you some good and ease your mind, then let's have it done. We've got bigger things to focus on."

Korbos growled. "We'll be the judge of that. Now talk."

I was worried. This was the crux of his questioning; the rest of her tale was just extraneous information, as far as he was concerned. How would he react if he didn't like what she said?

Cassidy shot him a look of disgust. "Quit being rude, Patches. I'm getting to it."

He twirled his fingers again. Hurry up.

Cass blew out a hard breath. "Like I said, I grew up in Nordinaar. Land of floating mountains. The airways full of rawn. Home of the Skyriders. My parents were...well, highly-placed, let's say that. I was raised with free run of wherever I put my mind to go. So, naturally, I made friends in and around the Palace of the Heavens. That's where I found the signara."

"In Nordinaar? Not bloody likely," scoffed Korbos. He gave Cassidy a strange look that took me a moment to work out. Disbelief mixed with intense curiosity. He wanted her to continue, but wasn't sure if she was telling the truth.

"Like you'd know?" she snapped. "This will go a lot easier if you'd just listen and stop assuming I'm a liar."

"Not an assumption if it's been proven true."

"Oh, frok you, man. If you're not gonna believe me, why are we even doing this...this interrogation?" She crossed her arms, petulance settling in.

Korbos patted the air with his hands. "Calm it down, Ryker, and finish the story. We'll decide then if we believe you or not."

"Whatever," she huffed. "I don't really give a damn if *you* do or don't. I'm telling this for *them*." A finger shot out, pointing to me and Mariyana.

"So, okay," she continued, "my folks and I didn't get along, to put it mildly. I never wanted for anything, but I was also stifled by them. Be a proper lady. Do this. Don't do that. No risk-taking. You'll marry this boy when you grow up. You'll have *x*-amount of children. You'll follow in our footsteps. That sort of thing.

"It was like they had my entire future planned out from the time I was a toddler and over the edge with whatever *I* wanted. The only thing I ever saw eye-to-eye with them on was rawnhandling. It was the one passion I had that they actively cultivated, which of course eventually made me step away from it.

"But that's neither here nor there. Suffice it to say that, as a surly preteen, I rebelled against them every way I could think. Friends they didn't approve of. Sneaking out at night, out rambling until middle of the next day, so on, so forth. One of my favorite things to do was explore the lower levels of the Palace of the Heavens. The deep levels, where no one has been in centuries. It was the one place I could lose myself for hours. Just miles and miles of ornate tunnels, halls and ballrooms carved into the very rock of the mountain. That exploring may have been why I took so quickly to being a Seeker."

She scratched her arm. "Eventually my ramblings and absences came to a head with my dad. I missed an important function and got into a fistfight with the guards he sent to bring me back. I put one in the infirmary with a ruptured eye and broke the sword arm of the other. Definitely made Dad regret all those combat tutors they made me study under my whole life.

"He went berserk, threatened to cut me from the family. To marry me off, even though I'd only just turned thirteen. Mother had no idea how to handle me, so she just went along with my father's rantings. Order only knew if they'd have done it or not. Looking back, I don't think so; he was just frustrated and unable to contain a rambunctious kid. But I'd be lying if I said hearing those things from him didn't hurt. Even if he might have been justified."

Cass reached over my lap, snatching up a glass of water and taking a long sip. I inhaled sharply as her body brushed against mine, and she gave me a wink as she drew back.

"Being a rebellious teenager," she continued, "of course I ran away. Grabbed some rations and a pack and hauled my backside down into the catacombs, deeper than I'd ever been before. Maybe deeper than anyone had been since the islands were first colonized. I don't know. I stayed down there for three days, exploring at least twenty-five different levels I'd never visited before. Atia herself only knows how many floors are actually down there, because I sure don't.

"By the third day, I was almost out of food. My glowlamp was nearly exhausted. I figured it was time to make my way back up and see if my absence had shown my parents what was what. I imagined that they'd be so wracked with guilt and worry that I'd finally be able to dictate my own terms for my life's trajectory. Wishful thinking, but hey, I was a kid.

"I decided to make one round of the floor I was exploring, and that's when I came across the door. A *wooden* door, unusual enough in an underground stone palace with no other doors at all. But what made it downright weird was the lock. Say what you like about Nordinaar, but locks just aren't a thing there. It's a small kingdom, and the culture doesn't allow for mistrust. I mean, the penalty for thievery is getting pitched over an island's edge and enjoying the Long Fall. So it just doesn't ever happen. The locked door stood out like a thundercloud in a clear sky."

Korbos was nodding. Was he familiar with the area? What was I thinking…of course he was. I didn't figure there were many places within Elarin that he hadn't embedded himself within at *some* point over the past nine hundred years.

"It took me a few minutes, but I found an old iron candelabra and managed to break the lock. Inside was a narrow closet, like you'd use to store brooms and mop bins, but the only thing in it was this pedestal containing a black box.

"I was worried the box would be locked, too, but it opened right up, flooding the area with that soft gold glow the signara puts out. I had no idea what it was, but it was beautiful. Something that definitely had no place being locked forty floors down inside a floating tomb. I picked it up and spent a long time handling it, just turning it over and over, trying to figure out just what in the skies I was holding."

Korbos looked troubled, muttering to himself. I couldn't make out much, but it sounded like "What would be the odds…"

"I was returning it to the box when I found the note. It was written in Coretongue, which confused me. Those rooms were at least two thousand years old, from before Coretongue was even a language, so *who put the box there*? Truth be told, I was kind of disappointed. I'd thought I was the first one to explore those levels. But here was proof that someone else had beaten me to the punch."

Korbos leaned forward, his earlier apprehension forgotten, entranced by the unfolding mystery. "What was on the note?" he asked.

Cassidy leaned forward as well, holding his gaze.

"Your name, big man."

Korbos grunted, his eye blazing. "How the…? Tell me *exactly* what it said."

"I can do you one better."

She bounced up, running out the door before popping her head back in. "Gimme just a minute."

The rest of us sat in thoughtful silence. Well, near-silence. Mari fed treats to Omari and Bastin, who had rejoined us during Cassidy's tale. The scuridai lay near the game table, curled into himself and chomping merrily as his fluffy tail beat a rhythm against the furniture legs.

Cassidy came jogging back in, holding a stiff scrap of parchment in her hand. Shiny reflections bounced from the paper, as if it had been treated somehow. As old as it looked, there had to be some sort of preservative on it, judging by the careless way she was waving it around.

She handed it over to Korbos, who sat down hard, eyes scanning the words again and again. His eye welled up, and he suddenly burst into great heaving sobs, startling us all. His hands clenched, though he was careful not to damage the paper.

I moved to his side, gently taking the note from him. There was indeed some sort of protective coating on it—a transparent slickness that extended slightly past the deckled edges of the paper. I stood and cleared my throat to read it aloud.

"To whomever unearths this treasure: its importance cannot be overstated. Keep it hidden, safe. Keep it from the Host. Take the cube to Korbos, he will reward you. Take my love for him as well. May he ever walk in the light of his own mind. —Rin Colsen"

My jaw dropped. "Wait…*RIN*? As in your…?"

Korbos nodded, his sobs changing to an ecstatic laugh. The big man was happier than I'd ever seen him, an enormous smile beaming out at us.

"Yes! Yes, Pyk! Rin left it for me—for *us*! Order bless that sweet, secretive, trusting *bhaka*! I have *no* idea where he'd have gotten it, but he must have hidden the signara away, hoping someone would one day find it and honor his request. Ha-ha! It only took nine hundred years, but it *worked*!"

He wiped a joyful tear from his good eye, still grinning like a fool. "Oh, gods above and below, Cassidy, I can't tell you the absolute joy this brings me. Bless you." He took her hand and kissed it, bowing low.

She looked uncomfortable, clearly not expecting such a turnaround from his earlier attitude.

"Sooooo," she drawled, "does this mean we're good? Stories squared away and accepted?"

Korbos couldn't stop smiling as Mari pounced and threw her arms around him, hugging him for all he was worth.

"Yes, we're…we're good. And then some. I…I never…" A quiet sob escaped him as he wiped his nose. "I've mourned Rin for centuries, Cassidy. I never expected to hear his words again. To hear his voice speaking anew in my mind. But you've earned the gratitude of a member of the Host. A diminished one, but I hope it counts toward something. What you've given me…I cannot repay this." He held out his massive hand.

Cassidy took his hand in both of hers, her fingers barely covering his first three. "Well, you can start with eighty thousand karani," she smirked, "then maybe keep going." A deep belly laugh exploded from him in response.

I smiled. It was good to see the big guy happy—truly happy—for once.

"What happened after you found the signara, Cassidy?" Eljin asked from right behind me. "Finish the story." I jumped, startled. He'd barely spoken during Cassidy's tale, and I'd nearly forgotten he was there. He moved quietly for a man his size.

"Oh, right. Well, long story short—I made it out, caught a rawn flight out of Nordinaar, and eventually wound up in a small village called Newsome. You know the rest from there. Not much to it, really, other than the fact that I spent nearly nine years hauling that box around with me, waiting to run across a man named Korbos."

"Not exactly a common name, eh? Heh."

"Only one like it."

I cocked my head, jerking a thumb at Korbos. "You've known this whole time that he's the man you've been looking for?"

She at least had the grace to blush. "Well, I *might* have been playing my cards close to the vest on that one. Imagine my surprise when I heard about a skilled local blacksmith by that name while I was racing to unload my ship before a real storm hit Hightide. I never expected to actually find him, you know?"

"Well, yeah, who would?"

"What matters is that she *did* find me," Korbos boomed. "She *did* get the signara to us. Miss Ryker here has kindled hope for a new future."

He stepped forward, placing his hands on her shoulders. "There *is* one more question I would like to ask, Cassidy, before we move on to…other business. Strictly out of curiosity."

Her eyebrows raised. "Okaaaay, I guess?"

"I've spent time in Nordinaar, in and around the court, many times over the centuries. Who is your family? I wonder if I might have had dealings with them."

Cassidy grimaced. "I'd…rather not say."

"Now, Cass," I wheedled, "I thought the secrets were done."

She shuddered, wrapping her arms around herself. Looked up at Korbos, standing a head taller than her, a kind smile on his elated face. Then she sighed in resignation, shoulders drooping.

"Why not? I'm sure you'll badger it out of me eventually." She ran both hands along her topknot. "I was raised by Aelfir and Norun Luftgaard, the Skylord and Cloudmother of the Rahirsken. King and queen of Nordinaar." She shrugged. "Mom and Dad."

My eyes nearly bugged out of my head. "Wait...you...you told me you weren't a princess!"

She glared at me like I was an idiot. "*Adopted*, drekface."

Korbos's eye widened in surprise, hands jerking away from her as if she was burning hot. His mouth opened to say something, but he caught himself and snapped it shut. A troubled look washed over him, just for an instant, before his wide grin returned. I looked around at the others, but no one else seemed to have noticed.

"Well, that's unexpected," he said.

I snorted. The man had a gift for understatement. "Frokking princess..." I muttered.

The big man clapped his hands together. "Okay, Your Majesty," he began.

"Oh, Order above, don't frokking call me that, Patches!"

"Duly noted. Absolutely not, Your Highness. As Mariyana would say, we've got bigger blackfin to bake." Mari giggled from between the two, where she was still hugging Korbos's waist, her laughs muffled by his long coat. "Let's check out this armory of yours and see what sort of trouble Pyk can get himself into." He gently—but with some measure of effort—pried Mari away from him, her eyes wide and grinning big enough to nearly split her face in two.

I tilted my head, not sure what to make of the blacksmith's newfound giddiness. He seemed almost...bubbly. It was a weird contrast to his moodiness and anger—not to mention the drinking—over the last few days, but I wasn't about to complain. I'd take a happy shark over a hungry shark any day of the week, to use a terrible analogy.

And, being honest, I was just *really* glad to finally see unbridled joy on the big man's scarred face.

THIRTY

Cassidy led the way to the armory, with me bringing up the rear. Korbos walked in the middle of our pack, staring intently at the message sent down through the ages, tuning out everything else to the point of a few stumbles as we navigated fallen storage racks and other hazards of the motor pool. Occasionally his lips would curve in a tiny smile. As we approached the weapons room, a decently-sized offshoot of the vehicle depot, he tucked the preserved scrap of parchment inside his coat, in the hidden pocket that lay just over his heart.

His face fell a little as we entered the armory.

"Damnation," he rumbled. "You weren't kidding when you said it had been picked over."

The room was a mess. Rusted, disassembled gun parts—at least that's what I assumed they were—lay scattered on every surface; benches, mesh-fronted lockers, a few small tables in the corners. The lockers themselves were empty, though a great stack of sealed crates stood against the far wall. Hope rose that they might contain some useable firearms. I knew I'd feel a lot better trying to break into a Host's home if I had better weapons than they did.

That hope was dashed as Korbos walked directly to the stacks, running his finger along a few inscribed plates welded to the sides.

"No guns that I can see," he intoned, "though it's still not a bad haul. Cassidy, is this where you found your pistol?"

"No," she replied. "It was in a sealed case I found in one of the smaller offices. Looked like a commander's desk, maybe?" She patted the gun strapped to her thigh. "Just Jasmin here and a single good-sized box of ammunition. Remember, the one Pyk tried to blow up on my ship?"

I rubbed my neck in chagrin. I was never going to live that one down.

"Anyway," she continued, "I tried to get these crates open, but they're shut tighter than Mari's bung. Couldn't even get them to budge."

"Hey!" cried Mari, indignant. She crossed her arms and huffed. Cassidy chuckled, patting the Chek on her back to ease the sting.

"Mmmm," Korbos hummed. "Pyk, see that bar over there, with the pry on one end? Toss that over here." I complied, and he pressed a few buttons that were completely hidden from view.

"How'd you know about…never mind," I said. "Stupid question."

He smirked as three latches popped free of the ridged surfaces of the crates. The pry bar slammed into one of the gaps, and he heaved it open with a loud hiss of air.

"The contents should be in good…ahh, yes," he said. "Magnetically and vacuum-sealed. Too bad all the guns weren't in here." Muscles bulged as he moved the heavy crate to the floor and set about opening the rest.

I swung open the lid and lit up with excitement as I saw the contents. No firearms, but still pretty good nonetheless.

The first crate contained an assortment of well-crafted bladed weapons I assumed were carried as backups for close-quarters combat. Why else would the bygone soldiers need such things when they could fight and kill from a distance? The blades would certainly come in handy for us, though. Well, as handy as an edged weapon would be against someone who could launch you into space with her brain, if she so chose.

Eh, I'd go up against a legion of Hostguard over Kaira any day. It's not like I thought I could actually put her down myself. Korbos could handle the High Lady. I hoped.

We sorted through the offerings Korbos set before us, everyone searching for a weapon that appealed to them.

Mari nearly fell headfirst into a tall crate, disappearing from the waist up—legs flailing—before emerging with a pair of daggers. Strange patterns and whorls saturated the blue-white metal of the blades, which curved slightly and tapered to a needle-sharp point. The hilts and crossguards curved slightly as well, giving the knives a serpentine feel. She brandished them both, small arms raised to the sky as she cackled like a villainous stage actor.

I fished around a bit. Daggers just didn't have the range I wanted, and I was more likely to cut myself than any enemy with a standard sword. Korbos held up a sort of mace-like truncheon, but I shook my head. Too heavy. I'd be skewered before I could ever get the thing around. What I needed was something light and maneuverable, almost like a…hang on…

A row of throwing knives rested on a long cloth, their points slanted up a touch. What was that under them? I gathered them up and set them aside, inhaling sharply when I removed the cloth from beneath. Under it was…I'd never seen anything like it. It was *almost* a sword, half-harpoon, three feet of razor sharp blade that curved to a thick tip and then doubled back upon itself to a second point, like an elongated gut hook.

The metal was the same as Mari's daggers, and I nicked my finger just touching it to the edge. It had an oversized hilt, much longer than a normal sword's, and a five-inch cylindrical pommel for counterweight. Laying within the case was a fitted sheath on some sort of shoulder harness.

There was no way the thing could be wieldable, but it fit my hand as though it were made specifically for me. Light, with a perfect balance. I stepped back and took a few swings, and the blade sang as it cut the air. A closer inspection of the grip revealed two interlocking rings just below the circular crossguard. They rotated slightly under my prodding. Curious. I gave them a sharp twist, and nearly dropped the weapon as the counterweight shot out to the side and the hilt extended a good four feet. It was a spear!

"Thaaaaat was *cool*," said Mari, eyes wide and staring.

I grinned like an idiot. A spear, I could work with.

"Mari, give this a try," said Korbos, tossing her what looked to be a child's toy. I squinted. It *was* a child's toy—a slingshot to be precise. One made of sturdy metal rather than wood, with some sort of stretchy material in place of a traditional leather sling strap. A curved metal piece folded down and flowed from the handle, offering support to her wrist. She squealed and gave it an experimental tug. Korbos smiled and handed over a hefty pouch filled with small metal balls, gesturing for her to try it out on a nearby locker.

She loaded the cup, pulled back to her cheek and let fly. I winced, preparing to duck and cover if the metal ball rebounded throughout the room. To everyone's amazement but Korbos, the projectile rocketed through the air and, with an extremely loud *SPANG!*, punched a hole straight through the steel door. Mari stared at the sling, and I shuddered, imagining what that sort of velocity would do to a person's head.

I glanced over to Cassidy, who stood with a huge grin on her face. "Not gearing up?" I asked.

She patted Jasmin's thigh holster and the hilt of her collapsible sword. "Nah, I'm good, Guts. Already got everything I need."

I shrugged, going back to fawning over my new spearswordharpoonthing. I was going to have to name it something fierce and menacing. As if she'd read my mind, Cassidy walked over and slapped a hand on my shoulder.

"It's name is now and forevermore Chum, chum."

The others burst into laughter. I frowned at them. "Absolutely not. This is Sharkslayer. Or Waveslicer. Or…or…"

"Or Chum!" Mari howled, doubled over and gripping her sides.

"Or…or Fish…Fishguts!" Cassidy screamed, unable to catch her breath, rocking side to side on the bench where she'd plopped down. "Fishguts for Guts!" Even Eljin was cackling.

I glared at all of them, throwing a rude gesture to each in turn before busying myself with an attempt at sizing the harness to fit me.

Korbos looked to Eljin, who was still strolling about, poking around the opened crates. "Can't find anything you like?" he asked the old man.

"Heh. Not as of yet, friend. I like something with a little more…heft, if you catch my meaning."

"Hmmm," Korbos rumbled, bending to scan the inscriptions upon the three remaining unopened boxes. He started, then leaned in closer to one.

"Ah!" he exclaimed. "See if this might suit you."

He slid out the bottommost case—a wide, flat thing that was nearly as long as I was tall. Eljin borrowed the pry bar and heaved it open. Inside was hands-down the biggest damn two-handed sword I'd ever seen in my life. Four feet of rippling steel, with a wide guard and a triangular blade that came to a point sharp enough to punch through a hull. The hilt was nearly as long as my forearm. It wasn't so much a sword as it was a battering ram.

"Heh…now, that'll do," hummed Eljin. It seemed ludicrous that the old man could heft such a weapon, but he surprised me by bending down with only a slight hitch and lifting the blade as easily as I would a fishing pole. Old or not, he sure wasn't decrepit. My amazement must have been plain, because he grinned and held it out toward me, blade pointed to the ceiling.

I took it out of sheer morbid curiosity and nearly dislocated my shoulders as my arms gave out and it clanged to the ground. The metal of the blade was surprisingly thick, with little edge to speak of. I heaved myself back to a standing position, barely able to hold the giant monstrosity parallel to the ground. Eljin laughed and took it back, laying the flat against his shoulder.

It…fit him, I thought. He'd been looking better and better as we'd traveled—not necessarily younger, but rejuvenated. The hunched old man from the Lau Tuai was gone, and in his place stood a powerful warrior; thick with muscle and ready for fresh adventures. I just prayed to Atia that we weren't leading him to his *last* adventure.

Korbos picked up the spearswordharpoonthing I'd set down and turned it over in his hands. The patterns in the metal rippled in a blue-white sheen as he ran a palm down the flat of the blade.

"A riphook," he murmured. "Haven't seen one of these in an age. It suits you." He turned to Mari, nodding approval of her daggers. "These are carbsteel-forged. You can tell by the patterning and the light hue of the metal. Virtually unbreakable, and with proper care they'll hold an edge through some pretty hard abuse." His arm swept a lazy gesture at Eljin. "That one's more a bludgeon than an actual sword, of course, but that tip will punch through a steel wall, much less an armored opponent."

Mari holstered her new knives in fitted sheaths she'd attached to her belt. "Why would Imperium soldiers even bother with low-tech stuff like this if they had guns and rifles and ammunition and oh were they rare even back then I bet they were because there's not many laying around here unless they were all taken before the place got trashed I wonder what actually happened with that—"

She cut off as Korbos held up a hand.

"There's no way of ever knowing what happened to this base. I thought for a while that it might have been the one where Kaira captured me a few centuries back, but I've never actually been here before. Frankly, I'm amazed by the place. I thought I knew all of the Second Battalion storehouses, but apparently not.

"As for the guns, they weren't exactly *rare* pre-Ruin, but not every soldier carried one, either. Cassidy got lucky in finding her officer's pistol. You see how these around us have deteriorated? They would have to have been vacuum-sealed to last the ages. The things were mass-produced, too—not exactly the high quality of those handheld weapons you're fondling."

I stopped running my hand along the metal of my riphook, shooting a furtive look around the room. Everyone was grinning at me.

"There was also the matter of the Host's purge," Korbos continued. "You have to remember, we did incalculable damage to them at the time.

After the Ruin, and after the Resistance had faded into obscurity, Kalos and Kaira pulled a feat I'd have never thought possible. They rounded up and destroyed damn near everything more powerful than Mari's new sling."

He rubbed the back of his neck as we shuffled, eager to move on. "Those null bombs we used scared the hells of Chaos out of them. They wanted power. Wanted *control.* And the best way to maintain that was to eradicate any meaningful method of resistance from the populace. That's why Hostguard aren't armed with anything stronger than stunpikes. It took them over a century, but eventually everything but the memory of firearms was removed from Elarin."

"I dunno," Cassidy said, drawing her gun and holding it before her. "Given the time and inclination, I could probably figure out how to machine some of these things. They're definitely less complicated than steamcart engines."

"I'm sure you could, mistress Ryker, but I don't think you'd want to. Of all the things the Host deserve to be vilified for, making it harder for people to kill one another isn't one I'd necessarily disagree with. In any case, all it would take was the *rumor* of someone manufacturing firearms, and the Host would have razed wherever you called home to the ground. The entire region around it as well, most likely."

Cass whistled through her teeth.

"The Host are *adamant* that nothing spring up that can challenge their power. They can't afford to let that sort of knowledge evolve again to the level of null bombs or other weapons that can actually hurt them. And that's just the tip of the scientific advancements they've suppressed over the centuries. Why do you think so few of the ancient wonders are commonplace today? It's not for lack of people trying to recreate them, I'll tell you."

I paused, thoughtful. I'd never considered that the Host were keeping Elarin at a progressive standstill. It *was* curious that, in all the time since the Ruin, so few of the commonplace marvels had made a reoccurrence. No autocarts. So very few aerowings. I didn't miss the kill-everyone-and-their-mothers type of weapons Korbos had described, but there were so many things from the past that could make everyday life better for the common person, if only they were allowed to have them.

The big man shrugged Bulwark on his shoulder. "Just one more minor atrocity to lay at their feet. Now, if everyone's settled, we've got some planning to do. I'd also like to take a minute to check out the back of those trucks in the motor pool. If we're lucky, those armored vehicles were carrying some useful stuff."

The vehicles were indeed carrying some useful stuff.

Korbos was like a kid at a candy stall as we unloaded the backs of the autocarts. Crate after crate piled up around him, his nose pressed close as he squinted to read off the contents embossed on the sides. Most of it didn't make sense to me, and the stuff that did make sense wasn't exactly useful to us at the moment. Three crates of portable tents. Four full of ancient military fatigues. Several crates of body armor, but it was overly bulky and wouldn't serve too well where we planned to go. A crate with portable heating boxes. Mostly, they were full of items that were well-made—some incredibly well-preserved—but we couldn't afford to cart them about with us.

"Cassidy!" Korbos called out, waving her over, excited by whatever was written on the box he was currently examining. She jogged over to join him as he pried open the lid with a hiss of escaping pressure.

"Order above protect and preserve us," Cassidy murmured. "Is that… what I think it is?"

"I thought you'd like this one."

The pilot laughed, a high delighted sound, before clapping Korbos on the back.

"What?" asked Mari. "Whatcha got?"

Cassidy reached down and pulled up some sort of metallic belt, with what looked like bullets attached to it. They were far larger than the ones she used in her pistol; each was near the length of my hand. I couldn't imagine the size of the gun that would fire them…hold on. Maybe I could.

I looked to the *Storm*. The huge gun barrel mounted under the cockpit. "No *way*!" I breathed.

"Oh yeah," grinned Cassidy. She positively cackled. "We've got some teeth now. Once I figure out how to load the sucker."

I smiled back at her. A giddy feeling filled the air around us; luck was finally breaking in our favor for once. It helped that we had a nine hundred-year-old translator walking around with us. Order only knew how long it would have taken to go through each of these crates by hand, if we ever even managed to get them open in the first place.

"I'll help you with that in a bit, Cassidy," Korbos said. "I've done something similar before, though it *has* been a while. We should be able to figure it out."

He was trying, Order bless him. Since the revelation of Rin's note, the big smith had been almost *overly* friendly to Cassidy. I was happy for him, truly I was, I just hoped he didn't overdo it in his attempts to make nice with her. Or everyone else, for that matter. We needed him focused and battle-ready.

Only three of the dark crates were left. The first, Korbos skimmed the imprinted writing and dismissed, but on the second—the largest by far, nearly waist-deep and just as wide—he stood bolt upright and beckoned for the pry bar. The lid opened with a hiss, and he pumped a fist in triumph.

"Excellent!" he cried. "We're in business now." A wondrous laugh crinkled his scarred face.

Eljin and I strolled over to see what had the big man so worked up, but I had no idea what I was seeing. The box was about two-thirds filled with some sort of…yeah, no idea. They looked like blocks of gray bread dough, a tiny black device with several buttons set atop each. There looked to be dozens of them. The remaining third, divided by a rigid partition, contained a number of black metal globes with a type of sliding flat lever embedded on a thin equatorial line rounding each.

"And this is…?" I queried.

"This," Korbos said, drawing the word out, "is the good stuff, Pyk." He hefted one of the gray brick-like things, tossing it from hand to hand. "These are explosives. Strong ones. These could come in handy."

"Order above, stop doing that then!" I backed away from him and the block he was haphazardly tossing.

"Calm, Pyk, calm. They have to be primed and armed. They're inert, otherwise." He pointed to the buttons set within the device on top.

"Okay, sure, yeah, just…stop tossing it around, please. Let's not push the switch."

Eljin's face split in a wide grin, startlingly white against his dark skin, and Korbos smirked at my discomfort.

"What are these other things?" I asked.

"Plasma pulse grenades," Korbos replied. "Matter of fact…"

The blacksmith picked up one of the black globes and walked over to Mariyana.

"You might like these, little one," he said, handing over the globe. "Since we don't have any more of your wonderful boompowder on-hand."

"Ooooooh, what do these do?" she began, and—being Mari—immediately pushed the sliding switch forward with her thumb.

"*Damn!*" screamed Korbos, snatching the ball from her hands and hurling it as far as he could. Which was all the way across the tarmac, given his enhanced strength. It rolled to a stop beneath some sort of wheeled lift.

"*Everybody down!*"

Everyone hit the ground. Cassidy dove behind one of the vehicles for cover. I had an instant to wish I'd thought of that when the globe exploded with an almighty *WHAMP!*

A crackling ball of blue energy, similar to the blasts from Bulwark, burst outward for a brief moment before dissipating.

The lift—weighing five thousand pounds, easily—rocketed into the air as though it were a toy hurled by an angry child before crashing down with a deafening racket. The underside appeared to have disintegrated to the tops of the wheel wells. A spherical hole at least ten feet wide had been carved out of the floor and nearby wall, and the remains of the lift slewed to a screeching rest in the bottom of the hollow.

We all dusted ourselves off and turned to glare at Mari. Order anyway, that girl needed to get a grip on her impulse control. Korbos should have known better, too.

"Oops," she said with a sheepish smile.

Even Bastin hissed at her.

THIRTY ONE

"You're sure this will work?" I asked Eljin, wiping my brow against the incessant heat. "It's been twenty years. They might have changed things up."

We were stretched flat on an overhang of a tall, rocky hill, looking out across an expanse of hardpan that led into the Mohagan desert. Mariyana and Korbos stood further down the slope, out of view of anyone traveling the pilgrimage route Eljin had led us to find. Cassidy and the animals remained with the *Storm*, hidden two miles back behind one of the gargantuan sandstone buttes that sprouted like beanstalks throughout the region.

Miles away, nestled among the towering edifices, was the Temple of Kol. No real details were visible, but the pyramidal structure had to be frokking enormous to be seen at such distance. The desert extended behind it to infinity, nothing but sand and baking sun wavering with heat mirages. Entering such a fortress under cover of stealth was going to be damn near impossible.

My body shook with nervous energy. It was all well and good to talk and make plans, but were we *actually* about to do this? Sneak into Kaira's own stronghold? What had seemed exciting and adventurous in the planning stage now felt like slow suicide when confronted with the reality of having to, you know, actually pull it off.

Order anyway, what was I doing here? I wasn't a fighter, I was a bloody fisherman. I was good at finding fish. Fishing. That was about it.

Eljin chuckled. "Sure? No, not sure, friend Pyk. Heh. Not much to be *sure* about any of this." He shook his head, the white mane of hair flowing about like liquid in the dry wind. "But they'll be coming this way, of that I *am* sure."

I, for one, was beginning to doubt. We'd been camped out here for hours, and my bits and bobs were hurting. Korbos and Mari at least had the option of moving every so often, climbing up the slope of the outcropping to ask if we'd seen anything new. Each time the response was the same negative, and each time my body got a teensy bit more sore.

"We need a Plan B," I muttered. Order only knew when—or *if*—our quarry would make their way into the valley, but Eljin stood firm in his prediction.

"They'll come, Pyk," he told me. "Like clockwork, they come. Heh. Every tenth day of the month. Any moment now."

"Yeah, I'll believe it when I see—well, I'll be dipped in bait and thrown to the greatsharks."

A plume of dust appeared in the distance, growing larger by the minute. There was a steamcart making its way onto the hardpan, high rails extending along a six-foot long flatbed behind the driver's cabin. They were still a long way off, but near as I could tell there were five passengers bouncing around in the back, with one or maybe two in the cabin. A manageable number, just as the old man had said. Eljin was duly impressed with my eyesight, patting me on the back.

"Here we go," I said, rising to signal the others. I yelped as Eljin's thick hand dragged me back down by the seat of my pants.

"Don't raise up, boy!" he hissed. "You'll stand out against the sky and botch the whole thing! Bah!"

I cursed to myself. He was right. I should have known better. Stupid, Pyk. I wiggled my way backwards until I was past the rocky ridge and easing down the slope.

Eljin followed, a bit slower but with less wincing and grunting. It wasn't fair that the old man wasn't as worn out as I was from the blistering sun and long stretch of immobility on the hard rock. The closer we came to Kaira's lair, the more vitality he appeared to gain.

Revenge *was* a beast of a motivator, it seemed.

I wondered when my motivation had moved past revenge and into duty. Don't get me wrong, I still wanted to see Kaira burn, but truth be told I'd bought into Korbos's dream hook, line, and bobber. I wanted to see a world free to grow on its own, without the influence of immortal tyranny. Without the stifling of progress.

I wanted a world where I could find a good life with someone.

My eyes turned inexorably to the far-off butte the *Storm* lay hidden behind. I was thankful that Cassidy had stuck with us so far, though she had been a little *too* happy to stay behind with the ship in case we needed a fast getaway. I hoped she'd continue on after all this. Assuming, of course, that we didn't all die an agonizing death within the next few hours.

A guy could daydream.

"They're on the way," I told Korbos and Mari upon reaching the loose scree at the bottom of the rocks. "He was right."

"Damn straight I was!" Eljin chimed, sliding to us with a nimble little hop I wouldn't have expected just a few days prior. "Heh. Going by the eyes of your young friend here, there's about six or eight of 'em, so he says. Don't forget the plan. We need their livery intact."

"I still don't see what we need their livers for," I grumbled. "Seems a bit excessive."

"Their clothes, Pyk," chirped Mari, shaking her head. "We need their clothes."

"Right, I knew that. Just messing about." She rolled her eyes.

We rounded the stone formation and strolled out to the hardpan, taking our time. The dust cloud grew closer and closer. Korbos shrugged his rifle from his shoulder, holding it out for me to take.

"How did *I* become the designated gun carrier person?" I whined.

Korbos didn't reply, just moved ahead of us about ten paces before turning his head.

"You might want to spread out," he said over his shoulder. I could hear the rumbling of the steamcart's engine as it sped toward us.

The three of us split, edging out to the sides; Mari and I on Korbos's left, Eljin to the right. I switched weapons, shouldering Bulwark and pulling Chum from its scabbard, slung across my back. Gods above and below, now even I was calling the riphook that. Even if it *was* a stupid name, at least it conjured up images of blood and guts.

My nerves jangled as the vehicle drew closer, the sun glinting from the glass of the wind screen, blinding.

The others drew their weapons as well, Mari fitting a ball to the cup of her new sling. Eljin whistled a little ditty as he unslung that gargantuan cleaver of his, holding it up over his shoulder in a roof guard.

The driver of the steamcart, seeing an armed group blocking their path, floored it. White billows hissed as they shot forward at the cart's maximum speed, intent on running us down. I held Chum in a two-handed grip, standing my ground, with absolutely no idea what Korbos was going to do to stop the barreling engine.

Just as the cart was about to mow through him, the blacksmith raised his arms and, with a bellowing roar, smashed in the vehicle's front with his bare fists. I jumped as it flipped end over end, bodies flying in every direction, before crashing to the desert floor in a plume of dust. As the dust cleared and the debris settled, we disarmed and drug the groaning forms of five stunned Inori priests to the wreckage. Korbos grunted and, eye flaring silver, ripped one of the doors from the driver's cab. Two more bodies splayed out into the hardpan. No, three. A tiny robed figure slid out, coughing. We disarmed them as well and put them with the others.

"Lucky," murmured Eljin. "They have a Chek with them. Heh. Lucky indeed, eh? Now we won't have to adjust robes for Mariyana. Hah!"

I nodded. Lucky, indeed.

"This is most fortunate, friend Pyk. The High Lady doesn't often allow non-human courtesans or adherents. Heh. Pretty rare to find so much as a single Thrane or Chek in the Temple of Kol."

I nodded again as he slapped my back, nearly knocking me to the ground alongside the Inori.

Korbos finished lining up the priests, then glanced to the rest of us. "You know the drill. Grip 'em and strip 'em."

"How *dare* you!" cried one of the priests, a male by his build. His voice rang metallic from the dust-covered geometric mask covering his face. He stood, stalking toward Mari. "The fires of Atia's wrath will consume you for this abominable attack on the High Lady's adherents! The Great One herself will peel your flesh like the skin of a grape for this! You—"

He cut off abruptly as her curved dagger pressed against his robes, the needle-sharp tip poking a small hole in the region of his groin. A squawk rang from beneath the mask.

"Do sit down, sir," growled Mari. The Inori quickly scampered back, taking a seat next to his brethren and sharing glances with those nearest him. Mari glared at the Chek among them, incensed that one of her kind would willingly follow Kaira. I couldn't blame her, given what the culls had done to the Chek as a whole.

Korbos raised his voice. "Do as we say and you'll live through this. We're going to need you to kindly remove your clothing and stand together in a nice tidy little group."

A babble of negatives surged from the priests, two of whom were women. Their eyes widened beneath the masks, and fancifully-coiffed hair floated as they shook their heads.

Eljin sighed, and with a swift move brought his sword around in an overhead chop that sheared clean through the hood, engine block, and metal wheel of the wrecked steamcart before burying itself in the hardpan below.

There were no more objections.

Robes flew as the Inori scrambled to get them off. More than one of the fools were not wearing undergarments, and I smirked as they tried to cover themselves. Mari piled the clothing and masks aside as Eljin and I began restraining the priests with lengths of rope. One, sporting a ridiculous hairstyle of hard-greased spikes that stood out from his skull like the business end of a mace, tried to headbutt me. I kicked his legs from under him and conked him over the skull with my artificial hand. Made it a lot easier to hogtie him as he lay on the ground, senseless. Soon enough the rest were bound and seated in a loose circle.

A loud rumble rolled across the plain. Korbos stood before a nearby rock formation, eye flaring, as stones larger than the cart itself exploded into the air, hollowing out a small cave. Eljin, Mari and I poked and prodded the Inori into the hole. Their eyes were saucers as they saw Korbos grouping up the floating rocks. I tried to shut out the cries of despair as he moved them back into place, trapping the Inori within.

"Don't fret, Pyk," the big man said. "They'll eventually get themselves loose, and there's enough wiggle room in there for them to dig their way free. One of these days."

I nodded, exhaling in relief. As much as I disliked the Inori, I wasn't keen on the idea of trapping a group of clergy to die of starvation or asphyxiation.

I joined the rest as we sorted through the pile of robes, looking for a good fit for each of us. Mari was already garbed. Eljin was right; we'd gotten lucky there was a Chek in the delegation. The robes were only slightly too long for her, but the mask fit well. Her twin puffballs only added to the look, emulating the oddball hairstyles popular with so many of the Inori. She giggled and made a turn, looking around before her shoulders slumped. My heart went out to her. We kept forgetting Bastin wasn't with us.

As well as the robes hung on Mari, Korbos was another matter altogether. There was nothing even close to fitting him. It took a half-hour we couldn't really spare for me to stitch together an approximation of the Inori robes in the big man's size.

Yes, I could sew. When you spent weeks at a time out on a trawler in the middle of the sea, you learned how to repair your own clothing.

"And you're *sure* this will work?" I asked Eljin once we were all robed up and ready to set out. Korbos shoved his rifle into a heavy duffel. Mari shrugged on a matching one.

The old man gave me a wry grin, so like Cassidy's that my heart missed a beat. I wished she was with us. I didn't like the fact that she had to stay behind, but it was almost certain that we'd need her to provide an extraction. I hoped our luck would continue and the necessity wouldn't arise, but better safe than sorry.

"Yar," replied Eljin. "Just stick with me, let me do the talking. Heh." He adjusted his robes around the strap of his enormous sword and settled the metal mask upon his face. A mane of flyaway white hair surrounded the mask like a halo, giving him an even more authentic look than Mari. "Spent more time around these Inori whoresons than I'd ever admit, and you pick up a thing or two."

We set out in a brisk walk toward the temple, shimmering miles away in the heat haze. A necessary part of our plan, but this part was going to stink like last month's catch.

The Temple of Kol was further away than anticipated. It took us over an hour, counting a couple of stops to chug down water, to reach the gates. I was swimming with sweat inside the heavy robes.

The metal mask hid my slack jaw as we approached the entry thoroughfare, a long dirt path laid with fifty-foot wide marble slabs and lined with matching columns topped with cross-pieces. Workers dotted the stones, sweeping away the encroaching sand and dust in an unending labor. Poor sods on the windward edge were furiously brushing even as the breeze deposited piles on the areas they'd only just worked. They had a haunted, haggard look about them.

On the southern side of the compound was a raised steel platform, emerging from the sand of the desert itself, and what sat upon it took my breath away. A skipship, easily twice the size of the *Storm.* Maybe three times as big. Far less elegant—blocky and solid, it seemed made of sharp angles and bludgeoning edges—it rested on four landing legs like a glacier poised to crush everything in its slow path. Kaira's personal vessel.

A shudder ran through me. It was the same ship I'd seen rising through the skies above Emun.

The Temple itself was nothing short of stupefying. A seven-hundred-foot-tall pyramid, it rose in ten stepped levels, its primary face broken by two wide marble stairways leading to an open-air plaza lined with statues. I squinted. They were all depictions of Kaira herself, carved in unyielding stone and topped with large slabs much like the columns far below. The lowest tier of stone—the foundations of the Temple—were carved the same, friezes encircling the entire structure with decorative depictions of the Host destroying armies, rising above the common people, ruling the known world, so on, so forth. Self-aggrandizement on a massive scale.

A gaping maw was set into the lower two tiers of the structure, recessed into the Temple itself, surrounding a pair of enormously tall ornate doors cracked wide enough to allow passage to the numerous staff and pilgrims. They buzzed about, hustling on foot or riding on small steamcarts that

ferried them to and from the squat outlying structures we passed on our trek down the promenade. Six levels above us, a crowd drank and reveled upon the steppe, some leaning over the high rail fence and jeering out unintelligible shouts to those below. Hostguard patrolled everywhere.

The ostentatiousness of it all made me sick.

I kept my head on a swivel, expecting to be accosted at any moment, but nobody gave us a second look as we proceeded to a small gatehouse set into the wall near the enormous doors. A bored-looking Hostguard—his insectile helmet resting on a table within the tiny room—looked us up and down, taking in our sweat-stained and dusty robes with a slight sneer. He thumped his stunpike against the stone.

"Big one, ain'tcha?" the guard asked Korbos. "You must be the Crannick delegation?" he inquired. His eyes narrowed in suspicion as Eljin stepped forward. "You're two hours overdue" He looked down at a clipboard in his offhand. "And I have eight of you on the schedule." His hand tightened on his weapon.

"Right you are, sir," said Eljin, his voice taking on a more provincial accent. The old man shuffled forward, bowing slightly and projecting an air of obsequiousness. "Too right. Heh. Had a little accident on the approach. Damn rockslide smashed our cart a few miles out. Biggest stones you ever saw, rumbling right off the promontory. Crushed the cab completely, and took four of our brethren to the arms of Atia herself, may she cradle their souls from the fire."

"Is that right?"

"Correct, good sir. Couple of 'em got buried in the slide. Weren't a thing we could do for 'em, not with all that weight. Poor Jerris got flung out the back and up against the rocks. Smashed his head right in, poor soul. Had to bury him right there in the desert, which of course took us some time now, didn't it? Check for yourself, if you'd like...you'll find the wreckage about two hours west of us."

"Hmph," the guard grunted. He looked us over, suspicion clouding his face. "I don't have anyone to spare at the moment. I suppose you'll be wanting to get cleaned up before you report to the Inarium on Level Five then."

Eljin cocked his head. "I think you might be mistaken, sir. The Inarium is on Level Six. But sure enough, we'll be heading right there once we swap these dirty old rags for some fresh clothing and showers in the Level Four barracks."

The guard grunted again, nodding. His posture relaxed as he waved us through. "Welcome back, adherents."

"Our thanks, good sir, and may Atia's divine wroth avoid your days."

The guard rolled his eyes as he turned away from us and back to his duties.

We adjusted our gear and headed through the enormous doors. It took a lot of willpower to not stare, to act as if I were familiar with the Temple. I was glad I had on the featureless mask, because I couldn't keep my mouth from hanging open.

We entered into a gilded world, a massive open-floor chamber supported by rows of columns ten feet thick that receded into the distance. There were people everywhere; milling about in groups, walking with purpose toward whatever errand they currently found themselves on, chatting about the weather. Who knew? Eljin had been right, though. Mari was the only non-human I could see, earning us more than one sidelong glance as we made our way through the floor.

Gold embellishments covered nearly everything within sight. Palm trees ran the edges of the floor and surrounded a gigantic bathing pool set within the middle of the room, where a multitude of gilded men and women frolicked. Seriously, they were gilded; gold paint covered their naked torsos in fanciful geometrically-detailed patterns. I'm no prude, but the sheer amount of flesh on display made me blush behind my mask. Mari gave a low snort of amusement. Some of them were engaged in acts…well, acts best not described to those of a more sensitive constitution. Robed figures lounged on long couches nearby, munching fruit and enjoying the show as they were fanned by mostly-nude servants covered in that same gold paint.

Among the debauchery, Inori priests walked about, some fingering the weapons at their sides. Relief flooded me. I'd been worried about carrying our blades openly, despite Eljin's reassurances that it wasn't uncommon for Inori to go armed, even within the Temple.

"Into the cragcat's den," Korbos whispered.

"Yeah, and the cats are apparently in heat…" I replied. Mari slapped my arm.

Eljin led us through the mass of humanity, nodding here and there to other Inori yet moving rapidly enough that we appeared as though we were on a mission. No one tried to stop or converse with us, although I could have sworn a number of the expressionless masks were watching with disapproval at our filthy state of dress.

I glanced around at the multiple lighting sconces glowing bright and steady along the walls. Huge ring lights on the ceiling above added to the illumination, immersing the entire floor in a warm golden haze that gave the place a look of dreamy soft focus, reflecting from all the golden inlays and painted folk. So the Temple had power. Maybe that geothermical stuff Korbos mentioned back at the storehouse.

I shuddered as I realized our destination. We were headed straight for the bathing pool. In the middle of the water—the exact center of the Temple, near as I could tell—was a square column rising up through the ceiling. Two sliding metal doors were set into the marble, and a small causeway extended across the pool to them. I tried not to look at the carnal writhing surrounding me as Eljin reached forward to press an illuminated button centered between the doors. After a moment, one opened on its track, and we stepped into a small mirrored room designed to fit maybe twelve people.

I sighed in relief as it slid closed. Then I nearly wet myself as my stomach lurched and we began to rise further into the Temple of Kol.

THIRTY TWO

I ripped off my mask, hyperventilating. Lights shone bright within the lift, but it was almost worse than being buried in that tunnel under Cortian. Way tighter.

"Calm, Pyk, calm," Korbos soothed, taking my shoulder and staring me in the eye.

"I'm calm," I replied, attempting to deepen my breaths. "I'm very frokking calm."

Gods above and below, I wished Cassidy was there with me. I hoped she was okay. We'd hidden the *Storm* behind a particularly wide butte, but it's not like there was a lot of cover out there in the desert, especially for something as large as a skipship. All it would take was one of those Hostguard patrols on a steamcart to round the wrong way and—

No. Focus. Focus. Breathe in. Breathe out. She can take care of herself better than you can, idiot.

Within a few moments I was…well, not okay, but steady, focusing on my companions rather than the metal box we were trapped in. The tight, cramped metal box currently rising through the air on Order knew what sort of mechanical contraption that could fail at any second and send us plunging into the—

My friends jumped as I slapped myself across the face.

"Slight change to the plan," said Eljin as I got myself under control. "We go up to Four, grab new robes as we told the guard. Heh. We'll never blend in like this. You saw the looks we were getting."

Korbos sighed in irritation but accepted the necessity of the delay.

I glanced at the big man and was alarmed to see a tremor in his free hand. Thoughts of being trapped fled my mind. He noticed my concern and swung it behind his back.

"I'm good," he rumbled. "Been a while since I've had a drink, is all. Just my mind trying to convince me that I need one. I'm okay, see?" He brought his hand back around and stared at it, concentrating. The tremble slowed, then stopped. He exhaled, then quirked the scarred corner of his mouth into an apologetic grin.

I threw a mock punch at his gut. "Stay strong, big guy." Truth be told, I was in awe of the control he showed over his body. I knew sailors who had gone into debilitating convulsions over liquor withdrawals. What kind of iron will did it take for Korbos to tamp down the shakes coursing through him? If only I were so sure about his ability to master his emotions. I rubbed my neck unconsciously, remembering the feel of hard bulkhead at my back, his hand at my throat.

Any further conversation was stifled by a loud *ding* as the door opened before us. I slammed the mask back down over my face. Wouldn't do to be seen just yet.

We stepped out into a wide hall completely unlike the lower level. The stone walls and floors were replaced—or possibly plated—with dull gray metal, hammered into geometrical shapes that mirrored our masks. The hall was otherwise void of any ornamentation, just gray as far as we could see. No signs, no markers, no indication of where any of the cutaway doors led. Few lights shone from recesses in the metal ceiling, leaving parts of the hallway in shadow. The Inori aesthetic was decidedly gloomy. And featureless.

It would be *way* too easy to get lost here.

Eljin didn't pause for a second, leading us down the hall, then around the corner to an open door on the outer edge. A large open room ringed with metal cubbies greeted us, Inori robes and masks lining the shelves. Nozzled pipes extruded from the ceiling, hovering over short metal walls that reached as high as my waist in an X configuration. They looked like stalls.

It was a communal shower and changing room. Order above, did the people in this place do *everything* together?

"C'mon, hurry up and get changed," Eljin said, dropping the bag he carried before stripping off his robes. "Fast, like. Heh. We need to be in and out before anyone else comes in."

"Is this really necessary?" I asked.

Apparently it was, as everyone was shrugging out of their clothes as fast as possible.

"Stop being such an old lady, Guts," Mari japed. My heart ached at hearing Cassidy's nickname for me.

"Yar," continued Eljin, chucking his robes into a gray steel hamper built into the nearest wall. "It's expected of adherents to be presentable at all times within the Temple. We go wandering around covered in sweat and desert muck, it's a dead giveaway we're not supposed to be here."

I hopped around, struggling to get my leg out of my clothing. "We're wasting time."

"You'll be wasting more time in the prison block if we get caught, Pyk."

"There is that," I replied, snagging another set of Inori garb off the shelves.

Within minutes we were all changed and freshened up, looking for all the world like every other Inori we'd passed. Eljin led the way back out into the gloomy hall and back around to the elevator.

"Time to part ways," said Korbos, shouldering his bag. "Stick to the plan, and we'll be fine. But Pyk, if things go awry, *get yourselves out.* I'll protect Mari, and we'll find another way to get below. But don't take any unnecessary risks." The big man clapped my metal shoulder.

"Who, me?" I responded, arching an eyebrow. I tilted my head, realizing after the fact that he couldn't see my facial expressions behind the mask.

Korbos punched the call button.

"No, really. You think I'd take unnecessary risks? Order above, man, *I'm* not gonna try and go face-to-face with Kaira. That's your job, mate."

Korbos glanced at me, then barked a ringing laugh from the confines of his own faceguard. He shook his head, saying nothing.

The lift door opened, and several blank-faced Inori looked out at us. Goosebumps broke out across my arms. Korbos and Mari stepped in and took their place, nodding to the adherents, who tilted their heads at Eljin and me.

"Sorry, going up," I said, pointing my finger as the door slid closed. My gut clenched, and I prayed to Order above that this wouldn't be the last time I saw my friends.

"Here we go. Heh," murmured Eljin as the second lift door opened for us, thankfully empty. We stepped in, and Eljin punched a lit button.

"How far up are we going, again?" I asked.

"Kaira's audience chamber is on Level Eight," the old man replied. "Nine is off-limits to everyone except housekeeping, who have their own access cards. Private quarters. Heh. Ten?" He shook his head. "You don't wanna see Ten."

We arrived at Level Eight two minutes later, and I exited to chaos.

The massive floor was brightly lit by wide circular lights high overhead and ceremonial braziers blazing ominously every twenty feet or so. Couches rested haphazardly, indolent courtiers reclining upon them. The rest of the visible space was *filled* with people—most of them well-dressed sycophants, with some Inori adherents scattered throughout—standing shoulder-to-shoulder a hundred deep and facing an enormous dais at the far wall. A deafening chant filled the air, as arms flailed about in supplication.

The wall itself was something from a nightmare, filled its entire length with bleeding bodies nailed into the stone, arms and legs splayed wide. Sheets of blood ran down the stones to pool in catches set like baseboards. I saw more than one Chek among the victims and was thankful that Mari wasn't there to see. Most of the unfortunate beings hung limp, but a few writhed in agony, their thin screams echoing above the chants. Each time they wailed, the chanting increased in volume.

As a counterpoint to the thrashings of those on the wall, the steps of the platform were covered with writhing bodies in various states of undress, much like the bathers we'd passed earlier. Whenever the crowd crescendoed, the performers would thrash all the harder. It was a horror of pain and pleasure, a farce put on for the depravity of the fevered watchers.

We'd stumbled into some sort of ceremony. I was glad I was wearing the stolen mask, because there was no way I could hide the disgust and revulsion I felt.

Upon the stone dais stood a gigantic gold throne, shaped to resemble a kraykan or some other manner of sea beast. Suckered tentacles, delicately forged, arced over the plush cushioned seat, where a woman lounged with regal disdain.

Kaira, High Lady of the Host, in the flesh. She was even more stunning than when I'd last seen her in Hightide, none the worse for having had a four-masted carrack dropped on her head. A glass of wine—at least I hoped it was wine—floated lazily in the air near her outstretched hand.

Standing close to her throne on the right was a tall, rangy man, who looked out over the crowd with a tight, evil grin. His chin was held high, arms clasped behind his back, resplendent in a finely-tailored suit of black free of ornamentation save a purple swath of cloth draped over his left shoulder like a short cape. Blond hair like mine, cropped short and spiked stylishly, shone over a thin goatee. He projected an aura of arrogant and malicious power.

I elbowed Eljin. "That who I think it is?"

"Yar," he muttered in reply. "Kalos himself. High Lord of the Host."

"Frokking *great*," I murmured. Not just the one, but *both* Host. This didn't bode well for our plans.

We hovered at the back of the crowd, where the masses weren't packed in so tight. Kaira stood from her throne, stroking a hand along Kalos's face. An almost painful lust shone from his eyes, though his expression never changed. Kaira raised her arms to silence the cacophony. They obliged, and she stood motionless for a moment.

"My followers!" she cried out, voice carrying well across the open floor. "My devotees! Are we enjoying ourselves?" The crowd roared in approval.

"Has your lust been sated?" She waved a hand at the lovers engulfing the platform stairs. The crowd roared.

"*Has your lust been sated?*" Her arm swept to encompass the bodies upon the wall. An enormous cry of "No!" rose from the crowd.

"Nor mine!" Kaira yelled above the roar. "Look you all upon the fate of those who would defy the Host! Who would oppose our generosity, our divinity! Who would spit upon our benevolence and stoke the fires of rebellion! Those who would meddle with knowledge deemed unworthy of our civilized society! And what do we do with such perverters? Such fomenters?"

"DEATH!" cried the crowd.

Kaira smiled, flinging her arms wide. Her fists clenched, and seven still-living people upon the wall imploded in a shower of blood and gristle. I cried out, an involuntary reaction, but it was fortunately lost in the bloodthirsty roar of the rabble. Eljin laid a hand on my back, and I quieted, remembering why we were there.

Stay hidden. Stay inconspicuous. Get the job done.

Kaira lowered her arms, still grinning. "We thank you for your loyalty, my friends. Now please, go and enjoy yourselves in this paradise we've made for you. Eat. Drink your fill. Satisfy all of your desires! Know that you are cared for and loved by the gods walking upon this world!"

The crowd roared even louder, fists pumping in the air, chanting the Hosts' names. Eljin and I followed suit, so as not to attract undue attention. Kaira and Kalos descended the rear of the platform, exiting through a large double door surrounded by corpses. My metal hand clenched, grinding.

The old man nudged me. "That's the one, over there. With the hair ornaments." He nodded toward a plump middle-aged woman, head bowed, who stood to the side of the dais with a group of similarly-dressed women. Kaira's handmaidens.

Eljin stood rigid, muscles trembling, and I knew he was thinking of his slaughtered wife. My respect for the old man grew. I didn't know that I'd have been able to return to the Temple if that kind of horror had happened to me. Yet here he was.

We strolled about as the crowd began to break up, some waiting for the lift but most taking hidden stairwell exits on the outskirts of the room. Soon there was much less of a crush as people made their way to whatever hedonism awaited them.

Eljin nudged me again, and we were on the move, angling toward the handmaiden he'd chosen. We caught up to her just as she was about to exit the room.

"Mistress Jaini, might we have a word?" Eljin asked the woman. She started, clearly uneasy at being accosted by the blank masks of two unexpected Inori priests.

"'Ere, wot's this all about?" she asked. Her voluminous white and gold robes swirled about her as we herded her to an unoccupied space on the opposite side of the lift. A robust set of keys and cards jingled from the thick belt hanging loosely from her hips. I moved around to stand behind her, and she wheeled back and forth, trying to keep an eye on both of us at once.

"A...delicate matter has come to our attention, Mistress Jaini," said Eljin in a low, dire voice. "A matter concerning yer daughter?"

Jaini went white as a sheet. "Wot're you on about? I don't have a daughter."

"Not here you don't, at any rate. Our order was told of a most troublesome rumor. That a certain lady-in-waiting had paid off brethren to smuggle out a daughter. Born in secret. Right here in the Temple."

The handmaiden's eyes filled with tears even as her mouth dropped open, aghast. "But...but that was over twenny years ago! I've been a loyal servant, you cain't just—"

"Madam, keep yer voice down and a civil tongue in yer head," Eljin growled. Jaini snapped her mouth shut.

"Now," the old man continued in a milder tone, "you appear to understand the predicament we have here. Our High Lady would be most displeased by these events, and yer life would be worth less than a spit in the desert. But I myself have a more...personal stake in the matter. If you wish to keep yer miserable skin intact, you'll give me the names of the adherents you contracted to help with yer little illicit activity."

Tears leaked down Jaini's face, though to her credit she refrained from breaking down. "I...I...I can't remember!" she whispered. "It was such a long time ago, you know? I don't know the fellows' names!"

"Oh, but I think you do, madam. There are two ways this can go for you. Either I can march you to the High Lady herself right now and you can throw yerself upon her mercy, or you can give me those names and I will...forget you for a period of time. Long enough for you to make yer way from here, if you understand me. Personally, I'd suggest the latter. I have no real reason to see you flayed alive. My concern is solely with those less devout elements of my order. But I will need yer decision right now."

Jaini's shoulders slumped.

"Lofland. It was Lofland I paid, and he was helped by Morrow and Rahll."

Eljin played his role well, remaining silent and letting her sweat before nodding once. He looked to me. "Then we have our next course. We'll apprehend the appropriate parties and…see to their discipline."

He looked back to the handmaiden. "Our thanks for your cooperation, Mistress Jaini. Were I you, I'd make sure my face was never seen here in this holy Temple again."

She sobbed, once. "Yes! Yes, I'll leave tonight!"

"Not tonight. Now." He hooked a thumb toward the golden platform. "Unless you prefer to be on that wall by moonrise tomorrow?"

Jaini went even paler, nodding her head, eyes wide and terrified. She smoothed her dress, wiped the tears from her face, and began to step around the column.

"Oh, and Mistress Jaini…?" Eljin stopped her. She turned to look at him. He leaned in close, imposing with his bulk and that blank Inori mask.

"We'll be needing to take yer access keys. Can't have those floating in the wind along with you." He gestured for her to give them to me. They made a small *clink* as she dropped them into my metal hand.

She was smart enough to not run as she bustled away.

I let out a relieved breath. "Well, that worked better than I expected," I said to Eljin. "How'd you know all that stuff about her daughter?"

His eyes twinkled through the metal cutouts. "My wife, rest her soul in Order's light, loved her secrets."

"Well, hopefully Mistress Jaini will have enough sense to not get caught fleeing within the next hour or so. Be a shame if she did all that to get her daughter away from this place and then we get her killed in the end."

Eljin grunted and shook his head.

We made our way back around the column, making small talk and waiting until we were sure we could get a lift to ourselves. A thought occurred to me.

"Excellent acting back there, by the way," I said to the old man.

"Yar?"

"Yup. I was impressed." He hadn't injected a "heh" into the conversation even once.

As the lift door slid shut behind us, Eljin rifled through the ring of keys and cards, finding one with an orange stripe and sliding it into a slot beneath the floor buttons. A small beep followed, and the lift began to descend.

"We meeting up with Korbos and Mari on Three?" I asked. Order alive, it'd be good to see them again. I didn't like the fact that we were split up in this devil's den.

"Not just yet," said Eljin.

I turned to face him. "What does that mean?"

"We need to make sure this is gonna work. Heh. We'll just take a ride to the bottom, then come back up and meet 'em as planned. Won't take a minute."

I shrugged, not exactly comfortable with deviating from the plan, but I couldn't think of any real reason not to scout things out before the next phase.

The lift slowed, then stopped. The door opened on a long metal hallway that matched the plated walls of Level Four. A wide steel door capped the other end, flanked by another keypad similar to the one we'd just used. When we reached it, Eljin slid the card with the orange stripe into the slot. A green light beeped, but the door wouldn't open.

We glanced at each other, confused. The old man tried again, with the same result. He raised his mask, scratching his whiskered jaw.

"This should be working," he muttered.

A faint *ding* echoed down the hall, and then everything went to hell.

I wheeled around, flooded with terror. Cold sweat broke out across my body. There was nowhere for us to go. No other doors. We were trapped.

No fewer than ten men stepped out of the lift as the door slid open, Hostguard forming a wall three across and blocking the hallway entirely. Not that there was anywhere for us to go. Eljin pulled his enormous sword from his back, but I couldn't even muster the brain power to draw Chum.

"And what do we have here, now?" asked a deep, gravelly baritone, dragging the words out in mockery. "Rats, gnawing in the walls? Or mice, after the cheese?"

The owner of the voice, a behemoth of a man—bigger and more muscular than even Korbos—pushed his way past the Hostguard. He wore bits of Hostguard armor, though hammered out in the color and style of Inori, over plain gray robes. Perhaps thirty, the giant's bald scalp and face were covered in ordered, ritualistic scars, with an impossibly square jaw edged in a beard that left his upper lip bare. He carried a long-handled mace, its business end reminiscent of the geometrical Inori masks and bigger than my frokking head.

"I believe, my friends," he said to no one in particular, "that we've found the proverbial pirates in dark waters. That is, to say, brigands. Looters. Plunderers." He raised the mace. "Thieves."

I sagged, all hope dashed from me, no will at all to even attempt a daring escape.

Eljin, however, was under no such paralysis.

With a rabid yell, the old man dashed forward, his sword held parallel to the ground at shoulder height, the razor point thrusting at the giant's heart.

Where it was batted away by the sledgehammer of a mace. I barely saw the giant move, but his armored fist hit Eljin's jaw with the wet smack of a blackfin thrown down on a wooden dock. The old man reeled, then collapsed to one knee, woozy and bleeding.

The huge man looked to me. "Now that *that* unpleasantness is out of the way, I trust you'll be a bit more obliging about this whole process?"

I shrugged my shoulders, unstrapping my riphook and tossing it to the floor. The Hostguard rushed forward as the huge man stepped out of the way. Outwardly, he looked bored, but I could see his small, dark eyes darting between the two of us, always watching.

We were stripped of our disguises, our wrists were bound, and they led us into the lift. Eljin's snow-white beard sported a red stain where blood seeped from a gash in his jaw. His face was swelling.

"I guess Kaira learned her lesson twenty-two years ago," he mumbled to me.

"I'll thank you to be quiet, please," the giant rumbled. "If you're lucky—or unlucky, depending on one's point of view in such matters—you'll have a plethora of opportunities to speak, very soon."

Order anyway, *that* didn't sound good.

The lift opened, and we were prodded back onto the eighth floor. This time, there was no crowd of sycophants and hedonists. The entire level was empty save us, our escorts, and two *very* psychotic demigods standing on the stone dais. We were half-walked, half-carried to kneel before the Host.

Kalos stood there with that same depraved smirk. His eyes danced in mad glee.

Kaira…well, she just looked ticked.

I had no idea how to play this. I was more scared than I'd ever been in my life; it was taking every ounce of willpower I could muster to not soil myself. Eljin, however, was staring at the High Lady and shaking with impotent rage. She returned his glare with a sneering curl of her lip.

I had no ploy. No way out. No real dignity left in the face of annihilation. So, being me, I did the dumbest thing I could think to do.

I swallowed my fear.

I puffed out my chest and threw on my biggest, most charming smile.

"Hello there, *bhuta*," I spat.

THIRTY THREE

Kalos's eyes went wide, flaring silver just like Korbos's, and a loud, tittering laugh burst from his lips. I gave an involuntary shudder. There was madness in that jollity.

An invisible hand wrapped around me, crushing. My mechanical arm groaned from the pressure, the socket at my shoulder digging into the muscles and nerves attached to it. So much pain. It felt like a rib cracked. I'd been wrong, *that* was pain. I gritted my teeth, determined not to cry out at the end. I was lifted into the air and pulled toward the dais, hovering before those insane eyes.

"This one is disrespectful, my heart," giggled Kalos. "I believe he must be…disciplined."

I closed my eyes and waited to explode like a dropped sweetdew.

Nothing happened. I cracked an eyelid and immediately wished I hadn't.

Kaira stood between me and Kalos, her hand on his chest, halting him from whatever horrible evisceration he'd been about to perform. A broad smile—beautiful and terrible in kind—beamed out at me. A glimmer of recognition twinkled in her gold eyes.

"Oh, what fortune is *this*?" she mused. Déjà vu washed over me. Those had been her first words to Korbos back in Hightide, what felt like a lifetime ago.

"Atia truly watches over us, my love," she continued, "to drop such luck into our laps. I know this one." Her golden eyes looked me up and down, and I felt a sinking feeling in my gut. This couldn't be good.

"Yes, this is one of the flailing little baghdas that slipped away from me in that silly port town. Set him down, pet." She ran a caressing hand down Kalos's chest.

I grunted as the force surrounding me vanished, dropping me several feet with a jarring thump to the platform stairs. Order anyway, my ribs hurt. I held my side as I raised from my crouch and tried to keep my face impassive as Kaira beckoned me to the top of the stage. I couldn't help but flinch as she raised her hand, caressing my cheek and jawline.

Her eyes widened, just a fraction. "But this one and I had met even before then, no? That no-name little village near the Longshore garrison? I remember you, pet. Did you spread my message like I asked?"

"It was Emun, my home. And you *killed my family*, you *bhuta*!" I screamed.

The High Lady laughed.

"Have you come to bring me my signara, little one?" she purred, rubbing her body against mine—highly distracting, given the scantness of her clothing. I focused on the pain in my side, fighting down a wave of revulsion and nausea.

"No, but I know who's got it," I spat through gritted teeth.

"Pyk, no!" cried Eljin. His head rocked and blood flew as Kaira made a lazy motion and an unseen force pummeled him across his injured jaw.

"And who might that be, pet?"

"Your mother."

I yelped as I suddenly lurched forward, my toes dragging the ground, and my throat slammed into Kalos's outstretched hand. His eyes blazed once again, and white teeth snapped near my ear.

"Impertinent," he cackled. "Insubordinate. Our Mother would have actually liked you, I think. But you're a big, strong, defiant man, eh? Hee hee. Let's burn off your manhood, and then we'll see just how disrespectful you'll be." His free hand exploded into white-hot fire. The air around it distorted from the heat. A firemaker, just as Korbos had said.

I clapped my bound hands over my groin, like it would do any good.

"Kalos."

His silver eyes left mine, focusing over my shoulder.

"I can stomach a flippant tongue, my love, but what I *can't* stomach is this idea you have that I need *you* to defend my honor. How many times over the ages must we have this conversation?" Her tone was pleasant, even affectionate, but there was an undercurrent of steel that chilled me. "Now put him down."

I rubbed my throat as my feet touched ground again, gasping in big whooping gulps of air. Kaira ran her hand down my spine. Kalos just grinned at me and shrugged his shoulders. Steam trailed from his now-extinguished palm.

The High Lady walked around to face me. "It's no matter if this one cooperates or not, in any case. If he's here and trying to get into Mother's lab, Korbos is most certainly within the Temple somewhere."

She looked to Eljin. "Did you *really* think I wouldn't change my security measures after the incident with Hethera?" His eyes flew wide at the mention of his wife. "Oh, yes, I remember her. And you, Eljin Dhovra. We forget nothing."

Kaira grinned. "The years have not treated you kindly, I'm afraid. It was a pity, what happened to your wife; I rather liked her. Of course, I also enjoyed having to…liquidate her."

Kalos giggled as Eljin thrashed against his bonds.

"So what shall we do with them, dear heart?" he asked Kaira.

She tapped a finger on her chin. "Do? For now, nothing, I think. We have them in hand, best to keep them intact. We might need…leverage…against our brother. If he cares for these mortals, it will be of benefit to have their body parts available to present to him should he become unruly."

I gulped.

Kaira inclined her head. "Rayce?"

The giant of a guard who'd captured us stepped forward, clicking his heels together as he bowed at the waist. "Milady."

"Take these two to the holding cells, and leave them be for now. None of your…conversion tactics."

"Affirmative, my Lady," Rayce replied with a bow.

Kaira turned to her…companion? Lover? I couldn't quite figure out what her relationship to the other Host entailed. "You'll need to report to Mother, Kalos. Take the *Predator* and let her know that our wayward sibling will soon be returned to the fold."

He frowned, sticking out his lower lip in an almost childlike pout. "No, Kaira," he whined, crossing his arms. Order anyway, he *was* pouting like a kid. "I want to be here with you. You'll need me to help with Korbos. You *need* me here."

Kaira laughed. "I most certainly do not. You know better than anyone what you're like when things get…heated, and I prefer my Temple to remain in one piece." She grabbed the back of his head and pulled him into a deep, long kiss, her hand rubbing him suggestively. "Now go have the crew prepare the ship, and we'll be together again soon enough. Once I have him and the signara, there'll be nothing left to stand in Mother's way. In *our* way."

Kalos sighed, then burst out a mad cackle.

"Fair enough, sister. Fair enough. Mind yourself. I'll give Mother your love."

Rayce, the giant, took Eljin and me by the arms. "Come gentlemen, let us see you to your new lodgings."

"Oh, and Rayce?"

He stopped and turned. "Yes, Lady?"

"Once they're secured, be on the lookout." She pointed to me. "If that one's here, there'll be others with Korbos. A freckled woman with a dark topknot, and a…" Her mouth turned down in distaste. "Chek woman. They came in a skipship, so have a detachment search the surrounding plateaus."

My gut dropped. Cassidy.

Rayce stood straight, as if in surprise, then bowed. "Yes, ma'am."

Kalos tittered again as he strolled to the central column. We followed, prodded by our Hostguard escort.

My breathing became heavy. I'd mostly gotten over my anxiety of the lift, but I did *not* want to share that metal coffin with Kalos. The group stepped in, and Rayce punched the button for the bottom level.

Kalos leaned in to me. "I dearly hope you enjoy your new quarters. We only…host…the best there." He nudged my ribs, causing me to grunt in pain. "Get it? You get it? Host?" He cackled wildly, then pulled a rolled cigarette out of his pocket, lighting it with the tip of his finger. Smoke filled the tiny cabin. "Ahhh, I just kill me sometimes."

"If only…" I muttered. He just grinned at me, those white teeth promising pain and madness.

The door opened, and he strolled out past the naked flesh writhing in the pool. "Toodle-oo!" he called over his shoulder, waggling his fingers in goodbye.

I shuddered as the door shut once again. The man was insane.

My stomach lurched as the lift rose.

"Where are we going?" I murmured to Eljin.

"Level Ten," he replied in a whisper. "Heh. Cells are on Level Ten, to hinder escape."

My head rocked forward as stars bloomed in my vision. Rayce had slapped the back of my skull. With his mace, it felt like.

"Did we not discuss your silence, gentlemen? Once more and I'll have to get…well, creative, seeing as my Lady wants you intact for the moment."

I kept my mouth shut for the rest of the ride.

We exited to a dire scene. Rows upon rows of metal cages filled the area. They rode the walls, surrounded the support columns. A few hung from the ceiling, barely clearing the cells beneath them. And in most sat the thin, starving, forgotten dregs of humanity. These weren't prisoners, they were torture victims. Nearly all were emaciated to the point that they no longer resembled people, but skin-covered skeletons. One bony woman, who still had enough energy to moan and reach through the bars, wore the gold body paint we'd seen upon the entertainers downstairs. She stretched out her hand, then screamed as Rayce snatched her wrist and slammed it sideways, breaking her upper arm against the bars. He never broke stride as she wailed and collapsed back into her cage.

I was appalled by the casual cruelty of it. The horror of what was to become of us. I looked to Eljin, who carried a grim look of despair.

"Here we are, gentlemen, your new home. I do hope you'll enjoy your accommodations. Dinner is served promptly at never, and should you ever desire a sound thrashing, feel free to contact one of our fine employees. I am Rayce Yahn, your humble host, and it's our profound pleasure to have you…here." The giant spread his arms, encompassing the misery around us with a wide grin.

I sneered at Yahn as he closed our cell door with a clang, looking him up and down and taking in his gray armor, so similar yet unlike that of the Hostguard. "So what's your story, *Inori*?" I put every ounce of scorn I could into the word.

He beamed at me, the scars pulling taut across his face. Order anyway, were *all* these people crazy? A booming laugh echoed throughout the chamber while he drug over a chair and sat before us. Even seated, his head was nearly on a level with mine. Gods above and below, the man was enormous.

"So kind of you to ask!" he roared. "Most of our guests have just the worst manners. Never engage in any sort of meaningful conversation, you understand. Very refreshing to have a polite chat with a guest!"

"I remember you," Eljin spat in disgust. "A skinny little twerp of a kid, running about after your father, thinking you owned the place. This little drekface would always throw his unfinished meal in the floor of the dining hall, then watch as my people cleaned after him. His father was High Consul of the Inori, so the little *bhaka* would have my people flogged if they missed even a crumb."

Rayce Yahn bellowed laughter. "Yes, yes, very untoward of me, I agree, Master Dhovra. I remember you as well. Shame about your dear departed wife. She was always kind to me. Not that she had any choice in the matter, mind you."

The cage rattled as Eljin slammed against the bars.

"Now, now…temper, Master Dhovra," rumbled Yahn with a frown. "It wouldn't do to be impolite." His massive paws clenched, veins nearly bursting from the skin.

He turned his gaze to me. "We haven't actually been properly introduced yet. Might I inquire your name, sir?"

I hesitated, but didn't see any real reason to not give it. "Pyk."

"Then we're well met, Master Pyk!" he boomed. "Now, in answer to your question, I believe Master Eljin here has lain the groundwork. It's not a long story in any case. I was brought up Inori, in this very Temple, and from the time I was young I was always a bit more…martial, let's say…than my brethren. Childhood brawls and whatnot. Very frowned upon in our order, although the adults are of course allowed to carry weapons.

"By the time I became a teenager, my devotion to the High Lord and Lady were unparalleled. The Lady herself placed her hand upon me and blessed me above all my kin. This didn't sit well with the others, of course, so I was expelled from the Order. Her Ladyship intervened, took me under her wing, and saw to it that I had the finest martial instruction her influence could provide. And her influence is vast, as I'm sure you know."

"She wanted a loyal killer," Eljin spat through the bars. "Heh. Couldn't have picked a better candidate, you frokking little sociopath."

Yahn sighed. Faster than I could see, his hand flicked out, and then Eljin was stumbling back, clutching his shin where a thin metal dart protruded. The old man growled as he pulled it out and put pressure on the wound.

"I believe I warned you about your manners, sir," Yahn said in a conversational tone. He sounded bored. "The next time, it will be something more…vital."

The giant stretched his arms out to the side. "Now where was I? Oh yes. My training took years, and by the time I was a man I had grown into the fine specimen now seated before you. I wasn't allowed to rejoin my brethren, but I worshipped the High Ones in my own way, giving fealty through blood and the sweat of my brow. Kaira herself named me Guard-Captain and gave command of her legions." He gestured to his scars. "I was allowed to take the traditional marks of Atia herself. And ever since, I have dedicated myself to the glory of Atia and the divinity of her embodiments upon this world."

Great. Just what we needed. A *true believer*. I cocked my head. "But you kept the trappings of the Inori?"

"Yes!" He fingered his gray armor. "One mustn't forget one's upbringing, even if a rift sometimes develops. Family is important, wouldn't you agree?"

"If that's your idea of family, I'll pass."

"Indeed. In any case, I must be going. Things to do, guests to accommodate, matters of that nature."

He stood up—and up, and up, Atia's *bones*, the man was *huge*—and thumped his way to the cage nearest ours, where a young woman cowered. Keys rattled as he opened the grate and dragged her out. Her cries echoed as the giant pulled her by the hair to a room situated on the far wall; basically three metal walls that stopped short of the ceiling. I couldn't see what was inside as he slammed the door with a clang.

But I could imagine as agonized screams filled the entire floor. Meaty *thwacks* echoed, sounding for all the world like a butcher's stall at the Hightide market. That was the reason for a lack of roof on the enclosure. So that everyone imprisoned on this level would partake of the horrors of that room as they occurred.

A few minutes later, Rayce Yahn appeared through the door, dragging the woman behind him. He hurled her back into the cage, then gently eased the door shut.

"A taste of what's in store during your stay with us, my friends," the giant rumbled. "The High Lady doesn't take kindly to thieves, you see. Thus my nickname among the rank-and-file: The Hack. An unfortunate moniker, but I'll admit that it's appropriate. I look forward to our next meeting." He sketched a mocking bow, then clomped his way to the lift.

I couldn't take my eyes from the skeletal woman, whose pitiful wails tore at my soul as she thrashed around on the floor. Her arms and legs ended in bandaged stumps. He'd cut off her hands and feet, then cauterized and bound them to prolong her suffering. As she screamed, I saw he'd cut out her tongue as well.

My legs gave out, and I thumped to the floor of the cell, shuddering. Eljin sat beside me, saying nothing, merely pressing his hand to my neck in comfort.

A rumble, distant and faint, rolled through the Temple. Kalos, leaving in the skipship. Good riddance to the crazy *bhaka*. One less thing to worry over.

I couldn't see any way out of this mess. Three Hostguard patrolled the rows of cells. Even if we did manage to somehow escape the jail, we wouldn't be much good against them unarmed. And wounded, in Eljin's case. I looked to his leg.

"How is it?" I asked.

"Ah, just a scratch. Heh," he replied, chuckling. "Dumb *bhaka* hit my artificial shin." He pulled up his pants leg to show the undamaged metal.

"You sneaky son of a…" I murmured. The old man grinned.

"Never let an enemy know your true capabilities," he said with an evil smirk. "They think I'm wounded, they underestimate me. They underestimate me, they die."

"Yeah, if we can somehow get the hell out of here." I didn't have much faith in that possibility at the moment.

The wails of the injured woman slowly faded as she lost consciousness. I felt guilty for enjoying the silence that followed.

Minutes passed. Ten. Twenty. Thirty.

I wracked my brain, trying to think of a way to escape. I conferred with Eljin. We discussed the possibility of using our metal limbs to somehow bend the gate. The problem there was that, although they were sturdier than flesh and blood, the Seeker-made appendages were only marginally stronger than regular limbs. I could crush rock with my hand, but try and lift or bend something beyond my means and it would tear my arm off at the shoulder. Same went for Eljin's leg.

The old man paced about the small cell, muttering to himself and shaking his head.

No viable plan came to me. I gave in to despair, leaning back against the bars and dropping my head into my utterly useless hands.

We were going to die here.

Mari was going to die here, unless Korbos managed to get her out.

Cassidy would never know what became of me. That somehow hurt the worst.

A sob escaped me as I just...gave up, covering my head with my arms.

A faint *ding* echoed through the floor as the lift arrived. Yahn, returning for more of his torturous hospitality, I imagined.

Loud shouts followed, punctuated with a tremendous crash. I stood, pressing my face to the bars and trying to peer down the row, then stumbled back as an armored Hostguard hurtled past our cage to roll into a crumpled heap.

I looked to Eljin, who grinned. Boots thumped in front of the cell, and there was Korbos, bigger than life and twice as ugly. I'd never been so happy to see his scarred, grizzled face in my life. He was holding our weapons.

"Order anyway, what are you two gawking at?" he rumbled, eye flaring as his power ripped the door from the hinges. "Let's get the hell out of here."

I looked around as I gulped down free air. "Where's Mari?"

"Don't worry about her," he said, "it's a big Temple and she's a tiny woman. She's doing her job. Eljin, take a look through these." He tossed a thick ring of keys and cards to the old man, who fumbled them. "Any look familiar?"

Eljin quirked an eyebrow. "Yar...you're still set on getting to the synthmind?"

"We have no other choice. It's here or nowhere."

Eljin nodded and yanked a striped card from the ring. "This'd be the one, then."

"Let's get moving."

"Wait," I cried, snatching the ring from the floor where Eljin had dropped it. I turned around, looking for a prisoner that seemed to have strength left. Spotting a young man pressed up against the bars of his cell, eyes wide, I ran over and thrust the key ring into his hands.

"Get them out, if you can," I said. I didn't stick around to hear his reply, catching up with the others at the open lift.

"Always the hero," Korbos sneered at me. I glanced at him, worried. He'd been using his powers without the benefit of Bulwark.

His lip curled. "I'm all right for a while yet, so wipe that look off your face. It's ticking me off."

Great. I grimaced, baring my teeth as the pain in my side flared.

Korbos eyed me critically. "You're hurt?"

"Yeah, my ribs. Kalos had me for a second."

Concern on his face, Korbos reached out. "Let me see." I lifted up my shirt, nauseated by the large purple and yellow bruise forming just below the left side of my chest. "Hnnng!" I squealed as the big man laid a hand and pressed, ever so slight.

Followed by a harder nudge. "Ow! Damnation, Korbos!"

"You'll be okay, Pyk. Probably just a few bruised ribs, possibly cracked. If they were broken, you probably wouldn't be walking right now."

"You keep prodding me like that, I might not be!"

At least he no longer looked like he wanted to murder us.

We rode the lift down to Level Three, Eljin and I strapping on our blades as Korbos unzipped the bag on his back and pulled out his rifle. He motioned us to stay inside, then exhaled hard as the lift opened.

The third floor was much like the first, with hundreds of courtesans and sycophants puttering about, indulging themselves. Plants bloomed everywhere around couches and enormous support columns.

"MARIYANA!" Korbos bellowed as he stepped forward, half-in and half-out of the lift, Bulwark at the ready. The time for stealth had passed, I supposed.

Heads turned. Hostguard and Inori alike began to move toward the lift, hesitant at first, then running as they realized we definitely weren't supposed to be there. From the side of the room—frantically racing to stay ahead of the oncoming soldiers—ran Mari, yanking off her robes and flinging the mask away as her tiny legs pumped for all they were worth.

Attackers screamed as they rushed the lift.

Korbos offered no mercy or quarter. Blue fire leapt into the room, mowing down Hostguard, Inori, and civilians alike as Mari slid past the big man's legs to slam into the lift's back wall. I hauled her up and wrapped her in a tight embrace as Eljin frantically pawed at the keycard controls. Korbos stepped back, pouring a steady stream of death from his gun until the door shut and we began our descent.

Our final descent in that infernal contraption, I hoped. One way or another.

"Everything go okay?" Korbos asked.

Mari hopped, the black bag around her shoulders bouncing up and down with a clatter. "Oh yeah I got everything placed where they needed to be and we should be good to go so just let me know when you're ready for me to oh Eljin what happened to your face it's all bloody did you guys get in a fight without m—"

I threw my arms around the Chek, cutting her off. I was so happy to see her unharmed. She returned the hug with gusto.

"I missed you too, tall boy," she said, muffled against my belly.

The lift hit bottom, and we stepped into the long hallway where Eljin and I had been so recently captured. Imposing gray hammered-metal walls hemmed us in, and the green light of the doorway keypad blinked incessantly.

"Hold up," I said, "the card was a trap last time. It's not gonna work this time either."

"Hmmm…" Korbos murmured. "Don't worry about that." He walked right up to the recessed steel door, Bulwark held low at his side, and lowered his head. Silver flared, and the door *whanged* as it crumpled and ripped from the frame. He set it gently to the side, and we filed through into the lab where he was created.

Where the Host were born.

THIRTY FOUR

It was exactly as Eljin had described at the Lau Tuai; a vast expanse of open floor, broken by support columns lined with lights that bathed the entire room—if something so huge could be called such a meager word as "room"—in sterile white. It was far larger than the Temple's entry level. Far larger than any interior space I'd ever seen, excepting maybe the Second Battalion storehouse or the shipyard where we'd lost Amadi. A stained quickcrete floor stretched out before us, cracks riddling the false stone. The ceiling hung improbably high over our heads; it was difficult to believe this entire structure could exist beneath the Mohagan sands and not collapse under the weight of its own size.

Along the far-distant walls, seemingly endless rows of glass sectionals—partitioned into sterile laboratories—extended as far as we could see.

But it was the tubes that held the eyes.

Each twelve feet tall, the cylindrical tanks began as soon as one entered the expanse, two rows stretching off and forming a corridor that disappeared into a blinding light that seared our eyes even at a distance. They were filled with some terrible black—yet somehow translucent—liquid that shone almost blue from lights set within the thick glass of the tubes themselves.

Floating within the tanks, twitching from whatever obscene currents swirled within, were horrors. Crimes against nature. Things that would haunt my nightmares until I finally joined Order's light.

Monstrosities in the shape of men.

Dark, scaly skin rippled loosely from elongated parodies of human limbs, stirring within the bubbling liquid. I cringed upon seeing the faces—if they could be called such. Overlarge, pitch-black eyes stared sightlessly, the features off-kilter as if molded from melted wax. Each looked to have perished in some unspeakable agony, lips drawn back in terrible rictus to reveal broken maws of turned, jutting teeth. Black, dead nails tipped the spider-like fingers. The creatures looked to be around nine feet tall, and from what I could make out there appeared to be a roughly equal number of male and female.

"Mother's failed experiments," cried a voice from the center of that brilliant light. Kaira's voice. "Did you know, Korbos, that for centuries she strove to improve upon the formula she used to create us? She wasn't content with the Host, oh no. Refused to even entertain the idea of creating more of us…not that we encouraged her. Dozens of attempts to elevate our design. Each attempt, an utter failure.

"I guess there's no improving upon perfection, eh, pet?"

I pulled the riphook from my back, grunting as the motion stretched my injured rib. The others likewise armed themselves. The light blinded me. I couldn't see the High Lady. I couldn't see anything aside from the dark atrocities bobbing around us. Convinced the creatures were at any moment going to burst forth and attack, my head swiveled back and forth, checking for movement.

I nearly hit the ceiling as Eljin laid a hand on me. "Easy boy," he said, "they're not what we need to worry with."

He was right, of course, but I couldn't shake the feeling.

Korbos paid the monsters no mind, stalking directly toward the blinding ray of light. We followed, wary, unable to make out anyone in the haze.

"I've so missed you, pet," Kaira called. My neck began to ache from the tension.

"We had such *fun* the last time we were together, didn't we, pet?"

"You tortured me for two hundred years, Kaira," Korbos replied as he slowed to a standstill. "You kept my face under an acid drip for fifty years. You disfigured me. You tried to break me. You failed."

"Perhaps. You seem just fine to me, pet. It's been twenty years since you and I have rubbed noses, so can't we just let bygones be bygones?" She giggled, the sound far too similar to Kalos's mad cackle.

"I think not."

"When you left so suddenly, you stole something from me." She sounded almost…pouty. "Mother punished me most direly, you know. It took me six months before I was right again. So I'll be wanting that back. Oh, and the signara, of course."

"Not going to happen, Kaira."

I looked at the big man. What had he taken?

"Come now, Korbos, it's still not too late. Mother would be thrilled to welcome you back with open arms. You were one of *us*! A god among mortals. A superior organism! Why insist on seeking forgiveness from these...lesser beings? What need do such as *we* have of forgiveness? These creatures are bred to be ruled. To serve *us*! You were our brother, and you can be again."

Korbos gave a slow, single shake of his head.

"I'm not looking for forgiveness, Kaira. Some things can never be put right. My job now is only to make sure it never happens again. That you, Kalos, and Mother have no more influence on this world. For the people of Elarin. For Rin."

Kaira scoffed. "Nine hundred years, and you still pine over a lost love? I thought you made of better mettle than that, brother."

"Guess we'll find out."

"I suppose so. I won't let you take the synthmind. Not that any of you have the slightest chance of ever leaving this place."

The light suddenly dimmed, and I blinked rapidly as my eyes struggled to adjust. My legs trembled as I saw what stood before us.

Backlit by a gigantic wall of monitors—just as Eljin's wife had described to him—stood Kaira, surrounded by fifteen Hostguard. Rayce Yahn prowled at her side, pacing back and forth, his massive club twirling in a bear-sized paw. He raised it, pointed directly at Mariyana.

"Mistress," he boomed out, loud enough for all to hear, "might I be so bold as to request the privilege of taking the Chek? I always wanted one, but, alas, I was too young to have participated in your culls. More's the pity."

Mari said nothing, setting her face in a stony mask and affixing her new slingshot to her arm. Steel shot gleamed from an open pouch at her waist.

Kaira laughed, delighted.

Yahn chuckled in return. "Ten thousand karani to the one who brings me the Chek alive!" he bellowed. Two of the Hostguard raced forward, brandishing pikes. A whispered *twang-thapp! twang-thapp!* sounded from my right, and the soldiers dropped; one with a neat hole punched through the armor over his heart, the other with blood spraying from the ruins of his multi-eyed helmet. Mari calmly seated another shot into the cup of her sling and arched an eyebrow at the giant man.

Rayce Yahn roared, and everything went to Chaos.

We scattered—Mari flitting behind the nearest tank, Eljin and I splitting off to either side. Korbos bellowed and charged straight down the middle of the hall, his powers blowing Hostguard in every direction as he bore down on Kaira. The High Lady grinned in anticipation.

I had no time to think as one of the guards thrust a stunpike at my face. Another followed with a stab at my legs. I just managed to fling myself out of the way, twisting in the air as I desperately parried with Chum. A third ran at me as I was regaining my feet, only to fly sideways as a shot from Mari's sling took him in the head. There was no time to thank her as the first two pressed the attack. I was by no means a swordsman, but the riphook flowed in my hand as I parried strike after strike. Pain receded as adrenaline flooded me.

The guard on the left tried a wide, sweeping blow, and I blocked with my netanium hand, jumping in close as the pike's metal haft bent against my arm. I buried the riphook in his throat, just under the insectile helmet, then gagged as a spray of blood caught me full in the face. Chum's wide blade had nearly taken the guard's head off.

I staggered back, swinging wildly, trying ineffectively to wipe the blood from my eyes. Damn near impossible with a metal hand. I finally managed to clear one eye just in time to see the point of a pike aimed directly at my breadbasket. A line of pain streaked across my cheek as I flung myself backwards to the floor.

The guard stood over me, ready to drive his weapon down into my chest. A flash of motion from my right, and suddenly Eljin was running past, his colossal sword trailing gore. The two halves of my attacker flew away to land with a wet splat.

I scrambled to my feet, quickly wiping my eyes with a scrap of shirt. Blue fire flashed as Korbos unloaded on the High Lady. Eljin was exchanging brutal blows with another pair of Hostguard. Where was Mari?

There.

A line of downed foes trailed before her as she darted from tube to column, using the structures as cover, popping out to launch a shot before moving on. I was amazed. She'd dropped at least seven of the fifteen Hostguard with her sling. Mari leaned back and dodged a thrown stunpike, the spearpoint sailing past her torso, before pulling the cup to her cheek and nailing the Hostguard dead center in his forehead at less than ten feet's distance. The soldier's helmet imploded, and his corpse flipped backward before rolling to a stop at her foot.

She grinned at me.

And then she was flying, crashing into one of the dark tanks before sliding to the floor, unmoving. Yahn had rounded the column on her blind side and hurled her like a sack of salt.

I screamed, a bellow of rage and fear and worry, then charged the beast of a man. In the corner of my eye Eljin put down the last of the Hostguard, and then he was running to join me from my left. The old man had several shallow cuts across his arms, and his good leg had a pronounced limp. We converged on the Inori Guard-Captain.

A six-foot ball of fire roared through the space between us, the heat causing the quickcrete beneath it to bubble and roil. All three of us staggered backward, and turned to watch hell unfold.

Kaira and Korbos stood in the center of a maelstrom. The big guy was unloading with Bulwark, heavy blue fire licking out to be rebuffed by Kaira's telekinetic shields. His own shield—much smaller, with silver cracks running through the invisible barrier surrounding him—was bombarded by a torrent of loose objects and eldritch powers.

The High Lady flung forward a hand, and a blast of icy air splashed across Korbos's shield before dissipating. A second volley missed him entirely, coming close enough to our position that frost formed on my metal forearm as I raised it to shield my face. Anything not nailed down spun in the air about them; monitor screens, electronic boxes, chunks of quickcrete ranging from the size of my torso to loose gravel pelted both shields and the surrounding ground. The closest laboratories were shattered, the glass walls pulled into the whirlwind and hurled like flechettes.

The floor around us rumbled. The two Hosts, each opposing force working against the other, were causing the entire foundation of the Temple to quake. A large section of the ceiling collapsed at the front of the chamber near the door, sand and stone and a few dozen half-nude courtiers pouring in to shatter against the quickcrete.

It was mesmerizing. Eljin and I—along with Rayce Yahn—stood rooted, our enmity forgotten in the face of such destructive chaos. For a moment, at least.

Eljin, seeing his opening, streaked forward, swinging his enormous blade in a rising arc, intent on cutting the scarred giant in half. Yahn never turned his head, never moved his feet, yet his monster of a mace swung around to block the heavy blow. His knees bent, absorbing the shock as he slid back two feet before launching a counterattack. Eljin held his own, parrying and thrusting several sets. I stood frozen in awe.

The old man spun, knocking the behemoth's weapon aside and using the momentum to twist into a vicious overhand blow. His wounded leg, however, buckled at the wrong moment, and the chop that would have split Yahn's head in two—and probably cleaved all the way through his torso in turn—went askew. The Guard-Captain jerked sideways, losing an ear but otherwise evading the strike.

Yahn bellowed in pain and anger, dropping to a low sweep and hooking Eljin's metal leg. The old man fell, losing his sword and catching a powerful kick to the ribs that sent him sliding ten feet. My own injured rib twinged in sympathy. He rolled to a stop, face down, groaning.

"YAHN!" I roared, catching the giant's attention before he could stomp over to finish off my friend. Blood sheeted down his neck into cloth and metal armor as his snarling face turned to me. A lumbering step, then two, then the entire bulk of a ticked-off leviathan was hurtling toward me at a speed faster than I would have believed possible.

Reach. I needed reach.

I twisted the rings on Chum's hilt, spinning it wildly as the haft extended. Gripping the spear with wide hands, I ducked low underneath a swing that would have sent my head sailing the length of the floor and stabbed at his dominant arm. Maybe if I could get his weapon away from him, I'd have a chance. The riphook's tip clanged off his pauldron, but I yanked the hooked point back to tear a long gash in his tricep, just above the unprotected elbow.

Blood flew, and Yahn grunted in pain. The mace fell from loose fingers. I had an all-too-brief moment of satisfaction before the giant spun, catching the weapon in his off-hand as it fell and bringing it around in a brutal sideswipe. I barely got the haft of my spear around to block it, but the force of the blow sent me flying. A two-foot shard of glass impaled the quickcrete near my hand as I landed in a crouch. I rolled away as Yahn's enormous mace smashed the ground where I'd been a moment before. Gravel rocketed away from the head-sized crater.

I couldn't keep this up for long. Especially not with an injury. I just wasn't a fighter, and the massive Guard-Captain had decades of martial experience. It was only a matter of time until he mushed me into paste. I stabbed at the scars of his unprotected face. Blocked. I swept at his groin. Batted away. The big *bhaka* was toying with me. The loss of an ear wasn't slowing him in the slightest.

I shuffled backwards, hoping Eljin would recover enough to help me. A quick glance told me that wasn't going to be happening.

A whistling blow forced me to duck, and the return backswing caught the blade of my riphook, wresting it from my hands and sending it flying. Order anyway, I was dead. Yahn grinned, his gore-soaked face promising a painful demise as he stalked toward me. I dodged another overhead blow. Ducked a swing that shattered one of the monstrous tanks, sending foul liquid and an even fouler body gushing to the floor. The failed abomination struck my legs, knocking them from under me, and

then Yahn was standing over my prone body with his mace raised for a killing blow.

I closed my eyes and thought of Cassidy.

A roar of agony assaulted my ears, and I looked up just in time to see Yahn drop to his knees, the mace falling. I rolled away as it bashed the spot where my head had been. Mariyana was sliding across the floor, boots soaked in foul water, daggers soaked in blood where she had just sliced open Yahn's legs at the back of the knees—a spot where the armor left his hamstrings unprotected. She'd dropped her bag and the sling, and set about dismantling the gargantuan warrior with her blades.

The giant swiped a paw at the Chek, improbably fast, and she darted forward, even faster, burying one of her carbsteel daggers in the crook of his arm. She dodged another strike, stabbing at his hand as it passed, then swinging around behind him and leaping up to attack the exposed muscle between his neck and armor. He roared, and I raced toward him as he managed to snag Mari's shirt. A massive hand wrapped around her tiny, birdlike neck.

I screamed and threw every available ounce of mechanically-enhanced strength I could muster into a skull-shattering metal punch. His face collapsed inward around my artificial hand, and he dropped Mari, hands flying to his ruined features as he shrieked. Somehow, he rose to his feet, wailing, and Mariyana darted in, grasping at her belt. She pulled out a round black globe, thumbing a switch and shoving it as far under his breastplate as she could reach.

Panic flooded me as I snatched up my riphook, snatched up Mari, and then ran for everything I was worth.

We hit the deck next to a stirring Eljin—I threw my body on top of Mari, my side screaming—as the pulse grenade exploded. Blue energy burst outward, and so did pieces of Rayce Yahn. Not much was left of the giant except a greasy smear within a ten-foot crater and the front piece of his breastplate, embedded, quivering, in another nearby tank.

I rose to my feet with a sigh of relief, helping the others up. The ground below us shook, and more hunks of the roof caved in near us, sending us scrambling. We huddled around the nearest light column, staring with mouths agape as Korbos and Kaira battled.

The entire room quivered. Vibrated. The energies wielded by the two Host set our hair on end. Ice, fire, and wind blasted in crisscrossing waves, thrown and deflected by protective domes of pure will. Korbos was knocked back several steps as a huge stone—a gigantic marble block from the Temple above us—crashed into his shield. Kaira went to a knee as the fragments abruptly reversed themselves mid-air and slammed into hers. Flames splashed in waves like a storm-tossed sea, and thick ice crystals formed against the invisible bubbles, breaking off and joining the whirling maelstrom, becoming lethal daggers. The three of us cowered against our column, using its bulk to break the air currents and protect us from the larger projectiles.

I clenched my hands, helpless. There was no way to assist my friend; no way to even approach. We'd be sliced to ribbons in a heartbeat if we broke cover.

For long minutes, the two calamities raged against each other. Korbos kept a staccato rhythm of gunfire hurtling at the High Lady, his shield flickering as it dropped, allowing the plasma burst to filter through, then re-forming the next instant. Silver cracks surrounded both Host, each of their shields nearly at the breaking point. It was merely a matter of whose energy—whose Well—gave out first.

Korbos's shield began to chip away, bits of light flying away into the wind. Sweat poured down his scarred face.

I screamed his name. He glanced around, taking in the fallen Hostguard, the blotted remains of Rayce Yahn, the three of us alive. He smiled, his face lighting up in beatific relief. He nodded at us, then bellowed out "THROW THEM!"

And then his shield dropped.

Kaira gave a shriek of triumph as debris pelted Korbos. Fire licked his skin. Ice froze upon his clothing. Rocks and icy shards ripped through his meat like bullets. Yet he staggered forward, tapping into his vast Host strength, progressing step by step toward the High Lady. Blue fire streamed from Bulwark as he fired volley after volley. Kaira's shield was nearly down.

Eljin, Mari, and I looked at each other. Throw them? What did that mean?

A tiny voice echoed in my mind—thin, as if it were coming from a great distance, yet there was no mistaking it. Korbos's voice. "*Throw them, Pyk. Attack. Trust me.*"

I looked down at the weapons in our hands.

"Eljin, throw your sword!" I screamed over the screeching wind and crashing debris. Without waiting to see if he heard me, I reared back my arm and hurled my riphook as hard as I could toward Kaira, grimacing at the pain in my side. An instant later, Eljin's sword flew past, flipping end over end at her shield.

Korbos's left arm shot out and, roaring at the top of his lungs, he threw whatever arcane power remained to him behind the carbsteel-forged blades as he held down the trigger of his rifle.

Our weapons hurtled forward as though shot from Cassidy's pistol, just as an enormous burst of blue plasma erupted from Bulwark. Kaira screamed as her shield collapsed. The blades struck home, Eljin's massive cleaver plunging straight through her gut, my riphook burying itself in her heart.

She staggered back three steps as her blood sprayed across the shattered floor, a snarl of fury twisting her beautiful face. Her hands shot forward, the dwindling force of her power shoving against Korbos.

Bloodied and exhausted, he pushed through the assault, ramming Bulwark's barrel into her armpit. Her eyes went wide, and then he blew half of her upper body to dust in an explosion of red mist and blue flame.

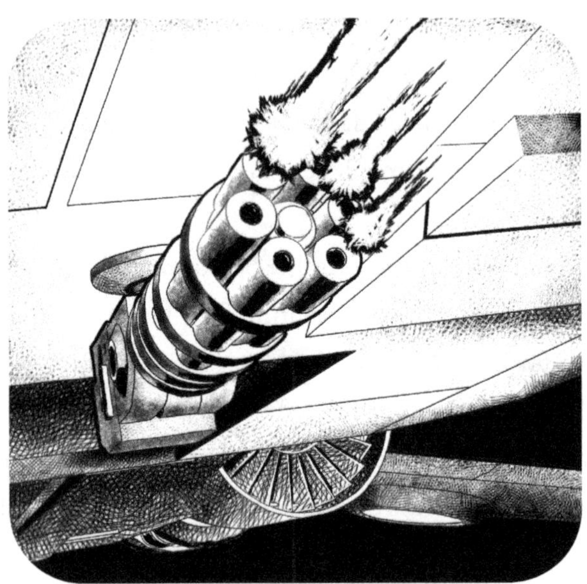

THIRTY FIVE

I raced over but pulled up short, cautious, as I stared at Kaira's twitching body.

"Frok me," I whispered.

Her entire left arm was missing. No, wait, there it was, over there. What remained of her torso was a ruined semicircular mass of meat, splashing blood into the shattered quickcrete beneath. Her head lolled, eyes rolling and unfocused, and her remaining hand clawed at the ground. Order anyway, that was creepy. How in the world was her body still alive without a Chaos-damned heart?

I picked up my riphook, wiping it on the ruins of Kaira's dress before returning it to the holster on my back as Eljin reached for his sword. The old man stood over Kaira for a moment, then spat down into her blood-spattered face. He bared his teeth before stepping back and wiping down his own blade.

Debris clattered to the side, and I looked up to see tiny, panicked faces peering down from the Temple above. Bodies and shattered masonry littered the quickcrete below the gargantuan hole.

"We…need to get…out of here," Korbos huffed, sagging beside me. He was a wreck; clothes shredded, his patch hanging on by an Atian prayer, skin lacerated into strips by Kaira's gravel storm. His Well had to have been running insanely low. The cuts began to heal, but slowly. He looked more exhausted than I'd ever seen him. Mari flung her arms around his waist, thanking Atia that he was okay, and he returned the hug with a weak squeeze.

"She's still alive, man," I said. "Shouldn't we, y'know, finish her off?" Rage filled me as I stared down at the dismembered remains. Flashes of Emun. My father's face. My little sister's hand reaching for me. I wanted the woman dead, but I had no idea how to make it happen. If this mutilation didn't kill her, nothing I could do would make any difference. I kicked her leg in frustration.

The big man snorted. "Nothing here would do the job. That's the problem with fighting her. We can't actually kill one another by any conventional means."

A *woosh-WHACK* echoed as we jumped. Eljin bent over, heaving his blade from the foot-deep furrow he'd bludgeoned into the quickcrete. Kaira's severed head rolled, coming to rest a few paces away.

"What?" he asked, seeing us all staring at him. "Heh. Can't hurt, right?"

Korbos grimaced. "Indeed. Let's get going." He staggered ahead, loping toward the ruined banks of synthminds and screens. Most had holes blown through them, fuzzing with static and sparks. My heart dropped. I heard Mari chanting another quick prayer to Atia, and I echoed the sentiment, hoping with all my being that all of this hadn't been for nothing.

"How'd you do that thing in my head?" I asked, trying to ease the tension. "The whole talking-in-my-mind whatsit?"

He grunted. "Telepathy. Speaking mind-to-mind. Just another Host trick. I'm not too good at it, but I guess it worked well enough."

"It was still pretty cool."

Korbos bent slowly to one knee, slinging Bulwark across his back and poking through the wreckage. He threw a few junked boxes out of the way, then stiffened. I feared the worst until he howled in triumph and held up a scuffed but otherwise undamaged charcoal gray casing. The big man snatched at a few cables and shoved them into the tattered remnants of his coat pockets, then laboriously stood and turned.

That was when the remains of the roof, far overhead, caved in.

The four of us cursed simultaneously and bolted for the exit, Korbos cradling the synthmind beneath his hunched torso. I slipped in the waste products of several tubes that had been smashed in the fight, but kept my feet pumping as debris rained down. Shrieking golden-painted figures and enormous chunks of stone splattered and shattered around us as we raced for the door, each of us limping in different ways. A palm tree crashed through one of the few intact laboratory glasses. An Inori woman was nearly torn in half upon impacting the jagged remains of a tank. Gilded couches exploded as they struck the quickcrete.

We got lucky.

About forty feet from the exit, the deadly rain halted, although the stone above the door creaked tenuously. I stood in the doorway and looked up at the gaping hole, where a large portion of Level One had fallen through. A small mountain of detritus filled the chamber we'd just escaped.

The lift, thankfully, was still functioning. Loathe as I was to enter it again, there was no other way up. We rode our way to ground level, and exited to a madhouse; adherents running every which way, scrambling for the giant doors that led to the dubious safety of the open desert. A vast section of the floor was just gone, a three-hundred-foot black maw that would, with any luck, serve as Kaira's tomb.

Our group joined the flow of deviants and hedonists headed for the gates. As we stepped through, a dry, hot, utterly fantastic breeze of evening desert air gusted across my face. I breathed deep, turning my face to the heavens.

When I looked down, a group of about twenty Inori stood before us, surrounded by hundreds of other adherents and sycophants, pointing and jabbering.

"Infidels!" one screamed. "They despoil the divinity of the High Lady and the sanctity of her holy Temple! Don't let them escape! Attaaaaaack!"

Korbos growled, shifting the synthmind to his left arm before swinging Bulwark on its strap and firing from the hip. The Inori disappeared from the waist up.

The rest scattered.

We limped on, taking the path of marble paving stones, the carved columns passing by slowly, so slowly.

"That's what we need, right there. Heh." Eljin pointed to a long steamcart, sitting abandoned near a low outlying building. Korbos nodded, then turned to stare at the Temple.

Emerging from the great Temple doors, a solitary figure could be seen, staggering along as one hand held her severed head to a healing neck. The remains of her arm were clenched between her teeth.

"Mariyana," Korbos cried. "Blow it!"

Mari stepped forward, a wicked grin on her pretty-yet-bruised face, and clicked a button on the boxlike device she held.

The third level of the Temple of Kol exploded outward, a shockwave flinging Kaira to the ground. Fireballs the size of dockside warehouses blew out the walls. For an instant I could see the bones of the structure—the wide support columns—before the intense heat and pressure shattered them. The upper levels collapsed, falling down, and down, and down upon one another as a chain reaction of explosions sent stones and people rocketing away.

The Temple of Kol became an enormous pyre.

"Let's get moving," Korbos said, a note of satisfaction in his exhausted voice.

We piled into the steamcart, Eljin taking the driver's seat and Korbos cradling the synthmind in the passenger couch as he took a long breath. Mari and I hopped into the back bed next to the old man's deposited sword. I grabbed a support strut attached to the cab as the metal wheels spun and the cart launched into the sands. Mari and I looked back to see the High Lady rising to her feet, head fully attached and jerking in our direction. I slapped the roof of the cab, screaming "Go! Go! Go!"

She receded into the distance as Eljin floored the cart.

Ten minutes later, we rounded a tall butte and reached our destination.

Despair shot through me, constricting my chest and shortening my breath.

The *Storm* was gone.

Cassidy left us.

But there *was* a company of Hostguard searching about the imprints in the sand and dirt where the skipship's landing gear had rested. Fifty insectile helms rose in alarm as the steamcart slewed to a sideways halt, a cloud of dust blocking us from view for a moment.

A scream of anguished rage ripped across the desert flat, and it wasn't until Mari shook me that I realized it was my own. The Hostguard raced to our cart, stunpikes extended, as the dust settled.

Mari pointed to her satchel—the backpack in which she'd carried a heap of Second Battalion explosives—lying between us in the cart bed. I hadn't noticed she'd picked it up in our flight from the laboratory. I snarled as I ripped it open and snatched up several of the remaining black globes. Without waiting for the others, we leapt out of the back and began hurling them into the ordered ranks of the guard.

Four went off almost simultaneously, blasting armored forms into the air, plumes of dust erupting as the remaining Hostguard scattered. Two more pulse grenades exploded a moment later, taking out a few more soldiers but doing only a fraction of the earlier damage to their numbers. The remaining twenty spread out, advancing in ones and twos to negate our advantage of arms. I threw my last grenade and pulled Chum as it blew two more Hostguard to the fires of Chaos. The pain in my side only added fuel to my rage.

She'd left us.

Suddenly Korbos was beside me, thrusting the synthmind into Mari's arms and opening fire. The remaining guard didn't have a chance. A few brave souls charged us at angles, hoping to avoid the blue annihilation, but Eljin and I stepped to the side and ended them in a swift exchange of blows. The rest were mowed down by Bulwark like wheat. Korbos slumped after the last had fallen. The big man was on his last legs.

I took a moment to be amazed by just how quickly we'd ruined an entire company of Hostguard. Had I really been so afraid of them back in Hightide? After facing down the likes of Rayce Yahn and being held powerless by Kalos, the soldiers didn't seem so much of a threat any more. Funny how one's perspective changes.

The skirmish was going to cost us, however. There was no way Kaira or any remaining forces had missed those explosions, not to mention the column of dust that rose into the air, giving away our exact position.

Korbos turned to us, wavering with exhaustion. "You…you have to get going. Take the cart and the synthmind and beat it. I'll hold them… as long as I can." He swayed slightly. I rushed forward, lending him my shoulder and nearly buckling under the weight.

"We're not leaving you here," I began.

"Yes, you are, Pyk. The task falls…to the three of you now. Take the synthmind, find Cassidy and the *Storm*. Get the signara back…and find a way to *end this*. End the Host. If I don't stay, then this…was all for nothing. I won't…let Kaira have you."

But Cassidy was *gone*. Our options were kind of limited.

My teeth ground together in frustration, but he was right. It was the only chance we had of escaping Kaira. But I couldn't lose him, too. Order only knew what would happen when the High Lady eventually disabled him.

Mari was shaking her head, arms wrapped around the bulky synthmind, tears in her eyes.

Korbos untangled himself from me, hobbling over to the Chek. "Yes, Mariyana. You have to go. Take the steamcart…and get as far away as you can."

A sob escaped her as Korbos leaned down and placed a delicate kiss on her forehead. "I love you, little one."

He turned and stuck a trembling hand out to Eljin. "Take care of them, Master Dhovra."

"I will, *Seta Sietau*. Heh. Just watch yourself."

At last, he turned to me, swaying where he stood. "Pyk, I…"

"Don't," I said. "No goodbyes. We'll meet again, either in this world or within Order's light. Kick the drek out of her for me."

"I love you, my friend. My son." A tear fell from his good eye. "For what it's worth, I'm sorry. About…everything. And thank you. Thank you for believing in me, even when I didn't have the strength to believe in myself. I'll…I'll never forget that kindness." He paused. "Or the backhand," he scoffed, rubbing his jaw. It sounded suspiciously like a sob. "I'll do my best to live up to…to your faith in me."

I threw my arms around the big man. My friend. My father, in place of the one I'd lost. He returned the embrace with crushing force. We held each other for a long moment, and then it was time to flee.

The three of us headed for the steamcart, only to stop short at the sight of a shambling figure rounding the cab.

Kaira.

I screamed in surprise and despair. How in the world had she caught up to us so quickly?

"*KOOORRRBOOOSSSS*!" she screamed. Her body was almost completely regenerated, and she was holding the remnants of her severed arm to her newly-formed shoulder. I could actually *see* the tendons and muscle fibers knitting themselves together.

A rumbling bass vibrated through the air, and things *really* went to Chaos as an enormous, blocky skipship rounded the butte, hovering forty feet off the ground.

The ship Kalos had taken. The *Predator*, Kaira had called it. He and his crew had come back.

I shook with fear. Panels slid aside as weapons systems activated and massive guns appeared from the sides and bottom of the ship. A chattering burst of fire blasted the steamcart into shredded hunks of metal.

We backed away as the High Lady advanced, staggering. Mari clutched at the synthmind, hugging it to her chest. Korbos stumbled forward and put himself between us. The *Predator*'s guns adjusted, targeting him.

Kaira raised her hands, a terrifying snarl painting her face, and a multitude of rocks and small boulders rose into the air around her.

Time stopped. All went still. I prepared myself to fight.

We were going to die here. I found I was becoming acquainted with the possibility.

Then the starboard gun on the bulky ship exploded in a rain of shrapnel.

A streak of blue-gray rocketed overhead, guns blazing as it raked Kalos's skipship with rattling punches.

It was the *Storm*. Hope exploded within me.

Cassidy *hadn't* left us!

Everything around us burst into sudden motion. Kaira began flinging stones at Korbos, at us, shrieking to the heavens. The Host ship peeled off to gain altitude and deal with Cassidy and the *Storm*.

I staggered as a melon-sized projectile nearly took my head off, knocking me sideways when I barely got my metal arm up in time to deflect it. The impact jolted pain through the muscles where my mechanical limb met flesh.

The three of us bolted for the nearest cover, a tall boulder in the lee of the butte. Blue flashes lit us from behind as Korbos engaged the High Lady. Dust exploded in runners around our feet as the *Predator* took a few wild shots at us before turning to engage the *Storm*.

Kaira was the more immediate danger to us on the ground, but as we cowered behind the boulder I couldn't take my eyes off the aerial battle unfolding above us.

The bulky *Predator* didn't seem to have much maneuverability, flying in lumbering, slow circles. The *Storm* was much more nimble and far faster. What the *Predator* lacked in grace, however, it made up in brute strength. Dense, never-ending arcs of white filled the air as the blocky ship's guns unloaded on Cassidy.

Gods above and below, Cassidy could *fly*.

The *Storm* wove and dove in swirling loops and rolls. The chains of bullets came close but never quite touched her ship as she danced with the wind. The skipship rolled upside down, then made a reversing half-loop straight toward the ground, a graceful semicircle path which ended with its cannon pointed straight at *Predator*'s engines. Gunfire chattered as she raked the enemy ship's stern. A loud boom echoed, fire erupting from the lowest of the three engine exhausts.

I winced as Cassidy shot past the main body and return fire chipped away at the *Storm*. She rolled at the last instant; it appeared nothing vital had been hit. A fast bank looped her around, putting her in position to attack the guns broadside, taking out another two emplacements. The

Predator was now weaponless on its port side, and Cassidy roared in to take advantage. The big ship attempted to rotate in order to bring their remaining guns to bear, but the *Storm* was just too agile.

Cassidy spiraled up and over the rear of the enemy vessel, nudging the skipship's thrusters and spinning it in a punishing maneuver that would have had me vomiting everywhere were I with her in the cockpit. The ship slammed forward, unloading a volley into the *Predator*'s engines. Another boom, and the enemy ship began to lose altitude, trailing smoke.

My freckled friend went in for the kill. Even as fear and worry enveloped me, all my heart went with her.

The *Storm* stayed in Kalos's blind side as it hurtled toward the ground, slower than I might have expected. Was the High Lord using his power to slow their fall? Was that even *possible* with a ship so big? The realization struck me that I had no frokking idea what was and wasn't possible any more when it came to the Host.

Cassidy goosed the engines, pulling ahead of the gigantic *Predator*, and executed another of those brutal flip-spins as she cut power. I goggled, then burst out into a ragged cheer. The *Storm* was falling at the same rate of speed as the Predator. Only…backwards.

With guns pointed straight into the windows of the enemy flight deck.

I like to imagine that Cassidy flipped a rude gesture at the pilot—maybe even Kalos himself—as she triggered the gun. Bullets roared in a deadly white stream from the cannon, liquifying the *Predator*'s cockpit and crew. Scraps of metal flew and an explosion roared out of the shattered viewscreens, belching fire into the sky between the two ships.

The *Predator* screamed toward the ground, a dark rainbow of smoke and flame following its descent. I'd been right. Kalos had been slowing their descent.

The *Storm* flipped around and rocketed away in a rising arc as the enemy ship plowed into the stony base of a nearby butte. Mari, Eljin and I ducked as the big skipship exploded in a mushroom-shaped cloud taller than the Temple itself. Hot wind rushed around us, and I whooped a victory cheer. Cassidy had come back! And gods above and below, what flying! Mari and Eljin were doing the same, pumping fists to the air as the *Storm* burst through the fireball, rolling and trailing fire and ash in a thick yellow and black streamer.

A ragged scream returned my attention to our more pressing problem. The High Lady.

Kaira had seen her lover go down in a blaze of flame and ruin. And she was *angry*.

Overall, however, the fight between her and Korbos was much less dramatic than it had been below the Temple. Kaira was limited to throwing individual rocks—no tempest of ice or fire this time. Korbos was dodging and shooting on the run. Both were sluggish and staggering; their Wells of power had to have been scraping the bottom of the barrel along with their physical stamina. They were scrambling to avoid hits; it appeared neither had the strength for a shield.

I had a thought.

I caught Korbos's eye as he swung near our hiding position and pointed frantically at the *Storm* and then Kaira. He nodded, then was moving past.

Order anyway, this was a dumb idea.

I scrambled up to the top of our sheltering boulder, ignoring the pain in my side and waving my arms as Cassidy sped past. I waited, nervous, as she wheeled the ship around. I was completely exposed up here; I could only hope that Kaira didn't see me and turn me into a smear of jelly.

"Atia's bones, Pyk, what are you doing?!" Mari cried below me. I waved her off, eyes fixed on the approaching *Storm*. I pointed to Kaira, then punched my metal hand into fleshy palm. I had a quick impression of Cass's hand waving at me, and then the ship was screaming past, looping around to set up an attack run.

I hopped up and down, waving to get Korbos's attention, then yelped as a stone the size of my torso hurtled toward me. The desert hardpan knocked the wind from me as I flung myself off the boulder, and agony burst through my injured rib. Mari rushed to my side.

"Tell…him…incoming!" I gasped, holding my side. She nodded and poked her head out, placing her fingers to her mouth and belting out her shrill three-note whistle—the one she used to summon Bastin. Rocks pelted our shelter as she ducked back. Eljin helped me to my feet as we tentatively rounded the opposite side of the boulder to watch.

Korbos was advancing on his sister, no longer dodging her strikes, taking the occasional hit to the shoulder or leg. As I watched, he slung Bulwark across his back and lifted a leg to pull from his boot a carbsteel knife as long as my forearm. A fist-sized stone clipped his temple, ripping away his tattered patch and exposing his hollow eye socket. He roared, challenging her.

A second explosion rocked the *Predator* crash site. Kaira shrieked. And went mad. The hail of stones ceased, everything from pebbles to boulders crashing to the ground around them.

"If you won't join us, Korbos, you cannot remain free from us. I will build a new Temple around the pulp of your ever-healing corpse! My glory will be your tomb! Yours, and that of your little mortal playthings."

She reared back, her hands outstretched, and unleashed a furious scream. High overhead, a building-sized hunk of the butte tore itself free and arrowed to flatten Korbos under tons of rock and mineral. He charged Kaira, closing the distance with a desperate burst of power-enhanced strength and speed. The High Lady backed away, too slowly. The gargantuan wedge of stone shifted course as she cursed. Guess Kaira didn't want to bury herself as well.

Korbos tackled her to the ground, and they rolled like schoolyard rivals, stabbing and punching, punching and stabbing. His skin sizzled as she pressed flaming palms to his face, and he roared as he buried his knife in her ribs. Clawed fingers razed bubbling, burning furrows over his unscarred eye.

The stone missile impacted, shattering the ground and throwing us from our feet, barely missing the two Host as they pummeled one another. Dust and rocks flew everywhere, and a blue-gray gleam cut through the air as the *Storm* made her approach.

"Korbos!" Mari screamed, pointing at the incoming skipship. "She's coming! Whatever you're gonna do, do it now before you run out of time and oh Atia protect us what do you even have planned it's gonna be—"

The big man roared—drowning out her words—then planted his feet and *heaved*, raising Kaira from the ground by her throat. Her feet dangled as she struck at his face and arm with burning hands. Korbos pivoted, and with the dregs of his strength hurled her a dozen feet up, above the dust and into the *Storm*'s path, where Cassidy opened up with the guns.

A piercing *BRRRRRT!* sounded, and white-hot ammunition tore through the High Lady's body, hundreds of rounds in less than a second. Her body jumped and jittered as it was shredded apart in a shower of viscera. Parts rained down to the hardpan.

Korbos dropped to his knees, wheezing, skin and clothing smoking from the vicious burns. Mari ran over to check on him while Eljin and I ran to examine Kaira's remains.

An incongruent thought ran through my mind. When had I last eaten? I couldn't remember. Maybe the protein bar before we left the *Storm*? And then I was hurling the last bits of food in my belly up, moistening the desert sands with bile.

Even the plodding dead of Cortian hadn't turned my stomach like this.

Kaira was strewn about in the dust and sand. One leg over here. The other over there. Bits of her hips and innards resting against that rock. The biggest remnant wasn't much to look at: her head—a large portion of her ethereal face was missing where a large bullet had bored a hole clean through—attached to a scrap of her upper chest and one still-flailing arm. I felt my gorge rise again, and tamped it down with no small difficulty.

Her one remaining eye rolled in its socket before fixating on me, and her sand-covered mouth worked in soundless fury, lacking any attached lungs to push air through it.

I gritted my teeth and knelt down, fist tightening around my riphook. Red rage coursed through my veins as I looked down at the monster who'd so irrevocably ruined my childhood. My family. My life. It was blind luck that I'd been fortunate enough to find another. And this… creature…wanted nothing more than to take that from me as well.

"This is for my father, Huk," I whispered. Chum descended, hacking off her remaining arm from the shredded shoulder. Her piecemeal features grimaced in futile wrath. "And this is for my little sister. Her name was Amiel, you *bhuta*." Her head rolled for the second time in a hour as I parted it from her elegant neck. Eljin nodded in grim approval and kicked it away.

She wouldn't be putting herself back together any time soon.

THIRTY SIX

The Host still wasn't dead. I didn't know how we were going to kill her for good. If we even could. But a sense of satisfaction filled me as I watched her head roll away. A sense of…closure.

Blood and sand flew as the *Storm* set down. We joined Korbos and Mari as the ramp descended. The big blacksmith had seen better days, although his wounds were healing slowly. He held the undamaged synthmind in his arm. It was so strange, that box. Such a seemingly mundane object for us to have spilled so much blood and sweat and tears to obtain.

"How you holding up?" I asked him, tapping a spot where his hair was still burned away. He winced, jerking his head.

"Ow. I've been better." An understatement. He was nearly white with exhaustion, the scars and burns on his face livid. What scraps of clothing remained on him looked like they'd been fed through a meat grinder.

"So what do we do about her?" I motioned to the pieces of Kaira, and my stomach churned again as her severed arms pulled themselves toward what remained of her torso. The fingers scrabbled against the hardpan. Eljin hobbled over and kicked them aside, looking at us in dismay.

"I…I don't know. We'll have to think about that," Korbos replied.

Eljin made his way back to us, and I turned my back to the ship. "Don't tell her I threw up," I muttered under my breath. A giant grin split his dark face.

Mari barreled past us as Cassidy descended the *Storm*'s ramp, hurtling into the pilot and bearing her to the ground with a muffled "Oof!"

"I knew you didn't leave us for good there was no way you'd ever do that I was gonna tell Pyk but we had to avoid the High Lady and Order anyway that was some great flying up there you took down that whole skipship gods above and below the thing was huge how did you know where to shoot it I'd have never—"

"Mari! Mari!" Cassidy yelled over the Chek, laughing fit to burst. "It's good to see you too! Now can you please get off me?"

"Oh right sorry about that didn't mean to knock you over oh Cassidy you should have seen it I got to plant all those explosives then Korbos let me blow up the whole…whole *frokking* Temple it was just like *boom* this huge firework—"

Cassidy couldn't stop smiling. "I heard it. Blast shook the *Storm* even way out here."

They both climbed to their feet as the rest of us approached, Cassidy dusting herself off as Mariyana let out a squeal and ran up the ramp to pounce on Bastin and Omari.

"He might need a bath!" Cassidy called up. She grinned at us, tossing a thumb over her shoulder. "He didn't do too well with some of those acrobatics up there. Reminded me of someone else I know."

I groaned.

Korbos clapped a hand on her, a bone-tired smile crossing his ruined face. "Well done, Your Highness. Well done, indeed." He waved for Eljin to follow him. The old man nodded and clasped arms with Cassidy, then helped a struggling Korbos up the ramp and into the ship proper.

"Don't call me that, Patches!" she yelled after him.

Then the two of us were alone, facing each other in the blowing dust. I didn't know what to say, just stood there with my jaw working, unable to articulate any of the feelings coursing through me.

A faint slither whispered behind me where Kaira's pieces were trying desperately to reform. Cassidy looked over my shoulder and raised an eyebrow, grimacing in disgust.

"So that's...horrible," she said, then grunted as I threw my arm around her and pulled her into a deep kiss. Our bodies melted into each other as she threw her arms around my neck, leaning into me and grasping my hair to return the passion. It was fire and ice, wind and rain. Order's light and the hells of Chaos clashing together in a storm of lightning. An eternal moment gone far too soon. The pain in my ribs faded away along with all other concerns.

As our lips parted, she smiled at me, a broad grin that crinkled her emerald eyes and set her freckles—and my heart—dancing. Had we actually just done that? I locked my knees to try and stop their shaking.

"So that...wasn't horrible," she joked.

"I...thought you were gone," I said. "Never been that glad to be wrong."

She feigned outrage, slapping me on the chest. "Well, thanks for the vote of confidence!"

I held her gaze. "Cassidy Ryker. You were…are…I…I don't have the words for it."

"Amazing? Stupendous? Fantabulous? Crushingly beautiful?"

"Modest?"

She laughed, hard and long. I cupped her cheek in my hand.

"Brilliant. You were brilliant up there, and you saved our backsides. My backside."

She smiled again, leaning in to kiss me. I obliged, feeling lightheaded.

"Yeah, well, it *is* pretty cute. Be a shame if I couldn't have it around." She reached around and patted the article in question.

I laughed, blushing, the horror of the last few hours put aside for the moment. We kissed again, and, as our ardor tapered off, I noticed a crowd of watchers. The others stood at the foot of the ramp, each sporting a broad drek-eating grin. Even Bastin was smiling, tongue lolling from the side of his muzzle. Omari prowled on the scuridai's back, licking his paws, unconcerned with everyone else.

"G'wan, show's over, folks!" Cassidy exclaimed, flapping her arm at our friends.

Korbos and Eljin were holding small crates from the ship's cargo bay. The old man gestured toward Kaira's remains. "Thought we could scoop her up and lock her away in these. Heh. Would keep the bits separate, at least."

I thought about it for a second, then nodded. Cassidy took one of the wooden crates from Korbos, who looked as if he could barely stand. I took the other.

"Sorry about taking off like that," she said to him. "I didn't have much choice when those Hostguard showed up. Would have been tricky evacuating you if I was in chains."

The big man nodded. "I figured as much. I meant what I said. You did well, Miss Ryker. You're a natural-born pilot, as good as any I've seen in all my years."

She smiled, pleased by his compliment.

We set about our grim task, collecting the mangled remains of the High Lady and placing each into its own separate crate. Mari seemed to take a perverse pleasure in nailing the lids shut. Korbos looked somewhat sad as he gently lifted Kaira's silent, screaming head. No sounds were audible, yet the remains of her face writhed and formed words.

Mari chuckled in wry amusement. "I think she just said something about 'eating your liver,' if my lipreading hasn't gotten too rusty."

Korbos carefully wrapped the gruesome trophy, swaddling it in an old cloak, and placed it into the smallest container.

He noticed my questioning look and shook his head. "I'm not remorseful at all, Pyk. We did what had to be done. But she was my sister, of a kind, all those years ago. I wonder what might have been had she made better choices. I'll always wonder if I could have helped her… guided her, the way Rin—and all of you—helped me."

He sighed, nailing the cover to the box with a hammer given to him by Cassidy. "But she brought her own fate upon herself. They all did."

My heart went out to the big man, even as I was glad to see the High Lady shut away. Though…I wouldn't feel comfortable until we could find a way to dispose of her with some measure of finality.

We hauled the crates back to the cargo hold, stowing them to one side beneath a web of netting—the only remaining after our trip to Cortian. Cassidy tsked and mumbled beneath her breath about needing another supply run.

Everyone shuffled our way forward, piling into the cockpit before collapsing into the seats and against the bulkhead.

Cassidy spun her pilot's couch. As she rotated back into view she held a tall canteen, taking a long pull at the contents. She coughed, handing it to Mari. The Chek raised it in salute and drank, then handed it to Eljin, who afterward passed it to me. I took a long gulp, exhaling with a low whistle as the heat from the whiskey spread through my chest.

I looked up to Korbos, leaning against the wall near me with a sad smile on his scarred face. He'd found another patch somewhere; he looked whole again, if exhausted. Despite my misgivings, I held out the canteen to him. What the hell. The man had earned it.

He held up a hand, stopping me.

"I think...I think I'm done with that," he said in a quiet voice, a slight tremor in his fingers.

Emotion flooded me, tightening my throat. Order only knew how difficult that had been for him to get out. I set the drink down, swallowing hard, then stood up and threw my arms around him. The big man stiffened for a moment, then relaxed into the hug, patting my back.

"Thank you," I mumbled into his tattered jacket. "Thank you, Father. If I may call you so."

A tear rolled down his lined face as I leaned back. "Pyk, it would be one of the great honors of my long, long life...but thanks for what?" he asked.

"For everything. For being you. For showing me something greater than myself. For keeping my friends alive. For your strength. For your love."

Korbos's face lit up in a beautiful smile that rolled away all the pain and hardship, all the centuries of strife and struggle. I saw the man he must have been so very, very many years ago, back at the beginning. It was a wondrous thing.

As Korbos struggled to get himself together, I moved closer to Cassidy, who took my hand and grinned up at me. Gods above and below, who was I fooling? I was in love with that smile. I rubbed a knuckle against the stump of her missing digit and returned the grin.

"Yes, well," Korbos coughed. "We still need to have a look at that signara. And we have to decide what to do with Kaira. I wouldn't trust those crates to hold her for long. I don't really have any options that don't involve world-breaking explosives. Anyone chewing on an idea? Maybe know a volcano nearby we can drop her into?"

I jerked, thoughts racing. A riotous laugh nearly doubled me over.

Everyone looked at me, heads quirked, with polite, curious smiles. The utter confusion on their faces set me off again, all the pain and stress and horror of the day bleeding out into hilarity like poison lanced from a wound.

"Order anyway, what's gotten into you, Guts?" Cassidy prodded.

"I just had a thought. You're gonna love this." I outlined my plan to them.

Korbos guffawed, then a wicked grin spread across his scarred features. "That should do it."

THIRTY SEVEN

We arrived near sundown.

The ship eased over ancient, dilapidated towers, the glass structures reaching up as if to pull us from the sky. Green forest extended to the horizon, rippling in the light rain that poured from low-slung clouds. Figures tramped about the hole in the massive wall to the east, busy in their repair work. A makeshift barrier of stone, braced with felled trees, served as a barricade to hold in the Devoid shambling around aimlessly within the wall. The Aka had been busy. Several waved hands in greeting, although they couldn't have been able to see us well. I smiled as I saw a Na'don raise his four arms in salute. I hoped Oben, Juni and the rest were doing okay.

"We'll have to find a spot to land later so Eljin can drop in and visit," I said. If he wanted to, that was. He hadn't actually been gone that long. I shook my head, unable to process that it had only been a few days since we'd left the Lau Tuai. Less than a week. It felt like years. A grunt was the only response I received.

Korbos, Mariyana and I stood on the *Storm*'s ramp, lowered and open to the air. Despite the safety harness around my waist, I kept an ironlike grasp on the hydraulic with my metal hand. I shifted as Cassidy nudged the ship further into the city of Cortian, coming to hover near the intersection where the Turris Imperialis strove for the clouds. She descended, navigating between the skytowers and coming to rest fifty feet above street level.

Wind whipped my hair as I leaned out and stared down at the sea of Devoid that had so nearly ended our journey. Their plaintive moan drowned out the whine of the *Storm*'s engines, although tens of thousands of hands reached toward the noise as if it offended their ears. Or holes, in some cases. Whatever they had.

"You really think this will work?" I asked Korbos. I wasn't so sure, now that we were here. The Devoid below undulated slowly, somehow reminding me of good fishing and calm seas.

"Yes, I think it might," he replied, his face stony as he held my eye. "I don't claim to know what happens to us after we die. Given that the Host are so hard to kill, I can't even say *if* we actually die. But I know that if she can't piece herself back together—can't regenerate—then she'll never again be a threat to the Elarin people."

That had been my thinking when I'd had the idea.

I turned to look up the ramp. "C'mon Eljin, send one down!"

A wooden crate, the top removed in advance, came sliding down the ramp to thump into my outstretched foot. I bent over to pick it up, cringing at the contents.

A leg. I turned the box over and shook, not wanting to touch the thing. Nothing fell out.

"Damnation!" I swore, before reaching in and yanking at the wedged limb. It squelched obscenely as it popped loose, and I hurriedly tossed it over the side of the ramp.

It struck the flurry of desiccated, outstretched hands, and immediately vanished as Devoid swarmed over it. I craned my neck, hoping that our plan would work.

Equal parts relief and disgust warred in me as a Devoid—particularly large—snatched away Kaira's foot from another walking corpse and promptly began gnawing on it. Others wrestled over the thigh and calf, tearing them apart and latching on like ticks. Within moments, there was nothing left, save a few shattered bones.

The creatures didn't even leave those.

A female Devoid stumbled away, crunching a knob of Kaira's femur between her exposed teeth. It was a feeding frenzy. More grabbed at the remaining bone, taking large bites before it was stolen by yet others. Soon there'd be no trace of her outside the swollen bellies of the undead.

"That's…that's frokking repulsive," Mari exhaled.

Yep. Looked like it just might work.

I slipped on a sturdy set of gloves from the back of my belt and nodded to Eljin. More crates began the trek down the ramp, and Korbos, Mari and I set to work.

The large chunks were easy; it was the wetter bits—the offal—that were hardest to dispose of. Thank Order's light for those heavy gloves. We spaced the task out, sending down one piece at a time, spreading them out far and wide, waiting to make sure little remained before tossing the next.

I was reminded of simpler times in Hightide—of sitting dockside, feet dangling in the warm ocean water, feeding the tiny fish that swarmed around and nibbled at my toes.

It was a disturbing thought, in context.

The last crate—the smallest—made its way down the ramp, where Mariyana caught it. Eljin followed it down, solemn in the moment but wanting to be present for this last, final, awful step.

"I'll take this one," Korbos said, his voice weary.

Mari nodded, hooking her thumbs into the safety belt and stepping aside to stand near me. I put a bracing hand around her shoulders. Harness or not, I didn't trust her being that close to the edge.

The big man tenderly unwrapped the cloak covering the head of Kaira, High Lady of the Host. One of the calamities of Elarin. A nine-hundred-year-old catastrophe responsible for the deaths of more innocents than any historian would ever be able to put a number. A woman of monstrous appetites, yet in love only with her own power.

I finally saw her for how small and pathetic she really was.

Her face had restored itself during her time in the box. Unimaginable beauty radiated from every pore, made all the worse for knowing the sickness that allure concealed. Bright golden eyes radiated malice as they took in her surroundings, and her mouth worked wordlessly, brows furrowed in unmitigated hate for Korbos. For all of us.

Korbos brought her up to eye level with himself, then gently leaned forward and kissed her brow. Her jaw clacked, trying in vain to bite, a last desperate attempt at violence.

We remained silent as he struggled with his farewell. Not that any of us actually wanted her to fare well. A long minute passed as Korbos opened his mouth and closed it, started and stopped. He finally bowed his head, exhaling a long sigh.

"I wish…" he began, "I wish things could have been different."

He stepped to the ramp's edge. Held the head over open air.

"Goodbye, sister."

Her brows shot up, those striking eyes widening in fear—likely for the first time in her exceedingly long life—and then she was gone, falling to the quickcrete below with a *whunk!* that fifty feet of distance did nothing to muffle. The head actually bounced before landing directly in a pair of outstretched hands. The Devoid mobbed her, gnashing and tearing.

And so ended the High Lady. Mari turned away, but Eljin and I watched, trying not to feel satisfaction and a sense of justice at seeing a monster devoured by monsters.

I'd love to be able to say I was successful.

But I can't.

After a few moments, the old man grunted, turned, and stalked back up the ramp. We followed, pausing to remove our harnesses, then made our way back up to the cockpit.

"Take us up," Korbos said, yanking a thumb toward the Turris Imperialis. "There should be enough clear space at the top of the building to set the *Storm* down."

"Oooookay," Cassidy drawled, "but why?"

He eyed her, expression deadpan. "Because I forgot to pick up a few things on our last trip."

She scoffed. "If you say so."

Centuries of grime flew from the roof, sending a shower of dust arching from the building like a brown waterfall as Cassidy set the ship down with a loud *clank.* There was barely enough room to accommodate the skipship, but she managed. Korbos was right, she was a fine pilot.

I followed the big man down the hall and through the cargo bay.

"Up for some company?" I asked, scratching the back of my head idly.

He glanced at me with a narrowed eye, then shrugged, moving onto the ramp as it lowered.

Truth be told, I was feeling a bit protective of Korbos at that moment. He'd slept for nearly an entire day after our fight with Kaira and still didn't seem at his best. The conflict had taken more out of him than he'd been willing to admit. And after my acceptance and embarrassingly heartfelt declaration of what the big man really meant to me, I wasn't about to just let him go haring off into a Devoid-infested building by himself. A quick shrug adjusted the strap over my shoulder, moving Chum into a more comfortable position.

"So why didn't we land here the first time?" I asked. "Seems like it would have saved quite a lot of trouble."

The big man grunted. "There was no way to know what sort of condition the towers were in. What if the entire roof had crumbled off when we touched down? Better to scout the place beforehand and see for sure. Besides, if things hadn't worked out the way they did, we'd have never met Eljin or recovered the synthmind."

And Amadi would still be alive. But I kept my mouth shut. I could see the same thought racing through Korbos's mind, and I knew he was beating himself up about it worse than anyone else ever could.

We strolled across the roof, winding around a few low structures until we found an access door. Locked. Korbos yanked it free with a snap, hinges and all, setting it down gently on the grime-covered floor beside us.

There were no windows on the stairwell, and I shuddered in the dark as I cracked one of Cassidy's glowsticks and led the way. One switchback flight of stairs and a locked door later, and we stood on the wide landing before the room where I'd been certain we were all going to die. Where Korbos had saved our lives. A faint moan came from below us, maybe only one or two floors down, and I pulled my riphook.

"Go on," I said, "get what you need, I'll keep watch." He nodded and ducked into the room, stepping over the mound of fallen Devoid left from our previous visit. A fusillade of clanks and crashes echoed out into the landing as he moved around the wrecked equipment in his search. The moan grew louder. Oddly, the noise didn't inspire quite the pants-wetting terror it had only a few days previous.

I moved over to the stairwell and waited, leaning against the wall. Soon enough, a pair of Devoid stumbled up the steps, shuffling footsteps hissing as one dragged a badly broken foot. I craned my neck, searching the visible stairs behind them, but it seemed to be just the two.

As the pair climbed, arms outstretched and wailing, I was struck with an unusual sensation. An emotion that I was woefully unprepared to feel in a situation such as this.

Pity.

I hadn't given it much thought during our previous trek through the city, mostly because I'd been running and fighting for my life, but seeing them now, my soul wept for the Devoid. These two, and the multitude on the streets below. The millions that Korbos and Cassidy said were trapped within other cities like Cortian.

They hadn't asked for this. They'd been regular people, like Mari. Like Ardis. People concerned with getting to work on time, wondering what was for dinner that evening, would their relationship last, would their kids do well at studies…

Oben and the Aka were somehow even worse. They *knew* what had been taken from them. And yet they'd adapted, carved out a relatively pleasant existence for themselves over the long years, despite their disadvantages. Their persecution. The horror of everlasting life.

My respect for them grew.

As did my corresponding hate for Kaira. Kalos. This creature they called Mother—the woman who'd created the Host and ushered in so many years of stagnation and suffering. The psychopath who'd murdered millions and turned millions more into these pitiful wretches before me. Even if Korbos were somehow struck down, captured, or otherwise incapacitated, I knew without a doubt that I'd continue on. Do anything in my power to end the monster and her bastard offspring. A so-called normal life would never again be an option, not with the threat of the Host and their creator still looming over Elarin.

I wasn't a religious man, but I whispered a quick prayer to Atia to deliver them into justice. Or into the range of our weapons, at the very least.

The two Devoid drew close, and I extended Chum's haft, stabbing out with the long reach of the spear. My ribs gave a muted twinge. Two quick strikes to the heads, and the creatures collapsed. Hopefully they were at peace now, their souls moved on to Order's light. The thought provided some small comfort.

No other sounds or moans reached my ears, so I exhaled and turned to see Korbos on the landing, holding a mishmash of cables and staring at me with a curious expression. Had he been watching? It felt like his eye saw clean through me. Maybe it was the look of pity and sorrow still marking my face.

He nodded once, slowly. "So you understand, now?"

Damn the man's intuition.

I returned the nod, agreeing in a quiet voice. "Yeah, I think I do."

Another of those youthful smiles appeared. "That's good, Pyk. I'm glad to have you on board."

"'Til the end," I sighed. "Be it theirs or ours."

I grinned at him. "But I'm betting on theirs."

Korbos laughed. "Good man. Now take some of these Chaos-damned cables before I trip and break my fool neck. I don't have time to wait on that to heal."

THIRTY EIGHT

"I've come to a decision," Eljin said, scratching Bastin's ears. "I think I'll be staying behind. Heh. If it's all the same to you." His voice grew soft. "There are some things of Amadi's back home that need tending before I leave out, since he…he won't be returning."

Mari looked stricken. She'd really grown to like the old man during his short time with us. But she knew we couldn't make Eljin stay. Omari hissed in her lap as she clenched his fur a little too hard, then arched his back into the followup consolation petting.

"Leave out?" she asked. "You won't be staying at the Lau Tuai for long?"

"Well, no, little one. Figured I'd see the world a bit, and to do that I'll be wanting a few things I had to leave behind. Then it's off to explore!

Hah! Twenty-two years I missed out on because I was hiding from that *bhuta.* Lots to see and do, young miss. Lots to see and do. Heh."

She looked sad, but nodded in understanding. Eljin couldn't be blamed for wanting to take advantage of a new lease on life. They embraced in a lopsided hug, his beefy arms enveloping her.

"If you need some travel tips, I can absolutely help you out there, old-timer," Cassidy said. "Got plenty of things to see and do that would curl that white hair for ya."

"Yar, I just bet you do, Yer Graciousness," he said. I burst out laughing.

Cass's mouth quirked as she shook her head ruefully. "I already regret telling you *bhakas* about any of that." She grew serious, taking him into a warm hug. "You take care of yourself, old man."

I nodded in agreement, clasping his forearm in the ancient show of friendship. We hadn't known him all that long, but battle makes brotherhood, as they say. I liked the old bugger. "I hope you find some peace out there, Eljin. I'd say it's been a pleasure, but Order above knows it hasn't."

He barked a laugh at that. "Yar, same goes double for you, lad. I don't envy you the road ahead."

"Agreed. It's apt to be short, steep, and right off the edge of a cliff."

The old man chuckled.

"You'll want to stick around for this, at least," came Korbos's voice from the vicinity of the deck. He scooted out from under a control panel, where he'd been fiddling with a rat's nest of cables and circuitry for hours. The synthmind rested nearby, wires jutting from one side to connect it to the *Storm*'s power grid.

"What, you think I'm gonna *walk* down this bloody tower and out through the Devoid?" Eljin said. "I'm gonna need a ride to the Old Tree, if it's not too much burden! Hah! Be a shame to ask for that before we open our prize, though."

Korbos smirked, taking his arm. "Give the Aka my best. We won't be staying."

"That I will, *Seta Sietau*. May Order's light shine on you and your quest."

Korbos grunted, eyeing us all. "Well, are we ready to see what all the struggle and headache was for?"

A chorus of affirmation answered him. "Atia's blessings, yes," said Mari.

A strange look flickered across Korbos's face. Almost pitying, although it was gone in an instant. I didn't think anyone else had noticed, but Cassidy took my hand and raised an eyebrow, prompting a shrug in return.

The matte gray of the synthmind reflected no light, not even the bright blue of the star-shaped insignia on the front of the casing. Korbos paused a moment, thinking, then pressed the glowing buttons in sequence. A low hum rose from the synthmind as he reverently took the signara—its gold glow a counterpoint to the blue—and placed it into the attached square clamp. Gears whirred as the cube slotted into place and the clamp…well, clamped.

The signara's color shifted violently from gold to a dazzling blue—the same hue as the Imperial Star—and a curtain of matching beams shot from the apex of the cube, forming a V-shaped display at our eye level. Motes of dust shone and danced in the light. My jaw dropped as shapes and patterns began to form within the light. They looked like letters, the same unfamiliar writing we'd encountered in Cortian. Cassidy's grip tightened on my hand. I tried not to wince.

"*COMEPI ILUGA OLAIGA*," boomed a voice from the synthmind. We all jumped in surprise, everyone except Korbos. "*PEFAPE FEONA AUNATU?*" Bastin sniffed the gray box and hissed, exiting the cockpit to return to the berth he and Mari shared.

Korbos closed his eyes, silent for a moment. "Order anyway, this thing is old." Hesitancy entered his voice as he replied. "Faaloga maiupu. Famatala laua gana. Fatino. Hear my words. Interpret. Execute."

The synthmind whirred for a fraction of an instant.

"*PULUPU. MEESAN. VAGA. FAMATALA.*"

"Bubble. Machine. Ocean. Interpret."

"*OLA. OTI. AMATA MA LEUGA.*"

"Death. Life. Beginning and end."

"Uh, what are you doing?" I couldn't help asking.

"Quiet. It's trying to learn modern Coretongue."

"Oh." It could *do* that?

Several more distinct call-and-answers followed.

"*Greetings, user,*" the machine said, in perfect Coretongue. I shook my head in astonishment. Cassidy was looking at the synthmind like it had just descended on Order's own light in a fanfare of celestial chorus. I imagined the thing's translative capabilities would be a Seeker's dream. Cassidy wouldn't need Korbos to teach her Imperial Standard if she could keep hold of the synthmind.

The strange writing on the display in front of us stuttered and resolved into more familiar letters, blurring from right to left so quickly I couldn't make out anything but the occasional word. Suddenly the writing disappeared, leaving the fan of light blank.

"*HELIX online,*" the machine stated. "*How may you best be served, user?*"

Korbos ran a nervous hand through his hair. "Order anyway, I haven't used a synthmind in nearly a thousand years…is that your designation? HELIX?"

"HELIX model 875-J, primary function: class-one self-contained archival data storage and retrieval. How may you best be served, user?"

The big man exhaled. Moment of truth. We all tensed.

"Hope this thing isn't nine hundred years out-of-date," Cassidy mumbled.

Korbos shot her an unreadable look. "I'm sure it is, but Mother wouldn't relocate no matter how much time has passed. She built her fortress for seclusion, and from what I've learned through the years of her dealings, her equipment was too specific and too large to be transported after the Ruin. There weren't enough of her Host left to dig her out afterward." He sighed. "There's also the fact that Mother *hates* people in general. Avoids them at all costs. She prefers the solitude of her science. So she's still there, I've no doubt."

"If you say so…"

"I do." He turned back to the synthmind. "I have to. We don't have many other options if this doesn't work."

"HELIX, access filedata on localized signara. Vestan. Location of primary research facility and engineering schematics. Execute."

"*Accessing.*" Images and data whirled across the blade of light, coalescing into an illuminated map of Elarin. Next to it shone an architectural diagram of a cubelike structure, reminiscent of the signara itself. Geographical data and technical schematic overlays popped up.

Cassidy stepped closer, examining the map on the left.

"It's the old names," she muttered, tracing a finger over the text. "Cortianis instead of Cortian, Ahrigar in place of Ahrimacia. Yikai is the same. Oh, wow, this was before Hylandet was wiped out and the Rippling Gulf created…"

More and more names appeared on the map—some familiar, some completely foreign—until a white square formed, honing in over an area in the northwest labeled Koram. We knew it as Qorun. A big iceberg, mainly, covered in glacial mountains and not much else. Something was off, though. Qorun was a large, hook-shaped island within the lifeless Crescent Bay, but on the map before us it was shown as a peninsula.

"*Primary Vestan facility location is marked, user,*" came the mechanical voice of the synthmind.

Korbos leaned forward, pointing excitedly to the spot, which fuzzed around his finger. "That's it! That's where Mother has been all this time!" He rocked back, placing a meaty hand to his forehead. "Order anyway, *that's* why Kalos wiped out the Thrane in Anchorage and Cranis a few centuries back. Mother was maintaining a perimeter. A dead zone." He laughed in disbelief. "I can't believe I didn't see that."

"How would you have known, mate?" I asked. "Every fisherman worth his salt knows those seas have always been dead waters. There's a reason people steer clear of Qorun."

"Yeah, because Mother wants it that way. Those seas weren't always barren, my friend. I always chalked it up to fallout from the null bombs, but it makes sense that she'd do something like this to keep people away on a more or less permanent basis. Order above, they'd have had to have killed every living thing within a six hundred mile radius…"

I stared at the map in horrified awe. If it and Korbos were correct, then the creature he called Mother had carved a swath of northwestern Elarin into dust. Towns. Cities. So many people, washed away by flood waters to create a private island. What sort of person annihilated that much life in order to be left to her own devices? What kind of power did it take to do something of that magnitude? How in Order's light did we stand a chance against it?

And what sort of unholy terrors had she been creating up there for the past nine hundred years?

"Atia protect and preserve us," Mari whispered, apparently arriving at the same conclusions. She clasped her hands and muttered a low prayer under her breath.

Korbos recoiled. The big man took Mariyana's hands, prying them apart and interrupting her prayer. I was a little shocked. They'd had their philosophical arguments in the past, but he'd never before interfered with her faith.

"There's...something else. Please believe me, I never, *ever* wanted to do this, but it's important that you know what we're going to be facing. The truth of it. The truth about my creator." He looked into Mari's large eyes. "It...it won't be easy for you, but you need to know."

She gave him a look of skeptical concern. "Korbos, you're kinda worrying me right now...what is it you think I need to know, and do you really think it's gonna freak me out like that wait is it something else you did in the past like causing the Ruin or oh something even worse because I don't know if I can handle—"

"HELIX," he interrupted, closing his eye as if in resignation, "access datafile: Maia Vestan. Pertinent background information and psychological profile. Three hundred year dataset."

"*Accessing. Maiatia Vestan, born 3243 Calendar Imperial Year. Second daughter of Juvio and Bellata (nee Carpadis). Graduated top-of-class, all honors, from Academy Imperium-Ahrigar in 3260. Academic emphasis in genetic biotechnology.*

"Vestan was singled out in literature by instructors and peers as being 'brilliant,' 'genius,' 'decades ahead of contemporary research' within her chosen field, contrasting with more critical descriptions of 'loner,' 'quiet,' and, in one case, 'antisocial.' It should be noted that in her first post-academic research, the supervising doctorate described her in an internal communique as 'the brightest genetic engineer I've ever had the fortune to work beside,' as well as 'intensely driven with borderline sociopathic tendencies.'

"Awarded Cross of Ahrigar in 3265 CIY, following discovery of recombinant cellular mitosis. Awarded Emperor's Medal in 3273 upon invention of self-replicating organ grafts. Awarded The Empress Veil in 3284 following perfection of biomatter/biotronic integration techniques."

I cocked my head. This lady was responsible for the tech in my arm and Eljin's leg? What was her name again? Maiatia...hang on...

Oh no.

"No records exist from 3285 to 3296 CIY, in which year Maiatia Vestan emerged from apparent self-exile. Utilizing aerowing transport, Vestan and an unknown cohort of scientific colleagues launched a biochemical attack on the walled cities of Missou, Panola, Oxfor, Sivanna, and the twin boroughs of Aidan and Nidan. Inhabitants were altered; ceasing to be human, yet no longer technically alive. Total casualties: Thirteen million, nine hundred seventy-six thousand, four hundred and twenty one—plus or minus three percent margin of error. Later bombardments claimed the cities of Cortianis, Longren, and Stoken. Statistical variances comparable."

Mari covered her mouth. I sympathized; it wasn't easy, hearing such precise numbers. I had a sinking feeling I wasn't going to like where this ended up. And that Mari was going to like it even less.

"Two months post-attack, Maiatia Vestan—along with her cohort and a considerable number of high-ranking military backers—overthrew the

Imperium, staging a coup that eradicated the line of Emperor and Empress Nishani. Military occupation was short-lived, owing to the emergence of Vestan-engineered metahumans, later designated Host. Metahumans waged war upon Imperial remnants, decimating military capability until Imperial capitulation in 3344 CIY.

"*Designates: Host fractured in 3352 CIY. One member, designate: Korbos, split from faction and launched insurgency. Maiatia Vestan faded from public view during this conflict, thereafter named Ruin War, which claimed the lives of seven designates: Host, in addition to three billion, six hundred and seventy five million, four hundred twenty nine thousand, seven hundred and two civilian casualties—plus or minus three percent margin of error.*"

I felt sick. Somehow, I knew what was coming, and I didn't want to hear it.

"*In early 3356 CIY, Maiatia Vestan—at this time aged one hundred thirteen—resurfaced in post-Ruin Northiniar with remaining Host, designates: Kaira, Kalos, Kaligos, and Kida. The four metahumans, unchecked, visited further destruction upon mainland continent of Elarin, conquering lands and citizens still distressed from aftereffects of bombardment by GCN-4815 Mk. 2 null warheads.*"

Korbos bowed his head, eye closed. His hands tightened around Mariyana's.

"*Alongside the campaign carried out by designates: Host, Maiatia Vestan established rule over select conquered lands. Subject Vestan, aided by self-inflicted biomechanic enhancements and alleged 'miraculous' abilities of her metahumans, established a compulsory religion, installing herself as figurehead deity and renaming herself as designate: Atia.*"

And there it was. Mari went stock-still. I could see the whites around her widened eyes.

"Vestan offered stability in uncertain times and constructed a fanatical base of worshippers and proselytizers. Designates: Host established a hierarchical position as demigods. In the century that followed, this self-styled 'Inor' belief system spread throughout Elarin, metastasizing into splinter and fringe systems.

"As the new belief system became self-sustaining, designate: Atia withdrew from public appearances. By late 3356 CIY, designate: Atia was presumed as, quote, 'ascended to Order's light,' unquote, and succeeded in rule over Elarin lands by her lieutenants, designates: Kalos, Kida, Kaligos, and Kaira. Last known location of designate: Atia is noted on map display. Facility schematics attached.

"*Further signara records are incomplete or inconclusive. End analysis.*"

Korbos bent forward and tapped the insignia on the synthmind. With a whirring diminuendo, the machine shut down and the fan of light scattered. The signara's light returned to a soft golden glow as he stowed it away from sight.

He turned to us, timid and hesitant.

"No."

Mari shook her head, arms wrapped around herself. "That's not true. That's *impossible*. Atia watches over us and protects us and…and…"

"It's the truth, Mariyana," Korbos said, soft as a whisper. "I know it's not easy, but I was there. I saw it happen. Her religion is just another system cooked up by a woman who, even with all her gifts, couldn't get enough power to sate her desire for control."

"No! I won't believe this! You mean…you're telling me…*the* Inori *of all people had it right all this time?!*" She tugged at her medallion, the symbol of her faith, as if she wanted to rip it from her neck.

"Mari, I'm saying *nobody* had it right. Atia is no goddess. She's just a woman in love with her own legend. Atia is the monster under the bed, the night terror that looms unseen over every man, woman, and child in Elarin. And she *must* be destroyed, or else the cycle will never end."

Mari shook her head again, sending her puffs waggling, breathing hard and fast. "Nope. Nuh-uh. Atia is kind and benevolent and... *it isn't true!* It can't be!" A sob escaped her. She didn't want to believe. She *wouldn't* believe.

But I think, deep down, she knew it just made too much sense. My heart broke for my tiny friend. It wasn't an easy thing to see someone's faith shattered. She struggled as Korbos wrapped his arms around her, slipping free and running to her bunk, slamming the hatch behind her.

Korbos himself looked stricken, scanning the rest of us, obviously hoping we wouldn't share a similar reaction.

Cassidy was nodding to herself, taking the revelation in stride. Eljin just sat back with his fingers steepled in front of his mouth, thoughtful. As for me, I believed the synthmind. How could I not? It wasn't like a nine hundred year old machine would fabricate something so outrageous out of thin air.

Still, it was a hell of a thing to realize that the foundation of a faith prevalent across the greater part of the entire world had turned out to be a man-made construct. I sighed—silently thanking Order for my general lack of piety—and nodded to the big man, easing at least some of his tension away.

He looked toward Mari's berth, leaning as if he wanted to go after her.

"Let her be, mate," I said. "Just...give her some time. She just took a hard blow."

His shoulders slumped, but he stayed put. The big man was in obvious agony. He truly loved Mariyana, and the pain of causing her harm was written all over his face.

"So," I continued, trying to keep his mind away from our small friend, "what happens now? What's our next move?"

"To start, you could drop me off. Heh," said Eljin.

"Still going?" Cassidy asked. "Even after hearing all that?"

"Yar, changes nothing to my mind. Heh. I've had my vengeance, and I want to see more of the world before my time comes. These bones aren't getting any younger, you know? Too Chaos-damned decrepit to be running about trying to tangle with any more gods and monsters."

I couldn't fault him that, after taking a long look at the old boy. During our escapade in the ruins of Cortian and our fight at the Temple, Eljin had shown a remarkably improved vitality, but now he seemed more frail; like he'd been when we first met him at the Lau Tuai. His thick shoulders hunched, the lines on his face deeper and more weary. Without the prospect of revenge fortifying him, he looked...well...*old* again.

"Our next move remains to be seen," said Korbos. "Now that we know where Mother is, we'll need to have a solid plan of attack. I've no doubt her defenses are...formidable. Then there's also the matter of Kalos. There's no possible scenario where he was destroyed when his ship went down, and he'll be looking for Kaira. Which means he'll be looking for us."

I grunted. I owed the *bhaka* for my hurt ribs.

"It'll be interesting to see what happens if and when he finds out she's been destroyed. I'm guessing it won't be anything good for the people near him. Whatever the case, there's still a damned lot of work to be done. Elarin will never truly be free until Kalos and Atia are dead and gone forever."

"Well that's the easy part, then, isn't it?" Cassidy snarked.

"Let me think on it," Korbos continued, ignoring her. "The important thing is that we remain focused, act with purpose and conviction. Together." He ran a tired hand over his face, looking toward Mari's berth again. "Maybe we *could* do with a bit of rest at the Lau Tuai, if Eljin and the Aka wouldn't mind putting us up for a few." He looked over to the old man.

Eljin laughed, delighted. "All the time you need! Hah!"

"It's settled, then. My thanks." The blacksmith scratched his whiskered chin. "I think I need rest *now*, actually. I'm still not one hundred percent after the last few days."

"Yar, I might join you, there," Eljin said. "Could do with a nap myself. Heh."

I cocked my head as they exited the flight deck, chatting amiably. What a couple of old farts. We'd be back at the Old Tree soon enough. It was only a few minutes' flight, assuming we could find a place in the clearing to land the *Storm*.

Cassidy had a strange smirk on her face.

She and I were alone on the bridge, discounting Omari. The felis wound his way around my legs, his six paws tapping pointed nails against the deck. I kneeled down and gave him an absentminded scratch behind the ears, lost in thought.

I hoped Mariyana would be okay. The Chek's faith was such a large part of who she was, how she defined herself. To find out the very goddess she'd spent her life worshipping was ultimately responsible for the culls, the near-extinction of her kind? It must have flayed her soul to its core. But she needed her space and time to work things through. Order willing, Korbos would have sense enough to give her that.

"So what do you think about all this?" I asked Cassidy as I moved to stand near the viewscreen. It wasn't just an idle question. Cass was one of the smartest, most capable people I'd ever met, and I valued her opinion. The moorings of my universe felt as though they'd come undone, what with the insanity of the last few weeks. It was strange how a person who'd only recently become a part of that life could provide such grounding. Could keep things sensible and manageable. In my head, at least.

Eljin and I had our revenge, but our responses to that newfound freedom couldn't have been more different. Not that I blamed him for wanting out, but after what we'd been through I felt a heavy responsibility settle over me that I couldn't shirk. A chance to make all things right again. I couldn't walk away from it, but it would be difficult without Cassidy at my side. I realized I couldn't do it—didn't *want* to do it—alone. So I wanted, *needed*, to know where she stood on the matter.

And Order anyway, I was absolutely smitten with the woman.

"I can't say I'm exactly *excited* about the proposition of further danger and near-certain death, Guts," she said after some thought, wrapping her arms around me and laying her head against my back. "But I also never thought we had a chance at that harebrained Temple scheme, either. We took down a living god, for all intents and purposes. Who's to say we can't do the same to a fake one?"

Straight to the point, mirroring my own cautious optimism. "So you're not just in it for the cash?" I joked. She swatted my arm before growing serious.

"Don't think Korbos is getting off the hook for his promise, but you know as well as I do the money's just an excuse. I'm…I'm with you as long as you need me." There seemed to be an unspoken question in her statement. I laid my hands on hers, savoring the moment. Her touch.

The feel of her against me as I turned and pressed my mouth to hers, our breath mingling like storm clouds merging before a hard rain.

Order above. Might as well just say it. I caressed her cheek, running my thumb across her freckles.

"Yes, we need you. *I* need you, more than you know. And we can't pull this off without you. Captain." Those bright green eyes sparkled as her nose crinkled with an utterly entrancing smile. Her hand ran through my hair.

She stood on tiptoe and grazed her lips against my neck, then I yelped as she—without a hint of a warning—pinched my backside and bolted around to hurl herself into the seat at the *Storm*'s yoke, cross-legged and bouncing in excitement as it spun in a lazy circle.

"Then grab a seat, Guts," Cassidy said, gesturing to the copilot's couch. "I figure it's high time I taught you how to fly this old girl."

—END OF BOOK ONE—

ACKNOWLEDGEMENTS

They say "It takes a village to raise a child." It's cliché as hell, but I'm here to tell you that in the case of this debut novel—my baby—the saying is entirely accurate.

Though I've always been an avid devourer of stories, be it in the form of movies, novels, comics, games, and what-have-you, I went most of my life without the gumption to try and craft my own. Order only knows how many fan-fics I've made up in my head over the years to go along with fan art and random illustrations, but it wasn't until 2008 that my long-time friend Sonny Willis convinced me to work with him on writing a fantasy story. I had recently been laid off, my wife and I were expecting our first and only child, and ghostwriting from his notes and plot wound up being a novel (haha) way to stave off depression and feelings of uselessness while I looked for work. Nothing ever came of the 500-page epic fantasy we created together (thus far, anyway), but I hold out hope that we'll eventually revisit that world and make something of it. There was some decent stuff in that early attempt, and it showed me that I could do (and really, *really* enjoy) something at which I never thought I'd be any good. So huge thanks go out to Sonny for finagling me into finally taking a shot at writing in the first place.

Riders on the Storm originally began as an illustrated short story—comprised of the first several chapters leading up to the companions' confrontation with Kaira on the Hightide docks (and a *lot* of bad art)—at around sixty pages. But the first seeds of Pyk, Korbos, and Cassidy reared their heads way back around 2014, when I was looking to put together a portfolio of character designs to send off to TTRPG companies. At Spectrum Fantastic Art Live 2015, an artist convention featuring some of the biggest names in fantasy and sci-fi art, I received overwhelmingly positive portfolio advice from a great many of my idols, including Justin Gerard, Annie Stegg Gerard, Greg Manchess, Donato Giancola, Cynthia Sheppard, Karla Ortiz, Tyler Jacobson, and the amazing Iain McCaig. Special thanks goes out to art directors Lauren Panepinto (of Orbit Books fame), Jon Schindehette (founder of Art Order), Taylor Ingvarsson (now of Wizards of the Coast), and Jeremy Cranford (who gave me the most hilariously brutal—and needed—portfolio review of my life). It's been a lot of years—and I was just one guy in an endless stream of wannabes looking for tips—but the advice and encouragement of these wonderful pillars of the SF/F art community have kept me going through a great many tribulations, and I'll forever be thankful to them. I can honestly say that without their feedback on those early designs, this book wouldn't exist.

Another round goes to my online artist network of friends, many of whom I've not yet had the pleasure of meeting face-to-face. I hope to rectify that soon, y'all, but for now I just hope you all know how much you mean to me and my journey thus far. Your advice and encouragement on all the art posts over the years—the good and the bad—and willingness to join in on my drekposting and stupid humor are insanely important to me. Thank you so much for being a part of my life, both online and hopefully out in the real world someday. You'll notice a few of their names scattered throughout the book. Special shout-outs go to my art buddies Jen Waldon, Crystal Sully, Bruce Brenneise, Stephen Najarian, Josh Hass, Matthew Stawicki, Shawn T. King, Darren Yeow, Luke Maddox, Luke Schroder, Chris and Delphine Malidore (thanks so much for taking a chance on me for 78Tarot!!!), Jason Rainville, Chris Bjors, Eunjoo Han, Reid Southen, Jeff Kristian, Felix Ortiz, Jay Yang, Jeremy

Gordon, Johnny Morrow, Henrik Rosenborg, Nick Beatrice, Kerovin Black and Order above there are too many others to even try and begin listing them all I'd be here all night typing this up and I just hope you all know this is in no particular order and if we interact on a somewhat regular basis that you're all so important to me and I appreciate each and every one of you blessed peop—

"*MARI!*"

Sorry…got a little carried away there.

Thank you so very much to my Buddy Down Under (and fantastic LitRPG author) Matthew J. Barbeler, both for his encouragement while I was writing this book and his excellent advice on publishing and writing in general. If you're interested in gaming-based fiction, *please* go check out his fun EDGE Force series (for which I did the covers) along with all his other fine works.

Big thanks to the people at PMQ Pizza Media, my day job of twenty-two off-and-on years, for helping me keep the lights on and our bellies full, and for just being all-around great people to work with. We haven't all strangled each other thus far, so let's keep it going. Steve Green, Linda Green, Tommy Boyles, Brian Hernandez, Blake Harris, Brandy Pinion, and Tracy Morin; you're good folks. All the love.

I'd like to make special note of my editor of eleven years (jeez, wow, yikes, *really*?) at PMQ, Rick Hynum. A great editor, a good friend, a fellow geek of comics, tv, and movies. He was instrumental in getting this book to your hands, helping me resolve a few plot points and providing excellent feedback on a genre (or five) that was new to him. Any grammatical errors you may spot are absolutely my fault, not his, and I owe him one hell of a steak dinner. Here's to the next one, bud.

Thanks to *you*, Reader, for taking the chance on a newbie author who waded into the deep waters without knowing how to swim. There's a bajillion books out there, but you picked up this one and decided to read it. (Hopefully you read through it, if you've gotten this far.) You didn't have to do that, but you did, and I'll forever be appreciative to you for taking this trip with me. I truly hope you enjoyed it, and let me just say; there's some good stuff coming in the next two.

Finally, to all my family…

I…I don't actually know what to say. We'd be here for another hundred pages. But Order anyway, let's try.

All the love to my grandmother Betty Summers, who heaped praise on that fledgling attempt at a novel back in 2008. I don't think she'd ever read a straight-up fantasy book in her life, prior to that, but she's been asking for years when the next book is coming. That meant more than I can ever express. Love you, Mamaw.

To Mom and Dad, Heidi and Donny Summers, thank you with all my heart for always encouraging me to pursue the things that made me happy, even when it was obvious I had no clue what I was even attempting. Thanks for the warped sense of humor. Thanks for the kindness and free reign in my young hellion days. Thank you for letting me know without words that I am enough as I am. Thanks for being wonderful examples and great frokking parents.

To my wife and my son—my rocks, my gloriously infuriating, funny, and amazing Tracy and Brady—I love you. All I do is for you. Thank you for making my life worth living. I'm so fortunate I get to share it with you.

—Eric, March 2023

Self-Portrait of an Idiot—iPhone, 2023. Not for sale.

ABOUT THE AUTHOR

Eric Summers is a geek. A dork. An easily-entertained nincompoop. A graphic designer and freelance illustrator of several decades' experience, with a deep, spiritual, and probably unhealthy love of all things comics, sci-fi, and fantasy. He's been known to bang on ye olde drum set from time to time for dreks and giggles. It's been a while, but he loves traveling, especially abroad. +10 points if there's a beach nearby, so he can enjoy the wonder and ecstasy of sand in his beard alongside a horrendous sunburn.

This is his first published novel.

www.ingramcontent.com/pod-product-compliance
Lightning Source LLC
Chambersburg PA
CBHW070644310726
48982CB00001B/415

* 9 7 9 8 9 8 8 7 2 2 4 1 0 *